W9-ADR-495

ONE SECOND AFTER

FORGE BOOKS BY WILLIAM R. FORSTCHEN

We Look Like Men of War

One Second After

William R. Forstchen

ONE SECOND AFTER

A TOM DOHERTY ASSOCIATES BOOK New York

This is a work of fiction. All of the characters, organizations, and events portrayed in this novel are either products of the author's imagination or are used fictitiously.

ONE SECOND AFTER

A Forge Book
Published by Tom Doherty Associates, LLC
175 Fifth Avenue
New York, NY 10010

www.tor-forge.com

Forge® is a registered trademark of Tom Doherty Associates, LLC.

Library of Congress Cataloging-in-Publication Data

Forstchen, William R.
One second after / William R. Forstchen.—1st ed.
p. cm.
"A Tom Doherty Associates book."
ISBN-13: 978-0-7653-1758-2
ISBN-10: 0-7653-1758-3
I. Title.
PS3556.O7418O54 2009
813'.54—dc22

2008038101

Printed in the United States of America

0 9 8 7 6 5 4 3 2

For my daughter, Meghan Marie Forstchen . . . and for those who protect her, that she may grow up in peace. And for my father, John Joseph Forstchen, who taught me what should truly be valued in life.

ACKNOWLEDGMENTS

All books are, in a way, the works of others . . . those who inspired me as a kid, taught me to be a teacher, a writer, a father. Those of you who grew up with science fiction during the Cold War will remember *Alas Babylon,* and the chilling movies *Testament* and *On the Beach*. The nightmares of that time did not happen, but one does wonder, if their warning insured that indeed such things did not happen, when I was a child. Their impact on me is obvious with this work, their warnings as real then as the warning of this book is a potential reality now.

Special thanks must go to my friend, Newt Gingrich, for kindly providing the foreword to this book, the encouragement, advice, and crucial contacts he helped me with along the way. Captain Bill Sanders, who serves with our Navy, is one of the world's leading experts on this topic; it was Newt who introduced me to him, and as I worked on this project his advice was invaluable, along with his friendship. I must emphasize that Captain Sanders is a true professional; at times I asked questions to which he replied, "I can't answer that," and there the discussion ended. Everything he did help me with is public record and not classified. Congressman Roscoe Bartlett, a true public servant, who headed up a Congressional committee evaluating the threat of electromagnetic pulse was a great inspiration as well.

An old friend, who might seem out of place in this acknowledgment is the author Jean Shepherd. So few recall his name today, though nearly all are familiar with his famous movie about a family Christmas during the Depression. His writing and radio show inspired me when I was growing up near New York City, and by incredible good luck, he was a neighbor of mine up in Maine. As a fledgling writer, I spent some incredible moments with Jean and always remembered how he said "write what you know, kid." After so many books set in the past, or future, for the first time I turned to writing one set now, and it was Jean's advice that led me to this story set in my hometown. Black Mountain, Asheville, and Montreat College, where I teach history, are all very real. Of course, being a work of fiction the characters are fictional, but friends and neighbors might sense something of themselves in this story, and to all of them I owe my deepest gratitude for their years of friendship. Particular thanks should go to Jack Staggs, chief of police, for his insights, to my family doctor and our local pharmacist, conversations regarding this story left all of us chilled. And as always Bill Butterworth (W. E. B. Griffin Jr.) one of the best darn editors and friends one could ever ask for.

As always my thanks to Montreat College, to the thousands of students I have taught there across the years, whom I love deeply, and who were indeed an inspiration as are some of my fellow faculty, the president of our college and the board of trustees, especially Andy Andrews, veteran of Omaha Beach and close friend for so many years. Thanks as well to the staff at a nearby nursing home, who guided my father and me through the last year of his life . . . truly everyone who works there is a guardian angel.

A writer cannot function without good editors, publishers, and agents. Tom Doherty will always stand in my view as one of the best, and Bob Gleason, though we had a few "moments" at times, moved this book forward and I am grateful. As for the agents who believed in this, Eleanor Wood, Josh Morris, and Kevin Cleary . . . all I can say is thanks. And there is someone else special, Dianne St. Clair, who has always believed in me, and whose loving encouragement always came at the right moment. And to Brian Thomsen, thanks for everything.

In closing, I hope that this book never comes true. The threat is real, frightfully real, made even more frightening when you take the time to study it, question the experts, and have a sense of history. The moment of a fall from greatness often comes just when a people and a nation feel most secure. The cry "the barbarians are at the gates" too often comes as a terrifying bolt out of the blue, which is often the last cry ever heard. There are those in this world today who do wish this upon us and will strive to achieve it. As was said by Thomas Jefferson, "the price of freedom is eternal vigilance."

I pray that years from now, as time winds down for me, critics will say this was nothing more than a work of folly . . . and I will be content . . . for the vigil was kept and thus my daughter and those I love will never know this world I write of.

William R. Forstchen
Black Mountain, North Carolina
July 2008

FOREWORD

BY SPEAKER NEWT GINGRICH

Though this book is a work of fiction, it is also a work of fact, perhaps a "future history," that should be thought provoking and, yes, even terrifying for all of us. I know this from personal study, across decades, of the very real threat to American security that is posed by this particular weapon that Bill Forstchen writes about in *One Second After*.

There has been much attention given, since 9/11, to a wide variety of threats to our nation . . . additional attacks by the hijacking of commercial airliners, biological and chemical attacks, even the potential of a so-called "dirty bomb," or even an actual nuclear detonation in the center of one of our major cities.

But few have talked about, let alone heard about, the terrible, in fact overwhelming, threat of EMP, which is short hand for "electromagnetic pulse weapon."

My friend, Captain William Sanders, USN, one of our nation's leading experts on this particular weapon, will provide the afterword for this book, explaining in greater detail, using unclassified documents, as to how such a weapon works. In short form here, when an atomic bomb is detonated above the earth's atmosphere, it can generate a "pulse wave," which travels at the speed of light, and will short-circuit every electronic device that the "wave" touches on the earth's surface. It is like a super lightning bolt striking next to your house and taking out your computer, except infinitely worse, for it will strike our entire nation, most likely without warning, and could destroy our entire complex electrical grid and everything attached into that grid. It is a real threat, a very real threat and one that has deeply worried myself and many others for years.

My friend, Bill Forstchen, has coauthored six historical novels with me across the years. I have gotten to know him closely. He holds a Ph.D. in history from Purdue, he has specialized in the history of military technology, and this is no wild flight of fantasy on his part. In fact, the start of this book was a conversation that Bill and I shared several years back, concluding with his announcing that he felt he should write a novel about the threat, to raise public awareness.

As I said before, I see this book as a terrifying "future history" that might come true. Such books have a significant tradition in their own right. H. G. Wells wrote frightfully accurate prophecies of what history now calls World Wars I and II. Two of the great classics of the Cold War, *Alas, Babylon* and the movie *Testament,* gave us a profoundly moving glimpse of what would happen to ordinary citizens if war between us and the Soviets was ever unleashed. In fact Bill will openly admit that those two classics were indeed models for this book. I also compare it to perhaps the most famous of the "future history" books of modern times, George Orwell's *1984.* If the evil of totalitarian regimes had been allowed to flourish in the rubble of Europe after World War II, that future history might have come to pass. Orwell, by his book, raised an awareness that just might have saved us from Big Brother and the Thought Police.

I'd like to think that Bill's novel may do the same. Few in our government and in the public sector have openly confronted the threat offered by the use of but one nuclear weapon, in the hands of a determined enemy, who calibrates it to trigger a massive EMP burst. Such an event would destroy our complex, delicate high tech society in an instant and throw all of our lives back to an existence equal to that of the Middle Ages. Millions would die in the first week alone, perhaps even you who are reading this if you require certain medications, let alone the most basic needs of our lives such as food and clean water.

The place Bill writes about is real; he has set this story in his hometown and the college that he works at. I remember when he was writing the book and we'd talk. More than once he was deeply disturbed by what he had researched, discovered, and was now trying to express as a story for all to read. What hit him the most, he told me, is that he kept picturing his teenage daughter in this nightmare reality, and I think as you read the book you will see that point of identification. It struck me deeply as well, for I have two grandchildren. As he wishes to protect his daughter from this fate, so do I wish to protect my grandchildren, to be able to pass on to them an America that is safe from such threats.

The threat is real, and we as Americans must face that threat, prepare, and know what to do to prevent it. For if we do not, "one second after," the America we know, cherish and love, will be gone forever.

ONE SECOND AFTER

For I have become death, the destroyer of worlds.

CHAPTER ONE

BLACK MOUNTAIN, NORTH CAROLINA, 2:30 EDT

John Matherson lifted the plastic bag off the counter.

"You sure I have the right ones?" he asked.

Nancy, the owner of the shop, Ivy Corner, smiled. "Don't worry, John; she already had them picked out weeks ago. Give her a big hug and kiss for me. Hard to believe she's twelve today."

John sighed and nodded, looking down at the bag, stuffed with a dozen Beanie Babies, one for each year of Jennifer's life, which started twelve years ago this day.

"Hope she still wants these at thirteen," he said. "God save me when that first boy shows up at the door wanting to take her out."

The two laughed, Nancy nodding in agreement. He was already enduring that with Elizabeth, his sixteen-year-old, and perhaps for that, and so many other reasons as well, he just wished that he could preserve, could drag out, just for a few more days, weeks, or months the precious time all fathers remember fondly, when they still had their "little girl."

It was a beautiful spring day, the cherry trees lining the street in full bloom, a light shower of pink petals drifting on the wind as he walked up the street, past Doc Kellor's office, the antique stores, the new, rather Gothic-looking art gallery that had opened last month, the usual curio shops, and even an old-style ice-cream parlor . . . at a dollar fifty a scoop. Next up the street was Benson's Used and Rare Books. John hesitated, wanted to go in just for a few minutes, then pulled out his cell phone to check the time.

Two thirty. Her bus would be rolling in at three, no time today to go in, have a cup of coffee, and talk about books and history. Walt Benson saw him, held up a cup, gesturing for John to join him. He shook his head, pointed to his wrist even though he never wore a watch, and continued to walk up to the corner to where his Talon SUV was parked in front of Taylor's Hardware and General Store.

John paused and looked back down the street for a moment.

I'm living in a damn Norman Rockwell painting, he thought yet again, for the thousandth time.

Winding up here . . . he never imagined it, never planned for it, or even wanted it. Eight years back he was at the Army War College, Carlisle, PA, teaching military history and lecturing on asymmetrical warfare, and waiting to jump the hoop and finally get his first star.

And then two things happened. His promotion came through, with assignment to Brussels as a liaison to NATO, a rather nice posting to most likely end out his career . . . and then Mary had returned from the doctor's several days after the promotion, her face pale, lips pressed tight, and said four words: "I have breast cancer."

The commandant at Carlisle, Bob Scales, an old friend who had stood as godfather for John's Jennifer, understood the request he then laid before him. John would take the promotion, but could it be to the Pentagon? It'd place them nearby to Johns Hopkins, and not too far from Mary's family.

It didn't work. Cutbacks were hitting as it was, oh, there was great sympathy from upstairs, but he had to take Brussels if he wanted the star and maybe a year later they'd find a slot for him stateside.

After talking to Mary's doctor . . . John resigned. He would take her back home to Black Mountain, North Carolina, which was what she wanted and the cancer treatment center at Chapel Hill would be nearby.

Bob's connections were good, remarkably good, when John first mentioned Black Mountain. A single phone call was made; the old-boy network, though disdained as politically incorrect, did exist and it did help at times when needed. The president of Montreat College, North Carolina, in Mary's hometown, did indeed "suddenly" need an assistant director of development. John hated development and admissions work but survived it until finally a tenure-track professorship in history opened four years back and he was slotted in.

The fact that the president of the college, Dan Hunt, owed his life to Bob Scales, who had dragged him out of a minefield back in 1970, was a definite mark in John's favor that could not be ignored between friends. Dan had lost his leg, Bob got another of his Bronze Stars for saving him, and the two had been buddies ever since, each looking out, as well, for those whom the other cared for.

So Mary got to go home, after twenty years of following John from Benning, to Germany, to Okinawa, sweating out Desert Storm, from there to the Pentagon, then a year, a wonderful year, at West Point and then three more wonderful years teaching at Carlisle. At heart he was a history teacher, and maybe whichever bastard in the personnel office at the Pentagon had nixed John's request to stay stateside had done him a favor.

So they came home to Black Mountain, North Carolina. He did not hesitate one second in granting her wish, resigning his commission and promotion and moving to this corner of the Carolina mountains.

He looked back down Main Street, frozen for a moment in time and memories. Mary would be gone four years next week, her last time out a slow, exhausting walk down this street, which as a girl she had run along.

It was indeed a Norman Rockwell town. That final walk down this street with her, everyone knew her, everyone knew what was happening, and everyone came out to say hi, to give her a hug, a kiss, all knowing it was farewell but not saying it. It was a gesture of love John would never forget.

He pushed the thought aside. It was still too close and Jennifer's bus would be pulling up in twenty minutes.

He got into his Talon, started it up, turned onto State Street, and headed east. He did love the view as State Street curved through town, past yet more shops, nearly all the buildings redbrick, dating back to the turn of the century.

The village had once been a thriving community, part of the tuberculosis sanitarium business. When the railroad had finally pierced the mountains of western North Carolina in the early 1880s some of the first to flood in were tuberculosis victims. They came by the thousands, to the sanitariums that sprang up on every sunlit mountain slope. By the early twenties there were a dozen such institutions surrounding Asheville, the big city situated a dozen miles to the west of Black Mountain.

And then came the Depression. Black Mountain remained frozen in time, and then came antibiotics right after the war and the sanitariums emptied out. And all those wonderful buildings, which in other towns would have given way to shopping plazas and strip malls, had remained intact, progress passing Black Mountain by.

Now there were conference centers for various churches and summer camps for kids where the sanitariums had been. His own college had been founded at such a site up in what everyone called the Cove. A small college, six hundred kids, most of them from small towns across the Carolinas and a few from Atlanta or Florida. Some of the kids were freaked out by the relative isolation, but most of them grudgingly admitted they loved it, a beautiful campus, a safe place, an old logging trail across the edge of the campus leading straight on up to Mount Mitchell, good white water nearby for kayaking, and plenty of woods to disappear into for partying for some of them, to get around the fairly strict campus rules.

The town itself finally revived, starting in the 1980s, but wonderfully, the charming turn-of-the-century look was maintained, and in the summer and fall the streets would be crammed with tourists and day-trippers coming up from Charlotte or Winston-Salem to escape the boiling heat of the lowlands, joined by hundreds of summer "cottagers" who lived in the Cove, many of the cottages darn near mansions for some of the older wealth of the South.

That had been Mary's family, Old South and wealth. Me-ma Jennie, Mary's mother and Jennifer's namesake, still hung on doggedly to their home up in the Cove, refusing to consider moving, even though "Papa" Tyler was now in a nearby nursing home, in the final stages of cancer.

John continued to drive east, the traffic on Interstate 40, coming up through the Swannanoa Gap, roaring by on his left. The old-timers in the town still expressed their hatred of that "darn road." Before it came in, Black Mountain was a sleepy southern mountain hamlet. With the road had come development, traffic, and the floods of tourists on weekends that the chamber of commerce loved and everyone else tried to tolerate.

Staying on the old highway that paralleled the interstate, John drove for less than a mile out of town, then turned right onto a dirt road that twisted up the side of a hill overlooking the town. The old mountain joke used to be "you know you're getting directions to a mountain home when they say, 'Turn onto the dirt road.'"

For a kid from New Jersey, John still got a bit of a kick out of the fact that he did indeed live in the South, on the side of a mountain, halfway up a dirt road, with a view worth a million bucks.

The home he and Mary had purchased was in one of the first new developments in the area. In a county where there was no zoning, the lower part of the hill had several trailers, an old shack where Connie Yarborough, a wonderful down-the-hill neighbor, still did not have electricity or town water, and next to her was an eccentric Volkswagen repair shop . . . the owner, Jim Bartlett, a true sixties throwback, his lot littered with dozens of rusting Beetles, vans, and even a few precious VW Buses and Karmann Ghias.

The house (Mary and John actually named Rivendell, because of their mutual love of Tolkien) offered a broad sweeping view of the valley below; the skyline of Asheville was in the distance, framed by the Great Smoky Mountains beyond, facing due west so Mary could have her sunsets.

When trying to describe the view he'd just tell friends, "Check out *Last of the Mohicans;* it was filmed a half hour from where we live."

It was a fairly contemporary-looking type of home, high ceiling, the west wall, from bedroom across the living room to the dining area, all glass. The bed was still positioned to face the glass wall, as Mary wanted it so she could watch the outside world as her life drifted away.

He pulled up the drive. The two "idiots" Ginger and Zach, both golden retrievers, both beautiful-looking dogs—and both thicker than bricks when it came to brains—had been out sunning on the bedroom deck. They stood up and barked madly, as if he were an invader. Though if he were a real invader they'd have cowered in terror and stained the carpet as they fled into Jennifer's room to hide.

The two idiots charged through the bedroom, then out through the entryway screen door . . . the lower half of the door a charade, as the screen was gone. Put a new one in, it'd last a few days and the idiots would charge right through it again. John had given up on that fight years ago.

As for actually closing the door . . . it never even crossed his mind anymore. This was Black Mountain. Strange as it seemed, folks rarely locked up, keys would be left in cars, kids did indeed play in the streets in the evening, there were parades for the Fourth of July, Christmas, and the ridiculous Pinecone Festival, complete to the crowning of a Miss Pinecone. Papa Tyler had absolutely humiliated his daughter, Mary, in front of John early on in their courtship when he proudly pulled out a photo of her, Miss Pinecone 1977. In Black Mountain there was still an ice-cream truck that made the rounds on summer nights. . . . It was all one helluva difference from his boyhood just outside of Newark, New Jersey.

There was a car parked at the top of the driveway. Mary's mother, Me-ma Jennie.

Me-ma Jennie was behind the wheel of her wonderful and highly eccentric 1959 Ford Edsel. Ford . . . that's where the family money had come from, ownership of a string of car dealerships across the Carolinas dating back to Henry Ford himself. There was even a photo framed in the house up in the Cove of Mary's great-granddad and Henry Ford at the opening of a dealership in Charlotte back before World War I.

Though it wasn't polite to be overtly "business" in their strata and Jennie preferred the role of genteel southern lady, in her day, John knew, she was one shrewd business person, as was her husband.

John pulled up alongside the Edsel. Jennie put down the book she was reading and got out.

"Hi, Jen."

She absolutely hated "Ma," "Mother," "Mom," or, mortal sin of all mortal sins, "Me-ma" or "Grandma" from her Yankee son-in-law, who was definitely not her first choice for her only daughter. But that had softened with time, especially towards the end, especially when he had brought the girls back home to Jen.

The two got out of their cars and she held up a cheek to be kissed, her height, at little more than five foot two, overshadowed by his six-foot-four bulk, and there was a light touch of her hand on his arm and an affectionate squeeze.

"Thought you'd never get here in time. She'll be home any minute."

Jen had yet to slip into the higher pitch or gravelly tone of an "old lady's" voice. He wondered if she practiced every night reciting before a mirror to keep that wonderful young woman–sounding southern lilt. It was an accent that still haunted him. The same as Mary's when they had first met at Duke, twenty-eight years ago. At times, if Jen was in the next room and called to the girls, it would still bring tears to his eyes.

"We got time. Why didn't you go inside to wait?"

"With those two mongrels? The way they jump, they'd ruin my nylons."

Ginger and Zach were all over John, jumping, barking, leaping about . . . and studiously avoiding Jen. Though dumb, goldens knew when someone didn't like them no matter how charming they might be.

John reached in, pulled out the bag of Beanies, and, walking over to the stone wall that bordered the path to the house, began to line them up, one at a time, setting them side by side.

"Now John, really, isn't she getting a bit old for that?"

"Not yet, not my little girl."

Jen laughed softly.

"You can't keep time back forever."

"I can try, can't I?" he said with a grin.

She smiled sadly.

"How do you think Tyler and I felt about you, the day you came through our door?"

He reached out and gave her an affectionate touch on the cheek.

"You guys loved me."

"You a Yankee? Like hell. Tyler actually thought about driving you off with a shotgun. And that first night you stayed over . . ."

Even after all these years he found he still blushed a bit at that. Jen had caught Mary and him in a less than "proper" situation on the family room sofa at two in the morning. Though not fully improper, it was embarrassing nevertheless, and Jen had never let him live it down.

He set the Beanies out, stepped back, eyeballed them, like a sergeant examining a row of new recruits. The red, white, and blue "patriot" bear on the right should be in the middle of the ranks where a flag bearer might be.

He could hear the growl of the school bus as it shifted gears, turning off of old Route 70, coming up the hill.

"Here she comes," Jen announced excitedly.

Going back to the Edsel, she leaned in the open window and brought out a flat, elegantly wrapped box, tied off with a neat bow.

"Jewelry?" John asked.

"Of course; she's twelve now. A proper young lady should have a gold necklace at twelve. Her mother did."

"Yeah, I remember that necklace," he said with a grin. "She was wearing it that night you just mentioned. And she was twenty then."

"You cad," Jen said softly, and slapped him lightly on the shoulder, and he pretended that it was a painful blow.

Ginger and Zach had stopped jumping around John, both of them cocking their heads, taking in the sound of the approaching school bus, the squeal of the brakes as it stopped at the bottom of the driveway, its yellow barely visible now through the spring-blooming trees.

They were both off like lightning bolts, running full tilt down the driveway, barking up a storm, and seconds later he could hear the laughter of Jennifer; of Patricia, a year older and their neighbor; and of Seth, Pat's eleventh-grade brother.

The girls came running up the driveway, Seth threw a stick, the two dogs diverted by it for a moment but then turned together and charged up the hill behind the girls. Seth waved then crossed the street to his house.

John felt a hand slip into his . . . Jen's.

"Just like her mother," Jen whispered, voice choked.

Yes, he could see Mary in Jennifer, slender, actually skinny as a rail, shoulder-length blond hair tied back, still a lanky little girl. She slowed a bit, reaching out to put a hand on a tree as if to brace herself, Patricia turned and waited for her. John felt a momentary concern, wanted to go down to her, but knew better, Jen actually held him back.

"You are too protective," Jen whispered. "She must handle it on her own."

Young Jennifer caught her breath, looked up, a bit pale, saw them waiting, and a radiant smile lit her face.

"Me-ma! And you drove the Edsel today. Can we go for a ride?"

Jen let her hand slip, bent over slightly as Jennifer ran up to her grandmother, the two embracing.

"How's my birthday girl?"

They hugged and Grandma Jen showered Jennifer with kisses, twelve of them, counting each off. Pat looked over at the Beanies lined up, smiled, and looked up at John.

"Afternoon, Mr. Matherson."

"How are you, Pat?"

"I think she needs to be checked," Pat whispered.

"It can wait."

"Daddy!"

Jennifer was now in his arms. He lifted her up, hugged her with fierce intensity so that she laughed, then groaned, "You'll break my back!"

He let go of her, watching her eyes as she looked past him to the Beanie Babies lining the wall . . . and yes, there was still that childlike glow in them.

"Patriot Bear! And Ollie Ostrich!"

As she started to sweep them up, he looked over at Jen with a bit of a triumphant smile, as if to say, "See, she's still my little girl."

Jen, rising to the challenge, came up to Jennifer's side and held out the flat box.

"Happy Birthday, darling."

Jennifer tore the paper off. Ginger, thinking the paper was now a gift to her, half-swallowed it and ran off as Zach chased her.

When Jennifer opened the box her eyes widened.

"Oh, Me-ma."

"It's time my girl had a real gold necklace. Maybe your friend can help you put it on."

John looked down at the gift. My God, it must of cost a fortune, heavy, almost pencil thick. Jen looked at him out of the corner of her eye as if to meet any challenge.

"You're a young lady now," Jen announced as Pat helped to clasp the necklace on, and then Jen produced a small mirror from her purse and held it up.

"Oh, Grandma . . . it's lovely."

"A lovely gift for a lovely lady."

John stood silent for a moment, not sure what to say as his little girl gazed into the mirror, raising her head slightly, the way a woman would, to admire the gold.

"Sweetie, I think you better check your blood sugar; you seemed a bit winded coming up the hill," John finally said, and his words came out heavily, breaking the moment.

"Yes, Daddy."

Jennifer leaned against the wall, took off her backpack and pulled out the blood-sugar test monitor. It was one of the new digital readout models. No more finger pricking, just a quick jab to the arm. She absently fingered the necklace with her free hand while waiting for the readout.

One forty-two . . . a bit high.

"I think you better get some insulin into you," John said.

She nodded.

Jennifer had lived with it for ten years now. He knew that was a major part of his protectiveness of her. When she was in her terrible twos and threes, it tore his heart out every time he had to prick her finger, the sight of his or Mary's approach with the test kit set off howls of protest.

The doctors had all said that, as quickly as possible, Jennifer had to learn to monitor herself, that John and Mary needed to step back even when she was only seven and eight to let her know her own signs, test, and medicate. Mary had handled it far better than John had, perhaps because of her own illness towards the end. Jen with her strength had the same attitude.

Strange. Here I am, a soldier of twenty years. Saw some action, but the only casualties were the Iraqis, never my own men. I was trained to handle things, but when it came to my daugher's diabetes, a damn aggressive type 1, I was always on edge. Tough, damn good at what I did, well respected by my men, and yet complete jelly when it comes to my girls.

"There's a few more gifts inside," John said. "Why don't you girls go on in? Once your sister gets home and your friends show up we can have our party."

"Oh, Dad, didn't you get Elizabeth's message?"

"What message?"

"Here, silly."

She reached up and fished the cell phone out of his breast pocket, tucked in behind a pack of cigarettes. She started to pull the cigarettes out, to stomp on them or tear them up, but a look from him warned her off.

"Someday, Daddy," she sighed, then taking the phone she punched a few keys and handed it back.

"Home late. Out with Ben," the screen read.

"She texted you and me during lunch."

"Texted?"

"Yes, Daddy, text message, all the kids are doing it now."

"What's wrong with a phone call?"

She looked at him as if he were from the antediluvian period and then headed inside.

"Texted?" Jen asked.

John held the phone so she could read the message.

Jen smiled.

"Better start keeping a sharper watch on Elizabeth," she said. "If that Ben Johnson has any of his grandfather's blood in him."

She chuckled as if remembering something from long ago.

"I don't need to hear this."

"No, you don't, Colonel."

"Actually, I kind of prefer 'Doctor,' or 'Professor.' "

"A doctor is someone who sticks things in you. A professor, well, they always struck me as a bit strange. Either rakes chasing the girls or boring, dusty types. Down here in the South, 'Colonel' sounds best. More masculine."

"Well, I am no longer in active service. I am a professor, so let's just settle for 'John.' "

Jen gazed up at him for a moment, then came up to his side, stood on tiptoes, and kissed his cheek lightly.

"I can see why my own little girl once fell for you, John. You'll lose both of them soon enough to some pimply-faced boys, so do hang on to her as long as you can."

"Well, you sure as hell didn't help, draping that gold necklace on her. What did it cost, a thousand, fifteen hundred?"

"Roughly, but then again, no lady tells the truth when it comes to her buying jewelry."

"Until the bill comes in and the husband has to pay."

There was a pause. He knew he had misspoken. If he had said such a thing around Mary, she'd have lit into him about a woman being independent and the hell with a husband handling the bills . . . and in fact she did handle all the family finances right up till the last weeks of her life.

As for Tyler, though, he no longer even knew what a bill was, and that hurt, no matter how self-reliant Jen tried to appear to be.

"I best be going," Jen said.

"Sorry, I didn't mean it that way."

"It's all right, John. Let me go up to the nursing home to spend some time with Tyler and I'll be back for the party."

"Jennifer was expecting a ride in that monstrous car of yours."

"The Edsel, my dear young man, was a generation ahead of its time."

"And the biggest flop in the history of Ford Motors. My God, look at that grille; it's ugly as sin."

She lightened up a bit with the banter. There were half a dozen cars in her huge garage, several newer ones but also an actual Model A, up on blocks, and, beauty of beauties, a powder blue 1965 Mustang convertible. A lot of bad memories, though, were tied to that Mustang. When John and Mary were dating, they had conned her parents into letting them borrow the car for a cruise up the Blue Ridge Parkway to Mount Mitchell and John, driving it, had rear-ended an elderly couple's Winnebago.

No one was hurt, but the car was totaled and Tyler had poured thousands into getting it restored . . . and swore that no one other than him or Jen would ever drive it again. And Jen still lived by that ruling.

"This Edsel will run forever, my dear, and just check on eBay to see how much it's worth. I bet a heck of a lot more than that SUV thing you've got."

He settled back against the stone wall as Jen maneuvered "the monster" around and cruised down the driveway at breakneck speed. The wall was warm from the afternoon sun. The Beanies were still there, and oh, that did hurt a bit; at least she could have carried Patriot Bear or the ostrich in.

Inside he could hear Jennifer and Pat chatting away about the necklace until the stereo kicked on. Some strange female wailing sounds. Britney Spears? No, she was old stuff now, thank God. What it was he couldn't tell, other than the fact that he didn't like it. Pink Floyd, some of the old stuff his parents listened to like Sinatra or Glenn Miller, or, better yet, the Chieftains were more his speed. He picked up one of the Beanies, Patriot Bear.

"Well, my friend, guess we'll soon be left behind," he said.

Leaning against the wall, he soaked in the view, the tranquility of the moment, broken only by the distant rumble of traffic on I-40 and the noise inside the house.

Ginger and Zach came back from their romp in the field behind the house and flopped down at his feet, panting hard.

The scent of lilacs was heavy on the air; if anyone wanted to truly see spring, they should live in these mountains. Down in the valley below, the cherry trees were in full bloom, just several hundred feet higher here at his home they were just beginning to blossom, but the lilacs were already blooming. To his right, ten miles away, the top of Mount Mitchell was actually crowned with a touch of snow, winter was still up there.

"When lilacs last in the dooryard bloomed . . ."

The scent always triggered in his mind Whitman's lament for Lincoln.

It reminded John that tonight, the second Tuesday of the month, was Civil War Roundtable night in the basement of the Methodist church. It'd be another fun round of the usual raucous debate, the other members all needling him as their one and only Yankee, whom they could pick on.

And then the phone rang. He pulled it out of his pocket, expecting it to be Elizabeth. There was going to be hell to pay if it was. How she could stand up her kid sister on her birthday to sneak off with that pimple-faced, horny, fast-handed Johnson kid . . .

But the area code was 703 . . . and John recognized the next three numbers . . . the Pentagon.

He opened the phone and clicked it on.

"Hey, Bob."

"John, how you doing? Where's my goddaughter?" He said it doing a halfway decent imitation of Marlon Brando as Don Corleone.

Bob Scales, now three stars, John's former boss at Carlisle and a damn good friend, had stood as Jennifer's godfather, and though Irish Catholic rather than Italian, he took the job seriously. He and his wife, Barbara, usually came down three or four times a year. When Mary died they had taken a couple of weeks off and stayed to help. They never had children and thus they considered Jennifer and Elizabeth to be their surrogates.

"Growing up," John said sadly. "Her grandmother gave her a gold necklace that must of cost a grand or more, which counted a helluva lot more than the Beanies, and the stack of Pokemon cards still waiting inside. I even got tickets to Disney World for once school lets out that I'll give her at dinner, but I wonder now if it will be the same."

"You mean when you took her there when she was six and Elizabeth ten? Hell, yeah, it will be different, but you'll still see the little girl come out down there, even with Elizabeth. How's Elizabeth doing, by the way?"

"I'm thinking of shooting her boyfriend later today."

Bob roared with laughter.

"Maybe it's best I didn't have daughters," Bob finally replied. "Sons, yeah . . ."

His voice trailed off for a moment.

"Hey, let me speak to Jennifer, OK?"

"Sure."

John walked into the house, shouting for Jennifer, who came dashing out of her bedroom, still wearing that damn necklace, and grabbed the phone.

"Hi, Uncle Bob!"

John tapped her on the shoulder.

"You take your insulin?" he asked.

She nodded her head; then chattering away, she walked around the house. John looked out the window across the valley to the mountains beyond. It was a beautiful, pristine spring day. And his mood began to lighten. Several of Jennifer's friends would be over soon for a small party. He'd cook up some burgers on the grill out on the side deck; the kids would then retreat to Jennifer's room. He had just opened the pool in the backyard over the weekend, and though the water was a chilly sixty-eight, a couple of the kids might jump in.

He'd flush them out around dark, go to his Roundtable meeting, and maybe later this evening he'd dig back into that article he was committed to for the *Civil War Journal* about Lee versus Grant as a strategic commander . . . a no-brainer but still an extra five hundred bucks when done and another vita builder for tenure review next year. He could stay up late; his first lecture wasn't until eleven in the morning tomorrow.

"Dad, Uncle Bob wants you!"

Jennifer came out of her bedroom, holding up the phone. John took it, gave her a quick peck on the top of her head and a playful swat as she ran back off. Seconds later the damn stereo in her room doubled in sound.

"Yeah, Bob?"

"John, I gotta run."

He could sense some tension in Bob's voice. He could hear some voices in the background . . . shouting. It was hard to tell, though; Jennifer's stereo was blaring.

"Sure, Bob. Will you be down next month?"

"Look, John, something's up. Got a problem here. I gotta—"

The phone went dead.

At that same instant, the ceiling fan began to slowly wind down, the stereo in Jennifer's room shut down, and looking over to his side alcove office he saw the computer screen saver disappear, the green light of the on button on the nineteen-inch monitor disappearing. There was a chirping beep, the signal that the home security and fire alarm system was off-line; then that went silent as well.

"Bob?"

Silence on the other end. John snapped the phone shut.

Damn, power failure.

"Dad?"

It was Jennifer.

"My CD player died."

"Yeah, honey." Thank God, he thought silently. "Power failure."

She looked at him, a bit crestfallen, as if he were somehow responsible or could snap his finger to make the CD player come back on. Actually, if he could permanently arrange for that damn player to die, he would be tempted to do it.

"What about my party? Pat just gave me a CD and I wanted to play it."

"No worry, sweetie. Let me call the power company. Most likely a blown transformer."

He picked up the landline phone . . . silence, no dial tone.

Last time that happened some drunk had rammed into a telephone pole down at the bottom of the hill and wiped everything out. The drunk of course had walked away from it.

Cell phone. John opened it back up, started to punch numbers . . . nothing.

Damn.

Cell phone was dead. He put it down on the kitchen table.

Puzzling. The battery in his phone must have gone out just as Bob clicked off. Hell, without electricity John couldn't charge it back up to call the power company.

He looked over at Jennifer, who stared at him expectantly, as if he would now resolve things.

"No problem at all, kid. They'll be on it, and besides, it's a beautiful day; you don't need to be listening to that garbage anyhow. Why can't you like Mozart or Debussy the way Pat here does?"

Pat looked at him uncomfortably and he realized he had committed one of the mortal sins of parenting; never compare your daughter to one of her buddies.

"Go on outside; give the dogs a run. They'll have the power back by dinnertime."

CHAPTER TWO

DAY 1, 6:00 P.M.

Flipping the four burgers on the grill, two for himself, one each for Jennifer and Pat, he looked over his shoulder and watched as the girls played tag with the dogs in the upper field behind his house. It was a beautiful sight, late afternoon sun, the eight apple trees in full blossom, the girls laughing as they dodged back and forth. Ginger, the younger and crazier of the two goldens, knocked Jennifer over with a flying leap as she tried to hold a Frisbee out of her reach, and there were more squeals as the two dogs and two girls piled on each other.

Months ago he had stopped wearing a wristwatch; the cell phone was now his timepiece. He looked through the kitchen window to the grandfather clock; it was just about six. The other kids should have been here by now; the agreement was they could come over for a brief party, but as it was a school night, the party would be over by 7:30. No one had shown yet. For that matter, he thought Jen would have been back long ago.

He lit a cigarette, puffing quickly—it was amazing how annoying a twelve-year-old could be when it came to a "quit smoking, Dad" campaign—and tossed the half-smoked Camel over the patio railing.

Burgers done, he set them on the patio table, went in, opened the fridge, pulled out the cake, and set it on the table, sticking twelve candles in.

Back out again to the deck.

"Dinner!"

The dogs responded long before the girls, racing out of the field, circled the table, and then sat at their usual begging positions. Pat and Jennifer came out of the field.

"Hey, Dad, something strange."

"Yeah?"

"Listen."

He stood there silent for a moment. It was a quiet spring evening, silent except for a few birds chirping, the distant bark of a dog . . . rather nice, actually.

"I don't hear anything."

"That's it, Dad. There's no traffic noise from the interstate."

He turned and faced towards the road. It was concealed by the trees . . . but she was right; there was absolute silence. When he had first purchased the house, that had been one disappointment he had not thought of while inspecting it but was aware of the first night in, the rumble of traffic from the interstate a half mile away. The only time it fell silent was in the winter during a snowstorm or an accident.

"An accident must of shut it down," he replied.

It was common enough, the long winding climb up from Old Fort; every month or two a truck would lose its brakes and roll or old folks in a forty-foot-long land yacht would lose it on the twisting turns as the highway zigzagged out of the mountains and down to the Piedmont. One such accident, a hazmat spill with a truck rolling over, had shut down traffic in both directions for over a day.

"Mr. Matherson. That's what we thought, but it's weird down there. No traffic jam, just cars stopped all over the place. You can see it from atop the hill."

"What do you mean?"

"Just that, Daddy. A bunch of cars, a lot on the side of the road, some in the middle, but no jam up, just everyone stopped."

He half-listened, while shoveling the burgers onto buns and putting them on the girls' plates.

"Most likely the accident's further on and people were told to pull over and wait," he said.

The girls nodded and dug in. He ate his first burger in silence, saying nothing, just listening. It was almost eerie. You figure you'd hear something, a police siren if there was indeed an accident, cars down on old Highway 70 should still be passing by. Usually if the interstate was closed, emergency vehicles would use 70 to access the highway and it would be jammed with people trying to bypass the interstate. At the very least this was the time of night the darn Jefferson kids, up at the top of the hill, would start tearing around into the forest with their damn four-wheelers.

And then he looked up. He felt a bit of a chill.

This time of day any high-flying jets would be pulling contrails, and directly overhead was an approach corridor to Atlanta for most flights coming out of the northeast. At any given time there'd be two or three planes visible. Now the sky was sparkling blue, not a trace of a contrail.

The chill . . . it reminded him of 9/11. How quiet it was that afternoon, everyone home, watching their televisions, and the sky overhead empty of planes.

He stood up, walked to the edge of the railing, shaded his eyes against the late afternoon sun. Up towards Craggy Dome there was a fire burning, smoke rising vertical, half a dozen acres from the look of it. Another fire raged much farther out on the distant ridge of the Smokies.

In the village of Black Mountain, nothing seemed to be moving. Usually, before the trees filled in completely, he could see the red and green of the traffic light at the intersection of State and Main. It was off, not even blinking.

He looked back at the grandfather clock. It was usually this time of day that the "million-dollar train" came through, so named because it hauled over a million dollars' worth of coal, mined out of Kentucky for the power plants down near Charlotte. When the girls were younger, an after-dinner ritual was to drive down to the tracks and wave to the engineer as the five heavy diesel-electric locomotives, thundering with power, pulled their load and crawled towards the Swannanoa Gap tunnel.

The silence was interrupted by a throaty growl as Grandma Jen came up the driveway in her monster, the Edsel.

She pulled in beside his Talon, got out, and walked up.

"Damnedest thing," she announced. "Power's out up at the nursing home. And you should see the interstate, cars just sitting all over the place, not moving."

"The power at the nursing home?" John asked. "What about the backup generator? That's supposed to automatically kick in."

"Well, the lights went out in the nursing home. I mean completely out."

"They're supposed to have emergency generation. That's required," John said.

"Never kicked on. Someone said there must be a broken relay and they'd get an electrician in. But still, it's a worry. They had to shift patients on oxygen to bottled air, since the pumps in each room shut off. Tyler's feeding tube pump shut off as well."

"Is he all right?"

"He was nearly done with the feeding anyhow, so no bother. They said he'd be OK. So I go out to the parking lot and all the five o'clock shift of nurses and staff were out there, all of them turning keys, and nothing starting . . . but that old baby, the one you call the monster, just purred to life. Had to be here for my little girl, and that monster, as you call it, worked as it always has."

She nodded back proudly to her Edsel.

"Can we go for a ride and see everything, Grandma?" Jennifer asked.

"What about your party?" John asked.

"No one else showed up," Jennifer said sadly.

Grandma Jen leaned over and kissed her on the top of the head.

"Lord's sake, child, you're a mess."

"They were up playing in the field."

"And wearing your necklace when doing that?" Jen asked, horrified.

John grimaced and realized he should have made sure Jennifer had taken it off before running around with the dogs. If she had lost it or it got broken in the roughhousing with the dogs, there'd have been hell to pay.

"A burger, Jen?" he asked quickly to distract her.

She shook her head.

"Not hungry."

"At least some cake."

"OK."

He went back into the kitchen and lit the twelve candles on the cake, a special one of course, no sugar, and brought it out singing "Happy Birthday," Pat and Jen joining in.

The other gifts were now opened, a card from Bob and Barbara Scales with a gift certificate for a hundred bucks for Amazon, the Beanies he had carried over from the wall and lined up on the table. Jennifer tucked Patriot Bear under her arm and opened the huge envelope, half as big as herself, that John had made up the night before, a collage of photos of Disney

World with a fake "Ticket for Jennifer, Daddy, and, oh yeah, Elizabeth" printed in the middle.

It was indeed a hit and now it was his turn to say, "Hey, don't squeeze so hard; you'll break my neck."

Finally it was over, past seven, and Pat started down the hill. Jennifer and the dogs walked her home.

"Guess there's no Roundtable meeting tonight," John said, looking back towards town, as Jen helped him load up the dishwasher, even though they couldn't turn it on.

"What do you think is going on?" Jen asked, and he could hear a touch of nervousness in her voice.

"What do you mean?"

"John, it kind of reminds me of nine-eleven. The silence. But we still had electricity then; we could see the news. All those cars stalled."

He didn't say anything. There was a thought, but it was too disturbing to contemplate right now. He wanted to believe that it was just a weird combination of coincidences, a power failure that might be regional, and would ground most flights due to air traffic control. Maybe it was some sort of severe solar storm, potent enough to trigger a massive short circuit; a similar event had happened up in Canada several years ago.

A thought hit him.

"Your monster, let's go turn it on."

"Why?"

"You'll see."

They went out to the car, John slid into the passenger seat, and she turned the key over, and the car instantly roared to life. The sound, even after but a couple of hours of silence, was reassuring.

He turned on the radio. It really was one of the old ones. With dials to turn, no buttons to push, the slightly yellowed face even had the two small triangles on them marking the frequency of the old Civil Defense broadcast frequencies.

Static, nothing but static from one end of the dial to the other. It was getting towards twilight, usually the time the FCC had most AM stations power down, but the big ones, the ones with enough bucks to pay for the license, should be powering up now to fifty thousand watts, and reaching halfway across the country if the atmospherics were right.

He could remember as a kid making the long drive from Jersey down to

Duke in his old battered 1969 Bug, killing the time by slowly turning the dial, picking up WGN in Chicago—that strange country and western station out of Wheeling, so alien sounding with its laments about pickup trucks and women—and throughout the night, if the atmospherics were just right, WOR out of New York, catching his favorite, Jean Shepherd, in the middle of the night.

Now it was just silence.

"You look worried, Colonel."

He looked over at her. The way she said "Colonel."

"Could be nothing. Might be one helluva solar storm, that's all."

That seemed to scare her and she looked to the western horizon to where the sun was now low, hanging over the Smokies.

"It isn't blowing up or something, is it?"

He laughed.

"My dear mother-in-law. If it had blown up, would we still be seeing it?"

A bit embarrassed, she shook her head.

"Major storm on the sun's surface will send out heavy bursts of various radiations. That's what triggers the northern lights."

"Never seen them."

"Well, you're not a Yankee, that's why. Sometimes the storm is so intense it sets off an electrical discharge in the atmosphere that short-circuits electronic equipment."

"But the cars?"

"Most cars today are loaded with computers. It might explain why yours keeps running and others stopped."

"People should have kept those old Fords," she said with a nervous smile.

"Let's do this, though," he said quietly. "I'm worried about Elizabeth; let's drive downtown, see if we can spot her."

"Fine with me."

She shifted the car into gear. At the bottom of the driveway he caught sight of Jennifer, shouted for her to pile in, and she ran over, delighted, climbing over her father and sitting between the two of them. That's the way it used to be forty years ago, he realized. Mom and Dad out for a drive, the kid between them, no bucket seats yet, except in sports cars, Junior not locked up in the back and, of course, belted in.

John just hoped Tom Barker, the town's chief of police, didn't spot them. Although John was now a well-confirmed local, Barker might just lay a ticket on them if in a foul mood.

They arrived to the bottom of the hill and Old 70 was empty except for a couple of abandoned cars by the side of the road. But out on the interstate there was indeed a "bunch of cars" as Jennifer had described it. Vehicles on the shoulders, some stalled right in the lanes. Not a traffic jam though, just as if everyone had shut their engines off at the same time and drifted to a stop. Nearly all the passengers were out, some looking over towards them as the Edsel pulled out onto 70 and headed towards town, driving parallel to the interstate.

"There's Elizabeth!" Jennifer cried, pointing down the road.

Sure enough, it was her, walking with that damn Johnson kid, his arm around her waist . . . not actually her waist but down lower, nearly resting on her backside. At the sight of the approaching Edsel, Ben quickly jerked his hand away. Jen pulled over to the side of the road and John got out.

"Where in hell have you two been?" John shouted.

"Hey, Dad, isn't this weird?" Elizabeth said with a smile, pointing towards the interstate.

She already had on her best con artist smile. Her head was tilted slightly, a bit of an "ah, Daddy, chill out," look in her blue eyes, playing every angle. She was, of course, a sixteen-year-old spitting image of her mother and she knew that would melt him. At this moment it also was triggering one helluva protective surge.

He turned his gaze on Ben. The boy had been a member of the scout troop that John had helped out as an assistant scoutmaster for several years. From that angle, Ben was a good kid, smart, made it to Life before dropping out because by ninth grade scouting wasn't cool anymore. A nice kid, his dad a member of the Roundtable.

But at this moment, Ben was a young man who had damn near been resting his hand on John's daughter's butt and lord knows where else over the last four hours.

"Mr. Matherson, it's my fault, sir," Ben said, stepping forward slightly. "Elizabeth and I went into the mall in Asheville after school; we wanted to get something special for Jennifer."

"Whatya get me?" Jennifer asked excitedly.

"We left it in the car," Elizabeth replied. "Dad, it was weird; the car just died a couple of miles west of town, near our church. It was weird, so we've been walking home."

John glared coldly at Ben and the boy returned his gaze, not lowering his eyes.

The kid was OK, John realized, didn't lower his gaze or try to act like a wiseass. He knew he had been seen and was willing to face an angry father. Elizabeth and Ben had been friends when in middle school, both were in the band together, and now, well, now it was obvious over the last several months he had turned into "something different."

It was just that as John gazed at Ben he remembered how he thought at seventeen and what the prime motivator in life was. Jen was looking over at John with just a touch of a sly grin.

"Ben, how's your grandpa?"

"Fine, ma'am. We was out fishing together on Saturday on Flat Creek and you should have seen the brookie he reeled in, sixteen inches. Made his day."

Jen laughed.

"I remember going fishing with him on that same creek. He'd always bait my hook," and she shuddered. "Lord, how I hated doing that. Tell him I said hi."

"Yes, ma'am, I will."

"You need a ride home?" John asked, finally relenting.

"No, sir. It isn't far," and he nodded to the other side of the interstate. "I can cross right over from here."

"All right then, Ben, your folks are most likely worried; get home now."

"Yes, sir, sorry, sir. Hey, shortie, Happy Birthday."

"Thanks, Ben." Like most kid sisters, she had a bit of a crush on her big sister's boyfriend. And Ben, being a smart kid but also, John grudgingly realized, a good kid, had a liking for Jennifer.

"Night, Elizabeth."

There was an awkward moment, the two of them gazing at each other. She blushed slightly. Ben turned away, walked over to the fence bordering the interstate, and in seconds had scrambled up and over it.

John watched him cross. Several people standing around their cars went up to Ben, and John didn't move, just watching. Ben pointed towards the direction of the exit into Black Mountain and then moved on. John breathed a sigh of relief.

"Excuse me. Excuse me!"

John looked over again to the fence that Ben had just scaled. A woman, well dressed, dark gray business suit, with shiny shoulder-length blond hair, was coming up the grassy slope, walking a bit awkwardly in her high heels.

"Ma'am?"

"Can you tell me what's going on?"

As she approached John, half a dozen more got out of their stalled cars and started towards the fence as well.

"I'm sorry, ma'am, I think I know just about as much as you do."

"I was just driving along," and she pointed back to the stalled BMW 330 on the westbound side, "and the engine just went off, the same with everyone else out here."

"I don't know for sure," John said, now choosing his words carefully as he watched more people approaching, four of them men in their late twenties, maybe early thirties, big guys, looked like construction workers. Some sort of instinct began to kick in as he watched them come up behind the woman.

"Hey, buddy, how come your car's running?" one of them asked. The man speaking was nearly as tall as John, stocky and well built.

"Don't know why it's running; it just is."

"Well, it seems strange, don't you think? All these cars out here dead and that old junker still running."

"Yeah, guess it does seem strange."

"What did you do to make it run?"

"It just turned on, that's all," John said quietly, fixing the man with his gaze and not letting it drop.

"Sir, can you give me a lift into town?" the woman asked.

He looked at the fence that Ben had scaled with such ease. John caught a glimpse of Ben going over the chain-link fence on the far side of the highway and then trotting up the road towards his house.

More and yet more people were approaching, an elderly couple, a woman leading a child of about six, a couple of teenagers, an overweight man in an expensive business suit, collar open and tie pulled down. A trucker over in the eastbound lane was out of his rig, slowly walking towards John.

"Ma'am, I don't see how you'll get over that fence," John said, nodding to the chain-link fence that separated them. "It's just over a mile to Exit

64," and he pointed west. "Don't get off at Exit 65; there's just a convenience store there."

He pointed to the lane for Exit 65 just a couple of hundred yards away that arced off the interstate just before the road curved up over a bridge spanning the railroad tracks.

"Go to Exit 64. You can walk it in twenty minutes. There's two motels there, one of them a Holiday Inn with a good restaurant as well. You should be able to still get a room till this thing clears up."

"John?" It was Jen, standing behind him, whispering. "Help her."

He let his hand drift behind his back and put his hand out forcefully, extended, a signal for Jen to shut up.

In many ways, eight years here had indeed changed him. Women were addressed as "ma'am" and doors were held open for them, no matter what their age. If a man spoke inappropriately to a woman in public and another man was nearby, there would be a fight brewing. The woman in the business suit looked at him appealingly. To refuse her went against a lifetime of thinking and conditioning.

Hell, there was even a touch of something going on here that he never would have dreamed of but ten minutes ago. Since Mary had died, there had been a few brief flirtations, even one brief affair with a professor at the state university, but down deep his heart was never in it; Mary was still too close. The woman on the other side of the fence was attractive, professional looking, early to mid-thirties; a quick glance to her left hand showed no ring. An earlier incarnation of himself, before Mary . . . he'd have cut the fence down to get to this woman and act as the rescuer. John was almost tempted now to do so.

But there was that "something else" now. A gut instinct that ran deeper. Something had gone wrong, what, he still wasn't sure, but there were too many anomalies, with the power off, the cars stalled, except for the Edsel, no planes. . . . Something was wrong. And at this moment, for the first time in a long while, his "city survival senses" were kicking in.

Growing up in a working-class suburb of Newark in the sixties and seventies he had learned survival. He was only seven when the big riots hit Newark in '67, dividing off for a generation any thought of what some called diversity. Italians stuck to their neighborhoods, Poles and the Irish to theirs, Hispanics to theirs, blacks to theirs, and God save you if you got caught in the wrong neighborhood after dark, and usually in daylight as well.

The interstate, at this instant, had become the wrong neighborhood. The way the four construction workers stood and gazed at him and the car—the one car with a motor still running—was triggering a warning. One of them was obviously drunk, the type that struck John as a belligerent drunk.

Something was changing, had changed, in just the last few hours. If alone, John might have chanced it, and chances were nothing at all would go wrong, but he was a father; his two girls and his mother-in-law would be in that car.

"Come on, buddy," the one worker said, his voice now edged with a taunting edge. "Help the lady. We'll push her over for you; then we'll climb over and you can give us a lift as well."

She looked back at the four.

"I don't need your help," she said coldly.

The drunk laughed softly.

John felt trapped, especially as he spared a quick glance back to Jennifer. Suppose the car was taken right now; it would be a long haul back for her.

At that moment he caught a glance from the truck driver. There was a slight nod and ever so casually he let his right hand, which had been concealed behind his back, drift into view. He was holding a light-caliber pistol. There was a moment of gut tightening for John, but the exchange of glances said it all. "It's OK, buddy; I'm watching things here."

John looked back to the woman.

"Ma'am, I'm sorry, I've got to get my kids home. You just walk a little less than a mile to the west and you'll find food and shelter."

"Rotten shit," the drunk growled, and moved to start climbing the fence.

"Girls, into the car," John snapped, and there was no hesitation. The doors slammed behind them. John backed up to the car, the drunk had a hard time negotiating his footing. John slipped into the driver's seat, slammed into reverse, and floored it.

"Son of a bitch, all we want is a lift," and as the drunk half-dangled from the fence he flipped John off.

Flooring the gas, John continued to back up all the way to the turnoff to their road, threw the gear into forward, and roared up the dirt road.

"John Matherson, I can't believe you left that lady like that. Especially with those men around her."

"I have a family," John said coldly, looking into the rearview mirror to where Elizabeth and Jennifer were in the backseat, both of them silent. He could sense their accusation, that Dad had chickened out. He shook his head and said nothing.

He pulled into the driveway, the dogs started to bound around him but then, sensing his mood, shifted their attention to Jennifer and Elizabeth.

"Girls, it's getting dark. Remember the hurricane last year when we all piled into my bedroom? It'll be like that tonight. Elizabeth, get out the Coleman lantern; you know how to light it. Jennifer, you help her."

"Come on, Dad; I think you're being a little uptight."

"Just do it, Elizabeth," he said slowly and forcefully.

"All right."

The two headed to the door, Jennifer pestered Elizabeth as to what her birthday present was.

"And Elizabeth, after you get the lantern lit, help Jennifer with her injection. Don't keep the medication out of the fridge any longer than you have to."

"OK, Dad."

"Then feed the dogs."

"Sure, Dad."

The girls went in. John fished in his pocket for a cigarette, pulled it out, and lit it.

"Are you going back to help that woman?"

"No."

Jen was silent for a moment.

"I'm surprised at you, John."

"I know I'm right. I go down to that highway and those bastards might take this car."

"But what about her? The woman? Does it bother you?"

He looked at Jen sharply.

"What the hell do you mean?"

"That woman. And there was another one with a small child. They could be raped."

He shook his head.

"No, not yet. Those guys weren't all that bad. The drunk was out of hand; the loudmouth one was just trying to show off in front of his buddies and the woman. Sure, it's strange, our car running, the others not, and if I went back down they'd be tempted to take it. Or worse yet, I'd be stuck all night running a shuttle service for everyone stalled on the highway, and running into yet more drunks with a bad attitude.

"But rape? No, too many others down there are OK. Everyone else is sober; the truck driver down there had a gun in his hand, though you might not of seen it. He'll keep order. That woman and the others will be OK. I wouldn't worry about that yet."

"Yet?"

He sighed, shook his head, let his finished cigarette fall, then fished out another one and began to smoke it.

"I'd like you to stay here tonight, Jen. The girls would love it."

"You worried about me?"

"Frankly, yes. I don't like the idea of you driving around alone at night in this monster," and as he spoke he slapped the hood of the Edsel.

"I'll stay."

He looked down at her, surprised there was no argument, about the cat needing to be put out or some other excuse. It was dark enough now he couldn't see her face, but he could sense her voice. She was afraid.

"It's so dark," she whispered.

He looked around. It *was* dark. There wasn't a single light down in the town, except for what appeared to be the flicker of a Coleman lamp, some candles. All the houses rimming the valley were dark as well. No reflected lights from the highway, none of the annoying high-intensity lithium glare from the service stations at the exit, not a light showing from the skyline of Asheville. There was a dull red glow, what looked to be the fire up on the side of the mountain towards Craggy Dome.

The stars arced the heavens with a magnificent splendor. He hadn't seen stars like this since being out in the desert in Saudi Arabia . . . before the oil wells started to burn. There was absolutely no ambient light to drown the stars out. It was magnificent and, he found, calming as well.

"Head on in, Jen. I'll be along in a minute."

She left his side, moving slowly. From inside the house he could now see the glare of the Coleman and, a moment later, heard laughter, which was reassuring.

He finished the second cigarette and let it drop, watching as it glowed on the concrete pavement of the driveway. It slowly winked out.

Opening the door of his Talon, he slipped in and turned the switch. Nothing, not even a stutter from the starter motor, no dashboard lights . . . nothing.

He reached under the seat, pulled out a heavy six D-cell flashlight, and flicked the switch. It came on.

When he went into the house the girls were already making a game out of camping out.

"Dad, Jennifer's new tester doesn't work," Elizabeth said.

"What?"

"The new blood tester. I found the old one, though, and we used that. She's OK."

"Fine, honey."

Somehow, that little fact now did set off more alarm bells within. The new testing kit was a high-tech marvel with a built-in computer that kept a downloadable record of her blood levels. In another week she was supposed to be fitted out with one of the new implanted insulin pumps . . . and something told him he should be glad they had not yet done so.

"OK."

Elizabeth started to turn away. He took a deep breath.

"Elizabeth?"

"Yeah, Dad?"

"Ah, you and Ben," he felt embarrassed suddenly, "you know, is there anything we should talk about?"

"Come on, Dad. Now?"

"Yeah, you're right. Get your sister settled in and let's call it a night."

"Dad, it's not even eight yet."

"Like the hurricane, kid. We went four days then and by the end of it we were asleep when it got dark and up at dawn."

"OK."

He looked into his bedroom and Jennifer was, to his delight, lining up her new Beanies along what she had already claimed was her side of the king-size water bed. Clutched under her arm was her beloved Rabs, the stuffed rabbit that Bob and Barbara gave to her the day she was born and which had been Jennifer's steadfast companion for twelve years.

Once a fuzzy white, old Rabs was now a sort of permanent dingy gray.

Rabs had survived much, upset stomachs, once being left behind at a restaurant and the family drove nearly a hundred miles back to retrieve him while Jennifer cried every mile of the way, a kidnapping by a neighbor's dog, with Dad then spending two days prowling the woods looking for him. He was patched, worn smooth in places, and though she was twelve today, Rabs was still her buddy and John suspected always would be . . . until finally there might be a day when, left behind as a young lady went off to college, Rabs would then rest on her father's desk to remind him of the precious times before.

The dogs had finished up chomping down their dinner and he let them out for their evening run. Ginger was a bit nervous going out, since usually he'd throw on the spotlights for them. At this time of year bears with their newborn cubs were wandering about, raccoons were out, and the sight of either would nearly trigger a heart attack. She did her business quickly and darted back in, settling down at Jennifer's feet.

"No school tomorrow?" Jennifer asked hopefully.

"Well, if the lights come on during the night, you'll know there's school. If not, no school."

"Hope it stays pitch-black all night."

"You want me in the guest room?" Jen asked, carrying the Coleman lantern.

"In with us, Grandma," Jennifer announced.

"That puts me in the middle," Elizabeth complained, "and Brat here kicks when she's asleep."

"All right, ladies, I'll be out in my office. Now get to sleep."

Jen smiled and went into the bathroom, carrying the lantern.

"Night, girls."

"Love you, Daddy."

"Love you, too."

He closed the door and went into his office. He sat down for a moment at his desk, setting the flashlight on end so that the beam pointed to the ceiling, filling the room with a reflected glow.

The office had always driven Mary crazy. She expected "better" of a military man to which his retort always was that she had also married a professor. Stacks of paper were piled up on either side of his desk, filed, he used to say, by "geological strata." A floor-to-ceiling bookshelf to his left held books two rows deep, the references for whatever he was working on at the moment, or what interested him, on the nearest shelf. The other walls were lined with photos, his framed degrees, Mary's degree, pictures of the kids.

He stood gazing at the bookshelf for a moment, pulled several books from the outer layer aside, found what he wanted, and fished the volume out. He had not opened it in years, not since leaving the war college.

Sitting down and propping the book on his knees, he held the flashlight with one hand, checked the chapter headings of the work, a mid-1990s dot-matrix computer printout, then sat back and read for half an hour. He finally put the report down on his desk.

Behind him was a locked cabinet, and opening his desk, he pulled out a single key, unlocked the cabinet, and swung the door open. He reached in, hesitated for a second, deciding which one, then pulled out his pump 20-gauge bird gun. From the ammunition rack he opened up a box of bird shot, and slipped three rounds in. The bird shot was not a killing load, except at very close range, but definitely a deterrent.

Next was the pistol. It was, he knew, an eccentric touch. A cap-and-ball Colt Dragoon. A big, heavy mother of a gun, the sight of it enough to scare the crap out of most drunks.

John had actually been forced to use it once for real, back in his undergraduate days, before he met Mary. He was living off campus, in a farmhouse shared with half a dozen other guys, all of them rather hippieish that year, long haired, the year he definitely smoked a little too much dope . . . something that Mary had made clear would stop on day one if they were to date.

Some local good old boys had taken a distinct dislike to "long-haired faggots" living nearby and one night did a "drive-by," blowing out the kitchen door with a load of buckshot, yelling for the faggots to come out and get what they deserved.

His roommates were freaked, one of them cried that they were in the middle of *Deliverance.* But their attackers had not counted on one of the "faggots" being from New Jersey, already into Civil War reenacting, and someone who knew guns. He had come out, Dragoon revolver in hand, leveled it, and fired off two rounds of his cannon. Not aiming to kill, just to make them duck a bit. After pumping out the two rounds, he lowered his aim straight at the chest of the redneck with the shotgun.

"Next shot's for real," John said calmly.

The rednecks piled into their truck and disappeared in one helluva hurry, his buddies standing on the porch, in awe as he walked back, feeling more than a little like Gary Cooper in *High Noon*.

"Peace through superior firepower," he said calmly, then went inside and poured himself one helluva vodka to calm down while his roommates chattered away, reenacting the drama for half the night.

What had truly scared him? The realization that he was ready to kill one of the bastards if they had tried to venture another shot. Reflecting on it later, he didn't like that feeling at all, and hoped he'd never have it again . . . though he would, years later in Iraq, but at least then he was not pulling the trigger just ordering others to do so.

The following morning, a Saturday, the landlord had come over with a case of beer, asked to see this now-legendary gun, and said that "you boys got some respect now."

A month later, stopping in a roadside bar with a couple of friends to get a beer, John had run into one of the four who had been his harassers. John recognized him, there was a tense moment, and the redneck broke out laughing, brought John a beer, and told everyone the story, concluding with "this Yankee boy's OK," and they shook hands.

Damn, even then he did love the South.

The revolver was already loaded, and he put it on his desk.

He suddenly realized someone was in the room and looked up. It was Jen in the doorway.

"This is serious, isn't it?" she asked.

"Go to sleep." He hesitated. "Mom."

She stood silent for a moment, nodded, then disappeared.

Without taking his shoes off, John stretched out on the sofa in his office, laying the shotgun down on the floor by his side.

It was a long couple of hours before he finally drifted to sleep. As he began to fall asleep, Zach disengaged himself from Jennifer's embrace, came out to the office, and with a sigh settled down by John's side.

CHAPTER THREE

DAY 2

The scream woke him up. He fumbled for the shotgun, got half to his feet, and heard Elizabeth cursing.

"There's no hot water, damn it!"

Putting the gun down, he walked into the bedroom as Elizabeth stormed out of the bathroom, a towel wrapped around her.

"Dad, there's no hot water!"

"What in hell did you expect?" he grumbled, heart still racing a bit.

Jennifer was sitting up, Rabs tucked under her arm, smiling.

"No school, Dad?"

"Nope."

"Great!"

"Dad, how am I going to take a shower?"

"Take it cold; it won't kill you," he muttered, and then wandered into the kitchen.

Coffee, damn it, coffee.

He pulled the foil bag down, the paper filter, made the coffee extra strong, filled the pot up, poured it in, and flicked the switch.

He stood there like an idiot for a good minute before the realization hit.

"Ah, shit."

He pulled a small pot out from under the cabinet, filled it with water and walked out onto the porch, flicked on the grill, and set the pot on it. Fumbling in his pocket, he got out a cigarette and lit it.

Though he was watching the pot, it finally did come to a boil, and a minute later he had a cup, doing it the old way he had learned in the Boy Scouts: throw a couple of spoonfuls of coffee into the cup, pour the hot water in, and to hell with the grinds.

"Got one for me?"

It was Jen.

"Sure."

He mixed a second cup and she looked at it with disdain.

She went back into the kitchen and opened the fridge, sniffing the plastic jug of milk after opening it, then came back out on the porch, taking a sip.

"Keep your teeth closed and that will filter out the grinds," John said, finally forcing his first smile of the day.

"Got to find an old-style percolator," she said. "Always thought that made the best coffee anyhow. Never liked those Mr. Coffee machines."

It was a bit chilly out and he found it invigorating. The coffee and cigarette were working their magic, bringing him awake.

Unlike the vast majority of men who had made careers in the army, he had never adjusted to early morning rising and hated all those who could do it, especially the cheerful ones. His instinct always was to be a night owl, to go to sleep around two or three, then wake up at nine or ten for his first lecture at eleven.

The college had learned that quickly and never scheduled a class for him prior to that time.

But he did have to admit, mornings were beautiful and he regretted missing them at times. Mary had been a morning person. He thought about her . . . remembering how sometimes at dawn she'd wake him up, at least for a few minutes to . . . The memory was too painful and he let it drop.

"That fire is still burning," Jen said, pointing to Craggy Dome.

He nodded. The flame had spread out, a plume of smoke flattening out, then drifting down towards the Asheville reservoir in the valley below. Looked like a hundred acres or more.

Far in the distance, out on the distant horizon, he saw two more plumes of smoke from fires.

The world was silent, no traffic; down in Black Mountain nothing was moving.

Nothing had changed.

"Can I have some?"

It was Elizabeth, hair wet, rubbing it with a towel, a heavy winter bathrobe wrapped around her, shivering.

"Sure, sweetheart," and he mixed up a third cup, which she drank without complaint.

Jennifer came out on the porch as well, Rabs tucked under her arm. She looked so adorable. When asleep, or half-awake as she was now, there was still that certain look, the eyes of a baby still there.

"You sure there's no school?"

"Doubt it."

She yawned, turned about without comment, and went back inside.

"You do your blood test?" he asked.

"Yeah, Dad, it's OK," and she wandered back to the bedroom to go back to sleep.

"I think I'll head down to town now, see what's going on."

"Can I come?" Elizabeth asked.

"No, I'd like you to stay here."

"Ahh, come on, Dad. Everyone will be down there; I want to see what's happening."

He took her gently by the arm and led her away from the screen door.

"I want you here to guard the house."

She gave him a sarcastic smirk.

"From what? Terrorists?"

"Don't joke about it," he said forcefully, and she fell silent, looking up at him.

"You know how to handle the shotgun. It's the 20 gauge, so don't be afraid of it. The safety is off, but I don't have a round chambered in it. So if need be, pump and then shoot."

"Dad, you're freaking me out here."

"Listen, Liz, I'm not joking around. I think something serious has gone down."

"What?"

"Look around. There's no power, nothing."

"It'll come back on."

He didn't say anything, just staring at her.

"Anyone you know coming up the driveway, OK. But if it's a stranger, I want you to stand in the doorway, but use the frame to cover yourself. Let them see you have a gun pointed in their direction. Don't take any bullshit or con lines. I don't care how pathetic they might look. If they're looking for a phone, water, help, just tell them to walk on into town and there'll be people there to help them. Got it?"

"Yeah, sure."

"Got it?" And this time his voice was sharp.

"Yes, Dad."

"If they try anything, anything at all, you don't hesitate, Liz. None of this warning-shot crap. You aim straight at their midsection and squeeze. If it's more than one man, drop the one closest to you, or anyone armed."

"Dad, you're scaring me."

He put his hands on her shoulders and squeezed them tight.

"I taught you and your mom to shoot. And remember what I said about what was most dangerous."

"A woman with a gun who doesn't have the guts to use it," she recited. Mary had always said it was such a sexist line.

"A guy like that drunk last night, he can sense it if you are not really going to shoot. You make it clear you're not taking," John hesitated, "not taking any shit and chances are you'll go through life and never have to pull a trigger."

"OK, Dad."

He forced a smile. "I'm just being paranoid, sweetie. Keep Jennifer close by; if Pat comes up to play, so much the better."

"What about Ben?"

He hesitated. Jen was inside.

"No problem."

"He really is a sweet guy, Dad, if you'd give him a chance."

He nodded.

"I know that."

"Why do you dislike him so much, Dad?"

"You know."

She smiled.

"Like he's going to get beyond a little making out with me? I think you used to call it past first base."

He stiffened a bit; it was the first time she was even being slightly direct.

All the "female"-related issues he had left to the care of Grandma Jen, including "the talks," other than the traditional old-style father routine of glaring at any boy who started to hang around.

John knew he wasn't much of a father for this new century, maybe a bit old-fashioned, but that was the way he was raised . . . and he had assumed for so many years that such things were Mary's territory.

"It's because of Mom in a way, isn't it?"

"How's that?"

"You know. We lost Mom, but you lost your wife, your friend and companion. Jennifer and I, we're filling in for some of the loss, and down deep you hate the thought that we're growing up and, in doing that, eventually we're moving away from you as well."

He didn't say anything, a bit startled by her insight.

"What makes you think that?"

"Oh, the therapist we went to after Mom died. But it's the truth, Dad. It's OK.

"I love you, Daddy; I always will," she said, going up on tiptoes to kiss him on the cheek. "You'll always be my number one guy."

He hugged her, eyes filled with tears.

"Thanks, honey."

They stepped back from each other, both feeling a bit awkward.

"I'll see what I can work up for breakfast," she said, and went back into the kitchen.

"Your girl is definitely growing up." It was Jen coming up to him, offering a second cup of coffee.

He sniffled a bit, nodded, then smiled.

"Mary was like that at sixteen. Wise beyond her years. Used to throw Tyler for a loop sometimes."

John drank the second cup. It was cooling, but that didn't matter, though two cups and two cigarettes without a breakfast did make his stomach feel a bit jumpy.

"You mind if I borrow the monster, go downtown, and see what is going on?"

"No," and she smiled. "The Mustang, though, that's still a different story."

As he drove past the interstate all the cars were exactly where they had been the night before. The road was empty, except for a lone trucker, sitting in his cab, door open, puffing on a cigar, the driver waving to John. It was the guy from the night before, and the sight of him was a reassurance.

John felt a bit of relief, fearful that something ugly might have indeed happened down here during the night, but all was quiet, no sign of any problems.

Coming up State Street, he passed the elementary school. The front door was propped open, and for a second he wondered if indeed school was open today but then realized that all the school buses were still parked in the lot. There was a hand-lettered sign out front: "Emergency Shelter."

Pete's Barbecue House, the restaurant across the street, had volunteered their big outdoor grill, the kind used at festivals and fairs, and there was Pete, set up in front of the school, wearing his absurd pink apron and pink chef's hat with a smiling pig painted on it, a couple of kettles on the grill, a line formed for coffee and barbecue for breakfast. Typical of Pete, always there for the town.

John honked and Pete looked up in surprise, as did those on the line, and Pete waved.

The light up ahead was off and John had to slow down, half a dozen cars blocking the road. It forced him to swing over to the eastbound side and he came to a stop first, looking both ways. It felt absurd doing it. Of course there was no traffic in sight other than all the stalled cars at the intersection. He weaved around, turned right, and pulled into Smiley's convenience store, got out of the car, and walked in.

"Hey, Hamid, how are you?"

Hamid had proven to be a fascinating addition to the town. He was Pakistani, married to a local girl, and purchased the store a few months before 9/11. Two days after "that day" the FBI had shown up and arrested him, claiming that there was a report that he had made a statement in support of the attack and would love to help out if anything was tried locally.

The arrest, to John's delight, had triggered a firestorm. The town turned out, rallied support, harassed the daylights out of the district's congressman to investigate, and finally Hamid had returned, a block party being held for him.

On the morning after his return, a huge hand-lettered sign was plastered across the window of his store. "I am proud to be an American. . . . God bless all of you, my friends."

Hamid was behind the counter; in fact, John suspected he damn near lived in his store.

"Crazy out there," Hamid said. "I had to stay here all night. People coming in from the highway. It's been nuts."

"How about a couple of cartons of Camel Lights?" John said.

Hamid shook his head.

John rattled off several more brands until finally he got a hit with Kool Lights.

"Still got three cartons."

"I'll take 'em."

John pulled out his wallet and started to draw out his bank card.

"John, that's down, you know."

"Oh yeah."

He pulled out some cash, fifty dollars, still twenty dollars short.

"Just pay me later today; I know you're good for it."

He hesitated before taking the cartons.

"Hey, look, Hamid, I think I gotta tell you this first. You've always been a good guy to me. I'm not even sure about giving you money at the moment. Things might be a whole lot worse than it looks right now."

Hamid looked at him quizzically.

"What do you mean, John?"

He pointed to the money on the counter.

"I mean that."

"The money?" And he laughed. "Maybe in my old country, but here, American money? You're kidding?"

"Just that I felt I had to tell you, the price of cigarettes might be a whole helluva lot more than twenty three bucks a carton in a few days."

Hamid took it in and, smiling, he pushed the cartons across to John.

"Thanks, John, I see your point, but take them, my friend."

John breathed a sigh of relief. At the moment he'd have emptied his wallet for one pack, but now he could take them without feeling guilty.

"Thanks, Hamid."

John took the cartons and looked around the store. Nearly all the beer was gone, most of the soda as well. Munchies, chips, pork rinds, all gone.

Hamid laughed.

"Best night of business I've ever done. Must have a couple thousand in cash here."

"Hamid, do yourself a favor."

"What?"

"Take down the rest of your cigarettes and stash them."

"Why?"

"Just call it an investment, a hedge on inflation."

Hamid shook his head.

"Can't do that. Maybe for strangers from the highway, but my friends here?"

John smiled.

"Just a friendly suggestion, Hamid. Stash them away; from now on, if you want to sell them to friends, do so just one pack at a time."

Leaving Hamid, who as soon as John was out the door began to pull the cartons off the display rack, he drove another block to the center of town, again weaving around the stalled cars, and turned up Montreat Road, usually the route of his daily commute to the college. The fire station and police station were on his right and there was a moderate-size crowd there, all looking in his direction. He pulled in, got out of his car, this time locking it and pocketing the keys.

"Hey, John, how the hell did you get that old beast rolling?"

It was Charlie Fuller, the town's director of public safety, which made him head of both the fire department and the police department. He was also a long-standing member of their Civil War Roundtable and often John's chief antagonist when it came to debates about the Constitutional justice of the Southern cause.

John looked around at the open parking area. All the fire engines were hangared inside the building along with the ambulance.

"Anything moving here?" he asked.

Charlie shook his head.

"Nothing. It's been a difficult night."

"How so?"

"Somewhere around a dozen dead, for starters."

"What?"

"Heart attacks mostly. One overweight out-of-shape guy walked in from the highway and collapsed right here, right where we're standing. I have no ambulance, nothing. We got Doc Kellor over, but the guy was already gone."

Charlie hesitated.

"Three dead up at the nursing home. Tyler's OK, though," he added quickly. "At least last I heard.

"Folks have been walking in, or riding bikes in, reports of accidents, and that fire up on Craggy."

"Yeah, I saw it."

"Someone said it was a plane, a large one, going in."

John didn't say anything.

"John, all my communication links are down. Everything, landline phone, radio. I have not heard a word from Asheville and I'm in the dark."

"What I figured."

There was the sound of a rattling engine, a sound he could instantly recognize, and around the corner an old Volkswagen van appeared, driven by Jim Bartlett, John's neighbor from down the street.

Jim pulled up by John's Edsel and got out. The sight of Jim always cracked John up; it was as if he had stepped out of a time machine from 1970, raggedy jeans, collarless shirt, headband like the kind Willie Nelson used to wear, the only giveaway of time passage the fact that Jim's chest-length beard and short-length hair were nearly all gray.

"**Hey** guys, what's happening?" Jim asked with a bit of a sardonic smile.

"So your old VWs are still running," Charlie replied.

Jim smiled. "Even if the world is coming to an end my man, they'll keep on rolling right up until the final big boom."

"Well," Charlie said quietly, voice pitched low so others wouldn't hear, "I'd prefer you not going around saying it's the end of the world."

"But it is," Jim replied, still smiling. "Been saying it for years. The Mayan Prophecy. They were saying December 2012, but somebody obviously got the date wrong.

He raised his voice a bit.

"This is it, my friends. The Day of Doom, just like them Mayans predicted."

John looked around, half a dozen small groups were gathered outside the station, and as Jim spoke people started to turn and look towards him.

"Been telling you all for years that this day was coming," Jim announced, strangely he was still smiling. "The Mayans had it right."

"My kid told me about that last night," someone replied, "yeah, some sci-fi guy wrote a book about it, my boy gave me the book and it seemed on the mark with all of this. Jim's right, this could be it."

John had always liked Jim, in almost every way he was a level handed, gentle soul, but he did harbor a few eccentric ideas, and now he had an audience.

"Power going off is just the starter. Wait until you see what happens to the sun."

"Damn it, Jim," Charlie hissed, "come over here."

Charlie forcefully put a hand on Jim's shoulder, moving him closer to the firehouse, John following.

"Are you crazy?" Charlie whispered hoarsely. "You want to start a panic?"

Jim looked at him confused.

"I should haul your butt inside right now for inciting panic."

"Just a minute," John interjected, putting his hand on Charlie's and pulling it off Jim's shoulder.

"Jim, maybe you're right," John said hurriedly. "But there are lot of kids standing around. You want to scare the crap out of them at a time like this? Come on, my friend, chill out, let parents tell their kids in their own way. Please."

Jim nodded thoughtfully.

"Sorry bro, didn't mean to scare anyone."

John made eye contact with Charlie. If his friend tried to collar Jim and make a scene, it just might very well start the panic rolling. Charlie got the message.

"Ok, sorry, Jim. Just I don't want the kids getting frightened any more than they already are. So do us all a favor, and don't talk about this Mayan stuff for right now. Got it."

"Sure, my man, got it."

"Now just go around and tell people you were joking, calm them down," John interjected, "it'd help a lot."

"Got it."

Jim made a show of turning back to face those who had been watching them.

"Just having some fun, that's all," Jim announced.

"Some fun," came a bitter reply. "We want to know what the hell is going on."

"That's what we're working on right now," Charlie announced, "so let's just stay calm."

"You two, we gotta talk." Coming out of the station was Tom Barker, the chief of police.

"Shit," Jim muttered. "Here comes the man."

"Tom, how you doing?" John said quietly.

"Like a legless dog that's covered in fleas and can't scratch," Tom replied, and John smiled a bit at yet another of Tom's colorful southernisms.

"Charlie, a question for you," John said. "Absolutely no communication whatsoever and all vehicles dead except for my car and Jim's here?"

"Yeah, that's about it. Also the old Jeep down at Butler's Garage still runs, though. We've got a couple of older mopeds and motorcycles, and Maury Hurt's antique World War Two jeep. We've got that out on the highway now, checking on some emergency cases that people reported."

"Not good," John said softly.

"I think we're on the same wavelength," Charlie replied softly.

"Where's Orville Gardner?"

John knew that Orville worked downtown in Asheville, as assistant director for the county's emergency preparedness office.

"Not a word from him. Guess he's stuck in Asheville."

"Tom, Charlie, can we go inside and talk?"

"Why?" Tom asked. "I'd like to know why you two have cars and the rest of us don't."

"Because nothing can kill a Volkswagen, man," Jim said with a grin.

John stepped between Jim and Tom.

"I really think we should go inside, gentlemen," John said. Though most of his career in the military had been spent behind books or up front in a classroom, he had led troops in the field and still did remember a bit about command voice, and he used it now.

Tom bristled slightly, but Charlie smiled.

"Sure, let's go. The mayor's inside; let's go to her office."

The three went in, Jim trailing along, and though John hated to insult the man, he turned and looked at him with a smile.

"Hey, look. You know you're a hair up Tom's butt."

Jim smiled.

"He's out in my back lot every year prowling for weed and never caught me once."

"Maybe you should skip this meeting. Keep an eye on the cars. Help keep people calm and no more of this stuff about prophecies. OK?"

"Sure, my man," and Jim gave him a friendly salute.

John walked into Mayor Kate Lindsey's office and she looked up from behind her desk, bleary-eyed. They were old friends. Kate and Mary had grown up together.

"You look beat, Kate."

"I am. Never should have run for a third term. Damn thankless job at the best of times, and now this. Did Tom tell you that someone came down from the nursing home? They've got three dead up there."

"Yeah, I heard."

"One of them was the Wilson boy."

John sighed and shook his head. The boy had been a freshman at the college. Car accident three years ago, the usual story, a drunk who walked away from it, had left the boy in a vegetative state, kept alive by a respirator, his parents clinging to hope. . . . Well, that was finished.

"I thought the law required all nursing homes to have emergency generation. Those folks up there are going to be facing one helluva lawsuit," Kate snapped.

"What about the highway?" John asked. "Any problems there? I had a bit of a confrontation with a drunk last night."

"I got four drunks in the lockup right now," Tom said. "Your boy's most likely one of them. You want to press charges or anything?"

"Naw, no bother."

"Someone came riding in on a bike a few hours ago from the North Fork, said a trailer burned there and old Granny Thomas burned to death in it."

"Damn," John whispered.

Kate looked out the window and then back to John.

"So why are your car and Jim's running?"

John looked around for a chair and sat down without being asked, then handed over the report he had pulled down from his shelf the night before and tossed it on Kate's desk.

"Something from my war college days."

" 'Potentials of Asymmetrical Strikes on the Continental United States,' " Kate read the cover.

"Some of us working at the war college put it together for a series of lectures. No one listened, of course, other than the officers taking our classes. I kept a copy as a reference. What you want is chapter four on EMP."

"EMP," Charlie said quietly. "Exactly what I thought when I saw all the stalled cars on the highway. Glad you came in, in fact was hoping you might know something."

"All right, not to sound like the dumb female in the crowd here," Kate said sharply, "but what the hell are you guys talking about?"

John couldn't resist looking over at Tom.

"Heard of it, but don't really remember. Are you saying this is some sort of terrorist thing?"

John nodded.

"EMP. Electromagnetic Pulse. It's the by-product of a nuclear detonation."

"We've been nuked?" Kate asked, obviously startled.

"I think so."

"Jesus Christ, what about fallout? We got to start moving on that right now."

John shook his head.

"Give me a minute, Kate. This gets a little complex. When you got some time, read the article; that will explain it better."

"John, have we been nuked? Is this a war?"

"Kate, I don't know. I know as much as you do at the moment as to what is going on outside of right here, in Black Mountain, but that alone tells me a lot."

"How so?"

John took a deep breath and looked at the Styrofoam cup on her table, the paper plate covered with crumbs.

"Look, guys, I hate to ask this. I'm starved and could use a little more caffeine."

No one moved for a second. Kate made it a point to remain firmly in her chair, not budging an inch.

"We got a pot boiling out back," Charlie said, and left the room and came back a minute later with a cup of coffee, black the way John always liked it, and, amazingly, some bacon and eggs.

"Picture an EMP as something like a lightning bolt striking your electrical line or phone line during a thunderstorm." John said between quick sips of his coffee. "Boom, and everything electronic in your house is fried, especially delicate stuff with microcircuitry in it. That bolt is maybe packing thousands of amps the microchip in your computer runs on hundredths of an amp. It just cooks it off."

Kate said nothing, giving him a moment to wolf down one of the eggs and a piece of bacon before continuing.

"Back in the 1940s, when we started firing off atomic bombs to test them, this pulse wave was first noticed. Not much back then with those primitive weapons, but it was there. And here's the key thing: there were no solid-state electronics back in the 1940s, everything was still vacuum tubes, so it was rare for the small pulses set off by those first bombs to damage anything.

"We finally figured out that when you set off a nuke in space, that's when the EMP effect really kicks in, as the energy burst hits the upper atmosphere. It becomes like a pebble triggering an avalanche, the electrical disturbances magnifying. It's in the report. It's called the "Compton Effect."

"Now come forward. When we did those articles back in the nineties, we were getting word that the Chinese were doing a helluva lot of research on how to boost the EMP from a nuclear blast, making it a helluva lot more powerful."

"So it's the Chinese who hit us?" Tom asked. "Damn bastards."

"I don't know," John said, a bit exasperated. "No one knows, at least not here, not yet. Maybe even the Pentagon doesn't know yet."

He hesitated after saying that, thinking of Bob Scales up there. Did the Pentagon exist? There was no news. One scenario that his group had kicked around was an initial EMP strike to take down communications, then selected ground bursts of nukes on key sites to finish the job . . . and of course D.C. would be the first hit.

It was maddening; John just did not know.

"How can nobody know anything around here?" Kate snapped.

"That's the whole idea behind an EMP strike," John replied. "Whether a full-scale strike from a traditional foe like Russia during the Cold War or a terrorist hit now. You pop off a nuke that sends out this strong electromagnetic wave, it fries off communications, and a lot of other things, then either sit back or continue. The frightful thing we realized was that some third-rate lunatic, either a terrorist cell member or the ruler of someplace like North Korea or Iran, with only one or two nukes in their possession, could level the playing field against us in spite of our thousands of weapons. That's what is meant by 'asymmetrical strike.'"

"So, is the whole country like this right now?" Kate asked. "Or is it just us?"

He shook his head.

"Look, I'm kinda tired, sat up most of the night keeping watch on the house, so let me try to explain this in order if that's OK."

"Sure, John, take your time," Charlie intervened.

"Well, at the same time the potential energy release of EMP grew, and believe me, I don't understand the technical side of it at all, just that I know that it happens when a nuke goes off and we suspect there's ways of calibrating a small nuke to give off a high yield of energy. Our electronic equipment was getting more and more sensitive to it."

"No one saw an explosion," Charlie said, "and believe me, I've asked around, kind of suspecting the same thing."

"That's just it, it's in the report," and John motioned to the article on Kate's desk.

She looked at it, thumbed through it.

"Mind if we run off some copies? . . ." And she fell silent, blushing slightly at what sounded like a dumb comment.

"We're all conditioned," John said with a reassuring smile. "I tried to make coffee in the machine this morning. It's OK, Kate."

She smiled sheepishly and nodded. "Go on, John."

"Well, to Charlie's question. EMP doesn't really hit unless you blow off the bomb above the atmosphere. Again the 'Compton effect,' and believe me, I've read about it, but don't have a real grasp on it myself; I need a tech head for that. Just that the burst above the atmosphere sets off an electro-disturbance, kind of like a magnetic storm, which cascades down into the lower atmosphere like a sheet of lightning and bango, it fries everything with electronics in it."

"Just one bomb?" Kate asked.

He nodded.

"Remember a TV back in the fifties, the early sixties, all those tubes, and hot as hell? That same thing now sits in the palm of my kid's hand when she's playing one of those damn games."

He wondered for a second if maybe all the pocket-size computer toys were gone. . . . If so, no regrets there at least.

"So the stuff gets more and more delicate, and more and more prone to even the slightest electrical surge."

"Someone could now fire off a nuke, calibrated to do a maximum load of EMP, and anything within line of sight from up in space gets fried, even from a thousand miles away. For that matter, anything hooked into our electrical web goes as well. Electrical lines are like giant antennas when it comes to EMP, and guide it straight into your house, through the sockets, and, wham, right into anything hooked up."

"Surge protectors, though?" Kate said. "I spent a hundred bucks on one for my new television."

He shook his head.

"Surge protectors don't work for this," Charlie interjected, and John looked over at him.

"We had one, exactly one, briefing on this about two years ago," Charlie said. "Hundreds on every other threat, just one on this, but I remember somebody asking that question. Seems like this EMP moves a lot faster than ordinary power surges like from lightning. Not faster in terms of speed, just that the impact hits and peaks faster, three or four times that of a lightning bolt hitting your electric line. So fast that the relay inside the surge protector doesn't have time to trigger off and boom, the whole system is fried. That's why it's so darn dangerous. It fries out all electronics before any of the built-in protections can react."

"You still haven't answered my question about your damn car," Tom snapped. "Why is yours working and I've got six squad cars out there that are dead?"

"The electronics," Charlie interrupted. "That's what got me thinking on it, too, but I didn't feel it was right to say anything about it."

"Why not?" Tom asked.

"Panic. That's why. I saw an article on the Web about this a couple of months back, and it was a lot worse than what we were talking about just two years ago. Some people who don't like us have apparently been spending a lot of time and money to get a bigger bang for the buck."

"So why didn't we just protect ourselves?" Kate asked. "Hell, what does it take to build a better surge protector?"

John sighed and shook his head. She was so damn right.

"Kate, it's some rather technical stuff, but it meant retrofitting a lot of stuff, hundreds of billions perhaps, to do all of it. And besides, a lot of people in high places, well, they just glazed over when the scientists started with the technical jargon, the reports would go into committees, and . . ."

"And now we got this," Charlie said coldly.

John nodded, frustrated.

"Global warming, sure, spend hundreds of billions on what might have been a threat, though a lot say it wasn't. This, though, it didn't have the hype, no big stars or politicians running around shouting about it . . . and it just never registered on anyone's screen except for a few."

"I don't get it with the cars, though," Tom interjected. "Computers, yes, but a car?"

"Any car made after roughly 1980 or so has some solid-state electronics in it," John said. "Remember carburetors, thing of the past with fuel injection and electronic ignition. That's why my mother-in-law's old Edsel is OK and Bartlett's VW out there. No computers in the engine, and vacuum tubes in the radio. The surge had nothing to fry off; therefore, it still runs. Now everything in a car is wired into some kind of computer. Better living through modern science."

John fished in his pocket for a cigarette, pulled it out, then hesitated. Kate was glaring at him, as was Tom. The town had a no-smoking ordinance for all its buildings.

John hesitated, but damn, he wanted one now.

"Look, guys, if you want me to talk, I get a cigarette."

"Mary would kick your ass if she knew you were still smoking," Kate said.

"Don't lay the guilt on me," John replied sharply. It was Mary's dying that had snagged him back into smoking after being clean for ten years. The army had started getting uptight on it, and amongst all the other aspects of grooming for the star, smoking was a checkmark against him with some of the bean counters and actuaries in the Pentagon who argued why invest the effort on a guy who might die early?

"Go on; light up." She hesitated. "And give me one of those damn things, too."

Now it was his turn to hesitate. He hated leading someone back into sin, but on this day . . . what the hell.

He lit her cigarette. She leaned back in her chair, inhaled deeply, let it out, and sighed.

"God damn, I've been wanting that for six years now. Damn, is it good."

A couple of seconds later she actually smiled, the first time she had done so since he walked in.

"Head rush," she muttered, then took another puff.

"Damn near everything has a computer in it now," John continued. "Cash registers, phones, toys, cars, trucks, but, most vulnerable of all, the complex web of our electrical distribution system. All of it was waiting to get hit."

Tom leaned against the wall and let a few choice words slip out.

"You think they'd of seen this coming. Done something about it."

"Who is 'they,' Tom?"

"Jesus, John, you know. The president, Homeland Security. Hell, I was getting e-mails damn near every day on terrorist alerts, training on what to do if they hijacked a truck loaded with nuclear waste, even a drill with the hospital last year if they unleashed some sort of plague. I got twenty bio and hazmat suits in a storage closet. Never even heard about this thing being talked about."

John sighed.

"Yeah, I know. It was off most people's screens. Seemed too sci-fi to some of them. But that doesn't matter now."

"I'm still worried about radiation, though," Kate said, "fallout."

"Don't."

"You sound rather assured of yourself."

"You don't have a single radio working here, nothing at all?" John asked.

Tom shook his head.

"I do."

"Where?"

"In the Edsel. It's an old tube radio. I checked it last night. Static from one end to the other. If this thing was local, if they had popped a bomb over Atlanta, Charlotte, we'd still be picking up radio stations from the Midwest and Northeast."

"Why?"

"It's a horizon event. Line of sight, like I said. I'll guess it was one to three nukes, lit off a couple of hundred miles up above the atmosphere, covered most, maybe all, of the United States. Fallout is a by-product of rubble blown up into the atmosphere from a bomb going off. Pop an EMP above the atmosphere . . . and, well, at least you don't have any fallout worries."

"Jesus Christ," Charlie sighed.

That caught John slightly off guard. Charlie was strict Southern Baptist, and for him to say that . . . well, it was a major sin, though a Catholic wouldn't think twice about it.

"Who do you think did it?"

"Does it matter?" John replied.

"Yeah, maybe it does to me?" Tom said. "I got a boy over in Iraq right now. You know that one of my nephews is with the navy out in the Pacific. I sure as hell would like to know who they're fighting. If it was the Chinks, my nephew will be in it. The rag heads and it's my son."

"Doubt if it's China," John said quietly.

"Why? You said they were the ones doing the research."

"Doing the research, but using it in a first strike? Doubt it. They are just as vulnerable to EMP as we are. Do it to us and we'd flatten them and they know it."

"We have it, too?"

"Sure we do. What the hell do you think the threat was to Saddam back in 1991? Charlie, you were over there then, same as me; you remember."

"Yeah, if they hit us with any weapon of mass destruction the word was we'd pop a nuke off about twenty miles above Baghdad."

"When a nuke goes off above the atmosphere or even in the high upper atmosphere, it sets off that electrical chain reaction I talked about. Again, just like a solar flare, usually the upper atmosphere absorbs the magnetic disturbance of a solar flare and up north we see that as the northern lights. But if it's big enough, the disturbance hits the ground and starts shorting things out. So we threatened Saddam with an EMP if he unleashed anything on us," John said. "It would have shut down the entire power grid of central Iraq and shut down their entire command and control system as well. They didn't, so we didn't."

"Wouldn't that have fried our stuff, too?" Kate asked.

"No. Remember, it's line of sight. Twenty miles up, our forces in Saudi Arabia would have been below the horizon. Besides, all our equipment was hardened against EMP to varying degrees. They spent a lot of money on that back during the Reagan years."

"So our military is still OK here in the states then?" Kate asked.

"Doubt it. That's the gist of the report I just gave you. Every administration since Reagan's has placed hardening of our electronics on the back shelf. Meanwhile the equipment kept getting more delicate and thus susceptible and the potential power of the burst kept getting one helluva lot stronger. Remember how we were all wowed by the high-tech stuff back in 1991. That equipment is now as primitive as a steam engine compared to what we got now. And in constantly making computers and electronics faster and better we made them smaller, more compact, and more and more vulnerable to an EMP strike."

He dropped the butt of his cigarette into his nearly empty coffee cup, offered a second to Kate, who took it, and lit another for himself.

"Who then?"

"For my money . . . maybe North Korea, maybe Middle East terrorists with some equipment supplied by Iran, Korea, or both. As for the warhead, we all know there's enough of those left over from the old Soviet Union that sooner or later someone would get their hands on, if for nothing else than the goodies inside that go bang. Iran and Korea were hellbent on making nukes as well. But they'd be crazy to throw three or four at us when we could make the rubble glow for a hundred years with a thousand fired back in reply. But turn them into EMP weapons . . . and they win, at least in terms of hitting us harder than we could ever have dreamed of.

"Maybe launched from a sub, hell, even from a freighter that got up a couple of hundred miles from the coast. Get that close and even an old Scud could just about get the package high enough. One like I said, maybe two or three, and you've just castrated the entire country."

"We'll flatten the bastards for this," Tom snapped.

"Most likely already have, but do they give a shit? Hell no. The leaders will survive; they're most likely down in bunkers a thousand feet deep laughing their asses off right now. Hell, if we flatten them, they'll tell their own people that survive that we struck first and then they got millions more followers."

"I can't yet believe this," Kate sighed.

"Sun Tzu," Charlie said.

John looked at him and smiled.

"The enemy will never attack you where you are strongest. . . . He will attack where you are weakest. If you do not know your weakest point, be certain, your enemy will."

All three looked at him in surprise.

"Hey, I remember a few things from college."

No one spoke for a moment.

"What happened out there," John said softly, "doesn't matter to us now. It's what happens here in Black Mountain that does."

"How long before the power comes back on?" Kate asked. "Or we get some word from Washington on what to do? Or even from Raleigh or Asheville?"

Strangely, an old Civil War song flashed into his mind, a line from "Lorena": "It may be for years, and it may be forever."

"Weeks, months, maybe years," John said, and he found he could not look into Kate's eyes as he said it.

Yesterday, her biggest concern was the hot argument in the town about who would be grand marshal this year for the Fourth of July parade, that and the continuing wrangle with Asheville about water rates.

"We've got to prioritize," Tom said. "Security for one thing. I've got five hundred strangers from the interstate on my hands this morning. What the hell should we do with them for starters."

No one spoke.

"Well, we just can't kick them out," Kate said.

John did not reply.

"Priorities for getting through this," Charlie interjected, and now everyone was becoming agitated. John realized that for the last fifteen hours they had been waiting for "someone else" to tell them what to do. The reality was beginning to hit, that there just might no longer be "someone else."

"Water first," Kate said. "Once the tank on top of the hill runs dry, the pipes will start emptying out. We don't have any means then of pumping more back up to the tank. Most of the town will be dry within a day."

"We're lucky in one sense," Charlie said. "We get our water gravity fed from the reservoir. The dam face is at twenty five hundred feet above sea level, so at least here in town we'll get some, but anyone above that elevation line is screwed."

John realized that meant him; his neighbor had a sign on his driveway: "Half mile high." They were 250 feet above the gravity feed point for water. *At least we have the pool, thank God.*

"Food," Tom said. "Jesus, no electric means no refrigeration."

John was silent, on his third cigarette as the other three argued about what to do next.

"I'm making a quick run up to the college, and once the pharmacy opens I've got a very important errand to run," John said. "I've told you all I know, so if you will excuse me."

He stood up and started for the door.

"John."

He knew this was coming. It was Tom.

"Concerning your car."

"What about my car?"

"I'd like to have it."

"Why?"

"I need to get around."

"Use a bike; it'll be good for you."

"John, don't bullshit around with me; I need that car. I'll give you a lift home, but I do need it."

John stared right at Kate for a moment, then back at Tom.

"That car is mine, my family's. You declaring martial law?"

"I think we'll have to," Kate said quietly.

"When you do, come and try and take it, Tom."

"What do you mean 'try'?"

"Just that. Just try."

Tom stood silent, no one speaking, and then finally he nodded.

"OK, John."

He looked back at Kate, who sighed and then nodded in agreement.

"Sorry, John, we were out of line."

"That's OK. Just a bit of advice, Kate."

"And that is?"

He pointed to the cigarette in her hand.

"Now that you are hooked again. You better go over to Smiley's and get several cartons. Cash only. If Hamid says he doesn't have cartons, pull rank on him. He's hiding them in the back of the store. You better load up now 'cause you're going to need them."

John turned and headed out the door and then realized that Tom had followed him out.

"What the hell is it now?" John asked.

Tom hesitated.

"Look, John. Sorry. I haven't slept since yesterday. Sorry about back in there," and he extended his hand.

John took it.

"Tom, I don't envy you your job one bit."

"Look, John. I know I might not be the brightest lightbulb in the pack.

You're the smart guy. I like my job, though, and try to do what's right. But I never thought I'd be dealing with something like this."

"Yeah, I know. Hard day. Damn, I hope I'm wrong about everything I just said back in there. My first thought was it was some sort of weird solar storm. Maybe I'm dead wrong and ten minutes from now the lights will come back on."

"Think they will?" Tom asked hopefully.

John reluctantly shook his head, went over to his car, unlocked it, and got in. He almost felt guilty as he turned the switch and the car roared to life. Everyone gathered in the parking lot looked at him as he drove off.

The run up to the college had been a quick one. He felt, though, that he had to go, just check on what was happening.

A lot of heads turned as he drove into the campus and pulled in front of Gaither Hall.

"Hey, Doc, cool wheels!" someone shouted, and John nodded and smiled.

The conversation with President Hunt only took a couple of minutes. He had basically figured out the same thing and was already organizing the place. The kids were feasting on steak and ice cream this morning; they were emptying out the freezers as quick as possible and stuffing the food into bellies. Anything preserved or canned could wait.

The kids on this small campus were a good crew and ready to help out. A group had been organized to push cars clear of the road; others were hauling buckets of water all the way from the lake up to makeshift tanks near buildings in case of fire. The water in the campus pool would serve as drinking water, and four Porta Potties, hauled with much groaning and complaining, had been commandeered from the construction site for the new gym and a couple of new houses going up in the Cove and placed in front of the dorms.

The head of campus security, Washington Parker, who until now was viewed by most of the kids as a "rent-a-cop" to be teased about falling asleep in the student union at three in the morning, now had a job. He was old ex-military, an actual marine sergeant from long ago, in his early sixties and the good-natured guy who usually had nothing more to do than bust a kid for being publicly drunk or shine a spotlight into a parked car to break up a hot and heavy session. Parker had already met with the heftier members of the ball team and their coach to discuss keeping the campus safe and setting up a twenty-four-hour watch.

Parker had taken his job seriously for years, in spite of the fact that if ever there was a "safe" campus in the mountains of western North Carolina, it was Montreat College up in the Cove. A year or two would go by without even a minor crime, let alone the far more serious issues of rape, assault, or heavy drugs. But he had religiously attended every conference on campus security offered by the government, especially the ones that dealt with the potentials of a terrorist takeover of a campus. He had once talked with John about that issue, pointing out that the fact that they were, in general, so darn safe up in these mountains meant they were exactly the type of campus that just indeed might be hit.

As John pulled away from Gaither Hall and turned to head back into town, he spotted Washington standing by the gateway that led into the campus. John slowed and came to a stop. Washington looked over at him and then actually saluted.

"Morning, Colonel."

It was an old joke between the two, colonel and sergeant, but today it felt more than a little strange.

"Inspecting the troops?" Washington asked.

"Just figured I'd drive up and see how things were here."

"It's EMP, isn't it?"

"How'd you know?"

"Your car for one, sir," Washington drawled, his deep South Carolina African-American accent rich and full, mingled in with that clipped tone of a former marine drill sergeant.

"Pre solid-state electronics. I bet Miss Jen's Mustang will run as well."

Her home was within walking distance of the campus. The realization caught him . . . everything was measured in walking distance now.

"You dropping a hint, Sergeant?"

"Yes, sir. I am. It'd be good to have at least one vehicle up here so I can move around quickly if needed. Besides, once people start figuring things out, it'll get stolen."

"She'll kill me if I ever tell her, so it's between us, Washington." John fished into his pocket and pulled out his key ring and snapped one off.

"That's to her house. Security code number is . . ."

He laughed softly and shook his head.

"The key to the Mustang, well, I never had security clearance for it."

Washington laughed.

"I can jump it."

"It's yours for the duration," John hesitated, "or until this old beast breaks down or someone gets it. Chief Barker and I nearly got on that very issue less than an hour ago. I managed to hang on to this monster, but Barker just might remember the Mustang, so I suggest you get over there now. Possession is always nine-tenths of the law."

"Deal, sir. I'll take good care of her, no joyriding, sir."

"Come on, Washington. It's 'John'; cut the 'sir' shit. I work for a living now."

Washington smiled.

"You said the duration, sir, when it came to the car," and now his features were serious.

Washington finally looked away from him and back to the gate.

"Good position here, you know that," Washington said.

John had thought about it more than once on his drive up the Cove to the campus. The gatehouse was a stone arch over the roadway, a tiny stone building, with nearly sheer ledges to either side, the road having been cut through the ledge a hundred years back. Long ago, back in the 1920s, it had been the entry to a tourist road that weaved up the mountains all the way to the top of Mount Mitchell. The gatehouse was a quaint leftover of that long-abandoned road. To the east of the gate, Flat Creek tumbled by; to the west, a near vertical cliff cut through the descending ridge to open the lane for the road. There was only one way in and one way out, and it was here.

Washington had obviously contemplated this fact long years ago.

John said nothing and he drove off heading back into town, crossing State Street and over the tracks of the Norfolk & Southern. He passed the Holiday Inn. A number of people were sitting around outside; a group of kids were playing tag. Several grills were set up, food cooking on them.

He slowed as he spotted someone standing down by the road, her arms folded, just gazing off towards the mountains. He pulled up, again a bit uncomfortable with how many people turned at the sight of his car.

The woman looked at him. There was a flicker of recognition.

"Ma'am, I owe you an apology."

"I think you do."

She was still dressed in her business suit, but the high heels were gone, replaced with a battered pair of sneakers.

He opened the door and got out and extended his hand.

"Look, seriously, I apologize. I had my kids with me, my mother-in-law, and frankly . . ." He hesitated.

She relented and extended her hand and took his.

"Sure; I understand. Guess I'd of done the same if the roles were reversed."

"John Matherson."

"Makala Turner."

"Curious name."

"My granddad was stationed in Hawaii during the war. Said it was a flower there. Talked my dad into using the name."

John couldn't help but let his eyes drift for a second. She was tall, even without her heels on. Five ten or so, slender, blond hair to shoulder length, top two buttons of her blouse unbuttoned.

It was just the quickest of glances, but he knew she was watching. Strange. If you don't check an attractive woman out, even for a second, it's an insult; if you do, there might be a cold, icy stare.

She smiled slightly.

"Where you from?" John asked.

"Charlotte. Supervising nurse for a cardiac surgical unit. Was coming up here to attend a conference at Memorial Mission Hospital on a new procedure for heart arrhythmias.

"Now, could you do me a favor and tell me just what the hell is going on?"

"That reminds me," John said. "Look, I've got to do something right now. Will you be here in ten minutes?"

"Sure."

He got back into the car, hesitated, and looked at her.

"I'm heading to the drugstore right now. I need to get something. If you want, you can come along."

She didn't move.

"I'm not trying to pick you up or anything. Really. I got to get some medication for my daughter. Just I can answer your questions while I drive."

"OK. Don't seem to be going anywhere else."

It was only several more blocks to the shopping plaza with Ingram's market and the CVS drugstore. The parking lot was nearly full, but no one was about.

He got out and looked at the drugstore, disappointed; it was dark. Damn, it must be closed, but then he realized the absurdity of that; all the stores were dark.

"I think it was EMP, like I just said," John said, continuing their brief conversation.

"Had the same thought."

"Why?"

She smiled.

"I help run a surgical unit. We had a lot of disaster drills, especially since nine-eleven. We did a scenario on that one, EMP. It wasn't pleasant. Kept me awake thinking for nights afterwards. Hospitals aren't hardened to absorb it; the emergency backup generators will blow out along with everything else, and you know what that means."

"You'll have to tell me more later on," John said. He pulled on the door and it swung open.

Inside was a minor bedlam, a harried clerk behind the counter shouting, "Please, everyone, it is cash only. I'm sorry, no checks. . . ."

John walked past her to the back of the store and the pharmacist counter. One of the regulars was there, Rachel, her daughter was one of Elizabeth's friends. One of a line of a dozen people, a heavyset man in his early forties, bit of a tacky suit, tie pulled down and half open, was at the counter.

"Listen to me!" he shouted at Rachel. "I need that prescription filled now, god damn it."

"And sir. I keep trying to tell you, I'm sorry, but we don't know you, we don't have a record for you on file, and that, sir, is a controlled substance."

"I'm from out of town, damn it. Don't you hicks up here understand that? Now listen, bitch, I want that prescription."

John caught the eye of Liz, the pharmacist. She was in her early thirties and, John always thought, about the most attractive pharmacist he had ever laid eyes on. She was also married to an ex-ranger. Unfortunately, her husband was nowhere around and with Liz at not much more than five two and a hundred pounds, she was definitely way out of her league.

Liz looked at him appealingly. John took it in, looked around, a book and magazine rack by the counter. Nothing he could use. The cooler for beverages, however, was about twenty feet away.

He backed over to it, not many had hit here yet, reached in, and pulled out a liter bottle of Coors beer. Makala was looking at him with disgust, not understanding what was happening.

Liz, coming up to the counter, tried to confront the belligerent customer, extending her hand for him to calm down.

"Listen, damn it. OxyContin, you hear me. I'll take thirty and you can call my doctor once the power comes back on and he'll confirm it."

"Sir. Please leave this store."

"That's it! Both of you bitches, get out of my way."

He started to climb over the counter, Liz backing up.

John was up beside him and slashed out, the bottle smashing across the side of the man's head, shattering.

As he started to collapse, John pulled him back from the counter, flinging him to the ground, and for good measure stomped him in the solar plexus, doubling him up.

The man was on the floor, keening with a high, piercing shrill. Everyone else stood silent, stunned. John looked over at Liz.

"Sorry."

He actually felt embarrassed by what had just happened. He had broken a societal taboo; folks around here did not go around smashing beer bottles across a guy's head, from behind, in the local pharmacy. John almost expected an alarm to go off, the police to come barging in. . . . There was only silence except for the pitiful cries of the man on the floor.

Still silence. John looked at the others lined up. Several turned and fled. One woman was shaking her head.

"Is this how you treat strangers in this redneck town?" she snapped. "I'll be damned if I ever stop here again."

She stormed out.

He recognized one of the men. Pat Burgess, a Baptist minister, part of his Civil War Roundtable club.

Pat nodded.

"Good work, John. Sorry, but with my heart, I'd most likely pitched a coronary if I had taken him on."

It snapped John out of the momentary haze, the shock, back to the reality of where they were and what had to be done, for that matter what he was here to do.

"Pat, can you see to him? Get a belt or something and tie his hands first. Maybe somebody can look at his face and see if I cut his eye."

"You did, you goddamn bastard. I can't see! My lawyer's going to rip you an extra asshole!"

The man started to scream again and John tapped him with his shoe. He cringed, falling silent.

John leaned over.

"Listen to me. You threatened these women. One more word and I will cut your eyes out," John said, and the man fell back to crying, clutching his face, blood leaking out between his fingers.

John looked back at Liz, then stepped around behind the counter.

"Liz, can we talk for a moment?"

"Sure, John."

He motioned to the back corner of the pharmacy area and the two went into the locked area and half-closed the door.

"Thank God you came in, John," Liz whispered hoarsely. "I've had three like that already. We bluffed the other two out, but that guy was crazy. Most likely addicted. Doesn't travel with any in case he ever gets stopped, and his supply is at home."

"Look, Liz, I need a favor."

Liz fell silent, the look of gratitude disappearing.

"I think we got a bad situation," Liz said quietly. "Don't we?"

"I won't lie to you. I think we do."

She looked back towards the counter, the line of customers, more coming in and queuing up.

"I've been here all night," she said wearily. "I live in Asheville, nothing was moving, I was hoping Jim might come to get me, but he hasn't shown . . ."

Her voice trailed off.

"How long before the electric comes back on?"

"I don't know."

"How long?"

"A month, maybe a year or more."

"My God," Liz sighed.

"Exactly, and you know what I am asking for."

"John, I have exactly forty vials in stock. There's one other kid in this town with the same thing your girl's got. Over a hundred adult diabetics with varying degrees of insulin needs.

"I've had four folks down here this morning already asking for extras. I can't give them out, John. I'm responsible to everyone here, not just Jen. . . ." She hesitated. "Not just you, John."

"Liz, we're talking about my daughter, my little girl," and his voice began to choke.

She pointed towards the neatly arrayed cabinets with medications.

"John, I've got hundreds of people I'm responsible for, and if what you said is true a lot of them will die, some in a matter of days. We just don't keep that much inventory in stock anymore. None of the pharmacies do; we rely on daily shipments."

"There won't be daily shipments for quite a while, Liz."

"Then my patients with pancreatic enzyme disorder? They don't take their pills daily they die. If what you told me is true, Mrs. Sterling will be dead within a week. . . ." Liz's voice trailed off and she stifled back a sob.

She took a deep breath and looked back up at him.

"Severe hypertensions, arrythmias, we got five people on antirejection drugs for transplants. Jesus Christ, John, what do you want me to do?"

He hated himself for doing it, but now started he couldn't stop.

"I lost Mary already, Liz. Please, dear God, not Jennifer, too. Not that."

He lowered his head, tears clouding his eyes. He wiped them away, struggling for control.

He looked back into Liz's eyes, shamed . . . and yet, if need be, determined.

Liz looked straight at him and John could see that her eyes were clouded as well.

"It's going to get bad, isn't it, John?"

He nodded his head, unable to speak.

Liz continued to gaze at him, then sighed, turned, and opened the refrigerator. She pulled out four vials, hesitated, then a fifth.

John struggled with the horrible temptation to shove Liz aside, reach in, and scoop all of them out. The temptation was near overpowering.

He felt the touch of a hand on his shoulder and started to swing, wondering if somebody was pushing their way in. It was Makala. She gazed at him and said nothing.

Liz quickly closed the refrigerator, opened a cabinet, took out a box of a hundred syringes, then bagged the vials and box up, wrapping several extra layers of plastic around the package.

"Maybe I'm damning myself for doing this," Liz said quietly. "That's five for you; there'll be five for the Valenti boy, and one each for the remaining thirty that come in here."

"That's fair enough," Makala whispered.

Liz looked at her, didn't say anything, then turned away.

"Stop at the cooler; there still might be some ice there. Grab up whatever candy bars are left as well. Go straight home, John. They should be kept stable at forty degrees; every ten-degree increase cuts the shelf life in half. So go home now. Once you run out of ice, try and find the coolest spot in the house to store them."

"Thank you, Liz. God bless you."

"Please leave, John. I got a lot to think about, to do today."

John nodded, still filled with a sense of shame.

"You want me to stop at the police station and bring someone back?"

Liz shook her head. "I'll send Rachel into town to get some help. She rode her bike in here, so she can be there nearly as quick as you."

Liz then opened a drawer in the locked room and pointed down. Inside was a .38 Special.

"It was against company policy, but my husband insisted I keep it here. You know how he is, ex-ranger and all that. I'd of used it if you hadn't showed up," and her voice was now cold. John wondered if he had tried to shove Liz aside, would that .38 have come out? From the look in his friend's eyes, he knew it would.

"Some advice, Liz."

"Sure."

"Get out of here."

"You know I can't do that, John."

"I mean once it starts to run short. Load up what you think you'll need for you and your family; then get out. When you start running out, it could get ugly."

She looked up at him and smiled, all five foot two of her standing with shoulders back.

"Jim taught me how to use that gun," she said. "I'll see things through."

John squeezed her shoulder.

"God bless you," and he walked out. The line behind the counter was growing. There were several nods of recognition; some were silent. Apparently everyone in line knew what had just happened with the bloody man whom Pat had thoroughly trussed up with, of all things, a roll of duct tape.

One woman saw the bag John was carrying.

"Matherson, isn't it?"

"Yes, ma'am."

She looked past John to Liz. "What did you give him back there?"

"Just some syringes for his little girl, that's all, Julie."

"I don't want to hear tell of any special treatment going on here, Liz. If so, I've been a customer of this firm for twenty years and let me tell you I have a list here. . . ."

John went down aisle four. Surprisingly, there was a whole stack of one-pound Hershey bars, and without hesitating he scooped them all up and dumped them into the bag. The high-school-aged girl behind the counter saw him do it, not sure what to say as he walked by.

"Don't worry. Liz said I can take them now and pay later."

The girl nodded, his action setting off an argument with a customer who had no cash and wanted cigarettes.

Outside John opened up the ice cooler. There were still a dozen ten-pound bags inside. He unlocked the car, opened the back door, and went back, pulling out four bags and tossing them in, went back again, and started to grab four more, then hesitated, looking at Makala.

He took just two, closed the lid, tossed them in the car, and slammed the door shut.

John got into the car, took a deep breath, started it up, and lit another cigarette.

"That'll kill you someday," Makala said quietly.

He looked over at her, unable to speak.

"You did the right thing. And so did Liz. Any parent would have done the same."

John sighed.

"Remember the old movies, the old cartoons from the Second World War. All the stuff about food hoarders."

"A bit before my time."

"Hell, I'm only forty-eight; I remember 'em."

She didn't say anything.

"Your girl has type one diabetes, doesn't she?"

"Yes."

"You better get home now like Liz said."

Makala reached over the backseat, and he felt like an absolute bastard, for he found himself looking at her as she stretched, dress riding up to midthigh.

She caught his eye as she pulled a bag of ice over, and said nothing as she broke it open. She dumped the box of syringes out of the plastic bag and then gently laid the bag containing the vials atop the open ice.

"That should do till you get home. Don't pack them inside the ice; they'll freeze and that will ruin them. Try wrapping insulation around the ice, but keep the top open and have the vials on top. That should keep them at roughly the right temperature. Stash the remaining ice inside your freezer; that's the best-insulated place for them.

"With some luck the ice should last you up to a week."

"I don't know how to thank you enough," John said.

"Well, helping me find some food might be a good starter," she said with a smile.

"I know where there's great barbecue."

"Sounds wonderful."

He pulled out of the plaza and headed back towards town.

"Hope you don't mind a personal question?" she asked.

"Go ahead."

"Who's Mary?"

"My wife."

"How long ago?"

"Breast cancer, four years back."

"I'm sorry."

"It's OK," he lied. "She left me two beautiful girls."

"I could see that last night. I kind of suspected your younger was diabetic. In my business you can spot it. That's why it didn't bother me too much when you took off like you did. Stress is bad for her situation."

"I know. Again, I'm sorry about running out on you like that."

She smiled.

"Oh, there was a truck driver there, a regular white knight. He finally beat the crap out of the drunk, then walked us ladies down to the motel."

She hesitated.

"You kind of surprised me, the way you took that man out in the drugstore."

"You figured I was running out at first, didn't you?"

"Well, to be honest, yeah, I did."

"I didn't, though."

She chuckled softly.

"You sure as hell didn't. Bit underhanded maybe, but you settled it."

"If you must fight, fight to win," John said quietly.

"You know you got a cut hand, don't you."

He looked at his right hand, and for the first time the pain registered. Part of the broken bottle had laid a deep slice into his right forefinger clear down to the crease with his thumb.

Damn, it suddenly hurt like hell.

"Pull over; let me look at it."

He drifted to the side of the road and came to a stop. She took his hand and gently spread the wound open; now it really hurt.

"You'll need stitches. Ten to twelve from the looks of it."

As she examined it, blood dripped onto her suit.

"Be careful, your suit," he said.

She ignored him.

"I don't have anything sterile on me. You should stop at a doctor's."

"Later. I want to get the medicine home first. Besides, the doc is most likely swamped right now."

As he spoke he nodded towards the road.

Maury Hurt's World War II Jeep was coming down off the exit ramp of the interstate, four people piled in, one a child with shoulders hunched over, pale faced, gasping. Lying across the back of the Jeep was an elderly woman who John could see was already dead.

"We don't realize just how dependent we are," Makala sighed, watching as the Jeep weaved around some stalled cars to head into town.

"I'd hate to be in my hospital right now. If the generators didn't kick on, everyone in ICU or under surgery is most likely dead. I watched one poor fool killing himself last night. Had a Beemer like mine. The drunks kind of scared him and he insisted on pushing the car as if somebody was actually going to steal it. Damn fool. Someone told me later that he collapsed. People are crazy and this is bringing it out big-time."

She let go of his hand.

"If you can find something I'll bandage it up, but you should get that medicine home."

He wondered if she was inviting herself over. And at that moment he honestly didn't know how to react.

He started the car back up and drove into town, turning onto State Street. More and more people were crowding in around the town hall complex. Poor Tom had a cordon of his officers out. A large hand-lettered sign was posted at the main intersection: "Emergency Medical," pointing towards the firehouse next to the town hall.

"Maybe I should go over there and help," she said.

"First get some food," John replied.

He had already turned onto State Street, and seconds later the elementary school was in view.

"Why not go back there and get some stitches?"

"My mother-in-law can handle it," he finally said.

"Sure," and there wasn't any reaction in her voice one way or the other. "Just make sure you dose it well with an antibiotic. If things are as bad as I heard you say to Liz, you can't risk any kind of infection."

"Yes, ma'am."

"Come on; it's 'Makala.'"

He smiled.

"Right."

He pulled up onto the lawn of the elementary school. Pete was still at his grill. The line was just about gone. John got out of the car and walked up; Makala followed.

"Hey, Pete, busy today?"

"You got that straight, Professor. Figure the stuff is gonna rot. Health inspector won't let me use the meat anyhow, going this long with no refrigeration, so what the hell, might as well put on a damn good barbecue."

John smiled. He genuinely liked this guy. Pork barbecue was something John had never really cared for, especially with the spices Pete threw in, but still he'd eat there occasionally just to hang out and chat.

"Professor?" Makala asked.

"Regular brain there," Pete said. "Professor at the college here, army colonel, too. They were even going to give him a star and make him a general, but he quit. . . ."

Pete's voice trailed off. Naturally, everyone in town of course knew why John retired early, but Pete was leading into private matters, and a bit embarrassed he stopped.

"All right, Pete," John said with a smile, breaking the nervous pause. "This lady's a good friend. So give her double of anything she wants. OK?"

John started to extend his hand to shake hers and she smiled.

"Get it bandaged, John; then we'll shake."

"Sure."

He started to walk back to the car, hesitated, and looked back. She was looking at him and he motioned her to come over.

"Look. I guess you're staying at the Holiday Inn?"

"I guess so."

"You know how to get back there?"

"Easy enough, turn left at the light and cross the tracks."

"Well, look, ahh. I don't want you to take this wrong. You need anything, you walk up this road just about a mile. Turn right on Ridgecrest Drive. I'm number eighteen."

"OK, John, maybe I will sometime."

"Thanks for your advice with the medicine. I better get it home."

"John?"

"Yeah."

"You were checking me out when I was leaning over the seat, weren't you."

He found himself blushing.

"It's OK. After a high-stress situation, men usually think that way. I wasn't insulted. I just want you to know it's normal. It might bother you later, you know, given you should be worried about your girl, memories of your wife, and such."

Now she blushed slightly.

"That came out awkward. Get home now. I'll be OK."

"Thanks, Makala."

He got into the car and drove off, carefully balancing the bag of ice with one hand, the vials of medication on top.

As he turned the engine off he was delighted to see Jennifer and Pat up in the field, tossing the Frisbee back and forth. Ginger gave him a quick look but then went back to chasing the Frisbee, but old Zach came down, tail wagging in greeting.

Elizabeth was out by the pool, dressed in shorts and T-shirt, sunning herself, Ben sitting beside her, acting as if he was reading a book. The shotgun was leaning against the wall by Ben's side.

He stood up at the sight of John and came up to the car.

"Could you help me get the ice in, Ben? There's some cartons of smokes in there as well."

"Sure, sir."

Still balancing the one bag with the vials on top, John headed into the house. Jen was in the living room, just standing quietly looking out the window, turning and smiling as he came in.

She didn't need to be told what he was doing when she saw the CVS bag.

"Get the basement door for me, will you, Jen?"

She opened it. He was suddenly paranoid that somehow he might drop the precious load, and he clutched the bag of ice with one hand to his chest, the other on top of the vials, holding them in place.

Going down to the basement, he looked around for a moment and spotted an old Styrofoam cooler. He laid the bag of ice in and placed it inside the shower stall and then carefully laid the vials on top. He put the lid on but left it cracked open and then with a pocketknife popped a small hole in the bottom of the foam cooler to let the melted water drain off.

It was getting to be a bit messy, blood dripping from his hand.

"How much medication did you get for her?" Ben asked.

John looked back and saw the young man looking at him intently.

"Five vials."

"Five months, not counting what's in the fridge?"

It caught John by surprise.

"Yes, something like that."

"I see," Ben said quietly.

John stood up.

"Look, Ben. I'm not going to lie to you. The situation might be bad. I suspect we've been hit by a weapon that has shut down the electrical grid nationwide. That means it might be months before we get power back again."

He took it in, nodding his head, saying nothing.

"But not a word of this to Elizabeth or Jennifer. Understood? Let me tell them in my own way."

Jennifer and again his throat tightened. She was one smart kid, very smart, and when she learned that the power would be off for a very long time she just might figure out that the clock was ticking for her.

He looked back into Ben's eyes, saying nothing.

"Yes, sir," Ben whispered.

"Fine then."

"You're bleeding, sir."

"An accident, nothing serious."

He went back up the stairs and sat down at the dining room table. Jen was already waiting with the first-aid kit.

"What happened?"

He looked up. Ben was standing by the door out to the deck.

"Everything's OK, Ben. But remember, I don't want those girls worrying about things. Given the way things are, I'm expecting you to be a man and keep a sharp watch on them."

"Anything you say, sir," and he left the room.

"You know, John, he really is a nice boy. By the way, while you were gone, we ran out of water."

"Already?"

"Poor Jennifer. She used the toilet, and well . . . it didn't flush and she was really embarrassed. Ben got a bucket, hauled the water in from the pool, flushed it, then filled the tank up again. He's a good kid."

John laid his hand on the table and she peered at it.

"You should of stopped to get stitches."

"No time. I wanted to get the medication home."

"I'll butterfly bandage it for now," and she set to work. "You can have Kellor look at it later.

"Now what happened to you? And fill me in on all the news."

He told her just about everything . . . except for Makala and, of course, the Mustang.

CHAPTER FOUR

DAY 4

The sound of the helicopter, a Black Hawk, after silence for so long was startling. It came in hot, about five hundred feet up, skimming over the interstate pass, leveling out.

He felt an emotional surge at the sight of it, the black star on its side. It roared past his house, which was high enough off the valley floor that he could almost see into the pilot's side window. Elizabeth was jumping up and down, shrieking, waving.

"We're saved!" Elizabeth shouted gleefully. "We're saved!" She sounded like a shipwrecked sailor on a desert island.

John found himself waving as well . . . and the helicopter thundered on, heading due west, growing smaller, the sound receding, then disappearing, the silence all-engulfing again.

The elation disappeared into a sense of overwhelming depression. Somehow, the sight of that lone bird was now symbolic of so much, and maybe it was a portent that within a few more minutes the electricity would come back on.

He stood for several minutes, shading his eyes, gazing westward.

And everything was as it had been.

Dejected, Elizabeth walked over to the side of the swimming pool and sat down, dipping her feet in, Ben came over and splashed her. The water was still cold. Without the pump, there was no circulation into the solar heating panels. The water was still clear, though. John was dosing it heavily with chlorine, since it was, for now, their drinking and bathing water. The kids swimming in it would at least keep the water stirred up.

Jen was already waiting in the car.

Ben waved, John casually pointed to where the shotgun was, and Ben nodded in reply. Jennifer was down today with her friend Pat, joining a couple of other girls who were going to play Monopoly for the afternoon.

Starting the Edsel, John rolled down the driveway, out onto Route 70, turned east, and drove the short distance up to Miller's Nursing Home, where Tyler was. Jen had gone up to check on him the day after the outage and said that though it was chaotic, Tyler was doing OK. She was silent now, tense, as they drove.

None of them had left home yesterday, except for one brief foray by John.

He had laid out a long series of tasks. All the meat still in the freezer downstairs was pulled out and cooked thoroughly, with everyone eating as much as they could before wrapping the rest in plastic and storing it. He wasn't sure if it would help or not, but what salt they had was liberally sprinkled on the meat.

Next came a privy pit dug at the edge of Connie's orchard, with a privacy screen made out of a tent. The girls had argued that the toilets inside were just fine, and there had been a rather delicate discussion about what the privy could be used for and what the toilets inside would be used for.

"Oh, for that, just do it like Zach does," Jennifer replied with a grin, "against a tree."

It took a bit of explaining as to the health hazard of that suggestion. Then a bit of retrofitting around the house. The water bed was already getting chilly without a heater, so extra blankets were dragged up from the basement to lay down as a covering, some old decorative candles pulled out, old clothes that might be cut into strips for toilet paper, and to his surprise an old chain saw, not used in years, actually started up after Ben fiddled around with it for a while.

He then made one quick run down to the market on the east side of town, the old Food Lion, hoping to stock up on some goods, canned food, toilet paper, but it had already been picked over clean. In fact, it looked more as if it had been looted. He could have kicked himself for not having seen to this shopping before the panicked rush.

One of the managers was still inside the darkened store, just sitting, reading a magazine when John came in.

"Helluva show here last night, Professor," he announced. "Never thought I'd see friends and neighbors act like they did. People running around, loading up baskets to overflowing. I kept trying to say, 'No cash, no sale,' and well, they just started pushing by me and that set it off. Place was pretty well cleaned out before the cops finally showed up."

He shrugged.

"Mind if I look around?" John asked.

"Sure, be my guest, sir."

There was not a basket to be found, so he just simply wandered up and down the aisles. A half dozen or so were in the store, doing as he did, one elderly couple was prowling through the frozen-food freezers, pulling out smashed and soggy boxes of vegetables and waffles, stuffing them into a plastic trash bag.

All the canned goods were picked clean of course. Underfoot were smashed bottles, busted cans, bits of meat, chicken, and seafood. The floor was slippery and began to smell in the heat, hundreds of flies were already buzzing about. Over in the bakery goods he found a busted twenty-pound bag of flour kicked to one side on the floor and immediately grabbed it. In the pet foods was a twenty-five-pound bag of dry dog food, torn open, maybe fifteen to twenty pounds still inside, which he grabbed as well. Near the door he saw a ten-pound bag of rock salt, left over from winter, and instantly snatched it. There was not much else and he headed for the door.

He looked at the manager.

"Just take it, Doc; it's OK."

John paused, curious.

"Why are you here, Ernie?" He motioned to the darkened store. The elderly couple slowly dragged the trash bag full of defrosted food: the air around him was thick with the rising scent of decay.

Ernie looked at him, slowly shaking his head.

"Don't know, Doc. Habit, I guess. No family. Dolores and the kids left me last year. Just habit, I guess."

John nodded his thanks and tossed the loot into the backseat of the car. Backing up to the Dollar Store, he went in and found much the same chaos, this store torn apart, with no one inside.

"Who's in there?"

Turning, he saw Vern Cooper, one of the town police, looking through the broken front window.

"It's me, Vern, John Matherson."

"Out of there now, sir."

He came out and felt a change, a profound change in his world. Vern had always been so easygoing, almost a bit of the town's "Barney Fife." Now he was carrying a shotgun and it was half-raised, not quite pointing at John but almost.

"Just looking around, Vern."

"John, I could arrest you for looting."

"What?"

"Just that, John. It got real bad here last night."

"Yeah, I heard."

"Just get out of here and go home, John," Vern sighed.

John didn't hang around to ask for details and did as Vern "suggested."

At the U-Rent store they had already sold out of extra propane tanks, and John didn't even bother to go into the hardware store; it was utter chaos, with a line out the door and halfway down the block. The mere fact that he had a car that moved caused nearly everyone to turn and look at him, a reaction that made him nervous. So he just turned around and went home.

The rock salt was a golden find, he realized, and they had then unpacked all the meat, salted it down, then repacked it. Next had come a wood detail, for sooner rather than later he knew the propane for the grill would run out, and by the end of the day they were all exhausted.

He had promised Jen they'd go see Tyler today, then make a run up to her house to get some clothes and of course, check on the cat, so John got back in the car. It was only a short drive up to the nursing home, just about a mile. They passed half a dozen abandoned cars, a family walking by in the opposite direction, mother and father both pushing supermarket shopping carts, one with two kids inside, the other stacked with some few family treasures. Who they were he didn't know, where they were going he could not figure out, nor did he slow to find out.

Again, such a change. A week ago, seeing a couple like that he'd have pulled over asked if they needed a lift; the sight was so pathetic.

As they pulled into the parking lot of the nursing home John instantly knew something was terribly wrong. Three people were wandering about outside. At the sight of them he could see they were patients, shuffling, confused, one of them naked.

"My God, what is going on here?" Jen gasped.

John started to go for the nearest of the wanderers, to guide her back inside, but Jen shouted for him to follow her.

And the moment he opened the door, he knew something was horribly wrong. The stench was overwhelming, so bad that he gagged, backed out, and gasped for breath.

Jen, made of far sterner stuff, just stood in the doorway.

"Take a few deep breaths. I'll be down in Tyler's room."

John waited for a moment, tempted to light a cigarette. He held back, having gone through five packs in just two days. That left him six packs plus two cartons and he was already beginning to count each one.

He took another deep breath, braced himself, and went in. Again the stench, feces, urine, vomit. He gasped, struggled, nearly vomiting, and fought it down.

The corridor, which a week before had been so brightly lit and spotless, was dark, a large linen gurney parked in a side alcove the source of the worst of the smell. He quickly walked past it, turned the corner, and reached the west wing's nurses' station. One woman was behind the counter and looked up at him wearily. Her gown of Winnie the Poohs was stained and stained again. He spotted her name tag: Caroline, and vaguely remembered she was usually part of the night shift.

He wanted to blow but could see she was exhausted, beleaguered.

"How are you, Caroline?"

"Fine, I guess," she said woodenly.

He looked down the corridor. The stench was so overwhelming that he felt it should be a visible fog.

"What in hell is going on here?" he asked.

"What do you mean?"

She was in shock. He could now see that. The poor girl was numbed, hollow eyed.

"When did you last sleep?"

She looked up at the clock on the wall. It was frozen at 4:50.

Feeble cries echoed down the corridor: "help me, help me, help me . . ."

"A few hours last night, I guess."

"Are any other staff here?"

"There's Janice down on the other wing. I think Waldo is still here."

"And that's it?"

She nodded.

"I'll be right back."

He braced himself and started down the corridor. All exterior doors were open, but there was no breeze and the heat was suffocating. Yet another building designed for complete climate control and year-round comfort with computerized environmental controls. The small windows in each room barely cracked open, and the temperature inside was as high, perhaps higher than outside.

The first room he looked into revealed an elderly woman; he remembered her as having Alzheimer's. She was rocking back and forth, sheets kicked off, lying in her own filth.

The next room: two elderly men, one sitting in a motorized wheelchair that no longer moved, the other lying on a bed, the sheets drenched in urine.

They both glanced up at him.

"Son, could you get us some water?" the one in the wheelchair asked, ever so politely.

"Sure."

He backed out of the room and went back to the desk.

"Can I have a pitcher for some water?"

She shook her head.

"We ran out last night."

"What do you mean, 'ran out'?"

"Just that. No running water."

"Don't you have a reserve tank? Aren't you supposed to have a reserve somewhere?"

"I don't know," she said listlessly. "I think there's an emergency well that runs off the generator."

"Jesus Christ."

He opened the door to the hallway bathroom and recoiled, gagging. A woman was sitting on the toilet, slumped over . . . dead, already the smell of decay filling the tiny room.

He turned and went back down the main corridor to the kitchen, storming in. One elderly man was there, balanced on his walker, heavy steel fridge door open, a package of hot dogs in his hand, and he was eating them cold.

"Hi there," the man said. "Care for one?" And he offered the pack up.

"No thanks."

John went over to the sink, turned the taps . . . nothing.

"Damn it."

Back out in the dining area, he took the lid off a large recessed canister that usually held ice. There was water in the bottom, and taking two juice cups, he filled them up and was back out and down the hall, returning to the room with the two old men. He handed each of them a cup.

"Thank God," the one in the wheelchair whispered, sipping on it, John having to hold the other cup so that the man in the bed could sip it down.

The man in the wheelchair was wearing an old commemorative cap, "Big Red One—Omaha Beach 1944–2004" emblazoned on it. Pins across the front, which John instantly recognized, Combat Infantry Badge, Silver Star, two Purple Hearts, miniature sergeant's chevrons. He felt sick looking at the man, sipping the last of the water in the cup and holding it back up.

"Son, I hate to bother you," the man whispered. "My chair just won't move. Would you mind getting me another drink?"

"John, where in hell are you?"

It was Jen, her voice shrill.

"Right there, Mom."

"Sir, I'll be back shortly," John said, and he fled the room.

He tried to not look into the rooms as he walked down the corridor. An elderly woman, naked, sitting curled up and crying, a sickly scent from the next room, and he dared to look in. . . . A body of a bloated man, face yellowing with the beginnings of decay, bedsheets kicked off from his final struggle, his roommate sitting in a chair, looking vacantly out the window.

John reached Tyler's room, Jen in the doorway, crying.

"We got to take him home," she said.

For a moment John thought Tyler was dead, head back, face unshaved. The IV was still in his arm. Gravity fed, it was empty. The feeding tube into his stomach was driven by a small electrical pump, the plastic container attached to it . . . empty.

He was semi-conscious, muttering incoherently.

The smell of feces hung in the room and John struggled to control his stomach. It was something that always defeated him. He prided himself on being a damn good father, but when Mary was alive the diapers was her job. Mary's chemo was a nightmare, but he had manfully stood by, holding her when she vomited, cleaning her up, then rushing to the bathroom to vomit as well. After she died, when the kids were sick Jen would come over to help. He was horrified by what he had to confront now.

"I'll clean him up," Jen said. "You find a gurney so we can move him out to the car."

"How in hell are you going to clean him up?" John gasped.

"Just find a gurney. I'll take care of the rest."

He backed out of the room and stormed back down the corridor to the nurses' station.

"I'm pulling my father-in-law out."

"Good, you should," Caroline said quietly.

"How in God's name can you allow this?"

She looked up at him and then just dissolved into sobs.

"No one's come into work. I've been here since . . . since the power went off. Wallace and Kimberly—they took off last night—said they had to get home somehow to check on their kids and would come back, but they haven't. I've got a kid at home, too. Her father's such a bum, shacked up with someone else now. I'm worried he hasn't gone over to check on her and she's alone."

Caroline looked at him, tears were streaming down her face.

"I need a smoke," John said.

She nodded and fumbled in her purse and pulled out a pack, as if he were asking for one.

He shook his head, reached into his pocket, and took two cigarettes out, offering her one. They lit up. It was a nursing home, but at this moment he felt at least a smoke would mask the smell and help calm her down.

She took a deep drag, exhaled, and the tears stopped.

"I need a gurney to move my father-in-law."

"I think you'll find one down the next corridor. Waldo took it a couple of hours ago."

"When was the last time these people were cleaned, fed, had water?"

"I don't know."

"Think, damn it."

"I think two days ago. Then it just all seemed to unravel. Mr. Yarborough died, then Miss Emily, then Mr. Cohen. No one's come to take their bodies. Usually the funeral home has the hearse here within a half hour. I think I called, but they haven't shown up. Mrs. Johnston in room twenty-three fell, I think she broke her hip, and Mr. Brunelli, I think he's had another heart attack.

"Now they're all dying. All of them. Miss Kilpatrick is dead in the next room. God, how I loved her," and she started to sob again.

He remembered Miss Kilpatrick, actually rather young. Bad auto accident, paralyzed from the waist down and in rehab and training before going home. Science teacher at the high school until she was nailed head-on by a drunk, one of her own students.

"She got some scissors and cut her wrists. She's dead in the sitting room."

He didn't even see her as they came in.

"She said she knew what had happened and wouldn't live through it."

"Caroline, you've got to get help up here."

"I don't know. I'm just an LPN. I'm not trained for this, sir."

She began to sob again.

"Where's the supervisor?"

"In her office, I think."

He nodded, left Caroline, and went down towards the opposite wing and turned into the administrative corridor. The door to the supervisor's office was closed, and without bothering to knock he pushed it open.

The woman behind the desk was fast asleep, head on her desk.

"Ira, wake up," John snapped angrily.

She raised her head.

"Professor Matherson?"

"Yes, that's me."

She rubbed her eyes and sat up.

"I know you must be upset."

" 'Upset' isn't the word for it. This is an outrage."

She nodded silently.

"I know. I've got four people in the building, maybe three; I think Kimberly took off. I sent the last of our kitchen staff down to the town to try and get help. But that was hours ago and no one's come back. No water, no air-conditioning, no refrigeration for food or medication . . ."

She fell silent, then looked down at a checklist on her desk. The woman was obviously pushed over the edge and reverting to an almost standard routine to hide in.

"Last rounds I counted seventeen dead. Six families have pulled their relatives out. . . . Let's see, that leaves forty patients and three staff on overtime. Normally during the day I have over thirty working here."

God, you'd think everyone would have pulled their people out, John thought, then realized the difficulties of that. Some had no family nearby at all. A couple retired here, the spouse died, the other wound up here, the kids somewhere else, New York, California, Chicago . . . the American way.

Even for locals, just five or ten miles away. How to get a sick, demented, or dying parent or grandparent moved? And many most likely just assumed or wanted to assume that "Grandpa is safe there; we're paying five thousand a month to make sure of that."

"But you've got to do something," John protested weakly.

"Pray, tell me what I should do first," she said quietly. "Did I tell you we were robbed last night?"

"What."

"Some punks. One had a gun, and demanded the drugs. They took all the painkillers, pills, the liquid morphine."

"Who?"

"I don't know. The one with the gun had a shaved head, earring, tattoo of a serpent on his left arm, red motorbike."

"Animals," John said coldly.

Tyler was on a morphine pump. Jesus, if he comes round it will be hell for him.

"That's what I called them and they laughed."

John found he couldn't answer her and was filled with a sudden pity for her. She was a good woman, her eldest son a member of his scout troop a couple of years back.

"I'll get into town and see if we can get these people evacuated somehow."

"Thank you."

"I'm taking my father-in-law out now."

"That's good."

"What about his feeding tube, the formula?"

"I wouldn't trust the formula anymore. It's supposed to be refrigerated.

We still might have some cans of Ensure. Use a funnel and gravity feed it into him."

John nodded, stomach rebelling.

"I better go."

He left her in her miserable solitude, and went into the next corridor. It was a deeper hell here. The entire wing was the "restricted wing," all the patients with Alzheimer's or another form of severe dementia. A number of them were out in the hallway, those capable of some mobility wandering aimlessly, at his approach reaching out with withered hands, some speaking, others just muttering or making incoherent sounds. He felt as if he had just fallen into a surreal nightmare. He could not stop for them, help them; to do so would trap him in the nightmare forever.

Passing an emergency exit door, he looked outside. There was a patient slowly shuffling towards the woods. With the entire security system down, the ankle bracelets that were touted as the newest thing in safety, which automatically locked the door and set off an alarm at the nurses' station if someone with dementia tried to open it, were now deactivated. It was a wonder that any who could still walk were inside the building, and he wondered how many had indeed just wandered into the woods.

He spotted a gurney at the end of the corridor, and as he approached it, to his horror he saw that the body of small, withered old man was on it, an elderly woman standing beside the body, stroking the man's hair.

John approached, determined to take the gurney, if need be, but as she looked up at him, his will failed and he backed away, then fled the ward.

He returned back to the wing where Tyler was. Somehow, Jen had indeed cleaned him up, a pile of torn soiled sheets tossed on the floor, a torn blanket wrapped around him. She looked at John, eyes calm, her strength amazing him.

"Did you find a gurney?"

"I'll carry him out."

She had already disconnected the hose of the feeding tube and the IV tube. John slipped his arms under Tyler and stood up. The man, in spite of his wasting away, was still heavy, and John braced himself for a second before daring to take a step. He turned to ease out the door and then continued out into the corridor, walking fast, a race against dropping Tyler. They went past the desk, Caroline said nothing, Jen raced ahead to open the back door.

In the corner of the sitting room John saw the slumped-over body of Miss Kilpatrick in the corner, a pool of drying blood was soaked into the berber carpet beneath her, flies were swarming on it.

Gasping for breath, John was out the door and down to the car, laying Tyler down in the backseat. He opened his eyes; there was a glint of recognition.

"It's OK, Tyler; we're taking you home. It's OK."

He couldn't speak. The cancer had long ago devoured his throat, vocal cords, and spread into his chest. His breathing was raspy, sounding like another bout of pneumonia was setting in.

Still, he had enough strength to grasp John's arm and squeeze it, then let go.

"Jen, start the car; I'll be right back," and John handed her the keys.

He went back in and returned to the nurses' station.

"Caroline, I need some Ensure."

She nodded towards the storage room. He went in, again a struggle for control. Someone had vomited on the floor. He gingerly stepped around the mess, tearing open storage cabinets; the bandage that covered his injured finger was soaked through with God knows what and finally just slipped off. Empty shipping cases of the precious liquid were scattered about, and when just about to give up, he found two cartons of twenty-four cans, grabbed them, and stepped back out.

He started for the door, hesitated, and then turned, going back to the room with the two old men. He took two six-packs and placed them on the old veteran's lap.

"Thanks for what you once did for us, Sergeant," he whispered.

The old man smiled and nodded. John felt a bit foolish at first but could not stop himself. He came to attention and saluted the old man, who stiffened in his chair, smiled, and returned the salute. John left him and headed to the car.

Dumping the cans onto the floor of the front seat of the car, John climbed in.

"Get us the hell out of here," John said.

He turned away, blocking out the sight of the demented patients wandering about outside. If he stopped for them he would be pulled back into the nightmare, with Tyler stuck in the backseat in the sweltering heat.

They drove out and several minutes later were back home.

"Ben, Elizabeth!" John shouted.

The two kids, soaking wet, came out of the pool, laughing, but then slowed as they saw John struggling to maneuver Tyler out of the car.

Elizabeth stepped back.

"Oh, Pop-pop," and she began to cry.

"You need help, sir?" Ben asked nervously.

"Just get the door."

John carried Tyler in, Jen following, and headed for Jennifer's room, putting him down on her bed, and then stood up.

Jen pulled a chair over and was by Tyler's side, gently brushing his cheek.

"It's OK, Tyler. We're home; we're home," she whispered.

John stepped back, suddenly feeling a terrible need to wash. Elizabeth stood in the living room, looking wide-eyed towards Jen's room.

"Elizabeth."

She was crying.

"It's going to be hard, but we've got to handle it. I want you to go get a bucket of water. Heat it up on the grill, find some soap, some towels, then go in and help Grandma."

Elizabeth stifled back a sob and nodded.

He was glad Jennifer was not home to have seen this.

He went into the master bathroom. He poured some water from a bucket into the sink and thoroughly washed his hands; then grimacing, the pain coursing up his arm, he doused his wound with some rubbing alcohol.

He cut a piece of old sheeting taken from the linen closet and wrapped it around the cut on his hand and went back to Jennifer's room.

"Mom, you OK?"

She looked up at him and smiled.

"Sure. I can handle this now, John. Thank you."

Ben came in carrying the warm bucket, Elizabeth hesitating before coming in with a towel and soap.

"Elizabeth honey. Your Pop-pop is a proud man," Jen said, her features serious. "I don't think he'd want his granddaughter helping with this."

Jen looked at John.

"And you, John, have the weakest stomach in the world. Why don't you two go outside?"

"I'll stay," Ben said quietly.

All three looked at him with surprise.

"Heck, I diapered my kid brother a hundred times. I'll help Miss Jen."

"Good man, Ben."

"Actually, I better go into town," John said. "I'll see if we can get some help up there."

"That's good, John."

He hesitated and looked at Elizabeth.

"Maybe you should come along."

"You sure, Dad?"

"It's OK."

She looked at him with relief and the two went to the car and got in.

"Sorry, Dad, I don't think I could have handled that. I'd of tried, though."

"Listen, kid, I barely handled it myself. Buckle up."

She laughed softly, though still shaken.

"This is a '59 Edsel, Dad, no seat belts."

They drove into town and he immediately felt as if he was now coming into an entirely different world.

Pete's free barbecue was shut down, the small-town feel of an outdoor fair atmosphere gone. Two police officers, both armed with shotguns, stood outside the elementary school, a large crowd standing in line. An open fire was burning, a kettle hung over it.

There were half a dozen more cops and an equal number of firemen in a loose cordon around the town hall, police station, and firehouse. Several men were at the back of Jim Bartlett's Volkswagen Bus, off-loading boxes. There was an assortment of bicycles, a few motorbikes, an old Harley motorcycle, a Jeep from the garage, the antique World War Two jeep, and a few old farm pickup trucks parked there as well, the doors into the firehouse open, the engines rolled out. Boxes, crates, containers filling up inside.

There was another line formed, an old military-style water tank on wheels, a guard by the side of it, the line of people carrying plastic jugs.

John rolled to a stop and got out with Elizabeth.

"One gallon per person," the guard was saying, repeating himself over and over, as John pulled Elizabeth closer in to his side and headed towards the mayor's office.

Though the downtown area had water, those living upslope were out and now having to do the long walk just to get a single gallon.

One of the guards saw John and nodded.

"Hi, Professor."

It was one of his old students, graduated several years back, now a teacher in the middle school, and he was embarrassed that he couldn't remember his name.

"What's going on?"

"Well, Charlie declared martial law. We're moving all medical supplies here to the firehouse and any food that can still be retrieved from the supermarkets, but most of that got cleaned out."

"I saw Food Lion, but all of the markets?"

"Well, sir, I guess you could say it was a riot. Folks just started storming into the markets taking what they wanted and then getting out. It got pretty ugly there for a while. Mostly the outsiders."

"Outsiders?"

"You know, the folks from the highway."

The way he said "outsiders" hit a nerve with John. It didn't feel right.

"We had a lot of people coming down the road from Asheville, a lot of them people who live here who got stranded, but a lot of people just getting out of the city as well. A thousand or more flooded in here last night. Word is it's pretty bad up there.

"The folks coming in from Asheville said a mob, mostly kids, started busting up the Asheville Mall, vandals, and part of it burned. Somebody said over fifty people were killed, hundreds of people rampaging through the stores along Tunnel Road."

He took it in.

"Quite a few dead on the road they say as well. People collapsing, bad hearts, elderly. Somebody said he counted at least twenty dead between here and Exit 53."

It was hard to believe.

"Thanks. Is the mayor in?"

"She sure is. They're having some sort of conference in there."

He didn't ask for permission; he just headed in and parked Elizabeth by the door, telling her not to move. As he walked in, his eye caught the commemorative plaque: "9.11.01 In Remembrance of the First Responders Who Gave Their Lives . . . Rest in Peace."

Half a dozen men and women milled about in the corridor. The door into the conference room was closed.

"I'd like to see the mayor," John said to one of the cops standing by the door.

"There's a meeting on in there, sir."

"I know, but this is urgent."

"I think, sir, you'll have to wait."

"This can't wait," John said loudly.

"Sir, please just go outside and wait."

The memory of the vet, begging for a drink of water, pushed John forward.

"I think I'll see her now," John said sharply. "Now step aside."

"Sir, don't force me to stop you."

He could see that the cop, not much more than a kid, was still out of his league. A week ago he was most likely the junior kid on the force, the biggest challenge ever faced a drunk on a Saturday night.

John reached past him, grabbed the doorknob, and pushed the door open.

"Sir! Please step back."

Charlie, Kate, and Tom were in the room, along with Doc Kellor and, interestingly, Washington Parker and an elderly couple who looked vaguely familiar.

"It's OK, Gene. That's Professor Matherson. Come on in, John."

John gave a curt nod to the young policeman and walked in. Everyone was gazing at John, and he suddenly felt a touch of embarrassment for barging in thus, but the memory of what he had seen in the nursing home stilled that.

"What is it, John, that's got you all fired up?" Charlie asked.

"I was just up at Miller's Nursing Home. My God, it's a hellhole up there."

"We know all about it, John," Kate said. "Mr. Parker here is sending a bunch of kids, volunteers from the college, to help out with some food and water. Kellor's canvassing the refugees for nurses to go help as well."

"I think it's going to take more than some kids and a few nurses," John replied, "but thanks, Washington."

"You know they were robbed? Some punks stole all the morphine and painkillers?"

"We're on that, too, John," Tom said softly.

Now John did feel embarrassed.

Charlie hesitated, made eye contact with Kate, and she nodded.

"John, actually, I should have invited you to this meeting," Charlie said softly. "We're talking some things over. Maybe you can give us some input.

"Do you know the Barbers?"

John looked over at the elderly couple. In fact, he did know them. They had a summer home, actually more of a mansion, up in the Cove, just up the road from his in-laws.

They looked haggard, Mrs. Barber pale, struggling, it seemed, to stay awake.

"They just got through from Charlotte."

Don Barber nodded slowly.

"Go on, please," Kate said.

"Well, as I was saying," Don continued. "By yesterday morning it was out of control. And what I was just telling you, absolute utter stupidity. A couple of helicopters flew in from Fort Bragg the morning after the power went off, landed near town hall, a dozen armed troopers got out, some ass of a major goes in, comes out twenty minutes later, they take off, and then someone comes running out saying we're at war."

No one spoke.

"War with who?" Tom asked.

"I don't know; nobody knows. That one idiot, running out, shouting we were at war, that we were hit with nuclear weapons and had already lost, set everything off. Just one loudmouth bastard."

He paused and looked over at his wife.

"Sorry, Wendy."

"Well, he was a stupid bastard," she whispered, barely keeping her eyes open, and John smiled.

"Look, I'm old enough to remember 1941. Kennedy in 1963, when Reagan was shot, 2001 of course. Always we at least had radios, television. Someone to tell us what was going on, what to do, offering leadership, and that rallied us together.

"This time it's a vacuum. Just that one idiot running out, and of course a crowd had gathered because of the helicopters landing, then taking off.

"I got down to the street and rumor was building on rumor; you could hear it. People talking about nukes, someone starts shouting about fallout killing them all, and that was it. Within an hour downtown was in chaos. People looting, fighting with each other, and impossible to control.

"The police were caught completely off guard. Things had been quiet throughout the night. A couple of old cars had been taken by the police and fire departments, driven up and down the streets, someone leaning out the window with an old megaphone and telling folks to stay calm, help was on the way, and so far it was working. But that panic ended it."

John hesitated but had to ask.

"Were we nuked? I mean a full attack?"

Don shook his head.

"I know the District Attorney for the county. I got my way into his office. That goddamn fool running out, some half-ass bureaucrat, heard a few minutes of the briefing, panicked, and was out the door.

"As for the truth of it, there's precious little. Remember it was a couple of days after nine-eleven before things started to sort out, and we had full communications then. Now, well, according to the District Attorney they were told that one, maybe two or three nuclear weapons were detonated over the United States, up high, a couple of hundred miles up."

"It's EMP for certain then," John interjected.

"That's what the DA said. Also, they were told some communications at Fort Bragg survived, aircraft parked inside protective shelters, some vehicles as well.

"Other than that, it's shut down the entire power grid of the United States, except for a few radios and machines that this major said were 'hardened.' He said the army was going to be working on getting things up and running and for folks to stay calm till then. But it was going to take several weeks."

Don shook his head.

"It'd of been better if he never showed up. The way he flew in, then took off, made it look like he was running out, and that helped the panic."

"Several weeks my ass," John muttered.

Don fell silent.

He looked at Kate.

"You read that report I left here?" John asked.

She nodded.

"Start thinking months, years. What Mr. Barber just told us confirmed it."

"I know, John."

Her tone indicated to him that she wanted him to stand back a bit, and he realized she was right.

"Sir, what happened then?" Charlie asked.

"Well, it was already edgy. Two planes had crashed in the downtown, one of them a seven-thirty-seven, right after the power went off. Hell of a mess. Some people were thinking it might have been some sort of failed terrorist strike. Like I said, without any radios, without any communications, rumors running ahead of the truth, the way they always do, no one knew and thus everyone was an expert, and everyone was soon scaring the hell out of each other.

"It was then that I realized I better get Wendy and myself out of Charlotte and up here."

"Why here?" Kate asked.

"Because it's safe here," Don said. He looked around the room as if seeking some assurance.

"Sure, Don," Charlie said. "You're OK now; you're with neighbors now."

"So I walked home from my office downtown. Four miles, at that moment I thought the toughest four miles I've ever been through since I got shot down over Korea and had to hike back to our lines.

"I got Wendy and from there it took us two days to walk to the airstrip where I keep my L-3."

"An L-3, what the heck is that?" Tom asked.

"Military designation for a World War II Aeronca recon plane. We used them in Korea as well for liaison and artillery spotting. It's nearly identical to the one I flew as an artillery spotter in Korea."

He smiled. "Found her as a junker about ten years back and fully restored her to original shape. She's a beauty to fly, slow and low."

John could not help but smile. Like a lot of older vets, when Don talked about something like that, the years seemed to drift away from his face and his eyes were young again as he spoke of a happy memory.

"All the time we were walking I was afraid she'd be taken or ruined. But sure enough, she was still in the hangar. Nothing fancy in her. Restored to original condition, maybe that's what saved her. No electronics whatsoever, could never find a period radio, so all I used was a small handheld GPS when I took her up. Of course that piece of equipment was fried, but the plane was OK."

He paused.

"In the old days, you worked your throttle, primed the cylinders by pumping, magneto switch on, and got someone to grab the propeller, and she started right up."

"So you flew here?" John asked.

"Sure did. Got airborne about four hours ago and circled over Charlotte."

He paused and lowered his head.

"I saw some bad things in Korea. I was there the second time the commies took Seoul. I never thought I'd see the likes of it here, in America."

"What did you see?" Kate asked quietly.

"Nine-eleven for example. The way people in New York and Washington acted that day and pulled together. No panic really when you think back on it. Guiliani on television, then the president, it pulled us together.

"But it's a vacuum now and in the cities especially it went out of control like I said. Downtown Charlotte was burning. I could see there was no firefighting equipment out. The water pressure was already failing by the time I decided to walk home, and at my house it was already dry.

"Looting, people running crazy." He paused. "I saw dead people lying in the streets. National Guard ringing a shopping plaza, thousands swarming around trying to break through to get at the food inside, and you could see the guardsmen falling back, shooting into the crowd.

"It looked, it looked like the old newsreels from the Second World War, or like Saigon when it fell, like what happened over there in Somalia. I never dreamed I'd see it here, never here."

He fell silent for a moment, gazing out the window.

"We flew along I-85, then up through Hickory Nut Gorge. My first thought was to land in Asheville, but then what? We'd still be thirty miles from home."

"Did you see anything moving?" Charlie asked. "Especially over in Asheville."

"It looked like a couple of cars, but nothing else. A lot of burning, some houses, several forest fires, I could see the one up on Craggy from fifty miles away. Passed over the wreck of a commuter plane just short of Asheville that was still burning."

"Why this talk about so many planes down?" Kate asked.

"Because nearly every commercial liner out there is so loaded with electronics now," Don replied. "Hell, the stick isn't even connected to a wire anymore like in the old days; it's computer links for the control surfaces. Pop that and most likely every last plane in America nosed in."

"Jesus," Tom sighed. "On nine-eleven we only lost four."

"Figure around three thousand planes falling out of the sky, which is the typical number airborne around that time of day," Don said coldly. "Two hundred passengers on average per plane . . . do the math."

He sighed again, looking off as if a great distance into a dark land.

"The mall was burning, big fire there. That convinced me to set down as close to home as possible. If I had landed at the airport, I'd never have gotten here. There was a couple of hundred yards on I-40 just west of town that was wide open and that little baby of mine just squeezed right in."

Tom grinned.

"Damnedest sight I've ever seen. A plane taxiing down the exit ramp, then parking in the Ingram's lot. Painted just like the old army planes, complete with D-day invasion stripes, hell, it made my heart leap at the sight of it."

"You've got it guarded?" Charlie asked.

"Of course I do. It's an asset for us."

"Thank you, Mr. Barber," Charlie said. "I'm glad you made it home."

"Look, we're kind of bushed. Is there any way we can find a ride up to our place?"

"I think we can arrange something special for you," Charlie said, "for a swap."

"And that is?"

"We can use your plane."

"As long as I'm flying it you can," he said defensively. "I put five years into restoring her, so no one else touches her but me. A little work and I can retro fit her to burn automobile gas. But wherever you want me to go, I'll do it."

"A deal."

Charlie stood up and went to the door, opening it.

"One last thing," Don said. "On the interstates. They're swarming with people. Thousands of them. Like an exodus . . . and they're coming this way."

He left the room and Charlie closed the door.

"What I figured," Charlie said softly. "We talked about it in some of the disaster exercises, the ones centered on a conventional nuclear strike, one or more weapons hitting urban centers. If the crap hits the fan, first there'll be rioting, people snatching what they think they need to survive; then like a homing instinct people will flee the city and literally 'head for the hills.' The same concern with a biological outbreak. Panic, then trying to head for the hills."

"Why?" Kate asked.

"Why are we here?" John interjected.

"What do you mean?"

"When you get down to the deepest core reasons. Sure I moved here because of Mary. But why were her parents here? There seems to be some sort of instinct, or call it a Mayberry fantasy, that up in the hills things are secure, safe, neighborly. People will help each other. When you think about it, before all this happened, that's exactly how we were."

"Well, it sure as hell wasn't neighborly yesterday," Tom said.

"How bad did it get?" John asked.

"You didn't see it?"

John wondered if Tom was making a jab at him, implying that Vern had talked to him about the foray into the Dollar Store.

"I was up nearly all day at home taking care of things. I came down late in the day to Food Lion and it was wiped."

"Yeah, Vern said he ran into you poking around the Dollar Store," Tom finally said coolly.

"Jesus, Tom, if I was going to be looting I'd pick a place a damn sight better than that."

He suddenly wondered if what few things he did pick up would now indeed classify him as a looter. Hell, in Russia and Germany during the war people got shot for a lot less; in Leningrad stealing a slice of bread could get you hung.

"Then why were you in there?"

"Go ahead and arrest me if that's what you're implying," John snapped.

"Both of you," Kate interjected, "cool it."

"Look, John, it got real bad here," Charlie said. "My fault maybe. I should have slapped down strict martial law the first day; I didn't. The night between the second and third days, it was as if a mass panic hit the town. Most people still don't have it really figured out what happened; all they know is something bad happened.

"First there was the run on the banks to get their money out, but all the banks use electronic records for accounts and digging up the paperwork for each takes time. Not like the old days when we still had bankbooks and they got stamped. They were mobbed, and that's where Tom had most of his people.

"The banks quickly ran out of money. Before I put a stop to it, one woman was actually trying to pull out fifty thousand dollars from First Charter."

John almost had to laugh at that one.

"It's nothing but paper now anyhow," he sighed.

"I don't need to hear that," Kate interjected.

"Sorry, Kate, but you better hear it. Until the federal government truly gets things stitched back together, and with that records retrieved and the same for financial institutions, what little paper money there is floating around out there is worthless. Our entire economy is built now on electronic money. It's all faith, and if a crack appears in that faith, then what?"

"It's going to be barter then, isn't it?" Charlie asked.

John nodded in agreement. "And you set the parameters."

"How so?"

"I'd suggest impounding anything still out there that has worth for survival . . . medicine, tools, auto parts that can be used to retrofit, construction materials, especially piping and such, and most of all food. Impound it, haul it up here, set up rationing, and the rations become the medium of exchange for various things."

"Sounds communist to me," Tom sniffed.

"Survival," John replied sharply, "and Tom, you know my politics, so don't insult me."

"Well, a lot of what you said is gone," Charlie replied. "Damn, we were caught flat-footed. Like I said, never a plan in place. The run on the banks triggered it, from there people storming into stores to buy anything and everything. Our people were basically on foot as well, and besides, we were all so used to having radios in our police cars to tell us what the hell was going on. The looting at the Ingram's was full-blown before one of the two officers stationed down there was able to run the mile up here to tell us. By the time we got people back down there to control it, it was already over.

"Hell, there were even people going through the fast-food places by the interstate waving hundreds of dollars wanting to buy up the burgers uncooked.

"The smart ones, though, they pilled into the three big markets in town, and it went from lines twenty deep to suddenly just people pushing out the door."

"Did anyone try to stop them?" And he looked at Tom.

Tom sighed.

"John, we're talking about our neighbors here. Damn it all, I saw folks from my church in there, parents of my kids' friends. Yeah, I tried to stop them, but I'll be damned if we were going to shoot them."

"Somewhere around twenty people died anyhow," Kate said. "Mostly collapses, heart attacks. A display case in Ingram's was shattered; someone fell into it, and bled to death."

"John, people just pushed past that woman even as she died," Tom said quietly.

John looked out the window to Bartlett's VW as it puttered off, leaving behind a stack of boxes, and headed back up Montreat Road.

"John, it was surreal," Charlie said. "Everybody on foot, the streets filled with people, I think the most coveted item yesterday was a supermarket shopping cart. Every last one has been looted and people were just walking up and down the street pushing their loads home."

"That's why the heart attacks," Doc Kellor finally interjected.

John looked at his old friend. Kellor, who as a very young general practitioner had brought Mary into the world, was with her when she left. He now tended to Jennifer and usually would drop over to the house once a month or so, to "check on my favorite girl," and then stay for a scotch and a round of chess. It rankled him that nine times out of ten John won.

"Fear, combined with people actually having to walk more than fifty yards," Doc Kellor continued. "There's been something like three hundred deaths since this started."

"Three hundred?"

"Why not?" Kellor said dryly. "You forget how fragile we really are, the most pampered generations in the history of humanity. Heart attacks, quite a few just damn stupid accidents, at least eight murders, and several suicides. To put it coldly, my friends, all the ones who should have died years ago, would have died years ago without beta-blockers, stents, angioplasties, pacemakers, exotic medications, well, now they're dying all at once."

John glared at Kellor for a moment, wondering what else he was thinking.

"It even hit pacemakers?" Charlie asked. "Good God, my mother has one."

Everyone looked at him.

"She's in Florida; I don't know how she is. . . ." And his voice trailed off.

"I'm sorry, Charlie," Kellor said, "but I've got to be blunt. Some yes, strangely, are still working, but how long the batteries will hold, well, I guess that's a countdown for them. But some died within minutes or hours."

John looked back at Charlie.

"You're going to have to take control, Charlie," and John said it sharply, a touch of the "command voice," in his tone, to shock Charlie back to the reality of the meeting. "Clamp down hard or it's going to get worse. So far we're just in the first stage of panic here."

"What do you mean?"

"People grabbing what they think they need, but not many thinking yet about a week from now, a month from now." He paused. "A year from now. Have you held a public meeting to discuss with people what happened and what to do?"

"What a disaster," Kate sighed. "Yeah, last night. Five or six hundred showed up; it was hard to get the word out. It almost made it worse. The moment Charlie started talking about EMPs and nuclear bursts, some folks just heard 'nuclear' and went crazy, saying they were going home to dig shelters."

"Same as in Charlotte, according to Don Barber," John said. "When the realization finally hits that this is the long haul, people will start looking at each other, wondering if a neighbor has an extra can of food in their basement."

"Or an extra vial of medicine hidden in a cooler," Kellor said quietly, and John knew he was talking about him but didn't react.

"That's when either we try to pull together and keep order or it will go over to complete anarchy."

"That old *Twilight Zone* episode," Kate said. "The one where a bunch of polite middle-class types are having a friendly social, the radio announces nuclear war, and by the end of the half hour they were killing each other trying to get into the shelter one had in his basement."

Funny how we think in terms of film and television now, John thought. *The Twilight Zone*. Last evening he'd been dwelling on the episode where the aliens started flicking lights on and off in different people's houses and soon everyone was in a panic, ready to kill one another, the aliens sitting back and laughing.

What would Rod Serling say about this now? "Presented for your consideration, America disintegrating when the plug is pulled . . ."

"To hell with *The Twilight Zone* for the moment," Tom said, "Refugees. We're starting to get swarmed with outsiders. That has me worried the most now. At least we know our neighbors who we can count on, but all these outsiders, who knows what they might do? And if too many come in, we'll all be starving in a matter of days."

"There's a million or more in Charlotte," Charlie said. "Even more in the Triad. If one in a hundred decides to make the trek, that means twenty, thirty thousand mouths to feed."

He fell silent and no one spoke for a very long minute.

"We'll have to have a plan," Kate said.

"Sure, a plan, what plan?" Charlie sighed. "We had a plan for everything else, but never for this one. Never once for this one.

"And that's why I got caught so off balance," Charlie said sadly, shaking his head. "I was waiting for someone to call, to do something. I'm sorry."

"Charlie, anyone would have been overwhelmed," John said, not altogether truthfully, but still he could see Charlie's thinking. Like the military preparing for combat: disasters were something they drilled for. No one had ever drilled for something at this level, had a master plan up and ready to go, and therefore the precious first few days, when so much could have been done, were lost.

"Maybe someone in Asheville is getting a handle on it," Tom said. "We all saw that Black Hawk go over. He was beelining straight for Asheville. Maybe they got some kind of link up there."

John was silent. Asheville. Exit 64 to Exit 53, eleven miles. A day hardly went by without Elizabeth trying to figure out some excuse to go to the mall. A week didn't go by when he didn't drop into the Barnes & Noble to browse the military history shelves and then have a coffee, or take the kids downtown to their favorite pizza joint, the Magic Mushroom, where all the weirdos and hippies, as Jennifer called them went, much to the kids' delight as they enjoyed a meal and "people-watched" the street scene.

Eleven miles, across unknown territory, it seemed like a journey filled with peril. My God, in just four days have we already become so agoraphobic, so drawn in on ourselves?

"I think we should go into Asheville tomorrow and see what the hell is going on there," John finally ventured.

"Agreed," Charlie replied.

John looked around and realized he had put his foot into it.

"OK, I'll drive."

CHAPTER FIVE

DAY 5

"This is impossible," Charlie announced, and John grunted in agreement.

Just past Exit 55, heading west, the interstate was completely blocked with scores of abandoned cars. During rush hour, it was this stretch of road where backups usually gridlocked, and when the EMP did hit, all the traffic had simply stopped, blocking the road across both lanes and the shoulder, where so many had drifted over as their engines stalled.

He went into reverse, weaving around the roadblock of cars back to the exit, swung around, and got off the road, then went down to Route 70, which paralleled the interstate on the north side.

"I wanted to go this way anyhow," Washington said, sitting in the backseat of the Edsel. "Maybe the veterans hospital has some sort of connection."

Flanking Washington were two of the boys from the college ball team, Phil Vail and Jeremiah Sims. At Washington's recommendation, which Charlie had agreed to, the two had come along "for the ride," and concealed down by their feet were two shotguns and in Washington's hand a Colt .45.

John nodded, took the turnoff onto 70, then headed west again, weaving around stalled cars, under the bridge for the Blue Ridge Parkway, and just past that, on their right, were the grounds of the veterans hospital.

They pulled through the gate, and John's heart sank. Somehow, he had hoped that here, a veterans hospital, a federal facility, maybe there was a miracle, a hardened generator, or at least some semblance of normal life, of orderliness. He half-expected to see troops lined up guarding the place.

Instead it was elderly patients scattered on the lawn, some lying on blankets, others just wandering about. A lane had been cleared of stalled cars approaching the highway, a "rent-a-cop" holding a shotgun standing in the middle of the road, motioning them to stop.

John leaned out as the cop came cautiously around to the side of the car, shotgun half-leveled.

"I'm Colonel John Matherson," he announced, feeling a bit self-conscious using that title again. He was so used to being called Professor or Doc these last few years, but Washington had advised him to revert to his old title for this trip.

"I live in Black Mountain. And this is Charlie Fuller, our director of public safety. In the backseat there is Sergeant Washington, a retired marine, and a couple of students from the college."

The cop nodded, saying nothing, but he turned the gun away from John.

"We're heading into Asheville to try and find out some information. Is anything running here? Electricity?"

"Nope. No power. You folks got any?"

"No, sir."

"Is there anyone in charge here who knows what's going on? Contact with Raleigh or Washington?"

Again the cop shook his head.

"Damn."

"Yeah, damn," the cop replied. "It's hell inside there. These old guys dying off left and right. Wouldn't think they could die so fast when without medicine for a few days."

John thought of the nursing home, of Tyler. He had been nervous about leaving Jen and the girls alone with Tyler. But Ben had become something of a permanent fixture at the house, and John's across-the-street neighbors Lee Robinson and his wife, Mona, parents of Seth and Pat, had volunteered to come up and give Jen some time off to sleep.

Tyler, of course, was failing. There was no IV, no oxygen, just pouring Ensure and water into him through his stomach tube. The agony was no painkillers. It was a blessing perhaps that the few days of neglect had pushed him to the edge of a coma. But when he was conscious John could see the agony in Tyler's eyes. Jen had stayed up through the night, and just before John left, Mona had walked up to lend a hand.

John looked around again at the grounds, the patients, a few nurses lugging buckets of water up from a creek at the edge of the hospital grounds. He could only imagine what it was like inside; it was already turning into one hell of a hot day.

"I think we best head into town," Charlie said.

The cop nodded.

"Good luck. And tell people up there we really need help here," the cop said. "Some of the staff, the doctors and nurses, have stayed on, but a lot left, and hardly anyone has come back."

"Why are you here?" John asked out of curiosity.

"Somebody came in yesterday and said a couple of the nursing homes in the area were hit by druggies. Well, there's a lot of that stuff inside that building. Figure they need some protection. Besides, I was a marine, took one at Hue, 1968. Those are my comrades in there. I don't have no family to worry about, so I guess these guys are my family."

He then thumped his left leg and there was a hollow echo.

"Semper fi," Washington said, and he leaned out the open window and shook the guard's hand.

"Some advice," Washington then said. "Don't stand out in the middle of the road. Set up some sort of road barrier and keep to one side; use a stalled car as protection. I could have blown you away before you even blinked."

The cop nodded.

"Yeah, guess you're right. Forgot. Tired, I guess."

"Good luck, Marine."

"You, too."

They backed out of the driveway, pulled out onto 70, and continued towards Asheville. A mile farther on, as they came up out of a hollow and started down the long hill that would pass the Department of Motor Vehicles; straight ahead they could see the Asheville Mall . . . a thick pall of smoke hanging over it.

"Get on the bypass," Charlie said. "Don't go anywhere near it."

Driving fast, John went up the ramp onto the I-240 bypass that led straight into the heart of Asheville. Once onto the bypass he began to wonder, yet again, about the wisdom of coming into the city.

It was like driving an obstacle course with all the stalled cars. Ahead, through the highway cut in Beaucatcher Mountain, he could see numerous fires burning in the city, plumes of smoke rising up, spreading out in the morning heat, forming a shadowy cloud.

A trickle of people were walking along the side of the road, and for all the world they reminded him of an old film clip of French refugees fleeing the German advance in 1940. Some were pushing baby carriages, supermarket shopping carts, a wheelbarrow, one family pulling a small two-wheeled cart like the type hooked up to the back of a yard tractor. All piled high with belongings, children, strange things like an old painting, a treasured piece of furniture, a stack of heavy books.

As he drove by going in the opposite direction all looked towards him, as if he were an alien. More than one tried to step out, to wave him down.

"Gun!" Washington shouted.

John hunkered down and hit the gas. A man was running towards them from the side of the road, waving a pistol, and lowered it.

"Damn it, Jeremiah, drop him!" Washington shouted.

Jeremiah picked the shotgun up from off the floor, but they were already past the man. He had not fired a shot, just waved the pistol angrily.

"You keep that gun ready, boy," Washington snapped, "and if I say shoot, you shoot."

"Yes, sir."

John looked in the rearview mirror. Jeremiah's features had gone pale. He was a good kid, a ballplayer. Like so many on the team he tried to act tough and macho, but down deep most of them were small-town churchgoing kids, who never dreamed that in less than a week they'd go from worrying about the next game, final exams, which should have started today, or convincing small-town girls to head off into the woods with them to aiming a gun at someone and squeezing the trigger.

The overpass to Charlotte Street had two cops on it, and as he weaved towards it, one of them motioned for him to take the exit ramp off and threateningly pointed what looked to be an AR-15 at him. The interstate bypass ahead was completely blocked.

He was planning to exit here anyhow, but still, he had never quite expected such a threatening welcome.

The ramp was cleared of vehicles and he turned left off the ramp and onto the overpass where the cop with the AR-15 stood, weapon leveled.

John rolled to a stop.

"Who the hell are you?" the cop asked.

Charlie held his hands up slowly, motioned to the door, opened it, and started to get out.

"Did I tell you you could get out?"

"Listen," Charlie replied sharply. "I'm director of public safety for Black Mountain. I'll show you my ID."

The cop nodded. Charlie slowly reached into his pocket, pulled out his wallet, and opened it up. The cop stepped forward and leaned over to look at it.

"Asshole," Washington whispered from the backseat of the car, his .45 tucked up against his left side.

"I'm here to see Ed Torrell, county director of emergency preparedness, to find out what's going on."

The cop nodded, then looked back at the car.

"I have orders to confiscate all vehicles that are moving."

"Listen, Officer. We drove up from Black Mountain. I need to see Ed right now. If you confiscate our vehicle, how the hell do we get back?"

"You walk. I've got my orders."

"Like hell. This is my car and we're keeping it," John snapped, and the cop turned towards him.

"Get out of the car, all of you. You can walk over to the county office; you'll find Ed there. If he says you can have it back and you got that in writing, fine with me. But for now I'm taking it. You'll find this car behind the courthouse if Torrell gives it back to you."

"How about the other way around?" Charlie replied, staying calm. "Get in, ride with us over to see Ed, and he'll take care of it."

The cop shook his head.

"I've got my orders. Guard this bridge and impound any cars. So the rest of you get out."

Charlie, exasperated, looked towards John, who shook his head wearily. Nothing worse than a corporal type, with limited intelligence, a gun, and his "orders." No amount of logic in the world could ever penetrate through to him.

"You know what you sound like with your 'only following orders'?" John asked.

The cop looked at him.

"A damn Nazi. We keep the car and Charlie here goes in to see Torrell."

"You son of a bitch, get the hell out of that car, all of you, and hands over your heads."

"Let me handle this," Washington whispered.

"Get out, you first, you loudmouthed bastard," and the cop pointed the AR straight at John.

"Move carefully," Washington whispered.

"I'm not budging," John said sharply, loud enough for the cop to hear.

"Out, asshole."

"It's not 'asshole.' It's 'Colonel,' " John replied sharply.

"Get out now," and the cop shouldered the weapon, pointing it straight at John's head.

"Better do what he says," Charlie said bitterly. "Get out, John."

"Hey, everybody chill. It's OK," Washington said, and his speech pattern had instantly changed from Marine DI to comfortable, laid-back African-American southern.

"Come on, bro," Washington said, patting John on the shoulder with his left hand even as he slipped the .45 behind his back. "It's cool; just do what the man says."

Washington carefully eased out of the car, putting his hands up in the air. He walked up to the cop grinning, his gait loose and relaxed . . . and a second later the officer was flat out on the ground. The second cop started to swing his AR-15 around, but the .45, that Washington had kept tucked into his belt behind his back was now leveled straight at the second cop's head.

"Move an inch, Officer, and you are history."

The cop hesitated.

"No one gets hurt," Washington said coolly. "Mr. Fuller is going in to see Mr. Torrell. Everything will turn out fine and then we drive away. We'll all just sit here, wait, and talk like friends. Now son, either drop the gun or I promise you, you will be dead in five seconds."

The officer laid the AR down.

"Boys, take their rifles. Their pistols, too."

Washington kept the pistol leveled as Jeremiah and Phil disarmed the two cops, the one who had been knocked flat with one blow sitting up, red faced, blood trickling down from a broken nose.

"Sorry I had to do that to you, son," Washington said, then turned to Charlie.

"Mr. Fuller, I think you should walk in. If the order is out to confiscate, we'll definitely lose this car trying to drive to the county office. We'll wait here."

"I'll go along," John said.

"Ah, Colonel, sir," Washington interjected. "I think you need to stay here."

"Why?"

"More cops might come along and I just have these two boys."

John nodded, took one of the AR-15s, and looked over at Charlie.

"I'll get back here as fast as I can," Charlie said. "Now listen, if for some chance I'm not back in," he looked down at his old-style wristwatch, "make it two hours, go for home. If it looks like you might lose the car, or have to fight, get the hell out and I'll walk home later. OK?"

"Sure, Charlie."

Charlie turned and set off at a slow trot to the twin buildings of the courthouse and county office. Watching him go, John had the same thought he always did when seeing the twin towers of Asheville, the famous local legend how back in 1943 the pilot of the B-17 bomber *Memphis Belle,* Colonel Bob Morgan, had flown his plane between the two buildings, a buzz job with him banking at a forty-five-degree angle to squeeze through.

Morgan was gone now several years, buried in the veterans cemetery in Black Mountain, and John turned to look back at the cop with the broken nose, the old Edsel, the two wide-eyed students of his. . . . My God, yet again, it was frightful to contemplate how much had changed.

"You all right?" John asked, trying to sound friendly, squatting down by the cop's side.

"Screw you, you asshole," he snapped. "That black son of a bitch broke my nose."

Washington looked down at him and shook his head.

"You're lucky that's all I broke," he said softly, all sympathy now gone. "And next time you address the gentleman, the first two words out of your mouth are 'Colonel, sir,' and as for me 'Sergeant' will be just fine.

"Boys, help him to the side of the road; put him behind that Honda SUV." He turned and looked at the other cop. "Would you mind going over and sitting down there as well."

The second cop nodded, saying nothing.

"Phil, get back into the Edsel. Turn it off, but be ready to fire it up if I give the word. Colonel, how about you and I stand sentry."

Washington leaned against the bridge railing, John beside him, and from a distance it would look like nothing had changed.

John pulled out a cigarette, lit it, and saw the second cop looking up at him.

"Want one?"

"Yes, sir."

John pulled one out, handed it down, the cop motioning to his pocket. Washington nodded and the cop drew out a lighter.

"Damn, thank you, sir. Ran out of smokes two days ago."

John, still holding the pack, looked down and counted. There were eight cigarettes left. He pulled two more out and handed them over.

"Hey, thanks, sir."

The universal gesture of a trade to cement the peace kicked in at that moment and John could see the second cop relax, exhaling with pleasure after he took a deep puff.

John looked over at the cop who was gingerly touching his now-swollen nose that was still leaking blood.

"You smoke?"

"Kiss my ass."

"Hey now," Washington said.

"Gus, you just don't know when to shut the hell up," the second cop said. "Stupid shit, you got what you deserved for once."

Gus shot him a bitter look, saying nothing but the gaze communicating that there would be payback time later for the comment.

"What's your name?" John asked the reasonable cop.

"Bill."

"What's been happening here, Bill?"

"I guess you can see it, sir," and though still sitting on the pavement, he gestured back towards the town.

"Looting, panic. Martial law declared yesterday. They actually executed a guy last night right in the middle of Pack Place. He had killed a cop."

"Got what he deserved then," Washington replied.

"How the hell would you know?" Gus replied, his voice thick.

"Because, you stupid shithead, I'm a cop, but unlike you I got some sense to me. Twenty-four years a marine before that. You might not believe this, buddy, but I'm on your side. But frankly, in your case, shore-patrol types like you I eat up for breakfast."

"Some people coming," Jeremiah announced, and nodded up Charlotte Street.

"I hope you guys cooperate," Washington said.

"Yeah, sure," Bill replied. "I got no beef with you. Besides, you guys were right."

"Wait until I tell the chief about this," Gus said coldly.

"Be my guest. I'm not the one who got thrashed."

John saw where Jeremiah was pointing and the sight was absolutely startling. It was like a procession, a hundred or more. Mostly the downtown weirdos as Jennifer called them.

Asheville across the years had developed something of a reputation as a throwback, a "Haight-Ashbury East," with a bizarre street life of aging hippies and New Agers, Wiccans, and just a lot of drugged-out kids. They were, to John's view, harmless, though the more conservative element of the city and county had real difficulties dealing with them. Frankly, he sort of got a kick out of their presence; there was still, within himself, a touch of them from his own youth.

It was indeed a procession, some guys up front beating on drums, a couple of girls, one of them definitely cute, with long blond hair and a sixties-looking nearly transparent dress on, with nothing on underneath, an old guy, gray beard and hair, wearing a robe carrying a sign that actually declared; "The End HAS Finally Come." Another sign read: "Stop Globalization," other signs "We Got What We Deserved" and several "Peace Now."

Jeremiah stood there grinning as the girl came up to him and did a bit of a provocative dance to the beat of the drum. As the group passed by the side of the Honda SUV, someone slowed.

"Hey, they've got some cops! Looks like they kicked the shit out of Gestapo Gus."

The procession began to grind to a halt.

"Wow, man. Revolution now!" someone shouted, beginning to approach Washington.

"Revolution my ass," Washington said coldly, and the protestor stopped in his tracks.

Bill stood up.

"George, you know me," he said, speaking to the bearded character carrying the end-has-come, sign.

"Yeah, Bill."

"Everything's cool here. Gus fell and broke his nose. These guys are helping out, so why don't you just move along."

The leader nodded, the beat was picked back up, and the parade moved on.

"Absolutely unreal," Washington sighed.

"Asheville," Bill replied. "You gotta love it, even now at times. I know a lot of those kids; most of them are OK, even if a bit misguided."

The dancing blonde came up to him and kissed him on the cheek. Bill actually patted her on the butt before she danced off.

He caught John's eye and grinned slightly.

"Monica and I had a little thing going a couple of months back."

"Wow, you and her?" Jeremiah asked.

Bill grinned but said nothing.

John pulled out two more cigarettes and gave another one over, both he and Bill lighting up.

"Poor kids," Bill sighed. "Strange when you actually think of it. What's happened, it's what many of them have wished for, for years. That one guy, though, with the 'Stop Globalization' sign, him I never liked. Talks the peace bullshit line to score with the girls, but down deep a potential killer. Real anarchist, hell, if he could have pulled the plug he'd of done it and laughed.

"Regardless of that, most of them are OK, and besides, it's a free country, isn't it?"

He chuckled sadly and shook his head.

"They don't get it now. If this is as bad as I think it is . . . they'll be the first to die. They don't know how to survive without a society that supports them even as they curse it or rebel against it."

He sighed.

"Once they run out of food, then the reality will set in, but by that point, anyone with a gun will tell them to kiss off if they come begging. And if those poor kids, if they have food, the ones with guns will take it. They're used to free clinics, homeless shelters when they need 'em, former hippie types smiling and giving them a few bucks. That's all finished. They'll die like flies, poor kids. No idea whatsoever how vicious the world can really be when it's scared and hungry.

"Damn, I hate to see it. Wish their idealisms were true.

"Gandhi and Stalin."

"What?" John asked.

"I used to tell Monica that when we'd get into politics. She'd always talk about how great Gandhi was. I'd tell her the only reason Gandhi survived after his first protest was that he was dealing with the Brits. If Stalin had been running India, he'd of been dead in a second, his name forgotten."

John filed that one away; it was a good point.

The procession disappeared around the corner, heading back towards their traditional hangout, Pack Place, in the center of town.

"A Black Hawk flew over yesterday." John asked, "Did it land here?"

"Yes, right down in Pack Place. From Fort Bragg."

"What did you hear?"

"That's when Ed finally declared martial law. We're at war. That's all I know. The guy on board, bird colonel, said he'll be back in a week or so, then took off."

"War with who?"

"No one really knows. Terrorists, North Korea, Iran, China. Just that we got hit with an EMP nuke, so he said that means we're at war. How are things over in Black Mountain?"

"About the same. Some looting, but Charlie got that under control."

"Memorial Mission Hospital, is it running?" John asked.

"No, sir. Generators never kicked on. I had to help take an old lady with a heart attack up there last night. We have some old trucks that run, a few cars we use as ambulances. My God, it was a damn nightmare up there. A hundred bodies or more lying in the parking lot . . ." And he stopped speaking, looking back towards the town where the old Battery Park Hotel, a hollowed-out shell, brick walls standing, was continuing to burn. Fires dotted the ridgelines beyond.

"The Doors," Bill said.

"What?"

"You know, the Doors. The song 'This Is the End,' been thinking it a lot."

"Here comes Charlie," Washington announced.

He was coming back up the slope, jogging, obviously a bit winded, and motioned for them to get in the car.

John looked at Bill and Gus, who was still on the pavement, eyes red rimmed, glaring.

John went over to the Edsel, pulled a notebook out from under the passenger side, opened it and scribbled a note, then signed it.

He handed it to Washington, who read it, smiled, then signed as well.

To Chief of Police, Asheville, NC:

The officer bearing this note, Bill Andrews, is a professional and has our highest recommendation. The incident between us was unfortunate but solely the blame of Gus Carter, a stupid ass who should be fired before he gets himself killed.

Signed,
John Matherson, Col. (Ret.)
Professor of History
Montreat College

Sergeant Major Washington Parker
U.S. Marines (Ret.)

Washington grinned and then added underneath a postscript:

Carter's lucky I didn't kill him; a baby could disarm him.

John tore the note out of the pad, folded it, and handed it to Bill.

"Hope that covers you."

"What does it say?" Gus asked.

"None of your damn business," John snapped.

"Get in the car now!" Charlie shouted, coming up the last few dozen yards.

"Colonel," Washington said, "clear Bill's weapon please, keep the ammo, and return it."

John pulled the clip, chambered out the round in the barrel, and handed it back to Bill. Gus was on his feet, looking at Washington.

"I like your gun," Washington said calmly. "And frankly, you are a danger to everyone but the bad guys when you are armed."

"Give it back," Gus snapped.

"I'm keeping it. Go explain to your boss how you lost it."

"You damn nig—" He didn't get the rest of the word out, Washington delivering a butt stroke to his stomach, knocking him back over.

Bill said nothing.

"Good luck, Bill," John said, extending his hand, shaking Bill's. John reached into his pocket, pulled out the rest of his pack. Two cigarettes left, he handed the one to Bill.

Again, a flash thought of the Second World War. A GI with a pack of cigarettes was a wealthy man, to share one with another man, or even a captured or wounded enemy, a significant gesture.

"We're out of here," Charlie said, coming up to the car, gasping for air.

Phil turned the engine over, got out from behind the wheel, and John piled in.

"I'll take shotgun," Washington said, getting into the passenger seat. Charlie nodded and climbed into the back with the two boys.

John went into reverse, swung around, then drove back down the on-ramp, feeling strange driving on the wrong side of the highway, moving fast.

Washington took the two pistols he now had, the .45 and the Glock, and placed the Glock by John's side. He kept the AR-15 at the ready.

"What happened back there?" Charlie asked.

"Oh, we made peace," John said, "and you?"

"Jesus Christ, it's a madhouse in the county office. Ed Torrell is dead."

"What?"

"Collapsed about four hours ago, dead in a couple of minutes. That really got people panicked. Ed was a good man, tough, but fair."

"Fair like with our car?"

"I'm doing the same thing."

John looked up in the rearview mirror.

"Like with me?"

Charlie hesitated, then shook his head.

"Course not, John. As long as you help out like this. I know I can count on you when we need it."

John relaxed.

"OK, what's happening?"

"That Black Hawk was from Fort Bragg."

"Yeah, we heard about that from one of the cops."

"Well, it's bad, real bad. There is no communication anywhere yet. They say they had some radios stored away that were in hardened sites and will start getting them out, but nothing prepositioned. Plans as well to see if any ham radio operators have old tube sets, maybe Morse code."

"Sounds like that movie *Independence Day,*" Jeremiah interjected.

"You're right, and almost as desperate."

"But news, I mean news from the outside?" John asked.

"State government's moving to Bragg. Some assets there did survive. Plus it's damn secure."

"Are we at war?"

"Nobody knows for sure with who. At least at this level. Rumors that we nuked Tehran yesterday and half a dozen cities in Iran and just blew the shit out of North Korea."

"So they did it?" Jeremiah asked.

"Like I said, rumors."

"How can we do that?" Phil asked.

"What?"

"I mean hit them when we can't get anything moving here."

"It must have been an event limited to the continental United States. Our assets overseas are still intact, at least for the moment.

"Oh yeah, there's a rumor the president is dead."

"What?" John exclaimed.

"Someone said the White House got word about fifteen minutes before the blast. Got the president airborne on Air Force One . . . and the goddamn plane wasn't hardened sufficiently, and went down."

"I can't believe they didn't harden Air Force One," Washington interjected.

"Yeah, we can't be that dumb," Charlie interjected, his voice bitter with irony.

"Here. Right now. What is going on?" John asked.

Even as he asked, it felt strange. At any other time in the nation's history, the word that the president might be dead froze the nation in place. John could still remember the day Reagan was shot, the incredible gaffe by Alexander Haig at the press conference when he said, "I'm in charge here." That mere misstatement had nearly set off panic with some about an attempted coup.

Air Force One went down? Horrible as the realization was, John felt at that moment it didn't matter to him. It was survival, survival here, at this moment, his family that counted, and he drove on, weaving around a stalled 18-wheeler, a truck that had been hauling junk food, potato chips, corn chips, and it was picked over like a carcass lying in the desert, hundreds of smashed-open cardboard shipping boxes littering the side of the road, bags of chips smashed and torn open lying along the side of the road. An old woman was carefully picking over the torn bags, emptying their meager contents into a plastic trash bag.

"They did get lucky with some vehicles in Asheville," Charlie said. "A scattering of cars parked in underground garages. Their big problem is water. At least we're gravity fed, but part of their downtown has to have the water pumped over Beaucatcher, though down by Biltmore, and on the east side of the mountain they're still getting supplied from the reservoir. They're badly screwed in that department; that's why there's so many fires."

He hesitated.

"Therefore Asheville is trying to organize an evacuation."

"To where?" Washington asked.

"Well, to Black Mountain for one. The new guy in charge, I don't even know him, he told me we're supposed to take five thousand refugees from the city. Didn't ask, no discussion. An order like he was now the dictator of the mountains.

"Almost the first words out of his mouth when I reported in to him. They want to spread their people out all over the region, as far west as Waynesville, north to Mars Hill, south to Flat Rock."

"Why?"

"Because they think we have food, that's why. The water thing is just an excuse. Hell, they're right on the French Broad River. I heard they even have a tank truck that can haul five thousand gallons at a clip. It's just an excuse. It's about the food."

"Do we have as much on hand as they do?" John replied.

Charlie shook his head, features angry.

"They got lucky with the stalled trucks on the interstates. A fair number with bulk food on board them, also the rail yard. Two trucks loaded with a hundred hogs even. They were roasting one right behind the courthouse. Dozens of railcars packed with bulk stuff as well down in the Norfolk and Southern rail yard. Got that from the assistant police chief, a good friend.

"I tried to raise with this new tin-plated idiot that the county should pool all resources and he wouldn't even talk about it, just kept ordering me to prepare to take five thousand refugees starting in a couple of days."

"Hell, it should be us moving in with them," Washington said.

"Why then?" John asked, a bit incredulous that control had so completely broken down that even on the county level there was no cooperation.

"He's planning ahead," Washington said bitterly. "Far ahead. Get rid of half the people and you have food enough for twice as long and let someone else worry about the rest. And I'll bet more than one of the inside crowd, some of the political heels up in that office and their cronies, will still be eating good six months from now.

"Besides, it's like all city folk, they somehow think there's more food out in the country."

John sighed. Scale of social order, he thought. The larger the group, the more likely it was that it would fragment under stress, with a few in power looking out for themselves first. Five thousand might be convinced to share and cooperate. A hundred thousand, self-interests, them and us, would begin to take over, especially with the breakdown in communications.

That had always been the power of media in the hands of a good leader. To get individuals to feel as if the leader was speaking directly to them, Churchill in 1940, Jack Kennedy in 1962, and Reagan in the 1980s. A single voice like that now could break the paradigm, but there would be no such voice and a few cronies of an old political machine in a county government hall might start thinking of themselves and their friends first, and the hell with the rest. John could barely imagine what it might be like, at this very minute, in a city of a million, of five or ten million.

"If we let them all in, it will cut in half the time we have before we run out," Charlie sighed, "and I doubt if they'll help us then.

"So I figured it was best not to stick around and argue. I just told him I'll take it back to the town council. He then said it was an order. I didn't argue. I just got out. As I left, a couple of cops asked me how I got into town and I lied, said I had walked it. Well, that's why I was running. I got a block or two and they started to follow me."

"I know this might sound stupid." It was Jeremiah. "But I thought we were all in this together. We're neighbors. . . ."

He hesitated.

"We're Americans. . . ."

John glanced back to the rearview mirror, unable to speak, then focused his attention ahead.

They were up to the turnoff onto Route 70. He went down the ramp, swung onto what he still felt was the correct side of the road, and floored it.

The line of refugees they had passed earlier was actually larger now, more people on foot, some on bicycles, others having already learned the old refugee trick that a bicycle can be a packhorse; loaded it down, properly balanced, it could be pushed along with a couple of hundred pounds.

"Gun," Washington announced. "Swerve left."

John swung the old Edsel across the highway. Strange, it was right in front of the DMV office. A week ago, a dozen cops would have been piling out to give him a ticket, the gunman cause for a SWAT team to jump in.

The gunman was the same as before, standing in front of a car dealership, now stepping out, waving his pistol.

Washington raised his AR-15, leveled it out the window. Some refugees were scattering, others just staring at the sight of the Edsel, some just oblivious.

"Don't do it," Washington hissed.

As if the man had heard Washington or, far more likely, seen the leveled rifle, he stepped back.

Washington tracked on him as they sped past, then exhaled noisily.

"Professor, I think your student just asked a question," Washington said calmly.

John, trembling from the tension, spared a quick glance back at Jeremiah, Charlie by his side.

"We're still Americans," John said softly.

An hour later they were back into Black Mountain. There was a roadblock up on the west side of Swannanoa; the chief there had chosen a good spot, a bottleneck where ridges came down on both sides, Route 70, Swannanoa Creek railroad track, and I-40 side by side. The roadblock had not been up when they had driven through several hours earlier.

John had slowed as they approached the barrier. Charlie leaned out of the car and a couple of the cops recognized him, asked for news, and he had confirmed the rumor that had already reached them that more refugees were coming out of Asheville.

John pulled back onto the interstate there, and once past the sign marking the town limits of Black Mountain he breathed a sigh of relief and he felt the others in the car relax as well, Washington finally lowering the AR-15. It was if they had gone to an alien land and were now safely back home.

But as they rolled into the parking area in front of the firehouse and police station, John tensed up again. A crowd had gathered, half a thousand or more, and for a few seconds he thought they were trying to storm the building for the emergency supplies.

The five of them got out, and at the sight of Charlie several came running up.

"They got two thieves in there, Charlie," someone said excitedly.

John shook his head. Hell, half of the people in this town in the last five days had stolen something. Even himself, he had never bothered to go back to the drugstore to pay for the medication or chocolate or the twenty bucks he still owed Hamid. Besides, there was no money anyhow.

"The bastards that raided the nursing home!" someone else shouted, and an angry mutter went through the crowd.

Charlie pushed his way through, and John followed along with Washington.

They got to the door.

"John, maybe you should wait."

"I got a stake in this. I was there; Tyler was affected."

"OK."

He followed Charlie in. There was a crowd gathered round the door to the conference room, and John stepped through the group with Charlie.

Kate looked up, visible relief in her eyes.

"You're back safe, thank God."

"What's going on here?"

"Got these two," Tom said.

At the far end of the room two men, midtwenties from the look of them, one as described by Ira, shaved head, distinguishing tattoo, earring; the other, almost an opposite, looking not much different from John's students now waiting outside: fairly well built, hair cut short, but his eyes . . . John could tell this kid was something of a stoner.

"Charlie, Tom wants to shoot them," Kate said quietly.

Charlie sat down against the edge of the table and looked at them.

"What do you got, Tom?"

"When I got the description from the nursing home, I knew where to look for him," Tom said, pointing at the serpent arm.

"Busted him three years back on a meth charge. Regular lab, a home just up over the crest of Route 9. Owned by his cousin here."

"I didn't have nothing to do with it!" the clean-cut one cried. "Larry here, he's the one."

"Shut the fuck up, Bruce," Larry snapped, trying to lunge towards him but unable to move. Both were handcuffed and bound to chairs.

"So I went up there this morning and sure enough found these two. Wasted as shit. You'll see the track marks from the morphine."

John looked closely at the clean-cut kid; there was some recognition.

"Professor Matherson. You know me, I took History one-oh-one with you four years ago. You know me."

John looked at him carefully. He was never that good with names, but faces he did remember. Yes, Bruce had been a student, showed some promise, then just disappeared from the campus after a semester or two.

Tom looked over at John.

"He was a student once. Several years back."

"That doesn't matter now," Tom said.

"I want a lawyer. A fucking lawyer!" Larry shouted. "I know my rights. You dumb-ass cop, you didn't even read me my Miranda, so you really fucked up this bust. I'm outta here once I get a lawyer. Brutality as well," and he turned his head to show a swollen cheek, right eye half-shut.

"We are under martial law now," Charlie said quietly, breaking into the argument.

Bruce looked over at Charlie, eyes wide.

"What does that mean?"

Charlie stood up and looked around.

"Witnesses?"

"We fetched the supervisor down from the nursing home. She's outside."

"Bring her in," Charlie said.

John stood up as Ira came in. She looked worse than yesterday, hair uncombed, dirty. It was obvious from the stains on her silk blouse, and the smell, that she had, at some point, snapped out of her shock and was trying to help with the patients.

She looked at the two young men.

"The one with the tattoo, that's definitely him."

"Lying bitch, it was dark; how could you see me?"

"How do you know it was dark when they were robbed?" Charlie asked.

"Heard it from somebody," came the muttered reply.

"The other one, I'm not sure. But that tattoo, I remember that."

"Thanks for the identification."

She nodded.

Charlie hesitated, looking around.

"Will you swear to this?"

"Sure, Charlie."

"Someone find a Bible."

Kate went into her office and returned a moment later with a King James. Charlie wasn't sure of the exact line, so Kate swore her in, and Ira repeated her testimony.

"You got the drugs, Tom?" Charlie asked.

"In my office."

"Go get them."

He returned with several dozen vials of liquid morphine, containers of other drugs in pill form.

"Tom, just look on the containers," Ira said. "'Miller's Nursing Home,' followed by a code number, should be on them. All controlled substances, when shipped, have tracking numbers and delivery ID numbers," and she repeated the coding.

"The same," Tom replied.

"John, would you witness to that?"

John looked over with surprise at Charlie, as if being dragged in. But the memory of the suffering in the nursing home filled him. Kate swore John in, he went over, picked up a container.

"It says: 'Miller's Nursing Home.'"

"Tom, you next," Charlie said.

Sworn in, Tom repeated his testimony as well.

Finished, he stepped back around behind the two.

"You men have anything to say?" Charlie asked.

"I want a fucking lawyer!" Larry shouted.

"Do you have anything to say?" Charlie repeated.

"Yeah, I sure as hell do; give me the damn Bible," Bruce said.

Charlie reddened, looking over at Kate.

"The Holy Bible please," she said slowly, forcefully.

Larry said nothing.

"I want the Holy Bible please," Bruce said.

Charlie picked it up, walked it down the length of the table, and put it down in front of Bruce, who was then sworn in.

"Tell us your story, Bruce."

For the next five minutes he rambled on. He had nothing to do with it, Larry just coming in with the drugs. Who the second guy was, Bruce didn't know. He and Larry had divided the loot.

John watched Bruce carefully. The man, still not much more than a boy actually, maybe twenty-one or -two, was obviously terrified. And, as well, John could sense Bruce was lying. All the years as a prof had sharpened his bullshit detector, as he called it.

Bruce finally fell silent.

"Ira?" Charlie asked. "How much morphine in liquid form was taken?"

"We keep individual vials for each patient using it, since dosage and strength vary. I think about forty or so."

"We confiscated thirty-two," Tom interjected.

"Not much of a cut between your friend here and his buddy," Charlie said. "You mean the other guy walked off with eight vials and Larry kept over thirty?"

"Yeah, that must have been it. No one argues with Larry."

"Or eight vials would be one hell of a party," Tom interjected. "It's a wonder they didn't kill themselves."

"You bastards."

It was Ira, her voice breaking.

"I got seven patients dying of cancer. Two are dead now, thank God, but the others are in agony and all I have for them is what was in their daily trays and then aspirin. I hope they shoot both of you."

She fell silent, eyes burning with rage.

"Larry?" Charlie said, motioning to the Bible.

"Why bother?"

Charlie nodded and then looked back at John.

"John, I want to keep this formal. I'm appointing you to speak on behalf of these two men."

"What?"

"You heard me."

"My father-in-law is tied into this."

"John, just do me the favor."

"Go get Norm Schaich; he's a lawyer. He can do this better than me."

"Norm's house is miles from here."

"I can drive it."

"John, I want this done now."

"I want a fucking lawyer," Larry stated yet again. "Yeah, go get Norm."

John looked at him, then to Bruce and over to Ira, and then out through the half-closed blinds to the crowd gathered outside.

John finally nodded and stood up.

"I'll say this for them. The world we knew, maybe it's finished, finished forever. Maybe not, but I doubt that. All that holds us together now are the things we believed in, the traditions of who we were, who we still want to be.

"Charlie, I guess you'll make the decision. Guide yourself with that thought, of what this country is supposed to be, even in these dark times. I know what you are thinking. I know what our neighbors outside are thinking. But whatever your decision, know it is a foundation point for what follows, but if we make a mistake here, Charlie, then we've lost that foundation. . . ." He paused. "We are no longer Americans."

He stepped back to the corner of the room.

Charlie stood silent, head lowered. Bruce started to cry.

Charlie finally raised his head.

"I dread this," he said quietly. "I never thought I would ever do something like this. But I must think of the community."

He stepped to the center of the room, behind the chair Kate was sitting in.

"Larry, Bruce—" he hesitated, "Randall and Wilson," Tom interjected.

"Larry Randall and Bruce Wilson," Charlie continued, "I sentence you to death by firing squad, for the crime of looting precious medical supplies, not only from this community, but from a facility where people were in desperate need of those supplies to ease their final pain. Execution to be carried out immediately."

"You bastard," Larry hissed.

"Son, you are about to go before God; I'm giving you ten minutes to make your peace. Someone go find a minister for them," Charlie said, and walked out.

John followed him as he went into his office and Charlie did not object as John closed the door. He pulled out the last cigarette in his pocket and lit it. Charlie looked at it longingly for a few seconds and John was ready to offer it over, but Charlie then shook his head.

"Did I do the right thing, John? Frankly, I'm so damn mad at those two animals, especially that Larry, that I'd do it myself without hesitation. But still, did I do the right thing?"

John sat down and didn't speak for a moment. He was torn as well. Again memory of his own temptation with Liz at the pharmacy, to snatch the medicine he needed for Jennifer.

"John, it's like we're back a hundred and fifty years. The Wild West. I kept thinking of that movie, *Oxbow Incident*. Remember they hang three guys in that movie but then find out they're innocent."

"Yeah, same thought here. It was just on TV last week. One of Henry Fonda's best."

"A week ago," Charlie sighed. "Just that short a time?"

"They are not innocent, though," John said.

"But still. A week ago we didn't kill screwed-up punks for stealing drugs. That Bruce kid, right guidance, he might have straightened out."

John shook his head.

"Look, Charlie, might have beens are finished. Charlie, we got six thousand, maybe seven thousand people in this town now. How much food? How much medicine? Water still works for downtown, as long as the pipe to the reservoir holds, but up on the sides of the hills we're out. Charlie, we don't keep order, in a month people will be killing each other for a bag of chips."

John felt the heat of the cigarette burning his fingers and he looked around, then dropped it into an empty coffee cup. "Or a pack of smokes. I'm sorry for that one, boy, but you did the right thing.

"Just keep in mind what I said on their behalf back in there."

Charlie nodded.

There was a knock on the door; it was Tom and Kate. Charlie motioned them in.

"Reverend Black is in there with them. Time is just about up," Tom said.

"Tom, you will not do the execution," John said.

Tom looked over at him.

"You are the police authority in this town. If someone must do the execution, it cannot be you or any other officer or official of this town. That terrible task has always been kept separate from the hands of those out in the field who directly enforce the law. If not, well . . ." He thought of Stalin, of the Gestapo. "It has to be someone else."

Tom nodded, and John was glad to see that in spite of his angry talk earlier, Tom was relieved.

John looked over at Charlie.

"Not me, John."

"No, it can't be you, either, Charlie. You're the emergency government; and Kate, the traditional government. No, not you."

"Then who?" Charlie asked.

No one spoke.

"You, John," Kate said quietly.

Startled, he looked at her. He had simply been advising as a historian; he never imagined it would come back on him like this.

"Damn all, I was not volunteering myself." John said, "I was just trying to keep us in touch with who we once were as a country."

"I'm not going out there to ask for volunteers," Charlie said. "I will not let this turn into a circus with some sick bastards mobbing in to take a shot. I want you to do it. You're the historian, John; you understand it, the meaning of it. You're a respected professor in the town. Everyone knows you, or knows your kin here."

"Oh Jesus," John whispered, knowing he was trapped.

Reluctantly he nodded his head.

"Where?" Tom asked.

John couldn't think.

"The town park," Charlie said. "It's the public gathering place. I don't want it here."

"Fine then," Tom replied. "We take them down to the park now and do it. We load them into Jim's van. The tennis courts have a concrete practice wall. I'll go outside and announce it for one half hour from now."

The mention of the tennis courts chilled John. It made him think of the Taliban and the infamous soccer stadium in Kabul. Is that what we have now, tennis courts?

"Maybe in private," Kate ventured. "Maybe in private. I don't like the thought of public execution."

"I don't either," John said slowly, "but we have to do it. There's fear in this town. I'm hearing people say that the refugees from the highway are 'outsiders.' We're already beginning to divide ourselves off from each other. We do private executions and I guarantee you, within a day there'll be rumors flying from those who don't live here that we are doing Stalinist courts and executing people in the basement of the police station. If we are forced to do this, we do it in public."

"Besides," Tom interjected, "it's a statement to anyone else who might be thinking about stealing."

"Wait a minute, Tom," John said. "I pray we aren't down to killing people for stealing a piece of bread."

Tom shook his head angrily.

"John, don't misread me. You might not believe this, but I don't like it any more than you."

John stared into his eyes and then finally nodded.

"OK, Tom, sorry."

"I'll go make the announcement."

"Tom," Kate said. "Adults only. I don't want kids down there."

Tom left the room and seconds later there was the crackling hiss of an old handheld megaphone and Tom began to speak.

There was a scattering of applause, even a few cheers, someone shouting a rope would be better.

Damn, it did feel like an old western, John thought, the crowd all but crying, "Lynch 'em!"

The crowd immediately broke up, many setting off for the park, some, especially those with children, staying behind. Long minutes passed, John silent, looking out the window.

He heard cursing from out in the corridor and crying. The two were being led out.

"We better go," Charlie said, and opened the door.

John felt as if he were being led to his own execution. Could he do it? All those years in the army, the training, but never a shot in anger or even in detached professionalism, as they were told they should act. During Desert Storm he was XO of a battalion, but even there, he was in a command vehicle a couple miles behind the main line of advance, never on the actual firing line pulling the trigger.

He thought of the taunting rednecks back when he was in college, the frightful moment when rage drove him to the point that he might very well have shot one, and the shock of it afterwards . . . and then the shaking of hands with one of them only days later and a shared drink.

He was outside. The two were in the back of Jim Bartlett's Volkswagen van, handcuffed, feet chained. The back of the van door was slammed shut, Tom up in the front seat with a drawn pistol, Reverend Richard Black crouched down between Jim and Tom.

John looked at the two as the door closed and realized when he made eye contact with Bruce, barely remembered but still a former student, there was one thing he could not do.

He saw Washington with Jeremiah and Phil and walked up to them.

"Washington, I need your help. God, do I need it," and John told him. Washington nodded, saying nothing, and got into the car with John, Kate, Phil, and Jeremiah squeezing into the backseat, Charlie up front with Washington and John.

The two vehicles set off and as they turned onto Montreat Road and then the side street over to the park, he saw people walking fast, heading for the park, others just standing there, staring.

"Killing is a sin!" someone shouted as he drove slowly, following the van that was dragging along at not more than five miles an hour.

It was like a damn procession out of the French Revolution, he thought.

They rolled down the steep hill to the corner of the park, a large crowd already gathered by the tennis courts and the concrete practice wall painted white, bits of paint flecking off.

The two were led out of the back of the van and all fell silent.

Swallowing hard, John stopped the car. He looked over at Washington.

"Just aim straight at the chest, sir," Washington said. "You try for the head and you're shaking at all you'll miss. First shot to the chest, he'll collapse. They don't go flying around like in the movies; usually they just fall over or sag down to the ground. Once he's on the ground, then empty the clip; just empty it. If you have your wits about you put the last shot into the head. Do you understand me, sir?"

Washington handed the Glock to him.

"A round is chambered."

John nodded.

He got out of the car and the crowd separated back, opening a lane, the two prisoners ahead of them. Bruce was crying, begging, Larry silent, Reverend Black holding Bruce's arm while Tom had Larry in a tight grip.

"This is wrong, Charlie!" someone shouted.

And there was an angry mutter, shouts back, arguments breaking out.

The condemned were led to the wall and placed against it.

More shouts from the crowd, some against, most for, a few yelling to string the guilty up rather than shoot them.

Sickened, John looked around, and before he even realized what he was doing he raised the gun straight up in the air and fired.

Bruce let out a scream of terror and collapsed to his knees. There were cries from the crowd and then silence, all eyes on John.

"I have been appointed to do something I never dreamed of in my worst nightmares!" John shouted.

No one spoke now.

"I will confess to you, one of these men I cannot bring myself to shoot;

he was once a student of mine. I have asked Mr. Parker, a former marine sergeant major, to do that task for me and he will do it."

"Our world has changed . . . ," and John's voice trailed off, but then he raised his head. "But this is still America. I want to believe this is still America.

"We are at war. Mr. Fuller will hold a town meeting this evening in the elementary school gym and share with you the latest news and information. This is a meeting for all of you, those born here, those who moved here like me, those whom circumstances now place here."

He paused again.

"All of you are citizens of our country. Mr. Fuller, who was director of public safety prior to this war and is thus now," he looked for the right word, "our temporary leader in Black Mountain, under martial law, will share with you the news we have from Asheville about what has happened, is happening, will happen.

"We are at war, and martial law has been proclaimed in this town. These two men have been condemned to death under the rules of martial law. They have been convicted and condemned for stealing vital medication, painkillers from Miller's Nursing Home, leaving the residents there to suffer in agony. Of that crime and the general crime of looting they have been found guilty beyond all reasonable doubt at a fair and open hearing."

"Fuck your trial!" Larry screamed. "This is a lynch mob!"

John was silent and no one from the crowd replied. There were no shouts or taunts.

"I am a citizen of this town," he said, his voice now softer. "By tradition, even in times of martial law, our police who directly enforce the law will not participate in what will now happen, nor our governing body. I want all of you to understand that. This is not a police state and it never will be. The condemned were found guilty at a fair hearing, and the sentence will now be carried out, not by those who are temporarily in charge of law and order, but by two duly appointed citizens who have volunteered for this task."

He lowered his head and swallowed, knowing he could not let a tremor get into his voice.

"I do not want this task. I did not seek it. I loathe doing it." He paused. "But it must be done."

He paused again for a moment, realizing something more still had to be said.

"We are all Americans here. There are hundreds of you, perhaps thousands, who did not live here but five days ago," again a brief pause, "but you do now. All of us are equal under the eyes of the law here. All of us. We must work together as neighbors if we wish to survive. The tragic justice to be dealt out here is the same for all of us, whether born here, moved here as I did some years ago, or arrived just yesterday. It must be the same for all of us. . . ."

His voice trailed off. Nervously he looked back at the two guilty men, Reverend Black holding Bruce up with one hand, open Bible in the other; Larry still held by Tom, his eyes glazed from the drugs, and with a boiling hatred.

John wondered now just how legal, how close to law in the tradition of Western civilization, his act and his words truly were, but he felt they were right, right for here, this moment, if the people of Black Mountain were to survive as a community.

He fell silent and looked over at Charlie. There was a pause until Charlie realized that ritual demanded that he say something.

He stepped in front of the group.

"By the power vested in me by emergency decree by the civilian government of this community, the town of Black Mountain, now under local martial law, I have found Larry Randall and Bruce Wilson guilty of looting of medical supplies and, in so doing, causing pain, suffering, and death. Their sentence is death by firing squad, to now be carried out by Dr. John Matherson and Mr. Washington Parker, appointed by me to perform this task."

Charlie looked over at John, nodding. John turned to face the condemned, his hand shaking.

"Remember what I said: first shot to the chest, let him drop, then empty the rest of the clip, last one in the head," Washington whispered.

The two walked the few dozen feet to the prisoners. Tom stepped back and away from Larry, who glared at him with cold hatred. But Reverend Black did not move, holding Bruce up.

"I think we should pray," Reverend Black said, and John nodded in agreement, embarrassed that he had not thought to do so.

Still holding Bruce, Reverend Black looked to the crowd.

"I ask God, in his divine mercy, to grant forgiveness to these two. But we must now render unto Caesar the law of Caesar. Forgiveness and redemption now rest between Bruce, Larry, and their Creator.

"Bruce, do you ask God for forgiveness?"

"Yes, please, God, please forgive me."

"Larry?"

He was silent.

"Our Father, who art in heaven . . ."

John repeated the prayer, hoping that the trembling of his hands would stop. He looked at Larry, making eye contact.

There was nothing but rage there, blind animal rage, and John almost felt pity.

"For thine is the kingdom, the power, the glory, forever and ever. Amen."

The last word, "Amen," echoed from the crowd.

John shifted the Glock to his left hand and, for the first time in years, made the sign of the cross; then he shifted the pistol back.

Reverend Black stepped away from Bruce, who now struggled to make a show of standing up straight. John suddenly realized there should have been something, blindfolds, sacks over their heads.

No, get it done; get it done quick.

"Move closer," Washington whispered. "Fire and I'll fire with you."

John looked straight at Larry, who was now only ten feet away.

"Go ahead; do it," Larry said coldly.

It all seemed to move so slowly. Without ceremony, flourish, John raised the pistol, centered it on the man's chest. At the very last instant Larry started to move, to try to fall to one side.

John squeezed the trigger.

He saw the impact; Larry staggered backwards against the concrete wall. The roar of Washington's .45 exploded next to him, startling him. He saw his second shot miss, striking above Larry's head as he slid down against the wall, leaving a bloody streak.

Two more quick shots from Washington's .45.

John fought to center his Glock, aimed at Larry's midsection; he was kicking feebly. John could hear screams behind him. He fired again, again, and then again.

A hand was on his shoulder. It was Washington.

"The head," Washington said softly.

John walked up to Larry. Was he dead? Blood was pooling out under his body, the front of his pants wet, another stench added in, bladder and bowels having let go.

There seemed to be a flicker of eye movement. John aimed at the center of Larry's head, standing over him, and fired.

A second later another explosion, the coup de grâce being delivered to Bruce.

Woodenly, John turned. All were now staring at him, all silent. Hands to mouths, a few were crying. The way they looked at him, it was different, different from anything he had ever seen before in the eyes of people gazing at him. Fear . . . awe . . . revulsion . . . from a few strange glazed eyes almost a look of envy and lust.

He felt the vomit coming up. He had to control it. He held the Glock up, not sure if he had actually emptied it or not. His student Jeremiah was standing in the crowd, and John made eye contact. Jeremiah stepped forward and John handed him the gun.

"Secure the gun and meet me at the car," John whispered.

He turned and walked away from the crowd, got behind the concrete wall, bent double, and vomited.

Gasping, he remained doubled over.

"It's OK, sir." It was Washington.

John looked up at him, suddenly ashamed.

"Puked my guts out the first time I killed a man. Sir, if you hadn't I'd of been worried about you."

"Stop calling me 'sir,' god damn it," John hissed between the continuing heaves.

"You did the right thing, sir. You did it well."

"Well? How can you say killing a man like that was done well?"

"No, sir. Not that. It's always a stinking mess. I mean what you said. That's why I call you 'sir' now. We used to joke about it before. Frankly, sir, you were a professor type, but I knew you were a colonel, so I played along. But today, sir, you led out there, you faced something horrible, and you led."

"OK," John sighed.

"Come on; let's get out of here."

John nodded. Wiping his mouth with the back of his hand. He winced with pain. His finger was infected and the act of shooting the Glock had ripped the cut wound open.

He came back around the wall and the crowd, mysteriously, was all but gone. Few had hung around. The bodies were gone, Bartlett's van already driving off.

John realized he must have been behind the wall for long minutes.

He was glad no one was around to see him now.

A bit wobbly, he headed for his car.

"John?"

It was Makala.

He didn't recognize her at first. Gone was the sexy business suit. She had on a pair of baggy jeans, a few sizes too big, and an old faded T-shirt from Purdue University.

"Thank you, John."

"For what, damn it?"

"What you said back there before you had to shoot those two."

He nodded.

"It's been getting a little tense between those who lived here before and people like me who have wandered in. What you said needed to be said. It reminded us we're one in this."

"OK."

He really did not want to talk and he slowly continued to the car.

"Let me look at that hand."

She stepped around in front of him and he winced as she pulled the bandage off.

"John, it's getting infected, badly infected. I told you to go home, wash it, and keep it protected."

He thought of the nursing home, carrying his father-in-law, the filth there.

"I need to clean that out for you, John; it really should be stitched up."

"It can wait," he said woodenly. "I just want to go home now."

"OK then, I'll go with you."

He glared at her coldly, a sick thought crossing his mind that perhaps she was turned on to him because of what he had just done, that or as an "outsider" she was ingratiating herself with a man who now obviously had power in the town.

She stepped back slightly.

"John. First, you're getting an infection; in this situation you could lose your hand, or maybe even your life. Second, I heard about your father-in-law and the nursing home. I volunteered to go up there to help clean and take care of the folks. After I'm done with you, it's a far shorter walk. Third, John, your little girl—Jennifer, isn't it?"

"Yes."

"Monitoring her diet now is going to be tough. She should be checked every couple of days by a nurse or doctor. So just take me home with you; I'll get done what needs to be done and then go up to the nursing home for the night."

"OK." It was all he could say.

He got to the car, Washington and the two boys standing by it. Jeremiah handed the Glock back to John.

"It's cleared and empty, sir. Tom gave me a fresh clip; you'll find it in your glove compartment."

Washington took the AR-15 and the two shotguns out of the vehicle.

"We'll walk back to campus, sir. Why don't you just go home?"

Phil stepped around and opened the door for Makala, who got in.

John looked back to the blood-splattered wall and then, almost ironically, fifty yards beyond it, the flagpole and the flag floating atop it. The sky beyond it was darkening. A late afternoon thunderstorm building.

He thought of Jeremiah's question and wondered. Can we still keep this as America? Are we still America?

As he drove home he did not say a word.

"Vomited, didn't you?" she finally said, breaking the silence.

"Yeah."

"I thought you were a soldier."

"I am. . . . I mean I was. Not many soldiers, though, are trigger pullers. I was in Desert Storm, exec for a battalion with the First Cav. Saw fighting from a distance, but never actually pulled a trigger. Most of the time I was just hunched over a computer screen trying to direct the action."

"Sorry, that came out wrong," Makala replied. "I didn't mean it as an insult. It's just the way you handled that guy in the drugstore the other day. You struck me as someone who had seen combat before."

"No."

"It's all right. I still get queasy at times during an operation. I damn near died when I walked into that nursing home last evening."

"Thanks for doing that."

"My job now, I guess."

The conversation died away.

They pulled into the driveway. The two fools Ginger and Zach came running up, and at the sight of a stranger they showed typical golden retriever loyalty and went running straight to her, ignoring John.

She laughed, scratching their ears as they jumped up to lick her, both starting to bark as they danced around her. John headed for the door where Jen stood.

"Thank God you're home," Jen said. "What happened? I've been worried sick all day about you."

"Went to Asheville like I told you."

She looked past John to Makala, who was coming up, the dogs trailing beside her. Jen's eyes widened slightly and John could sense she was not pleased, that this woman was an invader in her territory.

"Mom, I'd like you to meet Makala Turner. Makala, this is my mother-in-law, Jennifer Dobson."

The two nodded and shook hands.

"Mom, you might recall Makala; she was the woman on the road the first evening."

"Oh, oh yes. My dear, I didn't recognize you, given how you are dressed now."

"She's a nurse, Mom. Head RN with a surgical unit, actually. She came here to check on Tyler, Jennifer, and this." He held up his hand.

Jen's talons retracted and there was a smile.

"Oh, come on in, dear."

"How is Tyler?" John asked.

"Resting comfortably," she said quietly.

"The girls?"

"Jennifer's taking a nap. Her sugar level was up and she just took a shot. Elizabeth is out for a walk with Ben."

"Fine."

John walked into his office and left the two women, who went straight to what was now Tyler's sickroom.

John took the Glock out from his belt, looked at it, then laid it on his desk. He noticed now that the smell of cordite hung heavy on it, and on him.

Reaching around to the back corner of the desk, he pulled out a dust-covered bottle. There had been several times in his life when drinking had damn near won out, the last time for several weeks after Mary died. The dust on the bottle was a reassurance. He poured a double scotch out into an empty coffee cup and drained it down in two gulps.

The thunderstorm that had been on the western horizon rolled in, rain slashing against the window . . . a soothing sound.

When Makala came into the room a half hour later to check his hand, he was fast asleep.

CHAPTER SIX

DAY 10

"John, you look like crap warmed over."

He nodded, walking into the conference room for what had now become their daily meeting.

"Thanks, Tom. I needed that."

In spite of Makala's attention, John's hand was still infected and he was running a fever of just over a hundred and a half.

He settled into what was now his chair at the middle of the table. Interesting how quickly habits form regarding a meeting: sit in a chair once and the following day that's where you sit again, symbolism of who sits at the foot and head of the table the same. Kate still held that symbolic position at the head, but it was actually Charlie now, sitting to her right, who ran the morning briefing, Tom at the foot of the table. Doc Kellor had become part of the team as well, sitting across from John. Two more were present, he didn't recognize either, one dressed in a police uniform, a Swannanoa Police Department patch stitched on his sleeve, the second man in jeans and T-shirt, both in their midforties.

John picked up the cup of coffee that was waiting for him with his left hand.

"Let me look at that," Kellor said, getting out of his chair and coming around the table.

He eased back the surgical gauze that Makala had redressed the wound with the evening before.

"Good stitching job, couldn't have done better myself."

John said nothing. The dozen stitches Makala had sewed had been done without any painkiller other than a swig of a scotch, and he had sweated that out silently, though he had cursed a bit when she had dosed the wound with alcohol.

Kellor leaned over and sniffed the bandage and shook his head.

"How did it get infected like this?"

"I think when I was carrying my father-in-law, at the nursing home."

"Treatment?"

"Makala Turner, the nurse who volunteered to help run the nursing home, she put me on Cipro. Got some from the nursing home."

"Most likely fecal contact," Kellor said, nodding and looking at the wound. "But you can also get some pretty tough strains of bacteria and viruses growing even in the cleanest hospital or home, strep or staph.

"Let's talk about this later," Kellor said, and went back to his seat.

Kate cleared her throat.

"OK, let's get started. We got a new problem. Dr. Kellor, would you lead off?"

The old "town doc" nodded.

"We've got an outbreak of salmonella at the refugee center in the elementary school. It was bound to happen. I've got at least a hundred sick over there this morning. A mess, a damn mess."

"How did it get started?" Kate asked.

Kellor looked at her with surprise.

"Hell, Kate. People are used to running water, hundreds of gallons a day. Food with dates stamped on it; one day over the limit and we used to throw it out. There's six hundred people camped there. At least we still have enough water pressure for the toilets to flush, but no hot water and, to be blunt, no toilet paper or paper towels as well. It's getting nasty.

"Come on, people. Think about it. Most of us haven't bathed in ten days, toilet paper's getting scarce, soup line meals twice a day at the refugee center, food now of real questionable safety, I'll bet that damn near every person in there will be crapping their guts out and puking by the end of the day."

He sighed.

"Seven dead this morning. I checked before coming over here. Two of them infants, the rest elderly. Dehydrated out and couldn't get electrolytes into them fast enough. I'll need more volunteers to go down there to help out, because it will be full-blown by the end of the day."

No one spoke. The thought of a school building full of people in that condition . . . it left the rest in the room silent.

"Remember Katrina and that god-awful Superdome?" Charlie sighed. "Is that what we got?"

"Worse," Kellor replied. "Screwed up as their administration was, ultimately help was on the way, even though a lot of people started to panic with insane reports of murder and rape. We don't have that here at all, but on the other side, the cavalry is not going to come rushing in with helicopters loaded with supplies. We are on our own.

"We need to get some clean vats for sterile water; we can mix up an electrolyte batch like what is used in emergency relief in third-world countries.

"We are a frigging third-world country now," the police officer from Swannanoa said softly.

"It's simple enough. Just pure water, we still have that, don't we, Charlie?"

"What is coming out, gravity fed, from the reservoir is still clean, at least as of the last time our water department people tested it yesterday."

"I worry about that. All you need are some folks camping around the reservoir, one of them has a bug and relieves himself by the lake, and all of us are sick."

Charlie looked over at Tom.

"We better get a few men up there patrolling the lake. No campers."

The fishing in the lake was one of the more poorly guarded secrets of the community across the years. The reservoir, shared with Asheville, was supposedly strictly off-limits to everyone, even before all this had started. But many were the kids who would sneak in there with a rod and pull out a trophy brown trout of ten pounds or more. Until an activist type in Asheville had blown the whistle on it half a dozen years back, there was even a private fishing cabin in the woods just above the lake, a secret retreat for the higher-ups in Asheville and Black Mountain. A good-ole-boys club for a weekend of drinking and catching damn big trout on what they saw as their private lake.

Chances now were that people were already looking to that lake as a source of food, and it would have to be stopped.

"We need to mix up a batch of several hundred gallons of clean water, mixture of salt and sugar; it'll keep the electrolyte balance. Then start pouring it down the throats of those poor people. In nine out of ten cases they'll just be damn sick for a few days and then pull through."

"And the tenth case?" Charlie asked.

Kellor sighed.

"Without IVs, the elderly, children under a year, people already weak from other diseases." He paused and looked at the ceiling for a moment. "I'll estimate thirty dead, maybe fifty by tomorrow night."

Charlie folded and unfolded his hands.

"Who will organize the volunteers?" Charlie asked.

John sighed.

"I'll go up to the campus. See if we can roust out some kids."

"Promise them a damn good meal at the end of it," Charlie said. "One of my men got a deer last night. I got it hidden. Venison steak dinner in exchange for a day's work."

"I doubt if they'll be hungry after what we're throwing them into, but I'll see," John said.

Kellor nodded.

"Have them report to me by noon, right here. I'll have to brief them on their own safety before they go over there."

John nodded.

"OK, that brings me to something we might not want to talk about," Charlie said, "but I think we should. Burying the dead."

"We bury them as we always have, don't we?" Kate asked.

"There's no cemetery within town limits. The nearest one is over two miles away. I'm starting to think long term here, people. Not just this case with the salmonella but across the next several months."

No one replied.

"I'm thinking the town golf course across the street from the park."

"What?" Tom replied. "That's crazy. You're talking about the golf course?"

"Exactly. It's within an easy walk of the center of town. There was a lot of grading done when it was built, all of it soil, easy to dig. The approach up to the sixth green, that's all graded soil half a dozen feet deep or more. Remember, there's no more backhoes to dig graves, it's back to shovels, and I want graves dug deep and quick."

"Damn it, Charlie, that's the town golf course," Tom interjected.

"As if anyone is going out today to do eighteen holes?" Charlie replied sharply. "Hell, even you only play with an electric cart. I think we need a cemetery and close by, not out on the other side of Allen Mountain.

"Doc, do you agree?"

"Keep it at least a couple of hundred feet back from the creek that feeds into the park. On the slope draining away from the creek. Yes, I agree."

"Then that's where we take the dead now."

John remained silent. It was interesting how different things, different changes, shocked in different ways. Tom was a golf addict. Regardless of what was now happening, to turn his favorite piece of real estate into a cemetery . . . it was too much for him to absorb at this moment.

"We should get some of the ministers in to consecrate the ground," Kate said. "Folks will want that."

Charlie noted it down on his pad. "I'll talk to Reverend Black; he's sort of heading up the ministers here now.

"Any other health issues?" Charlie continued.

"Four more deaths up at the nursing home last night. They're dying off quick up there."

John thought of Makala. She had pretty well taken over the running of the place and he had not seen her in two days now.

"Three suicides as well. The McDougals and one of the outsiders."

"Greg and Fran?" Kate asked in shock.

"A neighbor heard the gunshots. Greg had shot Fran, then himself. They left a note. She had cancer, you know. She knew what she was facing without her twice-weekly treatments up in Asheville, so she asked Greg to end it for her. Then he did himself as well. Note said for us to use her remaining painkillers for someone who still has a chance of living."

"They sang in the church choir with me," Kate said softly, and for a moment her features reddened as she struggled to hold back her tears.

No one spoke.

"I'll post the notice about the golf course becoming the cemetery as of today and for the duration of the emergency," Charlie said, finally breaking the silence.

Several large whiteboards had been dragged over from the elementary school and tacked to the outside wall of the police station. This was now the official emergency notice board.

"We've got dozens of others who I suspect will not last much longer," Kellor continued. "Those with pancreatic enzyme disorder, the day they run out of pills they start dying. A lot of our severe coronary problems are gone now. Garth Watson dropped dead last night just hauling a bucket of water back up to his house."

"Damn, he was only forty-three," Kate said.

"And fifty pounds overweight with cholesterol of two-eighty," Kellor said. "I warned him. Well, so much for too much fast food.

"We got over a hundred people in town, though, on chemo- or radiation therapy for cancer. Their prognosis . . . Well, we saw what happened with Fran. God forgive her, but a lot might decide to take that way out, especially those on serious pain management. We've forgotten what a nightmare the final months of cancer can be like without readily available morphine."

He paused and looked around the room.

"I think we have to discuss that right now," he said. "We have a limited supply of pain meds. Do we impound it and use it only for emergency situations, or do we continue to let those who are terminal anyhow use up what's left?"

"My God, Doc," Tom interjected. "What in hell are you saying? One of those people you are talking about is my aunt."

"I know," Kellor said softly. "God help me I know. But your aunt Helen is going to die soon; we know that. But suppose I get a kid in here that needs major surgery. Shock and trauma kill, and managing the pain might mean the difference between his living and dying. We got to think of that."

"You're talking triaging the dying off, aren't you, Doc?" John said quietly.

Kellor looked at him and then slowly nodded his head.

"I'm not ready for that decision," Charlie sighed. "Most of the folks in question still have some meds in their homes. We'll cross that one later."

"But we'll have to cross it," Kellor replied, head half-lowered.

No one spoke for a moment.

"Accidents, you would not believe how many we got," Tom finally said, breaking the silence. "Cars are no longer killers, but chain saws still working, axes, shovels. Joe Peterson damn near cut his own leg off with a chain saw last night trying to cut firewood. We had three accidental gunshot wounds yesterday, one of them fatal, by idiots now walking around armed."

"It's food, though, that I think we got to start getting serious about," Kellor said.

"So what in hell do you suggest that we do different?" Charlie replied sharply, and John could sense the tension, as if this had been argued about before the meeting.

"By your estimate," Kellor replied, "we have enough food on hand to feed everyone for another seven to ten days. That means using meat any health inspector two weeks ago would have condemned.

"Charlie, after that . . . then what?"

Charlie sighed and wearily shook his head.

In spite of the fever and chills, John found himself focusing intently on this man, who after ten days of crisis, ten days most likely with not more than three or four hours' sleep a night, was approaching collapse.

"Half rations," John said quietly.

Charlie looked at him and then nodded.

"I don't know if that will work with some things," Kellor replied. "Meat that is beginning to spoil, for example, dairy products."

"Then pass that out now, use it up, if need be have a gorge feast tonight with the remaining meat that might be going bad. Just make sure it is cooked until it's damn near like leather. Then anything preserved goes to half rations."

"What about those holed up in their houses with food?" Kellor asked. "Charlie. There's at least half a dozen houses with electricity, old generators that were unplugged and survived. Enough juice to run a freezer. The Franklin clan, for example, up on the North Fork. I bet they're sitting on a quarter ton of meat in their basement freezer."

"And you want that I should go get it?"

Kellor nodded.

Charlie looked at Tom.

"I doubt that will work with the Franklins," Tom said, shaking his head. "At least with them and all my men being alive once we got the meat. Up in these hills we have more than a few of the old survivalist types, the kind that were real disappointed that the world didn't go to hell with Y2K. They're just waiting for us to come up and try."

"Let it go for now," John said. "If we start turning into Stalinist commissars hunting out every stalk of grain and ounce of meat for the collective, you know the fragile balance we have right now will break down and it will be every man for himself.

"And like any collectivization, whether true or not the rumors will explode that we took the food, but now some animals are more equal than others."

"What?" Tom asked.

"You slept through Mr. Quincy's ninth-grade English class, Tom," Kate said. "Orwell, *Animal Farm,* read it some time."

"Besides," John continued, "even if we looted the Franklins clean, that would be enough food to maybe give six hundred people one meal. It isn't worth the blowback, and in my opinion is a dangerous political and legal precedent. We don't want to be turning on each other at a time like this. Hell, if anything we want people like that Franklin clan working alongside of us. If they're survivalists like you say and we don't threaten them, maybe they got skills they'll teach to us."

Tom breathed a sigh of relief.

"I think it's fair that food we salvaged from the stores now belongs to the community. But what people have in their homes, whether it's one day left or six months' worth, that's theirs."

John looked around the table and there were nods of agreement.

He only wished that Charlie had acted faster, or for that matter that he had thought about it and pushed him to seize control of all food in the town on Day One. If they had done so and it was rationed out correctly, it might have been enough to stretch at half rations for two months or more. But that was too late now.

"What about farms, though?" Kate said.

"I can tell you right now, Kate," Tom said, "and you grew up here, too, and should realize it, the old farms are nearly all gone. When something like this hits, everyone seems to think people living in rural areas are up to their ears in food ready to be given away. But even the farmers now are dependent on the supermarkets at least until harvesttime. Up in the North Fork we have half a dozen small farms, one with about sixty head of cattle on it. Maybe a couple of hundred pigs. The usual mix of chickens, turkeys, some geese."

"Still," Kate said. "Stretched, that could be another month or so of food."

"I think we have to take that," Charlie said. "It's different from what's in people's basements."

John sighed and realized he had to agree even though it wasn't much different from his commissar imagery of a few moments ago.

Sixty cattle, two or three a day turned into soup, stew, could stretch things. But far more pragmatic, how to keep control, to prevent someone else from rustling them, from raiding the farm one night, killing the owners, and then just slaughtering what they could drag away quickly, leaving the rest to rot?

Again a film image, from *Dances with Wolves,* the Indians finding the hundreds of buffalo slaughtered by white hunters who just took their hides and tongues, leaving the rest to rot. It could be the same here, and yet again it caught him how movies had so defined so much of the country's image of self and now the screens were blank. A movie about us fifty years from now, if there are movies, what will it show?

"Charlie, we have to make a deal with the few farmers in this valley. We just can't go marching up there, take their cattle, and ride off. A deal. We protect their food, they get more than a fair cut because they are sharing with the rest of the community. In exchange we protect them, their herd and crops. And Charlie, we have to keep some stock alive."

"What do you mean?"

"For next year. A couple of males, enough females. We might be looking at next year and we're still in the same boat. We got to keep breeding stock alive even if it means we go hungry now. In the old days, eating your breeding stock was the final act of desperation."

"John," Kate said. "I don't need to hear this now. Are you saying this will still be going on a year from now?"

"Maybe. And if we don't plan now, there won't be a next year for any of us."

"OK, John," Charlie said. "We'll go up the North Fork later today and start talking."

"And suppose someone up there, shotgun in hand, tells us to go to hell and get off his land?" Kate asked. "You said I grew up here. I did and I know some of these folks. They're good people, but they don't hold much truck with someone telling them what to do."

"Then maybe you should be the one to go talk with them," John said quietly.

"Me?"

"Exactly. Everyone in town knows you, Kate, even more than they know Charlie or Tom here. You going first would be nonthreatening."

"Because I'm mayor or because I'm a woman?" she asked sharply.

"Frankly, Kate, it's both. Tom shows up, gun on his hip, it's commissar time. You show up, sit down with the family, have a chat, I think you can help folks with these small farms to see reason. They have to strike a deal because if they stay on their own, sooner or later someone will go for them and take what they have. We promise to post twenty-four-hour guards on their places, we offer protection, they trade some food back to the community."

"Sounds a bit like where you come from originally up in New Jersey," Charlie said with a trace of a smile. "Protection racket."

John tried to smile in spite of his light-headedness.

"Like it or not, that's the way it is now. I'm dead set against people's homes being cleaned out, but I think we can agree that farms have to be protected but something given back in return to help the entire community."

She nodded in agreement. "OK, I'll go."

Charlie looked down at his notepad.

"Transportation. Anything new?"

"We got three more cars running," Tom said. "Actually I should say that Jim Bartlett down in that Volkswagen junkyard of his did. Beetles, another van."

"He's become a regular friend of yours," Kate said, and there was, at least for a moment, a touch of a smile.

"Yeah, damn old hippie. Though I'm not buying his line that we should be using pot for medicine."

"I might agree with him now," Kellor said.

"It's breaking the law," Tom replied sharply.

"The cars, Tom," Kate interjected. "Let's stick with that."

"All right, other garages say they can get ten or fifteen more old junkers up and going, including an old tractor trailer down at Younger's."

"We'll have forty or fifty within the week," the policeman from Swannanoa said quietly.

No one spoke, looking at him.

"You folks up here in Black Mountain always kind of looked down on us in Swannanoa. Maybe because we was poorer, but that poorness makes us worth more now."

John smiled at that and knew it was true. He could remember Tyler calling Swannanoa a "poor white trash" town with its trailer parks, auto junkyards, a town that had essentially gone to hell ever since the big woolen and blanket mill closed down years ago. What had once been a thriving small downtown area in Swannanoa was all but abandoned, especially after the big mill burned several years ago. Route 70, which went straight through Swannanoa, was lined with aging strip malls, thrift shops, and repair shops. It was finally starting to turn around, at least until last week, as more and more "outsiders" came in looking for land with the spectacular views the region offered. The area north of the town was developing, with high-priced homes, but that was now a tragic loss; half a dozen old farms had been chopped up into "McMansion estates" over the last few years.

In the old trailer parks there were a lot of cars that a week before anyone in a Beemer or new SUV would have given a wide berth to on the interstate. Some of those rolling heaps were now worth a hundred Beemers.

"Folks, this is Carl Erwin," Tom interjected. "Chief of police for Swannanoa. I invited him here today to talk about a proposal we have."

Everyone nodded politely. Carl definitely had their attention with Tom's last statement.

"And the proposal is?" Kate asked.

"An alliance."

John smiled. Again the historian in him, picturing kings of the ancient world, riding to a meeting in chariots to discuss water rights, the exchange of daughters, to band their armies together.

"Carl and I have been talking about this for days," Tom interjected. "It's OK with me."

"What's OK?" Kate asked.

"That we band our towns together for the duration of this crisis."

"For what purpose?"

"Defense," Carl said. "We hold the door to the west; you have the one to the east. We cooperate, we survive; we don't, we are all in the deep dip."

Charlie stood up and pointed to the county map pinned to the wall.

"We have the bottleneck for I-40 and Route 70 in our town on the east side; that's up just past Exit 66. Just west of Exit 59 there's another bottleneck where the Swannanoa Mountain range has a spur that comes down. The two highways, the railroad, and the creek are practically side by side over there in Swannanoa. A defendable position only a couple of hundred yards wide. We have the front door; they have the back door."

"Maybe it's the other way around," Carl said, a bit of an edge to his voice. "Remember, we're closer to Asheville and they're still trying to force us to take five thousand for my town and five thousand for yours. I'm holding them back and it's getting ugly real quick. We've had half a dozen deaths at the barrier the last two days."

"From what?" Kellor asked.

"Gunshot, that's what," Carl replied sharply. "There's people that walked down here told they'd find food, we're telling them there ain't none, it's getting bad. I understand it's chaos on Old 70 and the interstate back towards Asheville."

"Why in hell didn't those idiots in the county office just tell people to stay in place?" Charlie snapped bitterly. "They just started this move even when we told them not to."

"Because they want to survive," John said, "and the numbers are not adding up."

"It'll be a die-off," Kellor interjected. "A bad one, and Asheville wants it to rest on us, not them. Can't blame them really."

"I sure as hell do," Charlie said coldly.

"Well, if you want to keep them out of your backyard," Carl said, "then we better get cooperating real quick."

"A smart move," John said.

"That sixty head of cattle you folks was talking about. If Asheville comes in here, they'll be gone in a day, and then what?"

He paused and smiled.

"Besides, we've counted over a hundred and twenty cattle in our town and three hundred pigs."

In spite of the horrifying severity of the crisis, John smiled. It truly was like ancient kings negotiating.

Carl looked around the room and all were silent. He had played his trump card and just won with it.

"There's one other back door," Carl finally continued, "that's up by the

Haw Creek Road, but we can seal that off as well. Our numbers, you have about a thousand more people here than we do, not counting all those that already wandered in."

"Will you share the cattle?" Charlie asked.

Carl hesitated, looked over at his companion.

"You have three pharmacies in your town; we only had one. You open up your medical supplies to us, we'll consider a transfer of some cattle and pigs."

"Consider?" Kate asked, and suddenly there was a shrewd look in her eye.

Carl looked at Charlie.

"OK. We'll share them out, as needed," Charlie said. "But it's full sharing on both sides, medicine, food, weapons, vehicles, manpower."

Charlie looked around the room and John caught his eye.

"Governance," John said.

"Go on."

"I'm sorry, folks, but I feel like I'm in an old movie, set in medieval or ancient times," John said. "We're like two kingdoms here negotiating."

"Well, I guess that's the way it's getting," Doc Kellor said. "But Swannanoa does have an outreach clinic from Memorial Mission. We could use that as a medical center. They had some equipment there for minor surgeries, emergencies, and such. Also three or four doctors in your town, that would give us a total of nine doctors for the community."

Carl nodded.

"We protected the clinic from Day One. Had the same problem you did with some druggies. . . ." He paused. "We shot them when they were trying to escape."

John did not ask for any details on that.

"Governance. We can't be divided off if we agree to work together on this. Everyone is in the same boat. So, what will it be?"

Charlie looked at Carl.

"I've known you for years, Charlie Fuller. As long as you are not tied into Asheville, I'll be willing to take orders from you. Damn, I'll be glad not to have to make some of these decisions."

Charlie nodded.

"Then Carl sits on this council," John said.

"Who are you?" Carl asked, looking straight at John.

"He's a history professor at the college. Ex-military, a colonel with combat experience."

John looked at Charlie. "Combat experience," that was stretching it.

"He advises us on legal stuff, moral issues, a smart man to have around."

"So why is he here in this meeting?" Carl asked calmly.

John bristled slightly. How he had evolved into being here, well, it had simply started with his barging in, but now, after but a week, he felt the need to be here, and a purpose.

"He is the one who executed the drug thieves," Tom said. "Let's just say he's our compass. Professor type but OK."

Carl continued to hold eye contact with John and he wondered if there was going to be trouble.

"My friend Mike Vance here, then I want him on this council, too. We didn't have a mayor like you, but he was town manager."

John could see that Vance was someone who did what Carl wanted.

"We're not a democracy here," John said, "though I regret to say that. We are under martial law and Charlie Fuller is in charge. We just advise. If we are to work together, it has to be Charlie's word that is the final say."

"Nice friend you have, Charlie," Mike said quietly.

"Mike, Carl," and now it was Tom speaking. "We've got to work together, and I agree with John. Either Charlie runs it for all of us or the deal is off."

The room was filled with silence and Carl finally nodded.

Charlie came around the table and Carl stood up, shaking his hand.

John said nothing. The formal ritual had been played out. The kings had shaken hands and the treaty been made. It was the smart move, though he wondered if all would feel the same a month, six months, from now.

Charlie went back to his chair and sat down.

"With the extra vehicles, I know the answer already, but gas supply?"

"We just drain it out of all the stalled cars on the highway for starters," Tom said.

"I know that, but should we start rounding that up now?"

"Wouldn't do that," Mike interjected. "Gas goes bad over time. You can't get it out of the gas stations until we rig up some sort of pumps. Inside a car, though, the tank is sealed, it will stay good in there longer than if we pull it out.

"I know; I own a wrecking shop."

Like him or not, John realized, this man's knowledge, at this moment, might be more valuable than his own.

"All right then," Charlie said. "Back to Asheville. Carl, you and I both got the same demand from their new director of public safety, Roger Burns."

"Asshole," Carl said quietly, and Tom nodded in agreement.

"That we're to take ten thousand refugees in."

"He can kiss our asses," Carl snapped back. "Ten thousand of those yuppies and hippies? You've got to be kidding."

John noted the change the alliance had already created. Now it was "we," against "them." He hoped that would last.

The debate flared for several minutes, Kate leaning towards accepting it, that these were neighbors as well, that some semblance of order had to be reestablished on a county level, Carl and Tom flatly refusing.

John wondered what was going on at this moment down in Winston-Salem, Charlotte, or far bigger cities, Washington, Chicago, New York. Most likely, by now millions were pouring out, at best organized in some way but far more likely in just a chaotic exodus, like a horde of locusts eating their way across the suburban landscapes. At least here geography played to their advantage, the choke points in the roads.

He had already seized on the idea last night. Brilliant in its simplicity but frightful for all that it implied but ten days into this crisis.

He waited for a pause in the debate.

"I have a simple answer," John said, "that will defuse the crisis without a confrontation."

"I'm all ears, Professor," Carl said sarcastically.

"Water."

"Water?" Carl asked, but John could already see the flicker of a grin on Carl's face.

"Their reservoir is in our territory. The deal is simple. Lay off the pressure, send their refugees somewhere else, or we turn the water off."

Carl looked at him wide-eyed for several seconds, then threw his head back and laughed.

"I'll be damned."

"I think we *are* damned if we turn off the water to Asheville," Doc Kellor interjected, and Kate nodded in agreement.

"So do I," John said quietly. "I don't know if I could actually bring myself to do it. There's a hundred thousand innocent people there, but this Burns character is playing power politics on us. But we hold the trump card. Send a message back. They still have their water but send the refugees somewhere else, that simple, no problem for them. If not, we blow the main pipe and the hell with them."

"Maybe that might provoke them to try and seize it by force," Kate replied.

John shook his head.

"No way. Remember the hurricane in 2004. The main pipe out of the reservoir ruptured and it was one hell of a mess. Special parts had to be flown in from outside the state to repair it. Well, after that they know how vulnerable the water supply is. We make it clear that if they make a move we blow it and they'll never get it back online."

"If we got that advantage, let's press it," Carl said. "I've heard they got dozens of railroad cars loaded with food and are hoarding it for themselves. We could demand some of that as well."

"Not a bad idea," Tom said quietly. "You might be on to something there."

"I'm not reduced to that yet," Kate snapped back. "Trading water for food. Not yet."

"Nor I; just keep it to the refugee problem. I think if we demand a cut of their supplies . . . they'll fight, and remember, they do have the numbers we don't have," John quickly interjected, "and we'll all wind up losers.

"But regarding the refugees, let's just say, we'll make them an offer they can't refuse."

Charlie smiled.

"That's right; you're from New Jersey originally."

John smiled.

"They back off on the refugee issue and that water just keeps flowing."

Charlie looked around the table and all nodded.

"Tom, send a courier back today. Use one of those mopeds we got running. I don't want to risk a car the way we did the other day."

"A pleasure, Charlie. Wish I could see Burns's face when he gets the note."

"Just remember this, though," Charlie replied. "Our sewage runs to the treatment plant in Asheville. The filtration is most likely not running, chances are they're dumping it straight into the French Broad, but still, if they close the pipe, it backs up clear to our town here. They could shut that down in retaliation."

"Then we threaten to dump our raw sewage right into Swannanoa Creek, which runs downhill to Asheville," Tom replied.

"Jesus Christ," Kellor sighed. "Are we getting reduced to this?"

No one could reply.

"All right," Charlie said, "the big issue. Our roadblock on I-40 at the top of the gap."

He looked to Tom.

"It's getting bad there. Like we agreed to yesterday. I had someone take a note down to Old Fort at the bottom of the mountain asking them to post a sign that the road above was closed. Old Fort refused. They've got seven, maybe ten thousand refugees camped there, all of them trying to get up into these mountains. They want us to let the people pass; in fact, they're encouraging them to hike up the interstate and, if need be, force their way through. The pressure is building. There's refugees strung out all along the highway.

"Last night one of my men shot and killed two of them."

"What?" Kate snapped. "I didn't hear of this."

"Figured I'd bring it up this morning," Tom said.

"What happened?"

"A crowd of about fifty just would not turn back. The men guarding the gap said they recognized several as folks who had been turned back earlier. They planned what they did and tried to rush us. Someone on their side started to shoot and my men fired back. Two dead on their side, about a dozen wounded."

Kate shook her head.

"It's going to get worse," Tom said. "Remember what Mr. Barber said when he flew up here last week, the interstate clogged with refugees pouring out of Charlotte and Winston-Salem. Well, Charlotte is a hundred and ten miles from here, Winston-Salem about a hundred and forty. Give a family burdened down with stuff about ten to fifteen miles a day. That means the real wave is going to start hitting us today; I'm surprised it hasn't been sooner. We might find twenty, thirty, maybe fifty thousand pushing up that road."

"Why I wanted this alliance," Carl said. "You're our back door. You let them in, we will be swamped. We'll be caught between Asheville on the one side and those folks on the other. They'll eat us clean in a day."

"Disease as well," Kellor interjected.

"I thought you said we have that already?" Carl asked.

Kellor sighed and shook his head.

"Salmonella, that's lurking in any community. I'm talking about the exotics now. Large urban population. You'll have carriers of hepatitis in every variant. What scares the hell out of me is a recent immigrant from overseas or someone stranded at the airport in Charlotte, which is a major hub. He might look well and feel well, but inside he might be carrying typhoid, cholera, you name it.

"We got one of those in a crowd, given sanitation for those people walking here? Just simple hand contact or fecal to water supply or food distribution supply contact and that bacteria will jump. We give someone a plate of food, they haven't washed their hands, we don't clean that plate with boiling water, and within a week thousands will be sick and dying.

"You ever seen cholera?" Kellor asked.

No one spoke.

"I did thirty years back. A mission trip to Africa. It makes salmonella look tame. People in those regions, most of them were exposed to it at some point in their lives and survived. We're wide open to it. We are six, seven generations removed from it and we have no natural immunity. America is like an exotic hothouse plant. It can only live now in the artificial environment of vaccinations, sterilization, and antibiotics we started creating a hundred or more years ago.

"We're about to get reintroduced to life as it is now in Africa or most of the third world. Not counting the global flu outbreak of 1918, the last really big epidemic, one that killed off a fair percentage of a population in a matter of weeks, well, I think it was the Chicago typhoid epidemic back in the 1880s that killed tens of thousands. Water supply got polluted with typhoid and they died like flies. It made the famous fire pale in comparison when it came to body count."

"Inoculations?" Charlie asked.

"Where?" Kellor said with a cynical laugh. "For typhoid or cholera? Those are inoculations administered by the county-level health department for travelers overseas, and even then they have to be special ordered. I bet there's not one person in a thousand in this valley protected against cholera, unless they've traveled to Africa or southern Asia, and damn few against typhoid.

"Thank God our elevation is high enough, our climate cool enough, that I'm not worrying about mosquito-borne diseases like malaria, West Nile, and others. And don't even get me started on how we better start looking out for parasitic worms, lice . . ."

His voice trailed off.

"We'll see infections running rampant that won't kill but will weaken, leaving the victim open for the next round. Kate, most guys don't even think of it, but do you have a good supply of what we euphemistically call feminine hygiene products?"

She blushed slightly.

"For this month."

"Right there, gentlemen, though I bet a lot of women are thinking about it now or finding out real quick. They're back to Great-grandma's days, and that combined with no bathing, poor diet, we'll see a soaring infection rate, and that's just one of a dozen situations we never thought about before last week.

"Johnnie steps on a rusty nail, get a tetanus shot. We might have a hundred of those left in the whole community. We might be staring at lockjaw come fall. Shall I go on?"

No one spoke.

John looked into his old friend's eyes and could see that this doctor, more than perhaps anyone else in the room, was haunted by just how medieval this nightmare might get.

As a historian John knew the horror. For every person who died in the westward migration prior to the Civil War from Native Americans attacking, the stuff of American legends, thousands, maybe tens of thousands died from water holes polluted by cholera and typhoid . . . but that doesn't make for a good movie.

"One thing we've neglected I want taken care of right now," Kellor said. "And I could kick myself for not thinking of it sooner. Get the veterinarians organized."

"Vets?" Carl asked.

"Hell, yes. They have anesthesia and antibiotics and, frankly, in a pinch can do emergency surgery as well. Inside a dog isn't all that different from a human. Same with dentists, podiatrists as well. Get the meds they still have, move them to the clinic we've agreed to set up in Swannanoa, and guard it twenty-four hours a day."

Charlie noted it down.

"Back to the refugees, what do we do?" Charlie asked.

"Seal it off," Carl said.

"We continue to seal it off," Tom replied, "and I tell you, there'll be fifty thousand piled up on that road by the end of the week and sooner or later they'll storm us, casualties be damned."

"A safety valve then," Kate interjected.

"How's that?" Charlie asked.

"We got a pressure cooker ready to blow on the interstate at the gap. Either we have it blow in our faces or we create a safety valve."

"Like I said, how?" Charlie said, a touch of exasperation in his voice.

"Let people through."

"God damn," Carl snapped. "I thought this alliance was so we can guard each other's backs and now you're talking about letting them in? If so, we pull out of the deal."

"You are already in the deal," Charlie said coldly, "and once in, you can't leave."

"Jesus, you're starting to sound like a damn Yankee and I'm a Rebel. If we want to secede out of this union, we'll do so."

"Kate has it right," John said.

"Oh, great, the professor speaks," Carl replied, voice filled with sarcasm.

"Damn you, listen to some reasoning!" John shouted.

The outburst made him feel light-headed, his hand throbbing.

It caught Carl off guard, though.

"She's right. We let people through a hundred at a time with the understanding that they don't stop until past the barrier on the far side of Exit 59. Then they can keep on going.

"They check their weapons in with us, just like when cowboys rode into town and the sheriff met them. We give the weapons back once they're on the far side of our territory. No food give outs, but for decency sake at least set up a watering spot, say by Exit 64. There should be enough water pressure to run a temporary pipe up there. A privy as well, with lots of lime thrown in and safe drainage."

Charlie nodded.

"We hold them back, like Tom said, and the pressure will build until they just overrun us."

"What about the threat of disease that Doc Kellor was talking about?" Tom asked.

"I think when comparing one threat to another what Kate and John are saying is 'the lesser of two evils.'

"If someone is visibly sick, we don't let them through. Quarantine like the old days. Everyone else, they can walk on through but no stopping; armed guards keep their distance while escorting them."

"We have hazmat suits," Charlie announced.

"What?"

"Twenty of them stockpiled in the storage area of this building. They were issued out by Homeland Security a couple of years back. Never thought we'd be using them like this, but would that serve?"

"Damn good," Kellor replied. "Anyone interacting at the barricades with those on the other side wears a hazmat."

"Good psychological impact as well," John interjected. "Conveys authority, and frankly, though I hate to say it, those on the other side will feel inferior and thus more compliant about being marched through without stopping."

He was inwardly angry for even mentioning that. Uniforms, and the white hazmat suits were like uniforms, had always been one of the means throughout history to control crowds, including those being herded to death camps.

"Water only like I said, sharp watch that no one relieves themselves other than at the designated privy. Armed guards in hazmats escorting them. They're allowed through and that's it."

"What about Asheville?" Kate said. "They might block the road as well."

"There's no defensive barricade there yet," Carl said. "They are assuming the flow is all towards us. We might get away with it for a few days before they organize. If they do, we try some logic on them to just let these people keep moving, or as the professor there said, we mention the water supply and make them an offer they can't refuse."

John looked around the room and there was no dissent.

"Good plan," Charlie finally said. "That's what we'll do."

"One change on it, though: some should be allowed in to stay," Kate replied.

"How's that?" Kellor asked.

"There's hundreds of people from right here who got stuck on the day everything went down. Driving back home, driving to meetings, flying in or out of Charlotte. They have every right to be here and we must let them in.

"Nearly everyone from Asheville who got stuck there is back, but we have people, several hundred, still missing. When they show up we got to let them in, along with those who own property here and are trying to get to it as a safe haven. They've lived with us for years; we owe them that chance if they make it here."

"What about the disease, though?" Charlie asked.

"Well, like the doc said, quarantine," John replied. "It's the way things were done a hundred years ago with ships coming into New York. A doctor inspected the passengers. If he was suspicious, they were put in an isolation ward."

Again a film image came to John.

"Remember *Godfather Two*? When the Don came to America as a little boy and was put in isolation because they thought he might be sick. We did it all the time then and it worked."

"Yeah, and look what we got with that guy, the Mafia," Carl replied.

John realized he had pulled the wrong analogy but pressed on.

"The practices of a hundred years ago did work and we have to step back to them. If a ship came from a port where they knew there was some outbreak of a contagious disease, the ship itself was anchored in the outer harbor until it was deemed safe to pass.

"We can do the same," John said, looking hopefully at Kellor.

Kellor hesitated, then nodded in agreement.

"Doc, what about the nursing home?" John asked, and Kellor shook his head.

"That place is crawling with every infection known to man. I'd suggest one of the larger buildings at the Baptist church conference center right up near the gap. It's right off the road."

He looked around and everyone finally nodded.

"Look, I know I won't be popular with some of you, bringing this up," Carl said. "But the outsiders, those that wandered in here the first few days before we sealed off. That boosted our numbers by maybe two thousand or more. Do we let them stay?"

No one spoke in reply, but Kate was shaking her head.

"We've settled that here," Charlie said, and John looked over at him, his thoughts instantly going to Makala.

"Why?" Carl asked. "I think we should of talked about this before our deal was made."

"What are you suggesting, Carl?" Charlie snapped. "They've been here eight to ten days now. Many have integrated in, found a friend or a job to do. What are we going to do, march around town and round them up at gunpoint? It would be one helluva sight and, frankly, tear us apart."

"We were once all Americans," Kate said quietly.

"Precisely," John now interjected. "Those that are here stay. We've already made that agreement."

He looked around to the others. In spite of his speech in the park, he wondered now if views were changing because a food shortage was now clearly evident.

"No different than keeping out those on the other side," Carl replied.

"Maybe not, God save us," John replied. "I don't have an answer for that. But those that are in stay."

He looked to Charlie for support.

"We change that view now and I am off this council. It contradicts what I said at the park and neither you nor anyone else objected then."

"What about what we did get off the road?" Kate said. "We're forgetting about that. We got six trucks loaded with foodstuffs, enough rations to feed all of them for a couple of weeks. Consider that as their payment."

John nodded to her, an adroit move on her part.

"They stay," Charlie finally said, and Carl nodded his head.

"One other thing," John interjected. "Those passing through. Anyone special, we should allow them to stay if they wish."

"Like who?" Kellor asked.

"Anyone that can help us survive now, or rebuild."

"Such as?"

"Military men, police officers for example."

He knew he'd get immediate nods from Tom and Carl on that. The "fraternal order" definitely looked out for its own, and John realized he was doing the same when it came to the military.

"But others. Farmers, they have skills we need, can help with the cattle, hogs, and what crops are planted. All that fancy machinery is dead and a lot of farming is reverted to backbreaking labor. I think we should grab any electrician we can find, power company guys, people like that, doctors, nurses as well. If they want to stay, we interview them; if they check out OK, they can join us."

There was a moment of silence again.

"Agreed," Charlie replied.

"That means their families as well," Kate said. "I wouldn't give two cents for a man or woman who would grab the chance to stay and walk away from their family."

"No argument there," Charlie finally replied.

"John, could you draw up a list of recommended skills you think we should have?"

John nodded.

"Frankly, I'd kill for someone who could build a steam engine."

There was a round of chuckles at that.

"No, people, I'm dead serious. A steam engine would be worth its weight in gold. Do any of you know how to make one, let alone repair an old one rotting behind a barn and then keep it running?"

Everyone was silent.

The thought started him rolling.

"Get a steam engine and you have power where you want it. To pump, dig, cut, hell, even mount it on the rail tracks and move things.

"I'd like to find some old guy who repaired phone lines forty years ago and could retrofit us. Prowl through the antique stores on Cherry Street and you'll find old crank phones that still might work if we could find someone who understood how to hook them up. It'd link the two ends of our community."

Several were now nodding.

"The guys I know in my Civil War Roundtable, Revolutionary War reenactors, many of them know skills that are lost to the rest of us. I want people like that. I'd trade a hundred computer-tech heads right now for one guy who understood steam engines. I'd trade a hundred lawyers for someone who could show us how to make gunpowder from what we can find here in this valley, or which roots we can dig right now and safely eat.

"An old chemist who could make ether or chloroform. Doc, we're going to need a lot of that in the months to come and I'm willing to bet we're short already.

"An old dentist who could get an old-fashioned foot-powered drill running. You folks think about that yet, next time you get a toothache? Care to have the tooth yanked instead and no painkiller while we're at it? Remember the old movies, the ones about a gang of kids and one of them usually had a bandage wrapped around his head to keep his jaw shut because he had an abscessed tooth. If we saw that two weeks ago the parents would have been arrested for child abuse. But I tell you, we'll be seeing that again, and real soon."

He suddenly realized he was rambling, the room silent, suddenly far too hot.

"Sorry. . . ."

No one spoke and he wasn't sure if it was because they were embarrassed by his rambling monologue or because he had indeed hit home with what they faced.

"I think we have it all for now," Charlie said. "Let's get to work. Meeting same time tomorrow."

The group stood up and John felt a stab of pain. Kellor was bent over the table, holding John's right hand down and taking off the bandage. The group looked over at them and he could see concern in Kate's eyes.

"John, I think you better go home. You're running a fever. I'll see if I can dig something up for it and come by later," Kellor said.

"I told you. That nurse, the tall good-looking one, Makala's her name. She's giving me Cipro."

"Well, it should have kicked in by now. I don't like this," and Kellor sniffed the bandage again, his nose wrinkling.

John looked down at his hand. It was swollen, red streaked, the exposed wound red, the edge of the flesh where it had been stitched puckered.

He was suddenly worried. God damn. An infected hand, now? He had images of Civil War era surgery.

"What the hell is it, Doc?" Kate asked, coming closer.

"Maybe staph, but I don't have the lab to test for it.

"Crops up in hospitals, nursing homes. Resistant stuff. Go home, go to bed, I'll be by later today or this evening."

"I said I was going up to the college to get some volunteers for the elementary school."

"Last thing I want is you walking around at the college or in the elementary school with that hand. If you got a staph infection, you're a spreader now. So just go home."

John nodded and stood up, feeling weak.

He headed to the door, Kellor walking alongside him. Starting the car up, John headed for home . . . and as he pulled into the driveway . . . he knew.

Jen was outside, sitting on the stone wall of the walkway leading to the door. Elizabeth was on one side of her, Jennifer on the other. As he got out of the car the dogs came up, but a sharp command warned them to back off.

"It's Tyler, isn't it," John said.

Jen forced a smile and nodded.

Jennifer started to sob and he put his good arm around her, his little girl burying her head in his chest.

"Pop-pop," was all she could get out.

Jen put a hand on her granddaughter's shoulder.

"Pop-pop is in heaven now, dear. But it's OK to cry."

Elizabeth leaned against John's shoulder, forcing back a sob, but then looked up at him.

"Dad, you're burning up."

"I'm OK," he said.

He looked at Jen.

"Let's go in," she said.

He followed her into the house, which was all so silent, and into what had been Jennifer's room.

Tyler's features were already going to a grayish yellow.

John remembered the first time they had met, Tyler coldly looking at this Yankee, worse yet from New Jersey, who obviously had but one intent only, and that was to seduce his only daughter and take her away.

John smiled. Oh, I understand that now, Pop, he thought.

And then so many other memories, of the gradual thaw. The first time they'd gone out shooting together while the "girls" went to the mall to go shopping, Tyler fascinated by the old Colt Dragoon pistol John had brought along, roaring with laughter over the encounter with the local rednecks that had happened but weeks before. That had been an icebreaker, father and potential son-in-law shooting, talking guns, then sitting on the patio and having a cold beer.

And then the grudging acceptance that had turned to friendship and at last had turned to the love a father would have for a son, a son who then gave him two beautiful granddaughters, granddaughters who allowed him once again to relive the joy of raising a child.

He was gone now. War or not, he would have died, but he had indeed died far sooner as a result of the war. In the cold figures of triage, he was an old man, someone whom villages, town, and cities all across America, this day, but ten days after an attack, were being forced to "write off."

For an old man in the advanced stages of cancer, there would be no medicine. . . . That had to be rationed now to someone who "stood a chance" or who, in a colder sense, could be of use. If the old man were not dying at home his would be a body whose departure would free a bed in a hospital flooded with the sick and injured. In a starving community his would be one less mouth to feed, even though his last meals were from a can poured into a feeding tube . . . but even that can of Ensure was now a meal, perhaps for an entire day, for someone else.

Tyler was dead, and there was a war, though it did not in any sense seem like a war that any had even conceptualized this way . . . and he was dead as surely as millions of others were now dead or dying after but ten days . . . as dead as someone lying in the surf of Omaha Beach, the death camp of Auschwitz, as dead as any casualty of war.

Frightened for a moment, John looked back at Jennifer, who stood in the doorway, clutching her grandmother's side. The last of the ice had given out two days ago, the bottles of insulin now immersed in the tank of the basement toilet to keep them cool. And there was a flood of panic in John. He knew, almost to the day, how much insulin was left.

He caught Jen's gaze; the way he was staring at her granddaughter, she pulled Jennifer in tighter to her side.

He turned back to look at Tyler.

"I think we should pray," John said.

He went down on his knees and made the sign of the cross. "Hail Mary, full of grace . . ."

It was close to sunset. To the north the hills, so affectionately known to all locals as "the Seven Sisters," were bathed in the slating golden light of evening. Beyond them was the massive bulk of Mount Mitchell, its slopes green as spring moved steadily upwards towards the summit.

"I think that's deep enough, Ben," John said.

Ben looked up from the grave he had been digging for the last three hours, helped by John's students Phil and Jeremiah.

Charlie had been right. The golf course was the ideal spot for the new cemetery, the earth easy to dig. Over twenty other graves had been dug this day or were being dug now. The seven who had died in the elementary school during the night, five others who had died during the day . . . and three suicides, though one minister had tried to protest that decision that they be buried in what was now consecrated ground. That protest was greeted with icy rejection from Charlie, who was now a former member of that congregation. There had also been two more heart attacks, four more elderly from the nursing home and perhaps most tragic of all, the Morrison family burying their seven-year-old boy, who had had an asthma attack.

John tried to block out the screams of the mother as the dirt was shoveled into her boy's grave.

Reverend Black drew away from the Morrison's and came over.

"Ready, John?"

John nodded.

Richard Black looked exhausted, eyes bloodshot. The Morrison boy had been part of his congregation, a playmate of his son's.

John looked over at Jeremiah and Phil and nodded.

The two boys went to the car, opened the backseat, and struggled to pull Tyler's body out, wrapped in a quilt. He was already stiff with rigor mortis. They carried him over and stopped by the side of the grave, looking down, and John realized no one had thought about how to put the body into the grave.

Always bodies had been in coffins, concealed mechanical winches lowering them in a dignified manner. Jennifer broke away from her grandmother's side, hysterical, and ran away. John looked at Elizabeth and she turned to chase after her sister.

"I'll help," Rich said. He eased himself down into the grave, Ben joining him. They took the body from Phil and Jeremiah and maneuvered it down, then pulled themselves out.

John found himself suddenly wondering why the old tradition of a grave supposedly having to be six foot deep existed. Fortunately, this one was maybe three and a half, four feet down and easier for the reverend to get out of.

Tyler rested in the bottom, face covered but bare feet exposed, and it struck John as obscene for him to be exposed thus, but there was nothing to be done for it now.

John looked at Jen, who stood at the head of the grave, almost serenely detached.

"I don't know the Catholic rite," Rich said. "I'm sorry."

"I don't think God or Tyler minds," Jen said. "You've been a friend and neighbor for years. I think he'd want you to do this for him, for us."

Rich opened his prayer book and started the traditional Presbyterian service for the dead.

Finished at last, he went to Jen, hugged her and kissed her on the forehead, then did something John had seen only once before, at a Jewish funeral years before. Rich picked up the shovel from the pile of earth, scooped up some dirt, and then let it fall into the grave.

The time John had seen that, it had shocked him, the funeral of the wife of a beloved grad school professor. The rabbi had thrown a shovelful in, then the husband, then family and friends, had done so also, filling the grave in while John's beloved professor stood silent, watching the coffin disappear and the earth finally being mounded over. It was such a sharp, hard lesson about mortality, the returning of dust to dust, when compared to the "American way," of concealing death in euphemisms, with green Astroturf to hide the raw earth, and the backhoe carefully hidden until the last of the mourners had left.

That set Jen off and at last she collapsed into tears.

Rich looked at John and handed him the shovel. Though it was agony, both physical and emotional, he knew he had to do it. He filled the shovel, turned, hesitated, then let the dirt fall, covering Tyler's face.

Light-headed, John stepped back.

"We'll take care of it, sir."

It was Jeremiah.

John nodded and handed the shovel over.

He walked away, heading towards the park. Jennifer and her sister were in the playground, Jennifer sitting on a swing, her big sister sitting on the ground by her side.

Jennifer looked up at his approach. Elizabeth stood up, tears streaming down her face, and came up to his side.

"Is it over?"

"Yes."

"I thought I should stay with her, Dad."

"You did the right thing."

"You've got to talk with her," and Elizabeth's voice broke. "She's thinking about . . ." Her voice trailed off.

"Go take care of your grandmother."

"Sure, Dad."

He went up to the swing and looked down at Jennifer.

"You OK, sweetie?"

She didn't speak, head lowered. She had brought Rabs along and was clutching him tight.

John fumbled, fighting the fever, not sure what to say, afraid of what might be said.

"Remember when I used to push you on this swing?" he said, filled now with nostalgia for that time when Mary was still alive and they'd bring the girls down here to play, to feed the ducks, and, while Mary still had the strength, to walk around the lake.

He got behind Jennifer, reached down with one hand to pull the swing back.

"How about we do it again? I'll push to get you started."

And with that she was off the swing, crushing herself against his side, sobbing.

"Daddy, when will I be buried here?"

He knelt down and she wrapped her arms around his neck.

"Daddy, don't bury me here. I'd be afraid during the night. I always want to stay close to you. Please don't bury me here."

He dissolved into tears, hugging her tight.

"I promise, sweetheart. You have years and years ahead. Daddy will always protect you."

She drew back slightly and looked at him with solemn eyes, eyes filled with the wisdom of a child.

"I don't think so, Daddy."

That was all she said.

Later he would remember that they remained like that for what seemed an eternity and then gentle hands separated them, Jen's hands. And strong hands. Ben, John's two students, helped him back to the car and then the fever drowned out all else.

CHAPTER SEVEN

DAY 18

He awoke feeling so weak he could barely lift his head.

"So the good professor is back from the dead."

He turned his head, focused; it was Makala.

She put the back of her hand to his forehead, a finger to his throat, and held it there for several seconds.

"Fever's broke. Figured that during the night. Good pulse, too."

She smiled.

"Well, John Matherson, I think you're going to pull through just fine now."

"What happened?"

"Oh, you had it bad, real bad. Doc Kellor was right, staph infection. I thought there was a chance that was your problem but hoped it was something simpler and the Cipro would knock it out.

"Thought we'd lose you there for a couple of days. Or at the very least your hand."

Panicked, he looked down. His hand was still there. Shriveled, sore, but still there.

"Twice its normal size three days back. Started to look like septicemia and gangrene. But we kept hand and soul attached. Charlie Fuller approved some rather rare antibiotics for you, just a few doses left now in our reserves, and Doc Fuller was up here pumping them into you."

"All that from a cut."

"I told you to wash it out thoroughly and keep it bandaged," she said chastisingly. "I regret now not coming up here that first night and doing it personally, but you might of seen that as too forward of me."

"Wish you had, forward or not."

She smiled and with a damp cloth wiped his brow.

"I'm hungry."

"I'll get you some soup."

"Bathroom?"

"I'll get a bedpan."

"Like hell," he whispered.

"Don't be embarrassed, for God's sake. I've been your nurse for the last week."

"Help me up."

"OK then, but if you feel light-headed, get back down."

She helped him to his feet. He did feel light-headed but said nothing; in fact, he felt like shit, mouth pasty, an atrocious taste. He brushed his good hand against his face, rough stubble actually turning into a beard, and just had a general feeling of being gritty and disgusting.

He pushed her aside at the bathroom door and went in. Used the toilet—fortunately someone had filled up the tank—and looked longingly at the bathtub. He so wanted a bath, to wash off.

Later, we'll have to boil up some water, I'll be damned if I take a cold bath. He brushed his teeth. The tube of toothpaste was nearly empty and beside it was a glass filled with ground-up wood charcoal. He used the toothpaste anyhow—that alone made a world of difference—and came back out.

There was a smell, food, and he felt ravenous and slowly walked back into the living room. Makala was out on the porch stirring a pot. The old grill was pushed to one side; it must have finally run out of propane. Someone, most likely Ben or a couple of John's students, had rigged up something of an outdoor stove out of an old woodstove, its legs jacked up with cinder blocks underneath so the cook didn't have to bend over.

Makala looked at him and smiled.

"Hot dog soup with some potatoes mixed in. I'd suggest a merlot, but the wine steward has the day off."

John smiled and sat down at the patio table.

"Where are the girls?"

"Jen took them out for a walk with the dogs."

Makala set the bowl down. Sure enough, it was hot dogs, cut up into bite-size pieces, mixed in with potatoes. He dug in, the first few spoonfuls scalding hot.

"Take it slow." She laughed, sitting down across from him, pushing the meat around with her spoon before taking a taste. She grimaced slightly.

"I'm definitely not a cook."

"It's great."

"It's just because you're hungry. What I wouldn't give for shrimp, chilled jumbo shrimp, a salad, a nice glass of chardonnay."

He looked up at her.

"If you hadn't saved my life, I think I'd tell you to shut up," he said with a bit of a grin.

She smiled back and he could not help but notice how her T-shirt, sweat soaked, clung to her body. His gaze lingered on her for several seconds until she made eye contact with him again.

"My, you are getting healthy again," she said softly, still smiling, and he lowered his eyes.

The potatoes were good, though still a bit undercooked. He scraped down to the bottom of the bowl, picked it up to sip the last of the greasy fluid, and set it back down.

"More?" she asked.

He nodded.

"Just take it slow. You had a rough siege of it there. Staph infections like that, well, you are one tough guy to be up on your feet."

She stood and refilled his bowl.

"The girls, how are they?"

"Jen, she's a remarkable woman. Tough as nails. Of course she misses Tyler terribly, I could hear her crying at night, but at the same time is able to accept it and then focus on those she loves that she feels responsible for. Actually, I think she was a bit upset that I moved in here for several days to see after you. Said she could handle it herself."

"You moved in?"

"Only temporary, John," she replied with a smile as she put the bowl down in front of him and sat to resume her meal. "Doctor's orders actually. Kellor and Charlie were damn worried about you. Said they wanted you alive and back on your feet, so I sort of got volunteered."

"Reluctantly?" John asked.

She smiled.

"Not exactly."

"I really don't remember that much."

"Well, you damn near had your brain fried. Temp up at one-oh-five, hand swollen like a balloon. Three weeks back and you'd of been in isolation in an ICU, ice packed, IVs. It got a bit rough there. Kellor thought he'd have to go to amputation to save you if the antibiotics didn't get the infection under control."

"Just from a cut in a stupid fight."

"I warned you," she said, half-waving her spoon at him. "Staph in a hospital is a twenty-four-seven fight. That nursing home, three days without cleaning, sanitation, you had a hundred different microbes floating around there and you just so happened to pick one of the worst."

"How?"

"How? You had an open wound damn near to the bone. Touching a counter, a patient, remember, John, the old days are gone; hospitals are more dangerous now than just staying at home."

"How is it up there?"

"Twelve left of the original patients."

"What? There used to be over sixty."

"Thirty-one dead. Six just disappeared."

"What do you mean, disappeared?"

"Alzheimer's that were still mobile. Remember, no security alarms. They just wandered outside, into the woods. Poor souls, most likely died within a day or two from exposure. We decided yesterday to abandon the place, move those who are left up to a dorm in the conference center. Without all the electronics you can't keep an eye on the Alzheimer's. I never thought I'd see such a thing again, but we have them restrained, tied to their beds."

She sighed.

"Sounds horrible, John, but it will be best when they're gone. We need at least four people staffing them around the clock. At least at the dorm there's only two doors in and out, and frankly, it's cleaner."

"What else?"

She sighed.

"It's been bad."

"How so?"

"A fight at the gap two nights ago."

"How bad?"

"More than two hundred dead on both sides, several hundred injured."

"Jesus, what happened?"

"Well, we were letting folks through a hundred a time, again your suggestion, good professor. It was going slow, though, and now the refugees from Winston-Salem, Charlotte, Greensboro, even some from as far as Durham were piling up on that road. God, John, it's positively medieval down on that road. Squatters' camps, people fighting for a scrap of food. Disease breaking out, mostly salmonella, pneumonia, a nasty variant of the flu.

"Well, a group was being escorted through and they broke. Started running to get off the interstate and into the woods. Two of them had concealed pistols, shot the two policemen escorting them. Shot them dead on the spot. And then they just started scattering.

"Tom ordered them rounded up, Doc Kellor was having a fit as well that they might be carrying something. It turned ugly. Most were too weak to get far, but some of them did put up a fight. About twenty are unaccounted for, disappeared up into the hills. Most are harmless, but a few, the ringleaders, they're out there and Tom is hunting them down.

"That triggered the riot back at the barrier. Charlie ordered it shut down until the mess was straightened out and they just rioted. I mean thousands of them just pushing against the barrier of cars and trucks. Tom did have some tear gas to push them back, but then they came back in. . . ."

"So we opened fire?"

She nodded.

"You could hear it all over town. Sounded like a regular war. Tom had a couple of men with automatic weapons posted up on the side of the pass firing down. John, I never dreamed we'd be doing this to each other."

She fell silent, poking at a piece of hot dog at the bottom of her bowl.

He looked at her, realizing how random fate had played out in her life. If she had not come to Asheville for a meeting that day, she'd have been in Charlotte when everything shut down. Maybe she'd be secure, given her job at a hospital. Then again, she could have been one of the refugees storming the barrier, desperate for a piece of bread, half a bowl of the soup he and she were now eating.

"I could have been on the other side," she said quietly. She looked up at him and for a moment there was rage in her eyes, as if they actually were from opposing camps, two enemies sharing a meal under a temporary truce before the killing started again.

"You weren't, though. You're here and you're safe."

"For how long, John? Some might say I'm still an 'outsider.' "

"Damn it, Makala, don't say that word again."

"Well, you should have heard some of the people talking after that fight. Twenty-seven locals were killed in it, a couple of them police officers, and there were more than one standing around the town offices yesterday talking about kicking out anyone who didn't belong."

"That's bullshit. Scared talk by scared people."

"Amazing, isn't it?" she said, shaking her head. "Three weeks ago we were all Americans. Hell, if somebody said an offensive word, made a racial or sexist slur, my God, everyone would be up in arms and it'd be front-page news. Turn off the electricity and bang, we're at each other's throats in a matter of days. Outsiders, locals, is the whole country now like this, ten thousand little fiefdoms ready to kill each other, and everyone on the road part of some barbarian horde on the march?"

He couldn't reply. He feared that it just might be true, but still, he couldn't believe it, in spite of what had just happened.

"We're still Americans," he sighed. "I need to believe that. We've turned on each other in the past. Remember, we once fought a war against ourselves with six hundred thousand dead. As a kid I remember the riots in Newark, the hatred that created between us, how that still lingered years afterwards. And yet, when it really counted, we did band together as one."

"But now?"

"People are hungry, scared. We were spoiled unlike any generation in history, and we forgot completely just how dependent we were on the juice flowing through the wires, the buttons doing something when we pushed them. If only we had some communication. If only we knew the government still worked, a voice that we trusted being heard, that would make all the difference.

"My grandfather used to tell me how back during the Depression the banks started to collapse; there was panic, even the scent of revolution in the air. And then FDR got on the radio, just one radio talk, reminding us we were all neighbors, to cooperate and help each other, and though the Depression went on for seven more years, the panic ended.

"Same thing on nine-eleven. I think it's the silence that is driving people crazy now. No one knows what is going on, what is being done, if we are indeed at war, and if so, who we are fighting and whether we are winning or losing. We are as isolated now as someone in Europe seven hundred years ago and there is a rumor, just a rumor, that the Tartars are coming or there is plague in the next village."

He sighed, motioning for another bowl. She refilled his and hers.

"In the past, any disaster, it was always local, or regional at worst. The hurricanes in 2004. It slammed us pretty hard here. Most of the news focused on Florida, but I tell you we got some of the worst of it right here, with two of those hurricanes literally crisscrossing over the top of us only days apart. But all along we knew help was out there. The guys who hooked my electric back up after four days were a crew from Birmingham, Alabama. The truck that brought in thousands of gallon jugs of water came from Charlotte actually, and always there were still battery-powered radios.

"If only we could get a link back up, I think that would calm a lot of nerves. Has there been any contact at all from the outside?"

She sipped a spoonful of soup, then shook her head.

"Not a word. A helicopter flew over two days ago. You should have seen people. It was like some god was passing by in a floating chariot, everyone with hands raised up, shouting. No, not a word other than rumors from those passing through. Global war, Chinese invading, help coming from Europe, plague in Washington, a military coup. A lot of talk now about some religious crazies forming into gangs, claiming it's the apocalypse and either join them or die. It's all crazy and they know about as much as you or me."

"It's the cars as well," John said. "They are such an ingrained part of our lives, right down to the fact that there are suburbs and people commute into cities. Hell, a hundred years ago this house never would have even been built, no matter how great the view. Too far from downtown, even if the town is just a small village. This isn't farmland; it's actually useless land other than for timber. But the auto made this valuable. Look at how people are migrating even now; by instinct they're following the interstate highways. Turn off all the cars, I think that is what scared us the most.

The damn things were not just about transportation; they were definers of social status, wealth, age, class. You for instance."

"Me?"

"Beemer Three-thirty? Told me right off you didn't have kids; if you were married you and your husband were definitely upwardly mobile types, professionals."

She laughed softly.

"Postdivorce crisis car."

He nodded.

"I really know nothing about you, Makala."

"Just that, postdivorce car. My husband and I met as undergrads at Duke. Both pre-med."

John laughed.

"Mary and I were Duke as well, though I guess around ten, fifteen years ahead of you. I was history; she was biology; we both wanted to teach. I got into the army through ROTC when they offered me a darn good deal."

"Saw that; your diploma's in your office. Rather impressive, John, master's from Purdue, Ph.D. from UVA in history. I thought you were army?"

"Hey, the army educates and they were crazy enough to pay for it and send me. For every hour I carried a gun I spent a hundred in a classroom or archive. Did have a few field commands. First with a recon company with the First Cav in Germany just before communism gave up the ghost. Actually enjoyed that posting, gave me a lot of time to explore history over there besides my duties. Then Desert Storm. My battalion mobilized over and I was looking forward to the challenge of command in a line company when I got promoted to major, then kicked up the ladder to battalion XO. It took me out of the front line and I always wondered since if I had somehow missed something as a result. But enough on me . . ."

She smiled.

"Well, we got married right after he graduated, two years ahead of me, and the classic old routine," Makala said with a sigh. "I switched majors to nursing to start the money rolling; agreement was once he got into residency I'd go back for pre-med."

"And let me guess," John interjected. "He got his M.D. and you got the divorce as a thank-you."

"Something like that. Just grew apart, I guess. Another woman wandered in, actually several women, and I got fed up and left. Young doctors with big egos, starry-eyed nurses saying, 'Oh, Doctor,' it's two in the morning, happens all the time."

He looked at her, the slight show of dimples when she smiled, clear blue eyes, tall, slender figure, and shook his head.

"He was an idiot."

"John, you hardly know me," she smiled, "so don't just judge by exteriors. I have my bad side, too."

"Well, I've yet to see it. Volunteering to go up and help at the nursing home. That took guts."

"Or it could have been calculation," she replied, "get into the community that way."

He looked straight at her, remembering what she said on the day he had shot Larry, and shook his head.

"No, you'd of done it regardless of the situation."

He hesitated, looking back down at the soup bowl.

"And any guys for you?"

"Why do you ask?"

"Just trying to put the pieces together."

"No one serious, if that's what you mean. Gun-shy."

"And no kids?"

"Thank God no."

"Why?"

"Now, with this? You think I'd want that worry on top of everything else? Suppose we did have children and I was up here the day it happened. I'd of been clawing through the tide of refugees to get back to Charlotte."

He nodded. The way she said "clawing through" told him a lot. She liked kids, maybe wished she had some, and had the instinct to kill to protect them, no matter whose they were.

"Let's talk about Jennifer," she said quietly.

"Is there a problem?" he asked, suddenly anxious.

"Of course there is, John. You got enough insulin for a little more than four months, though the water temperature where you are storing the vials is just over fifty degrees. I checked it. That will degrade the shelf life somewhat."

"By how much?" he asked, feeling a sense of panic.

"I'm not sure, John. We'll start to know when the regular dose doesn't control her blood sugar. Besides that, we have to start getting conservative with her testing kit. The new one, as you know, is junked, the old one, thank God, survived, but the test strips, no replacements now. So we're going to have to learn to just eyeball the situation more and only use the strips when we absolutely have to."

He couldn't speak, just staring off across the valley. It was all so peaceful. No noise, some plumes from small fires rising up, drifting with the westerly breeze. He reached to his breast pocket. No pocket; he was still in a sweat-soaked T-shirt.

"Cigarette?" she asked.

He nodded.

"I'll get them."

She came back out a minute later with two, struck a lighter and puffed one to life, hesitated for a second, then handed it to John, putting the second one on the table.

"Ex-smoker?" John asked.

"Yup. Surprising how many nurses smoke. But I looked at one too many cancerous lungs, though."

"Don't need to hear it."

She smiled.

"Well, you're going to run out in about two weeks anyhow. Stretch it and you might make it to four weeks or six, but sooner or later you will quit. Maybe one of the few blessings to come out of this. An entire nation going cold turkey on tobacco, alcohol, drugs. No cars, so we have to walk or ride bikes. Might do us some good."

"Back to Jennifer," he said, after taking several puffs. The meal was sitting well on his stomach, but the tobacco hit him after so many days away. He felt shaky and suddenly weak.

"Tyler's death, the funeral," she said. "If I had been around and knew, I'd of kept Jennifer home during the burial. It really traumatized her.

"It's tough enough on any kid of that age to lose their grandpa. But we, all of us, have really isolated death away, kept it hidden. Tyler died in her bedroom. In fact, she is terrified to even go back in there. When she'd come to see you when you were sick, she'd just stand by the doorway. It's just that she saw it all, and it registered.

"John, she's a diabetic, and even at twelve that makes anyone very conscious of their mortality. They know their life is dependent on that needle and the vial, but for seventy years now those vials just came across the pharmacy counter, no questions asked. She knows that's finished."

"How?"

"Damn it, John, she isn't deaf or blind. Every day since this started people have been dying and she knows she's on the short list once the insulin in the basement runs out."

He shook his head angrily.

"No, God, please no. That's four months off. By then we'll have something back in place. At least communications, some emergency medicines."

"John, you've been the very person going around saying that this is bad, real bad, that it might take years, if ever, to come back from it."

"I never said a word around her."

"Oh, John, you're such a father, but you don't understand kids. I've worked in hospitals with kids like Jennifer. Kids that were terminal. They had it figured long before their parents would ever admit it to themselves."

"She is not terminal," he snarled, glaring at Makala angrily.

She said nothing.

"Damn you, no," and he was humiliated by the tears that suddenly clouded his vision.

He struggled to choke back the sobs that now overwhelmed him.

She put her hand out, touching him, and he jerked back, looking at her, filled with impotent rage.

"My girl will live through this," he gasped. "Jennifer will live through this."

She leaned over, gently touching his face, paused, and then half stood up, kissing him on the forehead, and drew her chair closer to his side.

"John, with luck, if things straighten out, we'll get hooked back up to hospitals that work before the insulin runs out."

He noticed how she said "we."

"I've gotten close to her, John. Very close these last few days. She's a sweet child. Not a twelve-year-old dressing, talking, and sometimes acting like she's twenty-one. She still sleeps with Rabs in her arms, plays with Beanie Babies, reads a lot. The way perhaps twelve-year-olds were long ago. Rather nerdy actually."

He struggled for control as Makala described his little girl. He let the burned-out cigarette fall and without comment she lit the second one and handed it over, taking a puff on it first before doing so.

She smiled, and he realized that tears were in her eyes as well.

"It's just the poor child has really been obsessive about dying since she saw her grandfather go and the way he was buried, the way we're burying people now by the hundreds."

"I'll talk with her."

"I already have," Makala said quietly.

"About what?"

She hesitated.

"Go on; about what?"

"About death," she whispered. "She asked me for the truth. About how long she had if the insulin ran out."

"And what did you tell her?" he snapped, and she grimaced as he grasped her arm with his hand. "What did you tell her?"

"John, I told you, I've worked with kids like her. I know when to lie; I know when it is time to tell the truth. I reassured her that she'd be OK. That you and others were working to get things reestablished and soon medical supplies would start coming in."

He released his grip.

"Sorry," he whispered.

"But you've got to talk with her, too, John."

He nodded, head lowered, again struggling for control. He felt so damn weak. Not just physically but emotionally. Tyler's time had played out and though John had come to love that old man as if he were John's own father, he took solace knowing Tyler had lived a good life. But Jennifer?

"You better keep reassuring her if you want her to be happy." Makala paused.

"In the time she has left?" he asked, staring at her.

"Let's just pray for the best."

He finished his cigarette and sat back.

"You said hundreds have been buried?"

She nodded and then looked away.

He heard barking and then laughter. From out of the field above the house his family was coming. The dogs, seeing him up and about again, made a beeline straight to him. He could not help but laugh, both dogs grinning at him and dancing around his chair. And then with noses raised they were sniffing at the soup pot, Ginger standing up on her hind legs to peer in, nearly burning her feet as she lost balance and almost fell against the stove.

Jennifer came running down and jumped into his arms.

"You're better, Daddy!"

"Well, not exactly, but almost, pumpkin."

She buried her head against his shoulder and he wondered for a moment if she was crying. And then she pulled back slightly.

"Daddy, you really stink."

He laughed, tempted to play the old "armpit" game of grabbing her and forcing her up against his armpit. She loved it when she was eight, even as she shrieked in protest. But not now; he knew he really did stink.

"I promise I'll take a bath later today; I could use it."

"Outdoors now, Daddy," she said, pointing to a small kiddie wading pool and a rough-built shower made out of a six-foot ladder with a one-gallon plastic bucket suspended from the top rung by a two-by-four, the bottom of the bucket perforated with a couple of dozen small holes.

"Ben built it. One person showers; the other pours the water into the bucket while standing on the ladder."

Ben made that and John nodded and then suddenly wondered . . .

Makala laughed. "I do the pouring for Elizabeth, John."

"Well, Ben can pour for me and you ladies can go somewhere else."

Jennifer hugged him tight, let go, and looked into the pot.

"What is it?"

"Hot dogs and potatoes," Makala announced.

"Yuk, sounds gross."

"Really, it's quite good," John said.

"Can Zach and Ginger have some?"

The two dogs were by his side, tongues hanging out, panting, both with eyes fixed on his empty bowl. Across the years it had become an unconscious act: leave a little extra on the plate, set it down. When Ginger joined the family John would make sure two plates would go down at the same time, because no matter how much the dogs cared for each other, if there was only one plate there'd be a lunge and a yelp, usually from Ginger losing out to Zach, but now, as Zach was starting to show his age, he was becoming the loser in those squabbles.

"We ran out of dog food yesterday," Makala said quietly.

Damn, he had never even thought of that.

"Even the canned stuff?"

Makala didn't say anything and he realized with a shock that the reason she said nothing was because she or Jen had stashed the canned dog food for emergency use if need be. He suddenly wondered if they made a canned dog food of hot dogs but knew it was best not to ask.

"Come on, Dad; they're starving."

He looked down at his two buddies. His companions on many a late night of writing or research, they'd always be curled up in his office. Once it was time for sleep, Ginger would usually paddle off to Jennifer's room, Zach always to his.

He looked at Jennifer, then back to the dogs.

"Sure, come on, you two fools."

He picked up his bowl and Makala's, doled out one ladleful each of the soup, and put the bowls down. The two lunged, devouring the meal within seconds.

Jennifer smiled, watching them. Makala said nothing.

"I think I want to go into town to see what's going on, maybe over to the campus."

"Don't press your luck, John," Jen said, a bit breathless from hiking down from the field, coming up to his side and standing on tiptoes to kiss him.

"Damn, you really do stink," she said disapprovingly, stepping back.

"I'll drive," Makala interjected. "Besides, now that our patient is better, I think I should go back up to the nursing home and oversee the transfer up to the conference center."

Jen said nothing as Makala went into the house. Elizabeth pecked him on the check and sat down to eat.

"She's a nice girl," Jen said.

"I think she's in love with you, Dad," Elizabeth announced, saying it as if just commenting on the weather or the time of day.

Jennifer giggled at that.

John looked over at Jen.

"She sat up with you three nights straight. You were in a bad way there, John."

Jen smiled, but he could see she was just about in tears.

"What is it, Mom?"

"Oh, nothing," and she turned away. And he knew she was thinking of Mary.

The drive into town things looked pretty much the same, except for the fact that several of the men he passed were toting shotguns or rifles. At the elementary school there was a huge stack of firewood, a number of kettles set over a fire boiling.

"How are things in there?"

"John, people who just can't make it are dying off," Makala sighed. "Hundreds dead, but things are under control for right now."

At the station he found out that Charlie was up in Swannanoa, Tom up at the barrier in the gap. He read the town notice board, printed with red marker on the whiteboards tacked to the side of town hall:

MARTIAL LAW STILL IN EFFECT

John noticed the eraser marks for everything else on the board except for those five words; "Martial Law Still in Effect."

> **1.** It is estimated that twenty escapees from the interstate are still at large in the region. If they are sighted, apprehend, detain, or if need be use whatever force necessary, then report sighting to this office.
>
> **2.** Ration cards will be issued starting today for everyone in the community. If you are a resident with a home and you apply for a ration card, you must submit to your property being searched for food. If food is found it will be confiscated and then distributed to the community. Do not apply for rations unless you are in true need. Starting tomorrow, you will not be issued food at any public facility without presentation of the ration card, along with proper identification.

John paused at that one and thought about it. He realized it was a good decision. No threat of taking food, only if you asked for food. It'd keep hoarders from trying to eat off the public weal while continuing to sit on their own stockpiles. He continued to read.

> **3.** The outbreak of salmonella at the Emergency Refugee Center has been brought under control. Our thanks to the volunteers from Montreat

College and the staff, led by Dr. Kellor. We regret to report a total of sixty-one dead from the outbreak at the center. Community-wide it is reported that 310 have died from samonella, with over three thousand cases reported.

4. The new emergency hospital at the Ingram's shopping plaza in Swannanoa is open. If you need transportation to that facility, a public vehicle will leave here at noon every day hereafter.

5. Principal Greene, acting now as superintendent of schools for our community, has officially announced that all schools are now closed for the academic year. Classes will resume the day after Labor Day. Upon resumption of school, grades for the previous academic year will be posted.

John found that to be curious, that they had finally gotten around to canceling school. He'd have to tell the girls; they'd be delighted. Also, it was a touch of optimism that some sort of continuity would continue come fall and he was glad to read it.

6. Death notices: eighty-one deaths reported in the communities of Black Mountain and Swannanoa yesterday. Remember, all bodies are to be interred at the new community cemeteries, the golf course in Black Mountain, the upper grounds of the Swannanoa Christian Academy, above the floodplain for the Swannanoa River. Cause of death must be confirmed by the physician on duty in the respective town offices between the hours of eight in the morning and five in the afternoon.

The names were listed and John scanned it. One he knew, a student of his, cute girl, a sophomore, a bit overweight, with a smile that could light up a room. He remembered she suffered from severe allergies to bee stings, a notice having been sent around to all her professors at the start of each semester to be aware of that situation and immediately get her out of the room if a stinging insect flew in. He wondered if that had been the cause of death.

7. TAKE NOTICE. If there is a death in your family and your family has accepted ration cards and that death is concealed, all ration cards for the immediate family will be permanently confiscated except for those for children under the age of eleven, but said children will then be moved to the refugee center. If you are not a permanent resident of the community, you and all immediate family will be expelled except for children under the age of eleven.

That bothered him, the last sentence. It was still the defining of a different class within the community. Makala was standing beside him, reading the notice board, and he wondered how she felt about it.

8. NEWS! It is reported by one of our residents who has reached us after walking from Greensboro that there is an operating shortwave radio in Morganton. The resident claims to have heard a broadcast from the BBC in London. The British government has declared solidarity with America and even now is mobilizing massive relief aid. Long Live Our Allies of Old and of Today!

John smiled at that. And if true, it could mean that perhaps, just perhaps, communications gear was on the way to help reestablish links. The downside . . . why only Great Britain?

9. WAR NEWS! This same resident reports that the attack is now believed to have been three missiles, fired from a containership in the Gulf of Mexico. Our forces overseas are engaged in heavy combat in Iraq, Iran, Saudi Arabia, Pakistan, and Korea. There is progress on all fronts. Responsibility for the attack rests upon an alliance of forces in the Middle East and North Korea. Reports now confirm that a weapon similar to the ones that struck the United States has also been detonated over the western Pacific, creating the same widespread outages in Japan, South Korea, and Taiwan. A similar missile is also reported to have been detonated over Eastern Europe.

It is reported as well that the federal government, even now, is organizing the distribution of radios, which shall originate out of a stockpile kept in a secret reserve. Communications are soon to be reestablished with central authorities.

10. All announcements placed upon this board are official and in force from the time of placement. Claiming of ignorance of said laws shall not be accepted as an excuse for non-compliance.

Signed,
Charles Fuller
Director of Public Safety

WE SHALL WIN THROUGH TO ULTIMATE VICTORY. GOD BLESS AND PRESERVE THE UNITED STATES OF AMERICA.

John turned away from the board and looked at Makala.

"What are you thinking?" he asked.

"Feel like I'm in a bad movie or novel," she sighed. " 'Long Live the King,' or 'Long Live Our Glorious Leader,' or something like that should be on the board."

"We are nowhere near that yet," John said coldly.

"Might as well warn you now, I'm one of those old-style liberals who used to see conspiracies behind everything the right wing did."

He looked at her and saw a trace of a smile.

"I used to feel the same about the left," and now it was his turn to smile. "Seems absurd now."

"Still, to go from where we were three weeks ago to this, it's impossible to grasp."

They walked back to the Edsel. He noticed that the parking area around the police station had been cleared of all the newer and now-useless cars. There was a row of half a dozen VW Bugs, "Courtesy of Jim Bartlett" stenciled on the side of each with an old-fashioned peace sign added in. That must really rankle Tom, John thought. Two old Jeeps, one of them the antique World War II jeep with a white star stenciled on the hood, an assortment of cars from the fifties and sixties, a few from the seventies, the years that Detroit really started to turn out junk, which didn't survive as well as the older ones. A number of older motorcycles and mopeds as well.

To his surprise a couple of horses were tethered there as well, and he stopped to look at them.

"Stables at the kids' camps. Over forty horses in the community,"

Makala said. "Most were appropriated by Charlie for patrolling the back roads."

She walked up and rubbed the horse's nose and it nickered.

"Used to love riding. And you?"

"Actually, yes. The freedom of it when you're out on open ground. But it's been a while."

"Poor things."

"Why?"

"Charlie said we can use them through the summer, but once we go through the cattle and pigs, they're next."

He nodded, saying nothing.

They got into the Edsel, Makala still driving, and headed up towards the college. As they approached the arched stone gate, a huge hand-lettered sign greeted them:

HALT! YOU MUST STOP!

He rolled to a stop and two of his students, both with shotguns, blocked his approach, weapons leveled, but upon their recognizing him there were grins.

"What the hell is this?" John asked.

"Sorry, Professor. Interior defense. Some of those runaways from the interstate are still out there. Also, we're starting to get people trying to sneak in off the old toll road behind us. Sergeant Parker has posted a twenty-four-hour guard here."

John nodded, saying nothing as Makala drove through the gatehouse and then into the campus.

All was quiet here and then he saw them, lined up on the grassy slope in front of Gaither Hall. He motioned for Makala to pull over and stop.

He sat in the car for a moment and watched. Damn, it was like boot camp, fifty kids, a platoon-size unit, standing at attention, inspection arms, and every kid was indeed armed. Some had shotguns, others hunting rifles; a few stood there with pistols. Every weapon imaginable, from a Chinese SKS, to .22 semiautos, to a monstrous double-barreled 12-gauge shotgun, and he quickly recognized two boys carrying reproductions of Civil War .58 Springfield rifles.

He got out of the car to watch. A few of them looked his way. One girl grinned and started to wave; then realizing what she was supposed to be doing, she came back to attention.

And there was Washington Parker, walking down the line, grabbing a weapon from one student, levering the bolt action back, looking into the chamber, then slapping the weapon back into the student's hands.

"Not clean enough! You want to live? You keep your weapon clean!"

John slowly walked up and the eye contact from students was a tip-off to Washington to turn. There was the flicker of a smile and Washington came to attention and saluted.

"Good day, Colonel, sir. Care to inspect the troops?"

John found himself returning the salute.

"Are we feeling better today, Colonel, sir?"

"Yes, Mr. . . ." He fumbled for a second. "Yes, Sergeant Parker, I am, thank you."

Embarrassed, John turned to look at his students, kids of but three weeks back. He had spoken to them more than once about the privileges they had. That kids their age were defending them on distant fronts even as they sat half-dozing in class. Several graduates of the college had been in Iraq, another in Afghanistan, and whenever an e-mail came in from overseas John usually read it to these same students. And now they stood lined up with guns, in front of the main campus building that housed the admissions office, the registrar, the music department, and one of the two chapels on campus.

He knew they were expecting him to now say something, but words failed him. He saw his two favorites, Jeremiah and Phil, to the right of the line, sergeant's chevrons stenciled on the dark blue college T-shirts all of them were wearing like uniforms.

Jeremiah and Phil made eye contact and he nodded.

He wondered if these kids knew what he had done in the park. Of course they did, the whole town knew, and as he gazed at them he could see it in their eyes. They were looking at him differently. He had been the executioner. He was no longer the history professor who, though a former military man, was seen as having a soft heart.

"They look good," was all he could say as he turned to face Washington, who saluted him. John returned the salute and headed into Gaither Hall.

"Rather paramilitary, isn't it?" Makala asked, returning to his side.

John did not reply.

He walked into the building and for a moment wasn't sure what to actually expect. Of course the corridors were darkened, the air heavy and humid. Fortunately, the building was old, having been designed long before central AC, so at least there was some circulation. The door to the admissions office and registrar were closed, but he could hear a piano in the chapel. He motioned for Makala to follow and he opened the door.

The chapel had been built in the 1930s, just as the chestnut blight had ripped through the Carolina mountains, so the trees had been harvested off and now were the beams, paneling, and ceiling, a beautiful warm, dark golden wood. Austere to a certain degree, for this was, after all, a Presbyterian school, but still a wonderful chapel in John's eyes.

Up on the stage several kids were standing around the piano, Jessie, one of the music majors, just fooling around a bit.

A student whose name John did remember, Laura, said something, Jessie played a few chords, and she began to sing. Instantly John felt his throat tighten. Laura had sung this song in the spring musical review, and though it was from a play that he thought was way too sentimental, *The Fantasticks,* the song was haunting and, to him, such a metaphor for all that was happening.

"Try to remember the kind of September
When life was slow and oh, so mellow. . . ."

He felt Makala's hand slip into his and they were silent. He could feel a shudder run through Makala; she was crying.

Laura's voice echoed:

"Try to remember when life was so tender
That no one wept except the willow. . . ."

John could hear Parker shouting orders outside, the students now going through the manual of arms. It was almost to much for him to bear. It wasn't supposed to happen here, but it had happened here.

Laura finished the second stanza and drifted into the third:

"Deep in December, it's nice to remember,
Although you know the snow will follow. . . ."

"I can't bear this," Makala whispered.

They slipped out of the chapel, Laura, the others, not even knowing he had been there.

Makala leaned against him for a moment, sobbing, and his arms were around her and then she stepped back, breaking away from his embrace, looking up at him.

"Sorry."

"No, it was rather nice actually," he said.

The song finished in the chapel and he started out of the building, then noticed that the door to President Hunt's office was ajar. He tapped on it and walked in. The administrative assistant, Kim McMurty, was not behind her desk. That was a disappointment. She always reminded him a bit of the actress Nicole Kidman, perhaps better looking actually, and he had to admit he was smitten with Kim in a friendly sort of way, friendly, of course, because her husband, the director of computer services, was a darn good friend . . . and besides, Mary was still a haunting presence. What had just happened with Makala? He wasn't sure how to react to her now.

"President Hunt?"

"In here."

John walked into the back office and was startled.

Hunt seemed to have aged a dozen years in as many days, eyes sunken, hair disheveled, and then John wondered how he looked as well, still wobbly, unshaved, filthy, exhausted.

"John, you look like hell."

"Well, sir, if you don't mind me saying so, you look like hell, too."

Dan pointed to a chair and John sat down. He had always liked this office. John looked back and saw Makala out in Kim's office. Makala nodded and left, motioning that she'd wait outside.

The first time he had come to this office to be interviewed for the job that Bob Scales had engineered for him, what caught his eye was three paintings on the far wall. The first was what was to be expected of a president of a Christ-centered college, a nicely framed section from Michelangelo's Sistine Chapel, the hand of God reaching out to touch Adam.

The other two, though. The second was sort of a transition between religion and the military, a painting of Washington, kneeling in the snow at Valley Forge, praying. The third was Howard Pyle's *The Nation Makers,* a stunning portrait of a line of Revolutionary War infantry going into battle, men tattered but defiant, the American flag little more than a rag but going forward relentlessly to what could only be ultimate victory.

The paintings were still there, as always, but as John turned to look back out the window at the students drilling, Pyle's work took on new meaning.

Dan was silent and then, to John's surprise, reached into the bottom drawer of his desk and pulled out a bottle of scotch and a couple of coffee cups.

"If the board of trustees ever knew about this, they'd hang me," Dan said, and John wondered it he was being serious or just joking. It was, after all, a dry campus.

John took the offered cup and waited for Dan to pour an ounce. He held it up.

"For the Republic, may God preserve her," Dan said.

The two drained the cups down in a single gulp, Dan exhaling noisily as he put his down.

"What's up, John?" Dan asked.

"Well, sir, I guess you knew I was out of the loop for a week or so."

"You had us scared there, John. At chapel every day for the last week Reverend Abel and the kids offered prayers for you."

"Well, it most certainly worked," John said, looking down at his hand. "What about classes. Are they still meeting?"

Dan shook his head.

"Remember, most of our faculty live miles from here; no, classes are canceled."

"But you still hold daily chapel."

"Now more than ever," Dan said quietly.

That was reassuring, darn reassuring, a link to the past somehow. And yes, as well, in any time of crisis churches would fill up again. The Sunday after 9/11 John remembered the small chapel he and Mary used to go to over in Swannanoa was packed to overflowing.

"I felt I should check in, see what was happening on campus. After all, this place is my job." He hesitated. "No, actually my life in so many ways. I was wondering if there was anything I should be doing here now."

"Appreciate that," Hunt replied softly, "but I think you have other responsibilities now."

John said nothing.

"I heard about your role on what people are now calling the Council. I think it's darn good you're part of that. They need someone like you. Focus your efforts on that; don't worry about us."

"These are my kids, too, Dan. I worry about them."

Outside came the echo of Washington's voice, chewing someone out. He sounded like a Marine DI again, the right edge of sarcasm but, in respect to the traditions of the campus, at least no overtly sexual, scatological, or downright obscene phrases thrown in.

"To survive, to keep these kids alive, we're selling our services," Dan said quietly. "But there's a lot more behind this as well."

John stood up and walked to the window, empty cup in hand, and watched as Washington, finished with the inspection, now started to run the kids through some close-order drill.

"What is that out there?" John asked.

"First Platoon of Company A of the Black Mountain Militia," Dan said.

"What?"

"Just that. Charlie Fuller and I agreed on it a couple of days ago. A hundred and fifty kids so far. The other two platoons are out on a conditioning run up to Graybeard and back. We'd have more, but that's all the weapons we could find so far. Company B will start forming up once we get more weapons."

"Isn't this a little overboard?" John asked. "Hell, I know Washington's a good man, a great man actually, but come on, Dan. What is he doing out there, getting turned on with old memories, that it's Parris Island or Khe Sanh again?"

"In truth, John, yes. I guess you heard about the riot at the gap."

"Yes."

"It was then that Charlie realized something, and Washington had most likely put the bug in his ear already: we need an army."

John sighed.

"Three weeks ago those kids were dozing in classes, trying to sneak up to Lookout Mountain with their boyfriend or girlfriend, or maybe, just maybe, studying for exams. Now we're making them into an army?"

"I was younger than them when I lost this," Dan said, and he slapped his left leg, a hollow thump resounding. "You were a lieutenant at twenty-two yourself."

"Yeah, but Dan, this is a college. A small Christian college up in the mountains of North Carolina. Somehow it just doesn't feel right to me."

"Where else in this entire valley are there four hundred young men and women, in fairly good shape to start with, intelligence pretty darn good, already imbued with a sense of identity for the school and those who lead it, like you, me, Washington?"

"I don't know," John sighed, watching as the column went to right flank march and two girls screwed up, Washington in their faces and reaming them out so that one was crying as she tried to march.

"We had six hundred kids here, on the day before things went down," Dan said, now at John's side and watching the kids drill.

"About a hundred and fifty have left, trying to strike out for home. That was hard; you were not here for that meeting in the chapel. A lot of praying, soul-searching. I advised them to stay. Told them that if anything, their parents would want them to stay here until this crisis was over, knowing that they would be safe. Most who left are local, a day's walk away, but a couple of them are from Florida, said they felt they should try and get home."

John shook his head. The ones trying to get to Florida were most likely now facing hundreds of thousands heading the other way.

"The rest agreed to stay. Remember how several years back we had all those discussions in faculty meetings about orienting the college more to service? A couple of other colleges in the area, our rivals, were touting that all the time, so we put into the curriculum community service. That's what we're doing now."

"Dan, there's a helluva difference between kids working at a homeless shelter or community day-care center and drilling like an army."

"I don't think so, John. The times, as the old song went, are a-changin'."

The column of students turned and marched back across the green, weapons at the shoulder, and the sight of it sent a chill down his spine. He looked back at Pyle's painting and then back to them.

My God, no difference, John realized. The tradition of close-order drill was a primal memory left over from the days when armies really did go into battle that way, shoulder to shoulder. Today it was supposedly about discipline and spirit and the fact that soldiers were at least expected to march. But no different, no different from what he used to talk about with such enthusiasm at the Civil War Roundtable and see at reenactments.

The difference was, though, this was for real. From close-order drill Washington would take them to elementary tactics: fire and movement, holding a fixed position, laying down fields of fire, assault of a fixed position, marksmanship, leadership in combat, emergency first aid, infiltration tactics, hand-to-hand combat, how to kill with a knife, how to kill with your bare hands.

The sight of them drilling such struck home, as forcefully as what John had been forced to do in the park.

"Washington thinks the world of you," Dan said. "By the way, he told me what happened in the park. Said you handled yourself well."

"Handled myself well? I puked my guts out."

"No, not that. First time you shoot someone, if you got any heart in you, any touch of the divine spark, you should be horrified."

He looked off.

"I lost my leg during Tet. The day before that, though, I was on point, turned the corner of a trail, and there he was. . . ." He sighed, shaking his head. "The Thomas Hardy poem, remember it?"

John nodded. "'I shot at him and he at me, And killed him in his place. . . .'"

"Well, I got him first; he was walking point for his unit and we just ran into each other. Before I even quite realized it I emptied my M16 into him. Hell of a firefight exploded, and I was on the ground, lying by his side, and I could hear him gasping for air. Do you know what he said?"

John was silent, half-suspecting.

"He was crying for his mother. I understood enough of the language to know that. . . ."

His voice trailed off and John could see tears in Dan's eyes.

"The kid I shot," John said, "certainly wasn't calling for his mother. He died filled with hate."

"Perhaps he sees things different now," Dan replied. "I know it's not orthodox with some, but I have a hard time not seeing God as forgiving, even after death."

John tried to smile. There were some on campus who were rather traditionally "hard-line" in their views of salvation. Dan had never voiced this view before and it was a comfort, for the memory of that twisted kid's final seconds lingered like a recurring nightmare.

"Washington told me how you reacted and the kids know that, too. Remember, this is a Christian school and the reaction could have been bad if it seemed you were cold-blooded about it. So a lesson was taught there, John, but it's what you said as well that resonated.

"Washington and later Charlie Fuller told me that at that moment we as a community were balanced on a razor. Charlie had made the right decision, but he did not know how to see it carried through correctly.

"You did. At that moment we could have sunk into a mob or, worse, a mob that would then follow a leader, even a leader of good heart like Charlie, but still follow him with bloodlust and thus would start the slide.

"You're the historian; you know that of all the revolutions in history, only a handful have truly succeeded, have kept their soul, their original intent."

Though it struck John as slightly melodramatic, Dan pointed to the portrait of Washington kneeling in the snow.

"I don't think we are in a revolution," John said. "We're trying to survive until such time as some order is restored. Communications up, enough vehicles put back on the road to link us together again as a nation."

"But suppose that never happens," Dan said quietly.

"What?"

"Just that, John. Suppose it never happens. Suppose the old America, so wonderful, the country we so loved, suppose at four fifty P.M. eighteen days ago, it died. It died from complacency, from blindness, from not being willing to face the harsh realities of the world. Died from complacent self-centeredness. Suppose America died that day."

"For heaven's sake, Dan, don't talk like that," John sighed.

"Well, I think it did die, John. I think our enemies caught us with total surprise. We should have seen it. I'm willing to bet there were a hundred reports floating around Congress warning of this, experts who truly did know their stuff screaming that we were wide open. It happens to all nations, all empires in history. Hell, you're the historian; you know that. And at the moment it does happen, no one believes it actually is happening. They can't comprehend how their own greatness can be humbled by another whom they view as being so beneath them, so meaningless, so backwards so as not to be a threat. You know that, John. Nine-eleven, Pearl Harbor, were like fleabites in comparison to this."

"The Mongols hitting Eastern Europe in 1241," John said softly. "The Teutonic Knights, when they first saw the Mongols at the Battle of Leignitz, supposedly laughed hysterically at the sight of their opponents on horses so small they were the size of ponies. Ponies that would be crushed under the first charge of lancers. They lowered their lances, charged, and at a hundred and fifty yards the Mongols decimated them with their compound bows, unheard of in Europe, each bolt hitting at fifty yards with the kinetic energy of a .38. Thirty thousand Mongols annihilated tens of thousands of Europe's finest that day."

Dan nodded.

"The French knights at Crécy mocking the English longbowmen. The British mocking us at Monmouth and Cowpens. The Germans disdainful of the Russians in 1941," John said.

"And us in Vietnam," Dan said quietly, "though that was not a war for our national survival, but it certainly was for them. I remember going over there filled with a bunch of crap about how we were going to walk all over the gooks. Well, I've not walked right since.

"Nation makers out there, John. Some of our profs might think I've sold this college to the community, but the hell with them. I know a college nearby, one that put out a lot of majors in peace studies, and if there was a protest anywhere against our military, they'd show; it was almost required. If an army recruiter ever showed up there, they'd get mobbed, all in the name of peace of course. Can you imagine you or me ever getting a job there? Diversity worked for them only as long as you toed the line with their views, and now the whirlwind is upon us." He sniffed derisively. "They'll never make it now. I bet on that campus, today, they're sitting around like the French nobles did at Versailles even as the mob swarmed over the gates. I bet they're singing 'Give Peace a Chance,' even as they starve to death."

"Well, that's not going to happen to my kids," Dan said coldly, "and in our doing so our community will survive as well."

"A hundred and fifty for Company A. Another hundred for Company B once we get the weapons in. You take a close look and a couple of those kids are carrying reenactor Springfields from the Civil War by the way. The others are doing community service work or working on other projects. Kids that helped stop the salmonella outbreak, volunteering up at the isolation ward. Already have a crew of kids starting to cut firewood for the winter. Professor Daniels with the outdoor ed department figures we can retrofit a couple of the old oil boilers to burn wood in this building and the library and have steam heat. We'll need over three hundred cords of wood, though. Professor Lassiter is talking about rigging up a water turbine in the dam at Lake Susan. He thinks we could have it up and running by autumn and have electricity."

John could not help but smile.

Most of the towns in the area, back a hundred or more years ago, first got their electricity that way. Entrepreneurs would come in, sell the community a generator, show them how to hook it up to a mill dam, string some wire, and the miracle, what was then the miracle, of electricity arrived.

"Professor Sonnenberg tells me that in our school library are back issues of *Scientific American* all the way back to the 1850s. Also *Popular Mechanics*. In those golden pages are plans from eighty years ago, a hundred years ago, to build radios, telegraphs, steam engines, batteries, internal combustion engines, formulas for nearly every advance in chemistry.

"In our library we got darn near every issue of *Mother Earth News,* and the *Foxfire* books." Dan chuckled at that. "Most of the other profs had viewed such publications with disdain, but on the faculty was a beloved old professor from before your time, now dead, who was definitely, as the kids said, 'a granola eater.' That prof left us a gold mine. How to find food, how to preserve it, how to store it up. We got several groups out now, those books in hand, harvesting enough to keep us alive. Hard to believe, John, but rattlesnake shish kebab isn't all that bad.

"It's all at our fingertips if only we look down at our fingertips to see it there.

"But the kids out there must keep this place secure and, if need be, buy time."

"Buy time for what? We have the passes secured."

"You know about the fight there, don't you?" Dan asked.

"Yes."

"Well, that was a disorganized mob. Word is starting to filter in that groups are starting to come together. Most are just scared people banding together for survival and mutual protection, exactly what we are doing here. But some, John, there's rumors about cults. A family that was allowed to pass through here yesterday, actually heading east, coming out of Tennessee, said that over by Knoxville there's a guy claiming this is the start of a holy war."

"And let me guess, it's his vision of holiness you subscribe to or you die."

Dan nodded his head.

"Says that Jesus appeared to him just before the power went off and gave him his mission, that he is the new John the Baptist preparing the way for the final return. And good God, supposedly there are hundreds now following him and killing those who disagree."

"Several weeks, that's all it's taken," John sighed.

Dan rested a hand on his shoulder.

"Just remember Ecclesiastes, John: 'A time for war, a time for peace. . . .' "

"So now it's back to this. And back to kids drilling on the town green. I want to think that across America, today, there's a thousand such groups drilling in order to keep civilization intact so that we don't become a mob where one eats only because he is stronger than others or we kill each other in an insane frenzy of crazed beliefs."

"That's why those kids out there are drilling and that's why I want you to be in command of them."

"Me?" he asked, incredulous at the suggestion. "Hell, you're the one with the vision."

"I'm a college president," Dan said with a smile. "A one-legged college president."

"A wounded war veteran," John replied sharply.

"Yeah, a dumb eighteen-year-old kid from Mocksville, North Carolina, so damn stupid I couldn't see I was in a mine field. But I got the GI Bill, disability checks, and, since I could no longer run or play ball, a realization that I had to be something else. So here I now sit.

"John, while we work here, I want you to lead in the town. Charlie is a good man, a damn good man, but his focus, it's on the moment, on survival for the community, and God bless him for it. But we need something more. We need someone with vision who can see beyond, like the song said, 'to patriots' dreams . . .' You have the respect of everyone in this town now. The kids, the community, the police, Charlie, everyone."

"Why?" John said coldly. "Because I fumbled the job of blowing some junkie's brains out?"

"No, because of what you said before you blew his brains out, as you now so crudely put it. Maybe that poor devil-consumed kid really did have a purpose in life after all. Maybe it was to give you that moment.

"For some, the fact that you did shoot him, well, for some that created fear and awe. But for the rest, they heard your words and will not forget them. John, that gives you a power. And you did hold the rank of colonel and were offered a star, which you turned down for Mary's sake. Mary's family is an old family here and you tossing over being a general to bring her home was the talk of the town back then, and I think you saw on day one the respect everyone held for you."

Frankly, he did not; he was far too focused on Mary and, yes, somewhat bitter as well that the powers that be in the Pentagon had not found a way around his problem, but that was in the past and for so many reasons now especially he thanked God he was here in this place.

"Dan, my entire combat experience was a hundred hours in Desert Storm, nearly all of it locked up in a command Bradley, one minor jolt when a shell landed a hundred yards away, and that was it. Heck, give it to Washington. He's the DI; he's the guy who was at Kha Sanh."

"He doesn't want it and he fully agrees with what I'm saying here now.

"He explained it to me the other day when we began to plan this unit and the question came up of command. I left it open, at first thinking he'd take it, but he immediately said you should be the one."

"What did he say?"

"He laughed. Said he knew he was the best DI in the United States Marine Corps, but it takes more than that to lead an army. He wants someone with an advanced education, someone who will remain cool under stress, someone who's studied war and knows the history of it and can thus apply it in a crisis. Of course that means you, John. I think if it ever comes to a major fight it should be Washington on the firing line, but he wants someone like you behind him."

"I still think he should lead."

"He's von Steuben out there, John, even though his name is Washington, and he knows that. It's your job and Charlie agreed that if a crisis comes where a militia is needed, you lead it."

"Thanks, as if I wanted it."

"John, if you really did want it, I don't think your name would have been in the hat. We wanted someone who would see it as a service and, above all else, even while defending this community would be thinking ahead to afterwards.

"John, we dream of America. We want America to come to us. But I think it never will. The America we knew died when those warheads burst. If so, then it is up to us to not wait, but instead to rebuild America as we want it to be."

CHAPTER EIGHT

DAY 35

There was an air of celebration in the crowd that gathered about the town hall as John pulled into what was now his usual slot in front of the fire station.

The fire trucks, which had been rolled out over a month ago to make room for the emergency supplies stockpiled inside, were still in place, still motionless, no longer sparkling, somewhat dusty. Horses were tethered to the bumper of one of them.

The crowd stood around expectantly and many, seeing him approach, stepped back slightly, nodding greetings respectfully.

All were showing signs of the effects after thirty-five days. Faces were thinner, pinched on some. Clothing in general was dirty, sweat stained; hair, greasy, many of the men beginning to sport beards. And all of them stank. He wondered if this was indeed how people really smelled a hundred years ago, the scent of a crowd of unwashed bodies, or was it that thirty-six days ago people were used to sterility, terrified if their deodorant failed and they "offended," nearly all taking a shower at least once a day, many twice a day in the summer?

Was this now normal? Was this how Washington, Jefferson, and Lincoln smelled, so normal that it just was no longer really noticed?

Tom appeared at the door of the police wing of the building, grinning. "It works!"

A ragged cheer went up from the crowd, which then gradually began to drift apart, though many pressed up to the doorway and windows to look into the conference room as if what was inside was some sort of miracle.

John edged his way through and into the building.

"We'll start in a few minutes, but for right now, let's enjoy this," Tom replied.

John stepped into the conference room and had to smile at the sight of the old crank phone attached to the wall.

"Yes, yes, I hear you!" Charlie shouted, earphone in one hand, bending over slightly to shout into the speaker.

"Yes, I understand. It works; now keep setting up the wire. Yes, over and out here. Good-bye."

He hung up and turned to face the gathering.

"We got a phone system."

There was a round of applause picked up by those gathered outside.

John looked at the contraption, salvaged from an antique store, as he suggested, a comparable phone now set up in the police station in Swannanoa. It had taken the work of a dozen linemen, older employees of the phone company, several of them refugees allowed in through the gap.

Fiber-optics, modern wiring systems, were out. They had to find old-fashioned copper wire, a hard task, but bits and pieces were salvaged from a variety of sources, a golden find an old abandoned telephone or telegraph line of several miles along the railroad tracks. The wire had to be carefully spliced together, then strung on glass or ceramic insulators, most made out of soda bottles.

It was the first line, the goal now to run it into Asheville. Remarkably, an old-style switchboard had been found in the basement of the granddaughter of a phone operator from the twenties. When the system had been junked back in the fifties, apparently the old lady had her board toted home as a keepsake. A couple of the elderly phone company workers were now trying to remember how to rig it up, an actual switchboard that could handle dozens of phones.

There were other accomplishments. One of the junkyards in Swannanoa had successfully gotten a tractor-trailer diesel from the early sixties running. That had triggered intense debate as to who would get it, the fire department finally winning out, and on a flatbed were now attached hoses, ladders, and gear. They had even figured out how to use the engine as a power takeoff to run a water pump.

Fire had become a frightful hazard. Those who still had food were cooking with wood, and home fires and brush fires were commonplace. The community still had water pressure for those places lower than 2500-foot altitude, the height of the face of the reservoir dam. But above that, it was hauling buckets, and the potential of house fires turning into out-of-control forest fires kept everyone worried.

Between the two communities there were now over a hundred vehicles running and more coming online every day. Several mechanics had learned to bypass and yank out the electronics, especially on cars that only had minimal dependence on them, slap on some old replacements, and get the engines to turn over again.

A moped shop had become highly successful at getting their relatively simple machines running again, along with older motorcycles.

There were so many vehicles running now that a salvaged generator had been hooked up at Smiley's and the gas from Hamid's belowground tanks was flowing again.

Smiley's had become something of the old "general store." There was precious little to sell, other than his legendary horde of cigarettes, which were now doled out one at a time in exchange for a dead squirrel, old silver coins, or whatever might capture Hamid's fancy.

John almost regretted his sense of fair play that first day. He should have purchased a dozen cartons. He was down to five packs and rationing himself to no more than five cigarettes a day now.

"OK, everybody, time for the meeting, so let's clear the room," Charlie announced.

Those who had gathered to gaze at the phone reluctantly left the room. Charlie closed the windows and dropped the venetian blinds.

It was the usual group. Charlie, Bob, Kate, Doc Kellor, and John. Carl and Mike from Swannanoa came down from their end if there was something directly related to them at the moment but today were caught up with a forest fire up along Haw Creek that was threatening to turn into a real inferno.

A ritual John had insisted on was now enacted, the group turning to face an American flag in the corner of the room and recite the Pledge of

Allegiance, and then Kate led them in a brief prayer before Charlie announced the meeting was now in order.

"I hate to jump the gun on the agenda, but I've got something important," John said.

"What?"

"Outside news."

"Well, for God's sake, man, why didn't you say something when you came in?" Charlie asked.

"Everyone was excited about the phone, and well, frankly, some of it isn't all that good."

"Go on; tell us," Kate said.

"There's a station on the radio now. Voice of America."

"Wow. When?" Kate cried.

"I was driving last night, fiddling with the dial on the car, and it came in clear as day."

"The radio?" Charlie shouted. "Tell us about it. My God, we got radio again!"

"The old radio in the Edsel. I don't know, I was just fooling with the dial and suddenly it came in loud and clear, frequency at the old Civil Defense band. We sat there listening to it for a half hour or so, then atmospheric skip and it faded."

"We?" Kate asked.

He didn't reply. Makala had come down to join them for a meal and check on Jennifer and he was just driving her back to the conference center, which was now the nursing home and isolation ward for incoming refugees who were allowed to stay.

"So what the hell is going on?" Tom asked.

"They're broadcasting off the aircraft carrier *Abraham Lincoln,* part of our fleet stationed in the Persian Gulf when things started. They beelined it back here. They said the carrier was somewhere off the coast of the United States and was now the command post for relief and recovery operations.

"They said that help is on the way. Kept repeating that every five minutes. Said the nation is still under martial law."

"No news there," Kate said.

"What kind of help?" Tom asked.

"Didn't say, other than relief supplies are coming from Britain, Australia, and India and China."

"India and China?" Charlie asked.

"Yes, struck me as strange. That earlier report about a weapon detonated over the western Pacific."

"Who we fighting?" Tom asked.

"Didn't say. Just that allied forces are fighting, in Iran, Iraq, Korea. Good news is that Charleston, Wilmington, and Norfolk have been declared emergency restructuring centers."

"What the hell does that mean?" Kellor asked.

"I guess it means if we have some kind of functional assets overseas that didn't get hit, ships that can provide electrical power, aircraft, trained personnel, they'd be coming back here and those are three local places."

"Charleston is the nearest, two hundred and fifty miles away," Charlie sighed. "That won't help us a damn bit."

"I know," John said.

"What about the war?" Tom asked.

"Anything beyond the three cities?" Kate interjected.

"Nothing else. Oh yeah, the president is the former secretary of state. She's in charge."

No one spoke at that news.

"Apparently the president died aboard Air Force One; they got him up in the air and the plane wasn't hardened sufficiently to absorb the pulse. They didn't say what happened to the vice president or Speaker of the House."

"Nothing really that affects us directly," Charlie said, and no one replied. Strange, the death of a president and now we say it doesn't affect us, John thought.

"That was it. Then they played music."

"What?" Charlie cried. "Music?"

"Patriotic stuff. 'God Bless America,' it faded out with the 'Battle Hymn of the Republic.'"

John looked around the room.

"At least we know they're out there."

"The legendary 'they,'" Kellor replied coldly. "Doesn't help us here and now with what I've got to talk about."

"Go on," Charlie said. "In fact, what you just told us, John, depresses the hell out of me. The thought that they're so close. Hell, a month and a half ago a C-130 loaded with medical supplies could have flown here in an hour from Charleston. Now it's like they're on the far side of the moon.

"Doc, why don't you go ahead."

"Only thirteen deaths yesterday," Doc said, and there was a murmur of approval, the lowest number since they had started to keep count. "Two were heart attacks; two, though, were our dialysis patients. I think that is the last of them. Everyone in our communities who was on dialysis is now dead."

No one spoke.

"We also lost one of our diabetics."

Again no one spoke, but John felt eyes turning towards him. Of course they knew. He stared straight ahead, saying nothing.

"And we had a birth."

"Who?" Kate asked.

"Mary Turnbill. A healthy six-pound baby girl. Named Grace America Turnbill."

"Damn, that's good," Tom said out loud.

"Eight births so far, and only one lost child and mother. Not much of a statistical base yet, but still it's better than average compared to a hundred and fifty years ago."

"Good work, Doc," Charlie said.

"Well, I better go from that to the downside of things. In one sense we are in what I would call the grace period right now, the calm between storms. Our initial die-off in the first days, those needing major medical intervention, the first round of food poisoning, those woefully out of shape, as you know, approximately twelve hundred deaths out of ten thousand, five hundred total here in Black Mountain and Swannanoa. We still don't have an exact figure on those who got in the first few days, but it had to be well over a thousand, so let's put our total number at twelve thousand, now back down to roughly ten thousand or so."

"That doesn't count the casualties from the fighting at the gap, and refugees dying outside the barrier," Tom interjected.

"No, I'm only counting those who died of natural causes at the moment. What I'm saying is that those who would die quickly have pretty well died off. Across the next fifteen days or so the numbers should be fairly low as long as we keep the community stable and nothing exotic sneaks in on us, but then, I hate to say, it's going to start sliding up again and within thirty days be far worse than anything we've seen so far."

Kellor hesitated, looking at John for a moment. Kellor knew his secret regarding the stash of insulin.

"Nearly all our type one diabetics will die this month. The pharmacies, in general, allocated one bottle of a thousand units per person. That supply is now running out for them. So we can expect all of them, approximately a hundred and twenty in our communities, to start dying."

No one spoke.

"Other deaths in the coming month: severe asthmatics running short on their rescue inhalators, severe heart arrhythmia patients running out of beta-blockers, so I expect we are in the middle of the lull before the next wave hits.

"There is another issue as well, though, that I don't think many of us thought of, but Tom, you better start gearing up for it and we might have to start thinking about taking over a building as another isolation ward."

"What for?" Kate asked.

"Severe psychosis."

"You mean insanity?" Tom asked. "Hell, we're already seeing enough crazies coming in at the gap. And the suicides as well over the last month. I think we're all half-crazy now."

"Well, it's going to get a lot worse within a matter of days," Kellor said.

"Why within days?" Tom interjected.

"About a quarter of the population was on antidepressants or antianxiety agents. Prozac, Xanax, Lexapro, even just plain old lithium. Most of those people rushed to the pharmacies and stocked up, but even then, on average a person got at best a thirty-day supply.

"They're running out now. Withdrawal for some won't be too bad; for others symptoms will be quite severe, including hallucinations. Compound that with the stress we are under already. As an old-time doc I'll be the first to tell you quite a few on these meds were just mildly neurotic, living in a very pampered society where it was almost obligatory to have some sort of disorder. But seriously, roughly five percent of the population do have severe disorders, and one to two percent dangerous disorders that include severe paranoia and potential for highly aggressive behavior."

"In other words, expect a lot of insanity," Tom said.

"You'll be the one dealing with it," Kellor replied, "and I think your people better be briefed on it. Not too long ago in our past families suffered with it, keeping their crazy uncle Louie restrained or locked away, or shipped them to state hospitals which were indeed snake pits. Where do you think the word 'bedlam' came from? It was the hospital for the insane in eighteenth-century England and, if you saw the old prints, a true hell-hole.

"We haven't dealt with this ever since all the modern meds started coming out in the sixties and seventies. That and the changing of laws that pretty well stopped involuntary commitment except in extreme cases emptied the hospitals.

"If it was back fifty years ago, at least a hundred of our fellow citizens would be already under some form of restraint, either at home or in a state institution. Now they are with us and the medications that kept them somewhat stable are gone. Hundreds more are in varying degrees of instability as well. What I'm trying to get across is that we'll have upwards of a thousand people in our community who are in varying degrees of psychological unbalance, not related at all to the crisis but instead to their forced withdraw from medications. And at least fifty to a hundred will be extremely dangerous, to themselves or to others. Severe paranoids, schizophrenics, delusional personalities, several living here with criminal pasts but who were declared insane, treated, then released back into the community. I think, Charlie, you are going to have to authorize me to be able to declare people to be mentally unstable and to then incarcerate them by force. We'll need then to find people to tend to them, and also decide how we deal with food distribution to them."

Charlie sighed, rubbing his beard, and then nodded.

"I authorize you to have the authority to declare a person to be mentally deranged and to have them incarcerated, if need be against their will or that of their family. Tom, you will be responsible for arrest. I'll post that notice later today."

Kellor nodded.

"I think in at least thirty or forty cases we should move preemptively, meaning now, even if they still have some meds left. As a doctor, I know which of my patients were truly over the edge long before this happened. Patients who had repeated hospitalizations and incidents. Tom, you would know some of them, too, from incidents that led to their going to a psychiatric unit or jail. I think we should grab those people now before it gets bad."

"One thing," John said quietly.

"Go on."

"Keep in the back of our minds how that power was also used to lock up those that neighbors just didn't like, political dissenters, and, in a darker time, the belief that insanity was satanic and the resulting witch hunts. We got a couple small churches in this community that are already preaching that this disaster is God's punishment to a sinful nation, and/or that it is now the end-time. I never thought about what Doc here was saying in regards to mass psychosis, but we might see some of these deranged people being seen either as prophets if they have a good gift for gab even though they're crazy or, on the other side, demonically possessed."

"Damn, this is starting to sound medieval," Kate sighed.

"We are medieval, Kate," John shot back. "If we got people going off the deep end, and definitely if there is prior record of severe mental disorder, yes indeed, we'll have to lock them up, for everyone's protection. All we need is a bunch of people following some mad prophet around or a mob stoning a witch and it could come to that, but it's a fine line and we can't go overboard on it. We all know the news leaking in from Knoxville about that crazy cult; we don't want even the beginnings of it here."

John looked over at Kellor, who nodded in agreement.

"And one other item related to this," Kellor said. "Alcohol. The rush on the ABC store pretty well cleaned it out on Day One and the looting afterwards finished it."

John found himself thinking about single-malt scotch, the few ounces left in his bottle behind the desk.

"So the drunks, the hard-core alcoholics, are out by now, and that can get tough. My concern: some will try anything for a drink, trying to distill it."

"Every ear of corn goes to food," Charlie snapped. "We catch anyone trying to steal corn to turn into booze and there will be hell to pay."

"Not that, Charlie. I mean trying to distill out of *any* potential source, right down to people thinking they can get something out of hydraulic fluid. I've already got one idiot blinded because of wood alcohol. That's going to go up as well."

"A dry community," Kate chuckled softly. "We were for a long time after the Depression. Guess we are again."

"Now down to the harder issue," Kellor continued. "Food."

There were sighs around the table.

"With the cutting of rations yet again, we are, at best, doling out little more than twelve hundred calories a day per person. Our reserve stockpiles are down to not much more than ten days. I am going to have to suggest a further cut, by a third or so, to extend that out to fifteen days."

"What I was thinking as well," Charlie replied.

"What about the food on the hoof, cattle, pigs, horses?"

"We've gone through a third of that stock, and we must stretch that reserve out as long as possible."

"For how long?" Kate asked.

"The radio, though," Tom said. "If things are coming back online down on the coast, hell, help might be up here in another month or two. All they need is one diesel-electric locomotive and it can haul ten thousand tons of food and supplies."

"Easier said than done," John announced. "When we got hit, every train on every track in the country stalled. It's not like a highway, where you just move around it. Once they get some locomotives working, every stalled train on every line will have to be pushed somewhere to clear the line. All switches will have to be set manually.

"I've been hoping the folks up at Smoky Mountain Railroad might actually get something running with their steam locomotive, their track actually connects down into Asheville, but there hasn't been a word about it.

"Whatever help is coming in now, it will be from the coast. We are now like America of two hundred years ago. Get a day's walk in from the coast or a major river and you are in wilderness. So don't plan anything here with the hope that just maybe the legendary 'they' will show up."

"Maybe isn't definite," Charlie replied. "I agree with John on this one. Think of it, Tom; let's say the navy did steam into Charleston. There's a million people there without food. Anything beyond spitting distance of the sea I'm not optimistic for right now. Doc, tell us what you are thinking."

"The rations are running short," Kellor said. "Compounded by the fact that more and more of our locals are applying for ration cards as well, now that their own food stocks have run out. So even as we run out, there are more mouths to feed."

John had yet to apply for ration cards for his family. He had always been proficient with a rifle, and using the .22 he had nailed several possums, a number of squirrels for the dogs, and remarkably, just the day before, a tom turkey that had been such a feast that he had invited the Robinson family up to join them, Lee Robinson actually producing a quart bottle of beer and canned corn for the occasion. Makala had been there as well with a chocolate bar she had kept stashed away. Even the dogs had been given some scraps.

The possums, well, they reminded John of the old television series where Granny was always talking about possum pie. Jen was horrified when he had brought the first one in, she tried roasting it in the stove out on the deck, a disaster, but they were learning, even though the darn things were greasy as hell.

"You realize that if we cut back to around nine hundred calories a day we are at nearly the same level as the siege of Leningrad. Resistance is already down; the average person has lost at least fifteen pounds or more. For many that's actually damn good, but now we start getting into the body eating itself, and not just the reserve fat most Americans carry around.

"Strength will be impacted significantly and I want to talk more about that in a few minutes. For the general population on rations the impact is going to start kicking in within the next couple of weeks. Immunological systems in everybody are weakening, meaning if that flu down in Old Fort gets up here, it will be like the 1918 epidemic that killed nearly two million in America. I'd estimate ten percent of us dying in a matter of days if flu breaks out. I think, Charlie, that we will have to shut down our free passage through the gap or change the procedure. Lord knows how many flu carriers are walking along our interstate every day heading west."

Charlie sighed and looked over at John and Tom.

"We do that," Tom said, "there'll be more riots. Getting those people moving further west has prevented any more problems since the big riot of two weeks back."

"I agree with Tom," John said. "Block the barrier, we'll have a buildup of a couple of thousand again within days, even more desperate than the first wave, and it will be a bloody fight. Let them through, but drill our people on extra caution."

"They're wearing the hazmat suits already," Charlie said.

"Yeah, and most likely taking them off with their bare hands, not washing down properly."

He sighed.

"It'll most likely jump no matter what we do. People are not just staying on the roads; they're crawling up through the woods."

"I'm getting reports of that," Tom said. "Strangers breaking into houses, then running back up into the woods when someone shows up. Most likely outsiders."

John looked at Kate, who said nothing. The word was ingrained now across the populace. Even those who had not been inside the town on the first day but came in before the barriers went up were now using it, almost as if to say, "I'm here now; I'm not one of *them*."

"Nutrition-wise, thank God we're well into June. Scurvy is not a concern; we got enough greens of one sort or another, though the soup made out of boiled grass and dandelions is a bit rough to swallow. The first vegetables are starting to come in as well."

Throughout May Charlie, taking a page from the memories of some of the older folks, had called for a Victory Garden campaign. Every last seed in town had been snapped up and once beautiful lawns, yet another luxury of a pampered society, had been spaded over for lettuce, squash, beans, anything that could be eaten.

"Still, we are on the real edge now of running out."

"Damn it, Doc," Kate snapped. "We still got forty head of cattle here, a couple of hundred hogs, the horses, and Swannanoa maybe even more."

"One cow a day for ten thousand?" Kellor asked. "At best two ounces of meat, less than a cheap hamburger at a fast-food joint without the bread. OK, two cows a day and a hog. Five ounces of meat, barely enough, and the cows in both communities are gone in not much more than days, every last one. Then the horses, maybe another ten to twelve days. Then the rest of the hogs. Seventy days max and we've eaten our way through the lot. Then what?"

"And that's at everyone getting about a thousand to twelve hundred calories a day. Then we are out of food, one hundred percent bankrupt."

He looked at Charlie.

"You got to plan until next spring, four times longer than what we've been talking about."

Charlie looked at John, who reluctantly nodded in agreement.

"Don't count on anything from the outside, perhaps never. To get to us from Charleston, they'll first have to reestablish control in Columbia, then up to Greenville, Spartanburg. There are millions of people down there, just a couple of hundred thousand up here . . . and besides . . . they'll think we're OK up here in the mountains. Everyone always thinks that up the mountains there'll be plenty of food."

"What about trying to send Don Barber down there with his plane?" Tom asked.

There were several nods of agreement.

"At least it'd let them know we are up here."

Charlie shook his head.

"That plane is valuable beyond measure for keeping an eye on things locally. Its range, though, fully gassed is less than two hundred miles.

"We could rig up some kind of strap-on tanks to take it one way into Charleston," Tom said.

"Why?" Charlie asked.

"To get help," Tom said. "For God's sake, at least he could come back with some medicine. Doc Kellor could give him a list. Antibiotics, anesthesia . . ."

He hesitated and drew in his breath.

"Maybe even some insulin."

John looked at him, not sure how to react, it was as if a taboo had been broken, to not speak of the threat to Jennifer. He could see the look in the police chief's eyes, they were filled with compassion.

John couldn't speak, a flash thought that maybe Tom was right. Surely whoever was down there would answer their appeal.

"I'm sorry, Tom," it was Charlie, speaking softly. "And John, God in heaven knows I'm sorry for you, too, but I have to say no."

John couldn't speak, feeling that his worst nightmare had just been laid bare before this group, that a decision he now desired was obviously for himself, and the logical one that he knew Charlie would drive for he would be forced to agree with, even though he wanted to stand up and scream for them to agree with Tom or he'd quit being on the council.

He was embarrassed to realize he was actually trembling, eyes filling up with tears.

"It is a hard question of logic," Charlie continued, unable to look directly at John. "We definitely do have Don Barber's plane, we need that to keep an eye on the territory around us, it is crucial for the survival of all of us. We all know the rumors about various gangs starting to form up, only Don Barber and his L-3 can give us advance warning if they are coming this way.

"Sure the Navy might be down there in Charleston, but John, you yourself said there's millions of people along the coast they are already tending to. And besides, I think Doc Kellor would agree with me, how much insulin do you think they carry on board Navy ships, most likely none at all, and what was down there has most likely already been used."

John lowered his head, he did not want anyone to see his tears.

"If I was in command down there," Charlie continued, his voice sad, remote, "I'd give Don Barber some platitudes, maybe a few bags of antibiotics at best and a promise that help was on the way. I will not risk our only plane for that.

"And besides, worst case scenario, they just might confiscate Don's plane and that would be the end of it.

"If they are starting to rebuild down there it will be a step at time," Charlie continued, "restringing wire into the adjoining town, establishing order, then moving farther in. And with each step it'll mean more to feed; get as far as Columbia and they'll add a million or more extra people to take care of, or down the coast to Savannah another million or two. No, they're not going to come up here with relief supplies based on an appeal of a few thousand of us up in the mountains arriving via an antique plane."

There was a long moment of silence until John finally nodded his head in agreement.

"Charlie, I got a hard proposition to make," Kellor said breaking the silence.

"Go on."

"So far we've been very egalitarian about the food. Everyone on the same rations, young children and expectant and nursing mothers the only exemptions for getting extra, something absolutely no one would object to. But you do have to consider that we might have to categorize."

"What?"

John rousing from his shock regarding trying to get insulin could see it coming and looked over at Charlie. Charlie just did not seem to be in form; quick decisions were coming slower now. Was it just simple exhaustion, or could it be something else?

"Higher rations for the police force, those doing hard labor, and the militia," Kellor said.

"I don't like this," Kate interjected. "The old line from *Animal Farm* that pigs are more equal than other animals."

"Kate, the level for rations has dropped below maintaining efficiency for doing anything much beyond getting out of bed and then just sitting all day. We got people up trying to contain that fire along Haw Creek; guys fighting forest fires used to get high-energy diets of upwards of four thousand or more calories a day. Same with soldiers. You can't expect people to do hard work on nine hundred calories a day. If we do, in three more weeks everyone will be in collapse, too weak to even start bringing in the harvest from the few farms with corn, let alone defend the gap, contain people wandering around insane . . ."

Kellor's voice died off and he just sat there numb.

"We have to do it," John said.

"John, I kind of thought you'd be on my side in this," Kate replied.

John shook his head.

"Precedents throughout history. Ancient and medieval cities under siege, soldiers always received more rations. Though it was more for psychological and morale impact during World War II, our rationing was always directed towards getting resources to the men on the front line. In every other country in that war, the rationing was very real and at times," he hesitated, "a form of triage.

"Doc mentioned Leningrad. There they had to make the hard assessment that there simply wasn't enough food for everyone to stay alive, so it came down to soldiers and then essential workers getting enough to keep going, another level down for expectant and new mothers, children, and . . ."

He stopped speaking and looked back at Kellor.

"We have just over ten thousand souls in our communities. About enough food still on hand to keep a thousand, maybe two thousand in top health until autumn, when we'll at least get some small amount of food in from the cornfields and orchards. We try and feed everyone at the same level, I doubt if many will survive, dying from both starvation and also being overrun by desperate people from the outside more hungry than us. Long before that, what semblance of order we have will totally break down as well."

"Sweet Jesus, are we talking about deliberately starving some of our people to death?" Kate cried. "This is America, for God's sake."

No one spoke for a moment. For John it was the word "America" that hit. The land of milk and honey, the land where obesity had been considered a major health issue, almost a national right, with food chains boasting about who had the biggest, fattest burger. He often wondered, even then, what reaction there would be if such ads had been sent to Liberia, Yemen, or Afghanistan, showing America's excessive waste.

"'Deliberately starving people to death' is putting it rather bluntly," Kellor replied defensively.

"Death is rather blunt," Kate shot back.

"It's the harsh reality," John said, his voice distant. "It is that simple. We have *x* amount of food and *y* amount of people. The formula collapses in the next couple of weeks. The *y* amount of people is going to have to be subdivided if any are to survive."

"We have to do it," Charlie said, his voice soft.

"Well, I'm not going along with it," Kate said.

"Remember, Kate, this is not a democracy at the moment. If you wish not to go along with it and stop drawing rations, that is fine with me."

"The rest of you here?" Kate shouted. "Now you do have *Animal Farm*; you have the commissars and the famines in Russia. Do you think people will stand for it?"

"Personally, I'm not going to draw extra rations," Charlie said.

"Charlie," Doc interjected, "you have to. I know your health; remember, I was your family doc. You have a touch of hypertension and acid reflux. You're slowing down even now; everyone in this room can see it."

"It's just exhaustion," Charlie replied sharply. "Let me get a good night's sleep undisturbed."

"Bullshit," Doc snapped. "You're doing the work of two men and eating the same as everyone else. You'll burn out; you *are* burning out."

"Well, it'd be one helluva note to announce we're going to starve a lot of people around here and I'm walking around fat and happy. Screw that."

John lowered his head.

"He's right," John whispered. "Though I disagree on one point. Not a word of this is to be discussed publicly."

"You do sound like a commissar now!" Kate shouted.

He glared at her.

"Think I like what I just said?" John replied sharply. "But Charlie, if you go outside and say that some are now going to get more rations it will be a riot within the hour. I'd suggest we quietly move some extra rations up to the college campus. What we're talking about primarily applies to them anyhow. Those getting extra food get it there and there only. But as for Charlie's personal example, that's his decision and, I'll have to say, the moral one."

Charlie nodded and slowly sat down.

"Moving food in secret? Secret eating while others starve?" Kate shook her head. "I never dreamed we'd come to this point so fast, and agree to it, here, right here in our town."

"The first that would get hit by the rioting are the outsiders," John said. "There's been a semblance of acceptance, some bonding, that would disintegrate, Kate, and I'm willing to bet would turn into murders and lynchings, a massive scream to throw everyone out who wasn't living here the day of the event. Then our two communities will start glaring at each other. Frankly, Swannanoa has more food per person than we do, a lot more with their extra cattle and hogs. We'll split and those here will start screaming about marching there to take their cattle.

"You hear that, Kate? It's like something out of ancient history, the Bible; we'll be raiding each other for cattle. Then it will be every man for himself and we'll all die as a result if someone from the outside, with some organization and strength, then comes rolling in. There's your choice, Kate. Go ahead. What should we do?"

She glared at him, unable to reply.

John looked over to Tom, who had remained silent throughout the debate, and Tom nodded in agreement.

"I know I couldn't keep order. I'd have to call in the college militia, and even there, most of those kids would be defined as outsiders as well, and the mob ready to turn on them. It would be a helluva mess, Kate. John's right, we have to do this, but we have to keep it quiet."

"So in other words, horde some food for a selected few, do it in secret so that by the time the rest of the people figure it out, they'll be too weak to act."

John stared at her.

"Yes."

"You bastards."

"Kate, it's been this way throughout history. America, though, hasn't faced it since," he paused, "maybe parts of the South in the Civil War. Even then that was just limited. We've never seen anything like this before, but in reality, it has to be done if any survive. We can't keep social order, defend ourselves, and at the same time give out some kind of equal amounts of food to everyone else. If we try that, everyone will die."

"I won't accept extra food."

"No one is forcing you to," John said softly.

"Kate, you cannot discuss this outside this room," Charlie said sharply.

She glared at him.

"Or what?"

"I'll have you arrested."

"Sieg heil, mein Führer," and she raised her hand in the fascist salute.

"Damn it, Kate," Charlie snapped, his voice almost breaking. "I don't want this any more than you, so don't ride me on it."

She lowered her head.

"It has to stay in this room," John said sharply.

"Are you getting an extra?" Kate asked.

"Hell, no. We're still getting by."

"All right, Charlie. You don't take extra rations, none of us here do, and I'll go along with it."

"Tom has to be on the list for extra rations," Kellor said.

"Like hell."

John looked at Tom. His rotund pre-war form had melted away quickly, belt drawn in now by several notches.

"All police, firefighters, the militia, those doing essential work," John said, "and grave diggers."

There was a long silence.

"And Doc, you, too," John said.

Doc nodded.

"I won't hide behind false heroics. I hate the thought, but I know my performance is degrading fast. I set a compound fracture yesterday, one of the Quincy boys, fell off a horse. I thought I was going to faint towards the end of it. If we don't have doctors and nurses in this town who can function, well, we're all dead anyhow then."

"How many will we lose?" Charlie asked.

"When?"

"You said the curve is going to start going up again. How many do we lose in two or three months?"

Doc looked around the room.

"One-third to one-half if we follow the plan just outlined."

"And if we don't?" Kate asked.

"We drag it out a little longer, Kate, by not much more than thirty days extra; then everyone will be dead by winter."

No one spoke.

"Malthus is finally being proven right," Charlie said. "Our population here is three, four times higher than the carrying capacity. It was all about infrastructure. Out in Southern California right now I bet hundreds of thousands of tons of vegetables are rotting. The Midwest will be up to their eyeballs in unpicked corn in another six weeks. But there is no way to get that from there to here."

Silence, and John knew all were dwelling on food, the standard thoughts of someone going into starving and malnutrition. He could picture the hundreds of thousands of head of cattle out in Texas and Oklahoma. For that matter, just two hundred miles east of here, the hog farms. They were contemptible, usually rammed into poorer communities, five to ten thousand hogs raised at a clip in sheds where they could barely move from birth until slaughter, the stench and pollution killing property value for miles around . . . and to have one of them here now would be greeted with people falling on their knees and thanking God.

But even then, John realized, it wouldn't work. The farms were dependent on hundreds of tons of feed being shipped in each week. If those farms had not already been looted, the waste going on was most likely beyond imagining. The animals starving to death, people who almost thought meat was grown inside a pink foam package now trying to chase a hog down, kill it, and dress it. No, they'd cut off what they could, others would join in like vultures, and half of it would then just rot in the sun. If the hogs escaped, they would be into the woods now, wild boar in short order and damn dangerous.

Charlie finally stirred.

"Anything else?"

Silence.

"Minor point, but it's starting to get dangerous. Dogs."

John looked over at him.

"A lot of dogs are starting to run loose now. They're starving and they're going wild. We had an incident up on Fifth Street last night; two children got cornered by a pack of dogs. Fortunately, the father had a shotgun and dropped several of them; the rest took off."

After the grimness of the previous conversation John knew he shouldn't be reacting so hard, but he suddenly felt a tightness in his throat. The two fools Zach and Ginger were indeed getting hungry, begging ferociously at every meal, and yet still the family would share a few scraps. Most of the squirrels John had dropped over the last week had been tossed to the dogs raw.

"I think we have to order the shooting of all dogs in the town," Charlie said.

"No, damn it, no," Tom snapped. "I'll burn in hell before I'd go home and in front of my kids take Rags outside and blow his brains out. No way. If they're running loose and proving to be a danger, sure, but not that."

"What did the father do with the bodies of the dogs he shot?" Kellor asked quietly.

"Jesus, I never thought of that," Charlie replied.

"How many dogs in this town?" Kellor asked. "At least a couple of thousand. That's enough meat for full rations for three or four days at least, half rations for a week and a half."

"You can go straight to hell, Doc!" Tom shouted, and John was surprised to see tears in Tom's eyes. For the first time since this crisis had started, from the initial panic, the executions, the fight at the gap, it was now Tom who was breaking into tears.

"We got Rags the week my youngest was born. He's been with us ten years, as much a part of the family as any person. He'd die to defend us, and frankly, I'd do the same for him. I'm not giving him up and that's final."

"Tom, what I was talking about earlier," Kellor said, "that's only the first starve-off. I didn't even have the heart to talk about the second starve-off. Those that survive into the fall, chances are by the end of the winter most will be dead anyhow. Do you think any dogs will still be alive by then? And if so, they'll be feral, reverting back to packs of wolves, killing people to survive."

"Help will be here long before then!" Tom shouted. "It's starting already; you heard what John said.

"Charlie, I don't care what the hell you order, I will not do it to Rags or any other dog that the owners are still taking care of."

Tom was red faced, in John's eyes almost like a boy in a sentimental movie about a dog or other beloved pet, the obligatory scene when the kid is about to lose the dog, but we all know that at the end of the film, except in *Old Yeller* and *The Yearling*, things will be OK. And as for those two films, John had seen both as a kid and refused to ever see them again.

He was in tears now thinking of Zach and Ginger. How would Jennifer react? Ginger was her buddy, the two inseparable. It was terrifying enough trying to avoid the fate looming for Jennifer, but to do that to her, to kill Ginger? No, John would refuse as well. And he knew, as well, that in his heart, even without Jennifer, he would reach the same conclusion.

"I'm siding with Tom," John said.

"John, we have to leave sentiment behind," Kellor said.

"It's more than that," John snapped back. "It's yet another step backwards in who we are."

"John, ten minutes ago you agreed to letting some people starve faster than others. What in hell do you mean about stepping backwards?"

"I know this is illogical. It's just that we're Americans. We and the Brits especially are alike in this. We see something more in our pets than just brute beasts. For old people alone, they're a final source of comfort and love. For children, the beloved buddy that understands even when adults don't . . ."

He was ashamed, he was starting to cry.

"I'd kill every dog in the town if I could save one life by it," Kellor snapped back.

"That will take something out of us forever, maybe a line I don't want to cross, would rather not live in . . . No."

"The line is there," Kellor replied. "It is there no matter what."

Charlie stirred.

"How about this then? Loose animals will be shot and given to the communal food supply. Owners must keep pets inside or leashed. If an owner decides to dispatch a pet on their own, they can keep it for their own food supply. Is that agreeable?"

Tom jumped on it and nodded.

"Fine then."

"And every day they'll lose weight, that could be turned into food," Kellor snapped, "and eat food that people will give to them, even as they're starving."

"That's their choice," Tom replied.

He seemed ashamed of his emotional display, wiped his face, and stood up.

"Anything else, Charlie?"

Charlie shook his head sadly.

"John, that broadcast we should monitor from now on. We'll pull an old car radio, get some batteries, and rig out an antenna."

"Good idea."

"Maybe they'll be coming soon," Charlie said hopefully.

"Sure, Charlie. Maybe they will."

John left the meeting and started for home. The radio was now set on the dial to the Voice of America channel, but it was only static, maybe a whisper of a voice for a second or two, then static again.

He thought of stopping in to see Hamid, perhaps try to trade something for a few cigarettes to round out his day, even though it was still only mid-morning. The meeting had worn him to the edge.

He opened the glove compartment; extra ammo for the Glock strapped to his side was in there, along with what he called his reserve, a cigarette. He lit it up, inhaling deeply as he pulled onto State Street and drove past the elementary school. The once beautiful front lawn was now ragged, beat down, torn out in places. Some kids were down in the playground, playing baseball. They already looked skinnier to him, reminding him of photos of German kids playing in the rubble after World War II.

The cook fire was going. Today it was horse; one of the older beasts, close to death, had been shot. A crowd was gathered round it, butchering it, legs sticking up, yet another memory of a World War II film, of German civilians in rubble-strewn Berlin, hacking at a dead animal. One of Tom's men standing by, shotgun cradled casually under his arm, was watching the proceedings. Everything, every ounce of fat, bone, innards, everything would go into the kettle. Some greens would be mixed in, and there were at least fifty or more people standing around listlessly, watching every move hungrily.

John passed the school, continued on, the interstate to his left. Makala's Beemer still resting where it had rolled to a stop thirty-five days ago. He was tempted to drive the extra mile up to the isolation hospital, stand outside, and call for her. If he stepped in, he was stuck there for at least three days. He missed her. He slowed, drove past the turnoff to his house, and continued on, but then on reaching the turn to the conference center he figured he'd better not. So he continued on, driving several hundred more yards to a bridge that spanned over the interstate just behind the gap. He got out of the car, nursing his cigarette for one more puff before he got down to the filter.

The sound of the car running caused some of his old students, standing guard on the bridge, to turn. At the sight of him they waved.

His old students, my kids, he always called them. Hell, Mary and I were the same age when we met and no one could have defined us as kids to ourselves and she most definitely was not a kid at twenty . . . He remembered so many insane nights with her when neither got a wink of sleep till dawn and then they went to classes. And yet now, the years stretching away, those standing guard were indeed kids in his eyes.

They were uniformed. Blue jogging trousers of the college, blue long-sleeve shirts, college baseball caps . . . and guns. Several were in the baggy white hazmat suits. One of the girls, hunting rifle poised, was talking across the double barrier of stalled cars to a band of refugees on the other side. She had sat in his 101 class only the semester before. Cute, yes, a bit sexy looking with her long blond hair, blue eyes, and tight blouses, but still just a kid to him now, his own daughter not much more than two years younger.

And now his former student stood with rifle poised, drilled to fire if anyone did indeed try to scramble over the cars and break through.

One of the doctors, helped by a nurse, both in biohazard suits, was walking along a line of refugees who had been admitted through the barrier, looking at old driver's licenses, interviewing, maybe finding the one or two who might be allowed to stay, their skills on the checklist John and Charlie had created. . . . Anyone who worked with steam, electricians, doctors, farmers, precision tool and die makers, oil and gas chemists, the list went on.

Someone was culled out of the line and stepped forward. He anxiously looked back and was then relieved when a woman and three children were allowed to follow him. Five more mouths, John thought. He hoped the trade in skills was a damn good one as they were led off via a path to where Makala worked.

Someone with a hand-pumped weed sprayer now walked down the line, spraying down each person in turn with a mixture cooked up by Kellor. At least it would take care of lice, fleas, but also was a psychological tool, to remind them that they were somehow different once past the line and would be kept apart.

The group set off, led and followed by two students in biohazard suits who were toting shotguns. Behind the cavalcade a Volkswagen Bug followed, "Black Mountain Militia" stenciled on the side. Inside were a student and one of Tom's policemen, any weapons confiscated from the line of refugees piled in the back to be returned once they reached the far side of the barrier at Exit 59.

"Hey, Colonel, sir!"

It was Washington Parker up by the barrier.

John waved.

Parker waved for him to come down and there seemed to be an urgency to his gesturing.

The refugees were now filing under the bridge and the sight was heartbreaking. They wore ragged, torn, filthy clothing, several pushing supermarket shopping carts with children piled inside.

John went to the edge of the bridge to slide down the embankment to the road.

"Good morning, Colonel, sir."

Startled, he saw one of his students lying in the high grass, dressed in hunting camo, face darkened green. It was Brett Huffman, one of his ballplayers, a darn nice kid, backwoods type from up in Madison County, baseball scholarship with a real interest in history and wanted to teach high school. A kid who was a natural leader and looked up to by his classmates. John noticed the black sergeant's stripes stenciled on his hunting jacket. He had a wad of tobacco tucked into his jaw.

"Brett, just what the hell—," John started to ask.

"Vinnie Bartelli is on the other side of the bridge, staked out like me. If there's any trouble at the barrier, or any of them folks down there try and bolt . . ."

He said nothing for a moment, just patted the 30/30 Savage with mounted scope.

"I had to shoot one yesterday, sir. Good shot, though, got him in the leg, thank God, didn't have to kill him."

John couldn't reply. There was a bit of tightness in Brett's voice but already the sort of casualness John had heard so often in debriefings after Desert Storm. Good young kids trained to be killers and trying to be hardened to it, though it was still a shock.

"I guess, though, with a 30/30 through the leg he's a goner anyhow."

"You did what you had to do," John offered reassuringly.

"Still, sir. Reminded me of my first deer. Same kind of feeling, maybe a bit worse."

"Take care of yourself, Brett."

"Yes, sir."

John slid down the embankment and out onto the road. He looked back. Brett was impossible to see. It registered, so many of the college kids from small towns, more than a few hunters, or Boy Scouts or just outdoor types, of course they'd learn, and darn quick. The refugees were moving along on the other side, a long strung-out column.

They moved slowly, a few listlessly looking up at John. They were like something out of another age, some so obvious caught ill prepared, a man in a three-piece business suit, scuffed worn dress shoes, bandage around his head. Looked like a lawyer or upper-level corporate type . . . with no skills to sell here for a bowl of watery soup. Parents side by side, exhausted, pushing a shopping cart, the wheels worn, squeaking, two children inside, both asleep, pale faced.

Some refugees were actually barefoot. Few had realized on that first day what a premium would soon be placed on shoes, good shoes for walking, a lot of walking. He cursed himself for not thinking of it as well and grabbing some extra pairs from the camping supply store the first day. Civil War campaigns had often hinged on which side had better shoes, which usually wore out in little more than a month of tough campaigning. Those hiking a hundred and fifty miles in wing tips or even just plain old canvas tennis shoes were soon down to nothing, and more than one walking by actually had a different shoe on each foot.

A woman who reminded him a bit of Makala on the first night, very sexy gray business jacket and skirt, stockings still on but absolutely shredded, heels knocked off her shoes to try to make them more walkable, was limping along.

She caught his eye, forced a smile, and brushed back her greasy, limp hair.

"Hi, my name's Carol," she said, and moved towards the median barrier, her hand extended. He could see the lost world in her. Sharp professional-looking woman, intelligent face, sexy and using it to advantage, the hand extended for a warm handshake to start the meeting . . . which she was used to having go her way.

"Ma'am, step back and away." It was one of his students, face concealed in the hazmat suit, with rifle leveled. "Keep on the white line of the road as you were told."

Carol stopped, looking back.

"I just wanted to say hi."

The student shouldered her rifle.

"Ma'am, please move back. I will shoot if you try to go over that barrier."

The other refugees in the line looked back. A few froze; others immediately scrambled to the far side of the road.

"The rest of you," the student shouted, "do not attempt to leave the road!"

Carol looked at John appealingly.

"What kind of place is this?" she said, and her voice started to choke.

"We're a town trying to stay alive," John said.

"Ma'am!"

John held up his hand towards the student.

"At ease there, lower your weapon. I'll handle this."

"Colonel, sir, don't let her get any closer to you. I don't want to see you under quarantine."

"Colonel?" Carol asked, still forcing the professional business smile as if just introduced. "You are the officer in charge then. I'm pleased to meet you."

He tried to smile.

"Former colonel, college professor now. And no, I am not in charge here."

"I saw some of your people separating that family off and leading them away. Word on the other side of your fence is that if people have specialized skills you're letting them stay."

John took that in. If this was indeed known on the other side, security would have to be tightened. People would think up any kind of skill or profession and lie their way through the interview.

"Are they being allowed to stay?"

"I don't know," John lied.

"They asked us what we did. Is that it?"

"Really, miss, I don't know."

"Look, I'm a public relations consultant with Reynolds Tobacco."

She looked at the student with the gun still aimed at her.

"Colonel, to be frank, your operation needs some upgrading, a better interface with the public. I can help you set up a plan for that in no time that can help you avoid a lot of problems in the future."

It was a delivery, a sales pitch, cool, professional, and listening to her broke his heart. She actually was used to winning that way and believed it would work now.

"I'm sorry, miss. I don't make that decision here. The doctor and the police do. I'm sorry."

And in that instant her professional business poise, a vestige of the old world, collapsed.

She took a step closer and now it was both hands out in a gesture of appeal.

"Please let me stay!"

He couldn't respond.

She took a step closer.

"Do you want to sleep with me?" Carol asked. "I'm serious. Let me stay. You'll like me."

She looked down at herself and her ragged suit.

"Once I get cleaned up, believe me, you'll like me," and she looked at him with head slightly turned now, eyes widening. "You have a tub at home? I'd love a bath and when you see me then . . . you'll really like me. You can even help me bathe; I know you'd like that."

"Carol, please don't," John said. "Don't do this to yourself. Please don't."

She broke down sobbing.

"Don't do this to myself?" she cried, her voice rising to near hysteria.

"Offer you a piece to stay alive? Three nights ago I was raped. Raped by four men who said they had some food hidden in a shack. I half-expected it but was so damn hungry I no longer cared. Do you hear that?"

"I'm sorry."

She sobbed.

"And they gave me a bowl of watery soup in the morning, one of them did, and I felt it was damn near worth the trade. Please, Colonel, I'll spend the night with you if you let me stay and just give me a little something to eat."

And then she just stepped forward, heading towards the median barrier.

"I'll shoot!" the student guard screamed.

John held his hands out appealingly, looking towards his student.

"Don't!"

The rifle went off, Carol screaming, ducking down, the other refugees flinging themselves to the pavement.

Either the guard had fired high or in her nervousness had missed. But the girl was already working the bolt, the ejected shell casing ringing loudly as it hit the pavement.

"Next one is to the head!" the student was screaming.

"Carol, don't move!"

He started to move towards the median barrier, the hell with the quarantine.

"Colonel, don't!"

It was Washington Parker, running up, Colt .45 drawn, but something now seemed to tell him to holster his pistol, the sight of it ready to trigger a panic.

He stepped in front of the student.

"Point that gun straight up please," he said calmly, and she obeyed.

Next he turned towards the refugees.

"A mistake, people, nothing more. Please keep moving. There's plenty of fresh water at Exit 64, you can rest a bit and wash up there."

He pointed to the family with the children in the shopping cart.

"I bet your little ones need a bath. It's just around the bend in the road. But you must stay in the center of the road."

They started to get to their feet and moved back towards the white stripe dividing the two lanes.

Washington approached Carol, but not too closely.

"Ma'am, please stand up. No one will hurt you if you please stand up and back away from the median barrier."

"Do as he says, Carol," John interjected.

Shaking, she stood up.

John looked at her, and it was as if she was a different person. That the final shreds of pride, of decency, within her had disintegrated. A woman who but six weeks back most likely had a corner office, a parking slot with her name on it, a liberal expense account, and a damn good stock option had just tried to sell her body for a place to rest for a night and a bowl of soup.

"Carol, are you all right?"

She said nothing, features almost blank, turned, and fell back into the line of refugees.

Something told him with grim certainty she would not live much longer, shattered to the point that a razor blade across the wrists would be a welcomed relief. He was tempted to call her back and he stepped over the median barrier and actually took a step towards her.

"Colonel, sir."

He looked back. It was Washington, shaking his head no.

Washington turned back on the student who had fired the shot.

"Was that a warning shot or were you aiming at her?" Washington said.

"I'm not sure," and her voice was near breaking.

"You were wrong on two counts," Washington snapped, and the girl was now at attention, trembling. "That woman had not yet tried to go over the barrier. Your orders are only to shoot if they go over the barrier or try to turn on you."

"She was getting close to Professor Mather—I mean the colonel, sir."

"I am not sir; I am Sergeant Parker. Remember your orders and abide by them. Now the second count. Was that a warning shot or not? Remember I told all of you I am the only one to give a warning shot. If you shoot, then do it to kill. A warning shot is a wasted bullet, and we've got precious few of them."

"I think I aimed at her."

Washington snatched the gun from the girl.

"Go back up to the barrier; you can help interview the refugees. I'm sending someone who has the guts to aim right to your place."

The girl, crestfallen, turned and walked away, her shoulders beginning to shake.

Parker shouted for one of the boys by the barrier to walk escort with refugees and John came up to his side.

"A bit hard perhaps?" Washington asked.

John shook his head.

"I've told my girls repeatedly, if you are going to shoot, shoot to kill. But that pathetic woman did not deserve to be shot at."

"I know," Washington sighed. "What did she do? Offer to sleep with you?"

"Yes."

"I get it twenty times a day, and it's not because I'm good-looking," Washington said, his attempt at a joke falling flat.

"Sick. I'm hearing more and more stories up here about rape, murder, stealing even of baby formula. It's getting desperate on the road. You were going to offer to let her stay, weren't you?"

"Yeah. You could see it. She's far over the edge. I think she'll be dead in a few more days."

The two looked towards Carol, who was at the back of the column, staggering along.

Washington sighed.

"Yeah, God save her. You're right. You can look at these people and tell who still just might pull through. Poor woman, she's not one of them. No place in this world for her now, and what she has left to sell is fading."

John lowered his head.

"Damn all this," he sighed.

"I'm now seeing hundreds like her every day," Washington said wearily. "Sir, we let one in beyond those that can help us all survive, we break down."

He couldn't reply. He thought of the piece of a candy bar in his car, a survival ration if he got stuck. He was half-tempted to go get it, but if he did, it might not be there for Jennifer when she needed it.

"Maybe she'll get lucky," Washington said. "Maybe some guy farther down the road will take her in."

"God save us if we are really at this point already."

"Sir. I saw it in Nam. Hell, nineteen-year-old GIs thought it was heaven. A piece for a couple of bucks? But you looked at those girls, and I tell you southern Asian girls are some of the most beautiful in the world, and it made you sick. Fifteen-year-old kids that should have been in school, out selling their tail to feed their parents and kid sisters and brothers.

"And now it's come to America. . . ."

Washington shook his head.

"Damn all war . . . ," he sighed.

"You wanted me down here for something?"

"Some bad rumors starting to come in this morning; I think Charlie needs to know. I'm going to head back into town shortly to tell him."

"What is it?"

"Refugees are talking about something called the Posse taking over the interstate. They're down in the Charlotte area. Some said they're moving up Interstate 77 towards Statesville. Have a lot of vehicles that run."

"The Posse? Hell, it sounds like the Wild West."

"No. It's worse. The Posse was a name for a pre-war gang with branches all around the country. Punks, gangbangers who would pop a bullet into someone's head as a joke before this even started, drug dealers, the scum of the earth long before we ever got hit and the ones most ruthless to survive now than our worst nightmares have become real."

John realized just how really isolated their small town was. Several years back the Asheville paper had run a couple of articles about gang activity starting to flare up, but the local police had put it down fast.

"The Posse. One poor woman we let through with the last bunch said she was held prisoner by them for several days and escaped. Don't even want to talk about what they did to her, but it was beyond sick. Everyone's talking about it on the other side of the barrier. Sort of like an urban legend running with the refugee bands on the road. Some say a thousand or more and well armed. They're moving like ancient barbarians out there."

"Damn," John sighed, and yet again movie images, the Road Warrior films and all the cheap imitations of the genre back in the 1980s and early 1990s.

"I think we better start getting more vigilant. Just a gut feeling if this is real, they'll finally head our way. They'll figure Asheville, up in the mountains, must be loaded with food, and may be a good place for them to take over and hole up. They'll follow the trail of refugees and wind up here," Washington said.

"I heard a radio broadcast," John said.

"You mean Voice of America?" Washington replied.

"How did you know?"

"I was sitting up here last night, keeping an eye on things. The radio in that beautiful Mustang still works. Damn, I just turned it on. Sitting in an old Mustang, it was almost flashback time. Half-expected to hear Wolfman Jack or Cousin Brucie."

John chuckled.

"Yeah."

"And loud and clear had the signal for about an hour or so. Just wish they'd knock off the patriotic stuff, play some old R & B or rock. Yeah, I heard it."

"What do you think?"

"It's propaganda for morale, nothing more. Maybe the news about the coastal towns is on the mark, but for the rest of us, today, next week, it's bullshit. We got to look out for ourselves. I'm passing word at the barrier for people to turn around, to start heading for the coast. I know that's insane, none have the strength to make it now, but maybe it will be a counterrumor that will work back down the line."

John nodded.

"Downside, though," John said. "If the rumor hits that Posse crowd, that will move them up our way even faster. Under martial law every one of those bastards will be shot; the last thing they want now is any authority anywhere. We better work out a good tactical plan to defend this place against a serious attack right now and stop thinking about mob control or a few desperados trying to sneak in. If they have any ex-military types at all with them, they'll do a probe first, then hit us hard. We got to keep an eye on our back doors, the railroad tunnel and the old back roads down to Old Fort. We're no longer dealing with refugees; we'll be facing an army as ruthless as anything in history."

Washington nodded in agreement.

"I think I'll go home," John said.

The two shook hands and John went back up the slope by the bridge. He nodded to Brett concealed in the grass.

"Fran got a bit jumpy there. Glad she didn't shoot that woman."

"Same here," though John wondered if a bullet in her head might have been an act of mercy.

He got in the Edsel and headed for home.

As he pulled into the drive, the two fools Ginger and Zach came off the deck to greet him. He knelt down to pet both and found himself hugging them.

"Daddy!"

It was Jennifer, Pat with her.

"Everything OK?"

"Sure, Daddy."

He looked at Jennifer closely. She had lost a few pounds. At every meal Jen had been pushing as much food into her as possible, meat and vegetables, which right now were still boiled dandelions. He looked up at the orchard. If only the trees were peach trees; in another several weeks they could start to gather the peaches. The apples were growing, but far too slow, it seemed.

He had never had any real interest in the eight trees, other than their beauty in the spring. The apples were rather sour in the fall, and they usually just left the fruit there to drop, delighted when the apples lured in bears to feed on them.

"She had to eat a little chocolate earlier," Pat said. "Blood sugar went down."

"Snitch," Jennifer snapped.

"I promised your dad I'd keep an eye on you."

"I can take care of myself."

He hugged both of them, the two arguing as he went into the house.

Jen was half-asleep, book laid across her chest, an old book on the Civil War.

"Where's Elizabeth?"

"Oh, she and Ben went out for a walk," Jen said, and sat up, rubbing her eyes.

"They're out there walking a lot these days," John said.

"Well, Son-in-law, you better sit down."

"Why?"

"I think you need to talk to the two of them."

"About what?"

"Sex, getting pregnant."

"Oh, damn, Jen, not now, not today, I don't even want to think about it in relationship to her."

"Few fathers do. But frankly, my son-in-law, I think your sixteen-year-old daughter is now, how shall we say, a woman."

"Jesus, don't even talk to me about this now."

"Tyler and I had you and Mary figured out rather quickly."

He blushed. Jen had never said that before. And he looked over at her.

"Almost to the day, I bet. At least I did. Tyler, like any dad, went totally blind to reality, and John, I see it in your daughter now."

"Jen, not now," he sighed. "There's so damn much else going on."

Jen nodded slowly.

"And you don't want to face this issue. OK, but you better face up to it, John. Those two are scared, don't see much of a future ahead, the old restraints fall away. I'm old enough to remember the Second World War; it was the same then. Eighteen-year-old kids who knew each other just a couple days or weeks would figure 'what the hell' and either marry on the spot or have to get married within a few months. Our 'Greatest Generation' stuff tends to make us forget just how young and scared they were back then. So face up to the reality, dear son-in-law. You're the history professor; you know what happens inside kids when there's a war on."

Too much was happening today. He stood up, peeked into Jennifer's room. She and Pat were playing a game with Jennifer's Pokemon cards.

Her skin color looked off, a bit yellowish, pale.

Dear God, but one planeload of supplies into Asheville, but one, and my worst worry is gone.

"Would you talk to her?" he asked, looking back at Jen.

"Coward, and yes, I already have. But I think you as a dad better talk to both of them as well."

"OK, later," he said a bit too quickly.

Looking at Zach and Ginger, John went to the gun cabinet. He pulled out the 20-gauge and headed out the door, the two dogs slowly trotting along behind him, knowing that today there just might be some food if their master and provider got lucky.

CHAPTER NINE

DAY 63

He awoke to the dogs barking and instantly knew . . . someone was in the house.

They had drilled the plan after the murder of the Connors last week, their home at the top of the road, all four of them, parents, two kids, the house then ransacked from one end to the other for whatever scraps of food they might have.

He didn't hesitate, shotgun up as he stepped out of the office crouching low.

The two dogs were barking madly, snarling, and then he heard the crack of a gun and a high-pitched, yelping scream.

He stepped into the living room. The back door into the kitchen was wide open. Two men, at least it looked like two men.

So this was the moment and he did it without hesitation.

The first blast nearly decapitated the man by the door. The second turned; one shot fired wild and the second blast caught that one in the guts, flinging him back against the kitchen counter.

The girls had been drilled; if there was an intruder they were supposed to get on the floor behind the bed. The water bed where they now slept together was an excellent barrier. . . .

After several seconds Elizabeth started screaming "Daddy!"

"Stay put!"

Crouched down low, he came around the turn into the kitchen. The one man was definitely dead; even in the dark moonlight John could see that, the other whimpering, kicking spasmodically. By his side was Zach, crying pitifully, Ginger, with hackles raised, snarling at the wounded man.

There could be someone outside, John realized, but first he crawled over to the wounded man, grabbed his pistol, which was on the floor, a .22 revolver from the feel of it, and stuck it into his belt. The other man didn't have a gun, just a machete, and John took that with his free hand.

He headed back to the wide-open door, was about to step out, then thought twice, doubling back through the house, coming in low to first Jennifer's room and then Elizabeth's to make sure there wasn't a third intruder.

Past his old bedroom he looked in for a second.

"I'm all right. Now don't move!" he hissed. "Elizabeth, you have your gun."

"Yes, Daddy," and her voice was trembling.

"If I come back to this room, I'll call out first. If anyone else comes through, you shoot and don't hesitate."

"Yes, Daddy."

Back out through his office and then the front door, which he slipped open, circling back around the house.

No one else. He slipped through the rear door into the kitchen and touched the basement door; it was still locked. Then once more, down low, sweeping Jennifer's and Elizabeth's rooms yet again, nervously popping the closet doors open, both rooms still empty.

He went back into the kitchen.

"Jen, light a candle and get out here."

A minute later the flickering light illuminated the kitchen. Jen recoiled at the sight of the first man, face gone. The second was crying louder now, curled up. And then there was Zach.

John went over to his old buddy, his friend of so many years, who had saved their lives with his warning. He was shot in the top of the back, just behind the shoulder blades.

"Oh, God, Zach," John sighed. And like so many dogs, so desperately hurt, Zach licked John's hand as if by doing so he'd feel better.

John looked over at Jen, wide-eyed.

"You got to help me." It was the wounded man. "Please help me."

John actually felt stunned with how quickly he reacted. The Glock he kept strapped to his side even when he slept was out, round already chambered.

"John?" It was Jen.

He squeezed the trigger, the discharge of the 9mm round an explosion that set Elizabeth and Jennifer to screaming again.

"It's all right!" John shouted. "It's all right, girls, but stay put."

John looked at Jen, who stood stock-still, horrified.

"I'd of shot him in town if he lived that long."

John had executed five in the last week. Two of them locals, who had stolen a pig, killed it, and were gorging themselves up in a mountain hollow when finally tracked down, the two pathetic fools never fully realizing that hungry men could now smell meat cooking from half a mile away. The other three caught raiding a house, just like the two on the floor now.

"Jen, you'll have to help me drag them outside. I don't want the girls to see this mess."

Zach's whimpers made John turn around. Ginger was lying by Zach's side, licking her old friend.

John filled up. The execution-style killing had bothered him not in the least. Washington Parker was right. After the first one, it starts to get easier, and in this case, the men invading his home, threatening his girls, it didn't bother John in the slightest.

It was Zach, though. Zach and Ginger were down to skin and bones, ribs showing through their once sleek coats. Regardless of the ban on letting dogs run wild, John had let them out to forage since their old stomping grounds had been up in the woods that became Pisgah National Forest not a hundred yards away. Though he worried that others out hunting would bag them, so far they had been lucky.

He knelt down by Zach's side. Zach lifted his head and again licked John.

"Thank you, old friend," John sighed. "Thank you for everything."

"Do you want me to do it?" Jen whispered.

Startled, he looked up at her.

"No, he was our dog, Mary's and mine."

He pulled out the .22 taken from the dead man, cocked it, and put it behind Zach's ear. Ginger stood up, sensing something, whimpering loudly now . . . and John couldn't do it, dissolving into tears.

"I'll take care of him," Jen whispered. "You go outside, take Ginger with you. You don't want her to see it either. Now go on."

Jen left the room and was back seconds later with the last pack of cigarettes and the bottle of scotch that held a final precious ounce.

"Girls, we're safe, but you are to stay in your room, on the floor!" Jen shouted.

John looked at Zach and felt at that moment like a coward, completely unmanned. He knelt down and kissed Zach on the forehead. He was bloody, panting hard. He stood back up and then went outside, dragging Ginger by the collar, and let her loose. He lit the cigarette and uncorked the bottle.

"There, there, Zach," he could hear Jen in the kitchen. "Tell Tyler I love him. You remember our dog Lady. Its time to play with her now. . . ."

The muffled crack of the pistol had John leaning over the deck railing, crying, Ginger whimpering and nuzzling against his legs.

There was such a surreal sense of disconnect. I just killed two men, executing one without a second's hesitation. But this? Sobbing over a dog?

Jen came out the door a moment later bearing Zach, wrapped in a blanket.

"He's so light," she said softly. "He's better off now."

"I'll bury him once it gets light," John said.

"No, John."

"What?"

And then he realized. No, not Zach, no, he couldn't.

"I'd vomit. The girls, too. We can't."

"Take him down to the Robinsons. It won't be the same for them. Besides, poor Pattie is starving to death."

"They're on rations. Any food hoarding by getting something additional they lose their cards. According to the law we can eat him, but they can't. I'm supposed to turn him in to the communal food supply."

"Damn it, John. You are so cold-blooded logical in some ways and an idiot in other ways. Take him down to the Robinsons now. They can trade us something for him later."

John finally nodded.

She handed Zach's body to him.

"I'll get Lee to help with the bodies. You keep the girls out of the living room and kitchen."

"You'll tell them?" John asked.

She nodded.

John slowly walked over to the car.

"Don't move another goddamn inch." a voice hissed in the darkness.

He froze, cursing himself as an idiot. There had been a third man, maybe a fourth or fifth. John prepared to drop Zach, shout a warning before they got him, give Jen and Elizabeth time to be ready.

"John, that you?"

And now he recognized the voice; it was Lee Robinson.

"Jesus, Lee, yeah, it's me."

"I heard shots, came up to help."

"Thanks, Lee."

He stepped out of the shadows and drew closer.

"John, what are you carrying? Oh Jesus, not one of the dogs."

"Zach. If he and Ginger hadn't of warned us, they'd of had us, two of them. I killed both. Zach got shot by one of the bastards."

"I just heard a shot a minute ago."

"I couldn't do it," John admitted, and he found himself clutching Zach tighter. "What a piece of shit. Jen had to do it."

"It's OK, John; it's OK," and Lee's arm was around John's shoulder.

Southerners, he thought. Southerners and their dogs, they understand. He could feel Lee shaking a bit; he had been partial to Zach as well, their old dog Max a buddy. Max had disappeared a week ago, most likely poached while wandering in the woods, and Lee was absolutely distraught over him.

John gained control and the two stood there looking at Zach and each knew what the other was thinking.

"Take him, Lee," was all John could say.

"John, not in a million years did I ever think we'd come to this."

John handed the body over.

"I'll take him down to Mona. She'll be respectful as she . . ." He started to choke up as well and couldn't speak for a moment. "Thank you. I was getting frantic over Pattie. The damn rations just aren't enough. John, Zach saved her life, too."

John started his drive down to town several hours later. The bodies of the two robbers stretched out on the porch as he pulled away from the house. Bartlett's meat wagon, as they now sardonically called it, the old VW Bus, could be sent up later to get them.

John felt so cold about their deaths that for a moment he dwelled on the thought that two extra rations would now be spent, the reward for the digging of a grave, in the golf course cemetery. There were fifteen hundred graves there now, another five hundred filling the Swannanoa Christian School's soccer field.

Kellor had been right. The dying time was now upon them. Deaths from starvation were soaring. Yesterday there had been close to a hundred. Mostly the elderly still and then parents.

As a historian John knew that was the pattern, though a casual observer, an academic sitting in an armchair calculating such things, would have figured the children next. But what parent would eat while their child starved? The ration lines, now five of them scattered around the two communities, had nearly ninety percent of the surviving population showing up, for one distribution a day of soup and either a biscuit or a piece of bread.

That was another "state" secret. The bakery, closely guarded at a local pizza shop where wood heat had been rigged in, was now mixing in sawdust to give the bread bulk, to fill stomachs. It was the same as Leningrad, and actually that had been the inspiration for John to suggest it.

So the parents, many of them working to get an extra ration, were bringing the food home to their children, then dying off, and once both parents were gone it was hoped that neighbors or kin would take the orphans in.

Charlie and Tom had been forced to issue strict orders that personnel receiving extra rations were to eat them on site when the rations were issued, but even so, they'd stash a biscuit in a pocket, some even rigged up plastic liners in their pockets to pour the soup into when they thought no one was watching, then slowly walk home where two, three, four hungry kids might be waiting.

And yet ironically, at the same time, at least according to Voice of America, there were signs that some recovery was going on, down along the coast.

The federal government was reconvened, functioning aboard the carrier *Abraham Lincoln,* and martial law was still in effect. There were reports that the corn and wheat harvest of the Midwest would be brought in and train lines reopened to move the bulk goods. Headquarters for the south-east emergency government had been established in Charleston and daily reports now issued about the progress of rebuilding, even a claim that a nuclear power plant in Georgia had been brought back online, but it seemed like any progress being made was moving along the coast or slowly edging towards Atlanta. He wondered if someone up the command chain had decided to "triage off" upper South Carolina and western North Carolina.

There had been overflights, though. Fighters several times, a C-17 transport, and Asheville finally admitted that replacement parts for generators for the hospital had been airlifted in.

Asheville was playing its cards close. The phone line that Black Mountain had started had been run into the county office in Asheville, but the communications were rather one-sided, as if the director there resented the showdown over refugees versus water supply.

The thought that some kind of medical supplies had been lifted into Asheville had made John wild, Washington having to nearly physically restrain him from driving straight there and demanding some fresh insulin. He had personally telephoned Burns, who still was running Asheville, and begged for any information on insulin and Burns flatly announced none had come in and even if it had, he would not release any outside of the town no matter what.

Insulin, John was obsessed with it. Two days ago Jennifer's blood sugar was up. She had taken an injection, and it was still up.

He had finally gone for Makala and she carefully examined Jennifer, then took him aside.

"The three remaining bottles. They might have spoiled," was all Makala would say.

It had finally taken three times the normal dose to bring Jennifer's level back down.

Her time had been cut by two-thirds.

And help, if it was indeed help, was still as far away as the far side of the moon.

Of the other diabetics in the town, over half were dead, the others dropping off fast.

He turned off the motor of his car, sat back, and lit another cigarette, the sixth of the day . . . oh, the hell with it and the counting out.

He sat there, smoked, looking at the interstate, cars still stalled where they had died over two months ago.

Somehow we've all been playing a game of reality avoidance with ourselves, even on Day One, he realized.

Anyone with even the remotest understanding of EMP and the threat to the nation should have been going insane before it hit. During World War II the entire nation had been mobilized, all the talk of loose lips sinking ships, the scrap drives, the guards on railroad bridges in Iowa. Much of it was absurd when the threat was finally understood, long after the war was over. There were no legions of spies and saboteurs in America, and the few who were in place or attempted to infiltrate were caught within days by the FBI. There was a threat, and though remote, it was at least acted on back then. But this time? The threat was a hundred times worse and they did nothing, absolutely nothing. Angrily he stubbed out the cigarette and lit another.

If everyone had been educated to it, the same way Civil Defense had once been in the curriculum of every school back in the 1940s and 1950s, if people knew the simple things to do on Day One, Charlie already trained to react to an EMP, mobilize his forces and react quickly . . . if they had but a few simple provisions stocked away, the same way anyone who lives in hurricane or tornado country does, would they be in this mess?

The crime, the real crime was those who truly knew the level of threat doing nothing to prepare or prevent it. Bitterly he wondered if they were suffering as the rest of the nation now suffered or were they safely hidden away, the special bunkers for Congress, the administration, where food, water, and medicine for years were waiting for them . . . and their families? The thought of it filled him with rage. He knew what he would do if he could but go there now; show them Jennifer and then do what he wished he could do to them.

And he could see his own avoidance of it all since that first day even as he did scramble to at least get insulin. Food, bulk food, just a fifty-pound bag of rice or flour, shoes, batteries, an additional test kit for Jennifer, damn it, even birth control for Elizabeth, dog food, a water filter so they didn't have to boil what they now pulled out of the swamp green pool . . . I should have had those on hand.

It was over two months later and people in his small North Carolina town were dying of starvation. I pretty well understood it on Day One, and yet I avoided the worst of it ever since, he thought. Doc Kellor had alluded to it in their meeting of nearly a month ago, when the decision was made to reduce rations for most of the populace, but we did not fully face the horrible realities of it.

America, the breadbasket of the world, which could feed a billion people without even breaking a sweat, was dying now of starvation. The two frequencies of Voice of America were talking daily about the first harvests coming in from the southern Midwest, of cattle being driven, and it all sounded to him like the old Chinese and Soviet broadcasts of the Cold War when they boasted daily about their great strides even while people lived in squalor and indeed did die of starvation.

The food was there, but it would never get here, not to this place, not now. That meant that over twenty percent of the town was dead and upwards of half would die in another thirty days, while food by the millions of tons rotted because they still had no means of moving it in bulk to where it was needed most.

The medicines. Yes, they were out there, someplace. Some stockpiles overseas perhaps, but the factories that made them were in cities, and the cities had no power, or perhaps a few places here and there, and the people who worked in the factories were hunkered down or scattered refugees, perhaps some of the very people now lying dead below the barrier. And even if the factory did suddenly turn on, the insulin was processed from genetically altered bacteria in labs. But the labs, maybe in New York or Arizona, were a thousand miles away. The bottles it was then loaded into? Perhaps made in Mexico and trucked to the lab a thousand miles away . . . and then loaded back aboard climate-controlled trucks, and taken to airports and priority-shipped in containers specially designed, those containers perhaps made in Mississippi. And so it went.

IV bags. Nearly all the IV bags in America were made in just a few places. Million a day. And they were boxed in sterile environments and then shipped to other factories that filled them with blood drawn perhaps a thousand miles away, or various solutions mixed in Oregon and shipped to Texas there to meet the bags to be filled.

And so much, so much from overseas that were in containerships offloaded by diesel-electric-powered cranes, then loaded into trucks. Perhaps the plastic to make the IV bag first emerging from the ground as oil in Kuwait, and from there to Texas to be cracked and the appropriate chemicals siphoned off and shipped to Louisiana to be turned into plastics, some of them for plastic bags to come to Asheville.

Such a vast, intricate, beautiful, profoundly complex web, the most complex in history, and all along a few enemies, enemies whom Americans had for years ignored, and then in one day had come to hate, and that hate had slowly changed, as it does with Americans, to remoteness, disdain, and a smug sense of ultimate victory, perhaps even victory by the simple fact that they made a wish that the enemies were no longer there. For ultimately, what did 9/11 do in the coldest sense? It killed three thousand. Did the economy collapse the next day? Did John's Jennifer miss an insulin shot? Did the workers in a factory that made insulin scatter in panic on 9/11? No. And in spite of outrage, people's tears of empathy, unless it was a friend or one of their own blood lost that day, their world really did not change other than the annoyance of getting through an airport.

The web of our society, John thought, was like the beautiful spiderwebs he'd find as a boy in the back lot after dawn on summer days, dew making them visible. Vast, beautiful intricate things. And at the single touch of a match the web just collapsed and all that was left for the spider to do, if it survived that day, was to rebuild the web entirely from scratch. And our enemies knew that and planned for it . . . and succeeded.

He tossed the second butt out the window, lit another, and drove into town to report the attack on his house and get Jim to bring up the meat wagon.

The soup line at the elementary school was already forming up, even though distribution of the day's rations wasn't until noon. The carcass of a hog was trussed up to a tree, actually barely a suckling, already stripped down to the bones, which would be tossed into the pot as well.

The people on line were skeletal, their weight really falling away now. Many could barely shuffle along. Kids were beginning to have bloated stomachs. Out along the curb half a dozen bodies lay, dragged out for the meat wagon, no longer even given the dignity of a sheet to cover them. A man, three kids, most likely their parents dead and no one to truly care for them, and a woman, obviously a suicide, with her wrists slashed open.

It made John think of the woman on the road. . . . Carol, that was her name. Most likely dead by suicide long ago.

The refugee center was starting to empty out, people beginning to move into the homes of locals who had died.

In the short drive he could sense the collapse setting in. The bodies in front of the elementary school, the fact of just how dusty and litter-strewn the streets were. Without the usual maintenance, storm drains had plugged up with debris; several trees had dropped and were then cut back just enough to let a single vehicle through. One of the beautiful towering pines in front of the elementary school had collapsed across the road, smashing in the Front Porch diner across the street. Enough of the tree had been cut away to clear the road for traffic, the rest just left in place.

Nothing had been done to repair the diner's crushed roof, the inside now left open to the elements, the building itself broken into repeatedly by scavengers who were now willing to scrape the grease out of the traps as food.

That broke his heart every time he drove past it. The diner had been his usual stop on many a morning long ago. Mary would have freaked on his breakfast of bacon, eggs, and hash browns, but he so loved the place, the owner a man he truly respected, hardworking, starting from a hole in the wall a block away to create a diner that was "the" place in Black Mountain for breakfast. Truckers, construction workers, shop owners, and at least one professor type. How many mornings had John spent there, after dropping the kids off at school, for a great meal, a cigarette, the usual banter, playing one of the games the owner carved out of wood, trick puzzles, and then going on to his late morning lecture?

"What a world we once had," he sighed.

The parking lot of the bank at the next corner was becoming weed choked, though that was being held back a bit by children from the refugee center plucking out any dandelions they saw and eating them. The bank had been one of the last of an old but dead breed, locally owned, the owner's Land Rover still parked out front, covered in dust and dried mud.

John turned past Hamid's store. A few cars out front, a VW Bug and a rust bucket of a '65 Chevy, a couple of mopeds. Hamid had traded some smokes for an old generator, traded some cigarettes to someone else to get it fixed, and now he actually had some juice. It had been quite the thing when he fired it up, and the lights flickered on dimly. He had diverted the juice into two things: a fridge and one of the pumps for his gas tanks. John had instantly thought of asking Hamid to take the vials of insulin he still had, but Makala had vetoed it. The generator-driven power was variable, shuting down, fired back up again. Better to keep it at a steady fifty-five than at forty degrees that might suddenly climb to sixty or seventy before plunging back down below freezing.

But still his old friend had come through for him, a debt he could never repay, and he felt like a beggar every time he wandered in.

"For my favorite little girl," Hamid would say as he pressed a small package into John's hands, a piece of newspaper with a pound or two of ice inside. Ice, a precious pound or two of ice to try to keep the temperature of the remaining vials down a few degrees.

"I still owe you twenty bucks," John would always say, and Hamid would just smile, for he had little girls, too, and he knew, and he was proud to be an American helping a friend.

Makala. Funny, John hadn't thought of her these last few days. My own starvation, he thought. The unessentials of the body shut down first and after four years of celibacy after the death of Mary he had grown used to it. He knew Makala was interested in him; in a vastly different world they would definitely have been dating, but not now. Besides, he did not want to upset the delicate balance of his family. Jen had been Mary's mother; how would she react? The girls? They might like Makala as a friend, but as something more? For Jennifer, her mom was already becoming remote, but for Elizabeth, the death had hit at twelve, a most vulnerable of times, and her room still had half a dozen pictures of the two of them together and one that still touched John's heart, a beautifully framed portrait from Mary's high school graduation, the color fading but Mary very much the girl he had met in college.

He pulled up to the town hall complex. The rumble of a generator outside varied up and down in pitch as more power or less was being used.

One of the fire trucks was being washed down. The mechanics had finally bypassed all the electronics, done some retrofitting, and the engine had finally kicked back to life ten days ago.

He walked in. Charlie was in his office, cot in the corner unmade, looking up as John came in.

Charlie had lost at least thirty pounds or more, face pinched. He had a cup of what looked to be some herbal tea.

"Two dead up at my house, shot them this morning," John said matter-of-factly.

"That's eight reported now just this morning," Charlie replied, his voice hoarse.

John sat down, looked at his pack of cigarettes, fourteen left, and offered one to Charlie, who did not hesitate to take it.

"Damn it, Charlie. You got to get at least one extra meal in you."

He shook his head.

"Might not matter soon anyhow."

"Why's that?"

"We think the Posse is coming this way."

"What?"

"Don Barber flew his recon plane out a couple hours ago to take a look for us along Interstate 40 heading towards Hickory; he's yet to get back. Four days ago we didn't have a single refugee at the barrier, two days ago nearly a hundred, yesterday more than two hundred; it's as if something is pressuring them from behind. Rumors running with them that Morganton was just looted clean, a damn medieval pillage. Also, we had a shooting last night on the interstate."

"So, that's becoming almost a daily routine," John said coolly.

"This one was different. One of the few heading east. Big guy, looked fairly well fed."

"So what did he do?"

"Washington spotted him. He just had a gut feeling because he had seen this same guy, the day before, heading west; he stood out because he looked so well fed. Washington tagged along with the escort taking this guy and some other refugees east and played dumb. The big guy was peppering him with questions. How many folks lived here, how much food left, any organized defense."

"A spy?"

"Exactly."

"So Washington drew down on him just before the gap, and almost got killed for it. The guy had what Washington called an old-fashioned pimp gun up the sleeve of his jacket. Small .22. He actually got off the first shot and then Washington blew him away."

"Washington OK?"

"Nicked on the side. Kellor said another inch in and, given the way things are now, he'd of been in deep trouble."

"Where is Washington now?"

"Up at the college."

"I think we should go up."

Charlie nodded and the two got into John's Edsel for the short drive.

The drive up to the campus reminded him yet again of the lost world of but several months back, his daily commute of not much more than four miles, and he thought again of bacon and eggs. Damn, that would be good now.

He almost said it to Charlie. Food had indeed become the obsessive topic on people's minds, but now there was a ban on it being spoken of, a major breech of etiquette. It just made everyone crazy to talk about what they would eat when things "got better."

As they passed the turnoff to the North Fork road, there were two more bodies covered with sheets out in front of a home.

"Ah, shit, not the Elliotts," Charlie sighed.

Three children were out on the lawn, all of them skinny as rails, except that their stomachs were bloating, a neighbor clinging to them. That had started to appear over the last couple of weeks, kids with stomachs bloating out, even as they starved. Kellor told John it was edema, fluid buildup as their bodies inside began to shut down. It was the type of images he would always turn off when an infomercial ran for some save-the-kids type charity. Always it was kids in Africa or some disaster-stricken area in Asia with the bloated stomachs. He wondered if now, at this very moment, in a place in the world where electricity still flowed, such images were on their screens: "Give now to save the starving children in America."

God, it was a sobering thought. Would our friends overseas, those we had helped so many times, without a thought of any return, now be coming to us? Were ships, loaded with food, racing towards us . . . or was there silence or, worse, laughter and contempt?

"He was getting an extra ration as a grave digger, in fact two rations because he was digging two a day," Charlie said, interrupting John's thoughts.

"And taking them home to the kids and his wife," John said quietly.

They didn't even slow down but just drove on.

They passed three boys, early teens, two of them toting .22s, the other a pellet gun, and the youngest with, yes, a bloated stomach as well. All three moving stealthily, peering up at the trees, the interlacing telephone and power lines.

There was most likely barely a squirrel or rabbit left in town now, and birds were now becoming part of the pot. John's own hunts had started to come up empty unless he went deeper and deeper into the Pisgah forest. It knotted him up thinking about it. Zach had not even died with a meal in his stomach. He had come close to fighting with his Ginger for the rabbit he had bagged yesterday. Ginger was only allowed the bones after Jen had scraped off every bit of flesh for a rabbit stew.

"You know, we're actually starting to run short of small-caliber ammunition," Charlie said as they drove past the boys.

"Most folks who had a .22 in the closet rarely dragged it out and at best maybe had a box of fifty to a hundred rounds. Understand trading now is five bullets for a squirrel or rabbit."

Fortunately, John still had several hundred himself, but he was short on shotgun shells. The heavier-caliber stuff, he had kept that for other reasons.

The gate ahead was roadblocked. In the past the students guarding it recognized his car and waved it through. Not today. They forced him to a stop, one of them standing back with a 12-gauge leveled, while the other came around the side and looked in.

"Good morning, sir; are you OK?"

"It's Rebecca, isn't it?"

"Yes, sir."

She looked in his backseat, nodded, and two students started up the Volkswagen blocking the gate, let it roll forward for him to pass, then backed it into place and shut it down.

"Kids are getting more cautious."

"Well, with all the dead last night in break-ins," John said. "Lord knows how many others we'll find out today were successful and the families inside the homes are now dead and rotting.

"I think it's safe to assume that some of this Posse crowd have already infiltrated in, looked us over, and decided we are worth taking, at the very least to then move on to Asheville. Perhaps some are even holed up in some houses watching if we are getting prepared."

They turned into the drive leading up to Gaither Hall. And the troops were out. The days of close-order drill long past, they were practicing covering fire and withdrawing in front of the library, Washington pacing back and forth, yelling instructions as John pulled up and turned off the car.

Washington turned and went through the ritual, still the annoying ritual for John, of saluting, which he returned.

Kids were all around. Hunkered down low, concealed behind trees, under vehicles, up in windows of buildings. Farther up the road John could see what must be the red force, Company B, deployed out beyond the girls' dorm, a dozen vehicles running, some Volkswagens, again courtesy of Jimmie Bartlett, a few farm pickup trucks. One had a fake machine gun mounted on the back, technicals, John thought they were called in Somalia.

Washington held up his megaphone.

"Captain Malady. Now!"

Kevin Malady had been, of all things, an assistant librarian. With his strong, massive shoulders, thick black hair, and lantern jaw that made him look a bit like Schwarzenegger, the kids quickly giving him the nickname Conan the Librarian. He was ex-military, a sergeant with a mech unit in Iraq back in '03. He had just resigned from the library staff and had planned to go to Princeton Theological in the fall. Now he was the CO of Company B.

He knew his stuff as they simulated the assault. The technical supposedly laying down fire support, a vehicle with a plow bolted to the front driving straight at the barrier.

Of course it came to a stop, Washington shouting that the barrier had been pierced.

Malady had more of his troops storm from around abandoned cars, rushing the barrier.

If this had been done a few months ago, the kids would have been laughing, seeing it as playacting, shouting and whooping. Not now. They were silent, following directions from their officers, several of them staff and faculty with military experience, the defensive force pulling back, to try to lure the attackers into what would be the killing zone if the gap was pierced on the interstate. A couple of hundred yards back from the gap, the road was flanked on one side by a high concrete wall, a sound barrier erected for several hundred yards to shield the conference center.

Washington had already established firing positions on the reverse side of the wall. The campus chapel, the new one built several years back, which now housed a famous fresco, *The Return of the Prodigal,* by the famous artist Ben Long, was serving as a simulator for the wall, students suddenly popping up from behind the ridge of the roof.

"That's it!" Washington shouted. "Once up, it's fire superiority. Pour it down fast and hard, fast and hard. Panic them!"

The simulation was starting to break down, kids standing around. There could be no realism to it, no blanks, no miles laser packs.

They had used paintballs at the start, but the supply of those was used up in two days.

Washington blew his whistle.

"Stand down. That's it. Take an hour break. Dinner at noon."

To John's amazement, a fifer started to play and it sent a chill down his back. It was the D'Inzzenzo boy, not a student at the college, a local kid who had belonged to the reenactment unit and had taken to hanging around the college. Washington had taken a liking to him and he was now the official fifer for the militia, playing "Yankee Doodle" as the exercise ended.

"Good marching stuff," Washington said as John looked back at the kid, wearing a Union kepi. "The students love it and it's good for morale."

Students came out from buildings, crawled out from under concealment, all of them armed. Their equipment had been gradually upgraded. Most were armed with semiautos, heavier caliber, a great percentage of Company B with deer rifles, a lot with scopes. Charlie had already said that if a crisis came, he'd release the automatic weapons kept in the police station to Washington. A few civilians had come forward as well, one showing up with what had been an illegal full auto M16 with over four hundred rounds, saying as long as he could tote it in a fight, he'd be part of the militia, a vet from the early days in Nam.

Both companies were now rounded out by vets who had seen service, as far back as Korea, adding nearly a hundred to their ranks. These vets might be old, but they had combat experience and were now slotted in as squad and platoon leaders.

Others, the survivalist types, including the legendary Franklins, were teaching the kids how to concoct homemade claymores, land mines, satchel charges, and homemade rocket launchers fashioned out of PVC pipe. The reenactors in the town regretted they could not get their hands on an original cannon, but were now mixing up black powder for these weapons and rigging up a field piece made out of steel pipe that would be packed with canister.

As for the students, within seconds they were reverting back, a couple of the guys laughing, shouting good-natured insults. More than a dozen couples instantly paired up, a few of them, without any attempt at stealth, with arms around each other, heading down towards the woods behind the science building.

"There's a major problem brewing and figured we should check in with you," Charlie said, his voice thin, raspy.

Washington nodded and the three took the shaded path, walking over the old stone arch bridge that led from Gregor Dorm to Gaither. John had always loved this place in particular. On many a day he'd sit on the bridge to watch the creek tumble beneath him. Students were always passing by and it was a great place to just hang out, chat with kids, sneak a smoke with another smoker . . . a breaking of the rules since they were outside a designated spot, but the dean had given up a long time ago trying to hassle John about it, and the president actually thought it was good, a faculty member twisting the administrative tail a little with the kids joining in.

They headed into President Hunt's office. He rarely showed at the campus now, though his home was but a quarter mile away. In spite of the pleadings of John, Reverend Abel, and Washington, President Hunt had made a solemn statement that he and his wife would refuse extra rations. Every ounce of food had to go to "our soldiers and volunteers." It was typical of him, incredibly noble, and as a result he was dying.

They walked in and sat down around the conference table in the office, and as they did so, a humming sputter echoed and they were back up, looking out the windows.

It was Don in his Aeronca L-3, D-day invasion stripes starkly visible on the wings and fuselage, clearing the crest by Lookout Mountain and then dipping down into the narrow valley of the Cove. He circled the campus once, tight turn, not fifty feet above the trees, saluted, and then leveled out to head south into town and the landing strip at the Ingram's shopping plaza.

"So let me guess. The Posse is coming," Washington said.

John and Charlie nodded in agreement.

"It was inevitable; sooner or later they'd hear about us and figure we had something worth taking.

"He went out when, about two hours ago?" Washington asked.

"Make it two and a half," John said. "That plane cruises at about sixty. It ain't good news; they must be getting close."

They went back to the table and sat down.

"One of the boys bagged a bear last night," Washington said. "It's down in the cookhouse now. Meat for everyone at noon, maybe a pound apiece."

John instantly felt his mouth water. Twice now they had bagged bears, and though greasy as hell, bear was filling.

"I just wish we could get President Hunt to join us. I sent a couple of the girls up there to plead with him and they said he just smiled and refused. They were crying when they came back, said he looks terrible."

"That's Dan," John said quietly. "And maybe he's right. These kids have to be in good shape. We can't have them staggering like weak kittens if this Posse shows up."

"Are they ready?" Charlie asked.

Washington shook his head.

"Not very reassuring, damn it," Charlie replied sharply.

"Look, Charlie. I love these kids. Have known them for years. Down deep they're mostly small-town kids with good hearts, and remember, as a Christian college here, we were drawing kids with particular values and views as well. Or at least their parents saw it that way even if the kids didn't.

"But if you want the harsh reality, I can pick out a couple of the young men for you. Kids who grew up in the projects in Charlotte or Greensboro or Atlanta. And they'll tell you a different story about reality. Kids at twelve cappin' each other and boasting about being gangbangers. Kids at sixteen already with time in jail, maybe fathers already, cold-eyed as dead snakes, and most of them dead at twenty-five."

"The old sick joke," John sighed. "You won't find a drug dealer with a four-oh-one (k) plan."

"Exactly," Washington snapped. "These kids here, up until two months ago were thinking grades, fooling around, getting married after college, the more mature ones exactly that, their four-oh-one (k) plans. What they face, if we face it, will not just be gangbangers from cities. What will have gravitated to this Posse will be every lowlife scum with a will to do anything to survive. Mix into that the psychos that Doc Kellor was talking about. What happened to guys in prisons when this hit? Where are they now? Remember, our proud country had more people in prison per populace than damn near anywhere else in the world.

"Let them starve? Execute all of them? Maybe in some of the maximum-security houses the warden might have just done that. The food runs out and he lines them all up and shoots them rather than let them escape. But the minimum places, I bet those people were over the little chain-link fences by the third day. Most of the kids with a stupid-ass drug charge went home, but you already had some bad hombres in those places and they would gravitate together and now the world is a paradise, wide open, whatever they want if they have the balls to take it."

Washington shook his head.

"The food's run out here in the East," Washington continued. "If we were in the Midwest, the corn belt, cattle belt, I'd be more optimistic, but here? Density of population versus on-hand food, it's out, it's gone.

"And those barbarians, for they are barbarians, know only one thing now. Find food and gorge and take and inflict pain as they never dreamed possible before this happened. They're thinking that even as we sit around this table, talking about rations, the nobility of our college president, the debate whether to shoot and eat our dogs."

John winced at that. Of course Washington didn't know about this morning, nor did he notice John's reaction.

The phone rang.

The sound of it when it did happen was still rather startling. The three looked at one another and John stood up, went over to the president's desk, and picked up the receiver. It was an old rotary phone from the forties or fifties, receiver heavy, wire not even the coiled type yet, just jet-black and hanging down.

"Matherson here."

"John, is that you? It's Tom here."

"Go ahead, Tom."

"I'm here with Don Barber. I just picked him up and brought him to the town hall."

"What did he see?"

"Damn, John, he's pretty shaken."

"Can you bring him up?"

"Sure, John. We'll be there in five minutes."

"Over here."

The line continued to hum for several seconds until Judy, the switchboard operator at the town hall, pulled the connect and the line went dead.

John hung up.

"I think we got problems. Barber will be here in a few minutes with his report."

They just made small talk as they waited, John standing, looking out the window, smoking what was now his seventh cigarette of the day. A group of students was coming down from behind the upper men's dorm. Half a dozen girls and a couple of guys. The granola crew, they were called, and though they were mildly disdained before "the Day," no one mocked them now. Most of them were outdoor ed or bio majors and had become highly proficient at food gathering, knowing which roots to dig, which plants could be brewed into teas, which had some medicinal value. One of the girls had a copy of Peterson's guide to plants, dirty and worn, in her jeans pocket. Another girl was carrying a basket filled with mushrooms. So far there had been no mistakes on that score. Another was being helped by a boy, the woven basket between them piled high with greens. The boy and girl looked like some Rousseau ideal, a fantasy of the way the world was supposed to be if civilization went away.

The antique World War II jeep, which Tom had designated his official squad car, turned the corner and pulled up to Gaither. Barber got out along with Tom and they came straight in.

Barber saw the cigarette in John's hand and sighed.

"Damn, I haven't had one of those in years . . . ," he said softly. "John, could I?"

John hesitated, nodded, and handed one over. He was now down to eleven.

Don took a deep drag, sighed, went over to the table, and sat down.

"They're coming," he said.

No one spoke.

"Old Fort is a wreck. I flew down there first. At least fifty vehicles loaded with," he paused, took another drag, and then waved his hand in a gesture of disgust, "I can't even find a word to describe the scum. They were in the center of the town, most of it burning. There's fighting going on, even now, but that town is finished."

He sighed and looked out the window.

"Shit, it was like Korea in '51. If only I had a battery of 105s up here, we could have annihilated their advance guard with one salvo."

"Advance guard?" Washington asked.

Barber nodded.

"Give me a minute, Washington; my brain's a bit slower now. Let me tell it in order."

No one spoke.

"Like I said, about fifty vehicles. Most in the center of the town, those barbarians just running amok. I could see them gunning people down, right in the middle of the street, flushing them out of buildings they were setting on fire. Out on the interstate about ten more vehicles. They took a couple of potshots at me; you'll see a dozen or so holes in my plane by the way.

"So I figured to check up the road, fly up along Route 70, then come back down along the interstate. There wasn't much on 70, though it was obvious they had passed along it. Buildings burning, but a couple hundred yards back from the road I could see people out, still alive. It looked like they just were driving straight through. Marion wasn't hit hard. Just off the interstate enough, I guess, to be bypassed, plus they had well-manned roadblocks on the access ways in. Some evidence of fighting but looks like the scum backed off."

"Think they'll back off here?" Tom asked.

"No," John said forcefully. "First off, their spies have scoped us out; they know we still do have some resources. Second, to get into Asheville, a sweet big city to loot, they first have to go through us. Third, they are heading this way and there is now no backing off. Marion they might mark for later, but I think it's here first."

Washington nodded his agreement.

"What happened next, Don?" John asked.

"I pushed on to Morganton, down to Exit 103 on the interstate."

He lowered his head.

"I thought Charlotte was bad when I flew around it back when things started. That was different, though. In Charlotte there was rioting, yes, but people were mostly just trying snatch and grab, or just getting the hell out. This was different."

"How so, sir?" John asked.

"You know the mental hospital grounds there?"

All nodded. Broughan, the state mental hospital, was set back from the interstate about half a mile. Beautiful open lawn, surrounded by the old sedate southern town of Morganton, complete with some antebellum homes on the main street.

"A fucking nightmare."

John was shocked by Don's language. He was a devout church-going man.

"How bad?" Washington asked.

"My God, I think they're killing people and eating them," he whispered.

No one spoke for a moment, Don just staring off, puffing on his cigarette right down to the filter.

"You're kidding," Charlie whispered.

Don looked over at him fiercely.

"Would I joke about that?" he snapped. "There were a couple of hundred vehicles parked on the grounds of the hospital in a big circle, like they were circling the wagons. Old cars, Jeeps, trucks, even a couple of tractor trailers. Inside that circle the ground was blackened from a huge fire that was still smoldering. It was early when I flew over there; you could see them just sprawled out, sleeping it off. The hospital was burning, dead scattered all around it, most of the downtown burning as well, dead carpeting the streets. But it was what was inside that circle of old cars, trucks, motorcycles."

He finished the cigarette, stubbed it out in an empty coffee cup, and looked, appealing, at John. John handed him another and pulled one out for himself; it was down to nine now.

"They had something like a gallows set up. Bodies were hanging from it. . . ." Don shook and started to cry.

"They were cut open, some without legs and arms. Ten or more like that. Like hogs hung up to be butchered. My God . . ."

He fought for composure.

"You could see other people who were prisoners. As I flew over they were looking up at me, started to jump up and down, waving like poor bastards stranded in a nightmare. I sideslipped to get down lower for a closer look. One of those scum, I could see him looking up at me, and as I flew over he cut a woman's throat, cut it so I could see it.

"That's when I almost got shot down. They have an automatic and it opened up. Stitched my starboard wing. I dived down low, skimmed over not a dozen feet high, weaved and dodged."

He smiled.

"Like the old days. Damn, I was good then, could put my spotter between two trees not thirty feet apart with telephone wires waiting on the other side."

And then he seemed to unfocus again.

"I don't want to believe what I saw."

John sighed, sat back, lost in thought. Cannibalism. Leningrad, Stalingrad, with those cases it was civilians driven mad by hunger. Reports as well in China and, frightfully, documentation of Japanese soldiers doing it either out of desperation when cut off by the island hopping campaign, or ritualistically against American POWs.

"Not here," Charlie sighed, "not here. This is America, for heaven's sake."

"Yes, here," John said softly. "Why should we be any different?"

"Damn it all, we're Americans; it just doesn't happen here."

"Donner Pass, the *Essex* . . . Jeffrey Dahmer? Our sick fascination with films about that Lecter character. Sixty days with little or no food just because the electric suddenly shut off. Hell, yes," John said coldly.

"Most likely some damn cult down there. Like Doc said, psychotics running loose."

The cult over in Knoxville with its leader proclaiming he was John the Baptist reincarnated was still running. There were reports of others, some nutcase proclaiming he was the messiah, others speaking in tongues and looking for answers in Revelation, others just beyond madness believing that aliens had invaded. He thought of that one small coven up above Haw Creek, a couple of dozen families and a church, which according to rumors not too long ago was into passing snakes around. They had sealed themselves off completely, said that it was the end-time and God's wrath was at hand. No one dared to even get within a hundred yards of their barrier now, and John wondered what madness they were practicing up there.

"They have nothing to lose now," John continued. "A nation under martial law, they've looted, raped, murdered. They know that if civilization ever gets the upper hand again, any semblance of order, all of them will be put against the wall and shot. So nothing to lose.

"Mix into that the terror of it all. We figured out it was an EMP, but others . . . especially others who were already off-kilter? What's the answer? God got angry, Gaia the Earth spirit got pissed, Satan took over?"

He found he was almost on the edge of hysteria himself. His hands shaking slightly, he pulled out another cigarette and tossed yet another over to Don.

"Satan's taken over. Maybe whoever's leading them is preaching that. God has turned his back on America, Satan has won, so anything goes. I doubt if all of them are doing it; I want to think most of them are as terrified of whoever is running their crew as we are. But I'm willing to bet whoever is running it is shouting that he has the inside dope from God, Satan, whomever."

"It's insane," Charlie whispered.

"Remember Jonestown. Those were Americans, even though they no longer lived in the forty-eight. And nearly a thousand of them committed suicide because of some damn nutcase who told them to drink Kool-Aid laced with poison because God had ordered it through him.

"Look, you get people scared, then you knock out every prop that we've taken for granted. After these last sixty days I bet there's a dozen prophets running around this country saying, 'Follow me,' and even if but one-tenth of one percent of the survivors do so, that will still be hundreds of thousands of barbarians on the march and the rest of us running, scared shitless of them.

"Damn our enemies who did this to us, they knew us well," John sighed. "They knew human nature too well, and just how fragile civilization is, and how tough it is to defend it. Something we forgot."

No one spoke until Don finally stirred.

"I flew back along the interstate," he said softly. "I counted, between Morganton, Old Fort, and on the road, about two hundred-fifty vehicles total."

"A thousand to fifteen hundred people then," Washington said.

"And just remember this, gentlemen. I was a trained artillery spotter, so I know how to count and how to spot."

"We don't doubt you," Charlie said.

"In this case, don't doubt me. Now for the troubling aspect tactically."

"They're coming round the back," John said.

"Exactly. That's why I flew over here on my way back. I counted two dozen vehicles on the old dirt road, right at the base of the mountains by Andrew's Geyser. Some on the abandoned paved road. A couple more farther up, near where the railroad track crosses over the old dirt road. They know our back door, and not just the interstate."

"Any on the old fire roads?" Charlie asked.

Don shook his head.

"Hard to see, with the summer canopy," he said.

"I doubt it," Washington interjected. "Unless they have a couple of local boys, those old fire roads are mazes. My bet is they'll stick to the old abandoned paved road, the dirt road farther to the north, and the railroad track as their flanker, and they'll hit there first."

"I agree," Charlie said.

"They could be here trying to maneuver into a flanking position by late afternoon," Don said.

John nodded.

"They must have a good military leader in there, knows his stuff and has done a thorough recon on us by now and sees the flank roads as the opening move. They'll hit just before dawn," John said. "Hope to catch us sleeping. If I was one of them, Don here flying around would tell me that what's waiting for them has some kind of warning, so they will move fast rather than give us time to prepare.

"We can pray they're just a mob that overruns by numbers and surprise, but it looks like there are some ex-military with them. Worst case, they got a couple of recon types who know how to figure out the ground, the defenses, the approaches, and formulate the plan of attack.

"Their advance party is in Old Fort to secure the place for the rest of them later today. I'd bet by late afternoon their advance will start probing, and we've got to meet them forward of the potential line of battle. They see our setup, get a good judgment on our strength, we'll have even more problems holding. They'll laager in Old Fort tonight and tear the place apart, then hit us before dawn."

"We'll be prepared," Washington said sharply, and stood up.

"We feed the troops, then move them into position today. Washington, we've talked about this scenario, so we both know the plans. I want officers' briefing within the hour. Tom, start to evacuate all homes behind our fallback line beyond the old toll road as we've talked about before. Charlie, I want every citizen who can carry a gun as our reserve. Mr. Barber, I hope you can stay up in the air most of the day. Keep high, though, sir, real high; just keep an eye on their movements," John said.

Washington looked around the room, a thin smile on his face. Charlie, shriveled with emaciation, said nothing, but his gaze communicated volumes. John was now in charge.

"I think we should get to work, gentlemen," John said.

Tom headed back to his car with Don by his side.

Washington looked over at John and Charlie.

"Gentlemen, I think it's important you join us in chapel and for our meal."

Two hours later, after the officers' briefing and a map exercise, the 1:25,000 geological survey maps taken from the small map store in Black Mountain spread out on the table, John felt everyone understood their mission. Several of the platoon leaders were students, Jeremiah and Phil having been promoted to second lieutenants, in the first and second platoons of Company A. The others were vets from around the town, a good sprinkling of men from Desert Storm, a few from Nam.

John walked into the dining hall. Strange, it still looked basically the same. The counter where kids used to get their meal cards swiped with a laser scanner, circular tables, the twin doors leading into the food-serving area.

It was a room filled with a lot of happy memories and a few poignant ones. This school was unlike what he had expected when he had first come here. He feared that his old commandant, in his rush to get John a job where Mary once lived, had most likely hooked him into some fundamentalist camp meeting. Not that he had any particular objection on a philosophical level as an American, but still, he was a Catholic kid from Jersey. His fears could not be farther from the truth. It had turned into the warmest place he had ever worked in.

He had been greeted with open arms into a community where friendly intellectual debate was encouraged. Though a few might be a bit judgmental, most were actually very open-minded, saying that was the true spirit of what Christ tried to teach and not the nuttiness most outside the South believed of them, and all were guided by a desire to put their students first. The school was better than John ever imagined and now, at this moment, he realized yet again just how much he loved them all, especially "the kids" now sitting at the tables, decked out in camo gear, weapons stacked along the walls.

The tradition with faculty was not to eat segregated off but rather to join a table with their students, laugh, debate, argue, tease, stimulate.

Mary had attended this college her first year before transferring to far more competitive Duke, and coming here was coming home for her. Several of the professors had even taught her long ago.

Towards the end, she often came here to join John for lunch, and always kids would gather round their table and those who fully knew her condition would usually leave her with a kiss to the forehead, an embrace, and, "I'm praying for you every day, ma'am."

And then she was gone.

But still, in the four years afterwards, so many happy days here, of shared meals, of the absolutely ridiculous but still touching dumb skits by the faculty for the Senior Breakfast the day before their graduation.

But now . . .

The cafeteria lines were closed, the food service off to the far side, tables set up near the back door, the grill outside smoking madly with the slabs of bear meat. Most of the students had already taken their plates, each proportion carefully cut, a slab of bear meat, some greens, a cup of herbal tea, that was it, but still a pound or more of meat, while downtown, at this moment, everyone else was getting thin soup with just a couple ounces of meat mixed in.

And yet in spite of their hunger, they remained restrained. None had yet to cut in; all sat around their tables, talking, but not touching the food.

John looked over at Charlie.

"You will eat," John said sharply.

"John?"

"Charlie, you will eat."

He pushed Charlie forward and they joined the back of the line. It only took a few seconds before they were handed the plate, the piece of meat already cut. John noticed that the cooking staff actually had a scale behind the carving table, each piece of meat thrown on it before being put on a plate. Maybe the measurement would be off by an ounce or two one way or the other, but still it was a message to stifle any arguments.

John followed Washington to a table set directly in front of the now-closed doors that had once opened onto the cafeteria line. As they reached their table the room fell silent, all eyes turned towards them.

Without prompting Reverend Abel stepped forward and offered the blessing and finished, John and a few others making the sign of the cross.

But Washington remained standing.

"I am proud of you," Washington said.

The room was absolutely silent, no matter how longingly some looked at the feast before them, a largess of meat not seen in weeks.

"I am proud of all of you, everyone. Those who are bringing in food for us, especially our marksman Brett Huffman."

Brett, who had dropped the bear, stood up, and there was a round of applause and cheering.

"But also for all the rest of you. Those of you gathering, those of you searching, those of you in jobs some might think unglamorous, the work in the refugee center, the isolation ward, the infirmary, the woodcutting crews."

He looked around the room.

"Tonight or tomorrow we face battle."

A murmur swept through the room.

"You've heard the rumors about a group called the Posse. We just received intelligence they are headed this way."

No one spoke, but John could see the anxious looks back and forth.

"There will be battle by this time tomorrow and some of you will die. I have never lied to you; I never will. Some of you will die."

And now he had their attention like never before.

"You are now soldiers. Every one of you. Those of you who trained for it, and those who have not. Every student of this college is now mobilized as we previously discussed. Those who are not assigned to our two combat companies will fall in as medics, messengers, and in the other jobs you have been trained for. I expect all of you to do your duty as soldiers."

Washington turned and started to sit down. Before John even quite realized what he was doing, he stood up.

A few had started to cut into their meal, but as he stood they stopped, looking towards him.

"Tonight, tomorrow, you will fight. It is, tragically, the day you grow up and will never be able to turn back from. You are the defenders of thousands of people in this town who are now too weak to defend themselves. And now I will be blunt. I will fall silent for a moment and I want you to look at the meal before you. That food is food sacrificed by others to give you strength to defend them . . . and yourselves."

He did fall silent and no one spoke, nearly all looking down at their plates.

"Think of," and he actually chuckled sadly, "think of how two months back we complained about the food here, filled our plates, then tossed half of it out, and now, tonight, you will face men and women who will kill you and everyone else for that piece of meat on your plate you would have thrown out but two months back."

He hesitated but knew it had to be said.

"Or even your own flesh if they win, because not forty miles from here this evil band is slaughtering human beings for food."

There was an uncomfortable stirring.

"So for everything you eat now know that but two miles from here, down in the town of Black Mountain, half a dozen died of starvation this morning. Died so you can eat, and have strength to survive and defend."

He sighed, started to sit down, and then stopped.

"Some of you were in my classes on military history. You know how we so casually talked of wars past, the suffering remote. You remember some of the speakers I've brought in, veterans of that generation we now call the Greatest Generation."

He braced himself, looking around the room, and now there were tears in his eyes.

"Tonight, tomorrow, in years to come, you will, you must be, the greatest generation. You must win this fight; then remembering all that America was, you must rebuild her and never forget . . ."

He sighed, lowering his head.

"Never forget. . . ."

He sat down and for a moment there was silence.

Laura, the girl in the choir, stood up and raised her voice.

"Oh, say can you see, by the dawn's early light . . ."

Instantly all were standing, singing as well, and never had he heard it sung thus.

He looked at them and tried to sing, unable to do so, overcome by emotion.

The last stanza finished, a cheer erupted and all sat down, except for Laura. She smiled at John, and half a dozen of the choir came to join her.

And together they started to sing again, even as their comrades ate.

"Oh Danny boy, the pipes, the pipes are calling
From glen to glen, and down the mountainside. . . ."

John lowered his head, gazing at his meal. Perhaps half, maybe a quarter for myself, he thought, the rest for Jen, the kids, and Ginger.

The meal done, there was a procession, led by the American flag, the school banner, and their fifer playing, over to the Chapel of the Prodigal with its famous fresco painted by Ben Long. The service had to be short and to the point, for John had warned Reverend Abel that time was pressing.

They had opened with the Lord's Prayer, and just as they finished the back doors of the chapel opened and in hobbled President Hunt, leaning on the arm of a student for strength. All stood, many with tears in their eyes. President Hunt took the front, standing beneath the painting, and then slowly drew a Bible out of his pocket.

"I carried this Bible in Nam," he said, his voice husky, weak. "I held it close the night I was wounded and lost my leg. There is a psalm I read every night I was there and I wish to share it with you. . . . We call it the soldier's psalm, the Ninety-first."

He half-opened the Bible, but it was obvious he knew the prayer by heart.

" 'He that dwelleth in the secret place of the most High shall abide under the shadow of the Almighty. . . .' " As he spoke, his voice gained strength.

" 'Thou shalt not be afraid for the terror by night; nor for the arrow that flieth by day.

" 'Nor for the pestilence that walketh in darkness; nor for the destruction that wasteth at noonday.' "

It was midafternoon when John at last returned home. The entire town was astir, at least those still with the strength to move. Don had flown a second mission and returned with word that the Posse was indeed moving, already past Marion. The first skirmish had erupted halfway down the mountain in Swannanoa Gap, ironically not far from where, over 140 years earlier, in perhaps the last battle in the East during the Civil War,

Confederate militia had fought to turn back Yankee raiders. The half dozen advancing up the abandoned paved road had been wiped out near where the old overlook and hot dog stand had been.

Another skirmish erupted along the dirt road farther to the north, long-distance sniping, one student soon dead from it and another missing.

In town, those men still with any strength were forming up, deploying into a secondary line.

Charlie was in the town hall, and fuming with rage. He had called in the report to Asheville, begging for support. And they had written Black Mountain off. They claimed a group was approaching them from the south and had already torched Hendersonville and there was no defensive bottleneck to keep them back. Everything they had was committed to that direction.

Tom reported though that Asheville's barrier, just short of Exit 53, the narrow bottleneck of the interstate, and I-40, was now heavily manned by Asheville militia, but they were not coming forward to help pitch in.

Black Mountain and Swannanoa were on their own, Asheville most likely figuring they could take the blow and if the invaders were repulsed, that would be great; if the defenders were overrun, the opposition would be so weakened that they would not have the strength for a final push. Payback perhaps for the defiance over the refugees, even though Charlie had warned that if the town fell the last thing he would do would be blow the water main and Asheville be damned.

At three in the afternoon the militia, like something out of long ago, had marched through the town, fifer in the lead wearing his Union kepi and blue jacket, playing "Yankee Doodle" over and over, complete as well to a drummer from the high school and a flag bearer forming a tableau like the old painting. The street was lined with starving civilians who cheered them and wept as they passed.

A few could remember such parades from sixty years past and could not help but wonder at this, the sight in their own hometown, of kids marching off as from long ago, to fight others who but two months back were part of the same country.

Their training uniforms of college blue were now replaced with camo, donated by civilians of the town, a mixed lot of hunting gear, some military surplus, some of it way too big for the smaller girls in the ranks. But still it lent a military air. Some of the vets in the ranks sported helmets and more than a few of them were toting firearms that would have triggered an ATF raid in the old days . . . a couple of Thompsons, AK-47s, street sweepers, a frightful-looking .50-caliber sniper rifle, and a number of exotic-looking assault rifles. Piled in the back of a truck were satchel charges, some primitive mines, and hundreds of tin cans packed with scrap metal and a blasting charge, to be lit with a match, then thrown.

Making them had been a tricky business, and one student had been killed and two wounded just after church service while packing a "grenade" when the charge went off.

It was indeed like something from long ago, John thought, watching as they came down Black Mountain Road and turned onto State Street, heading east to the gap. He stood to attention at the corner and saluted, standing thus until the last of the two companies of infantry and the company of auxiliary supports had passed. Though it was a solemn moment, he caught the eye of more than one of his former students, a flash of a smile, a subtle wave, as if somehow they were still kids playacting even as they toted rifles, shotguns, satchel charges, homemade bazookas and grenades.

He and Washington had nearly come to blows arguing about the plan, and for a few moments John felt that the two months of Washington calling him Colonel had been nothing more than tradition and playacting. And yet, in the end, Washington had at last deferred, though he warned it would triple their casualties and maybe cost them "the war."

After the passage of the militia up to the gap, John then briefed the hundreds of civilian volunteers, some barely able to stand, as to their task and where to deploy, while Charlie made sure that two precious cattle would be taken up to the front and there slaughtered and cooked, with all being able to fill their stomachs before the fight. Kellor had pitched a fit over that, claiming it was better they went in with empty stomachs in case of gut wounds, but Washington and John had won out; better to lose some that way than have half the army collapse from hunger pains. The last few precious bottles of vitamins had been pulled out and each combatant swallowed a double dose as well.

Carl was leading down over five hundred more from Swannanoa, those still able to heft a gun and fight.

John finally felt that he had time to get away and get his family out. Their home was on what was being defined now as the front line and he had decided to move his family back up into the Cove near the college.

Jen's home, though abandoned for nearly two months, was still intact, though scavenged through, with a door broken along with some windows.

He pulled into his driveway, and with all that had happened he realized that he had left but nine hours before.

The two bodies were still out on the deck. The meat wagon had not come; in the heat, they were now drawing swarms of flies. Jen stood in the doorway, and as he got out of the car Ginger came up, head lowered, whimpering, almost scared, and Jennifer flung herself into his arms.

"Daddy," and she started to cry.

He suddenly realized that he had become so preoccupied with the approach of the Posse that he had all but forgotten what had transpired here just this morning.

Jen came up to him and the look in her eyes told him something was wrong. Had there been more of them?

"Everyone OK?" John gasped.

"Yes, we're OK."

"Thank God."

"You look beat, John."

"I really can't explain much now, Jen, but we only have an hour to pack up and move out. We're moving up to your house."

"Why, for God's sake?"

"There's going to be a fight here by tomorrow. We're evacuating everyone on both sides of the highway."

"John, we all need to sit down and talk."

He felt Jennifer still in his arms.

He hugged her.

"I'm sorry about Zach, sweetie. He was a brave doggie. The best."

"I know, Daddy."

"John, there's something else," Jen said.

He looked at her.

"John, come inside with me please."

Too much was happening and her tone set him to a near panic. Was it something about Jennifer?

He broke her embrace and looked at her. Her features, though pinched and yellow, had not changed much.

"Jennifer honey, I think Ginger needs to play," Jen said.

Her voice was not a suggestion and Jennifer registered it.

"OK, Grandma."

"And make sure she stays away from those bodies out on the deck."

The way Jen said it, the message of those words, struck John as yet another breakdown. Tell your kid to go out and play with the dog, but stay away from the men Daddy had shot during the night because your beloved golden might suddenly look at them as a meal.

He followed Jen into the living room. Elizabeth and Ben were sitting together on the sofa, holding hands, and somehow at that instant John knew. To his surprise, Makala was standing in the corner of the room, half-turned, looking at him.

Elizabeth looked up at him and took a deep breath.

"Daddy, I'm pregnant."

Absolutely thunderstruck, he couldn't speak. He looked at Ben, whose arm was now protectively around Elizabeth's shoulder. Ben tried to look him straight in the eye and then lowered his gaze.

John turned away, fearful of what he might say or do, lit another cigarette, and walked to the bay window.

Jen came up to his side.

Behind him Elizabeth started to cry and Ben was whispering to her.

"John?"

It was Jen, standing by his side, whispering.

"For God's sake, John, do the right thing."

He turned and looked back.

"How?" was all he could say, and he instantly realized the absurdity of it. At sixteen Elizabeth already so looked like her mother, and he remembered when they met she was twenty, he was twenty-one. Of course he knew how.

But this was his baby girl, who used to smother him with "smoochies" and say she would love him forever.

He walked towards them and to his horror he saw fear in Elizabeth's eyes. Ben then stood up.

"Sir. If there's blame, it's mine." His voice was trembling and broke into an adolescent squeak. "It's my fault, not hers."

"No, Ben. Both of us."

She stood up and put her arm around him.

"Daddy, we love each other."

He slowly sat down, shaking his head.

"My God," he sighed. "You're kids in high school. College ahead."

"Not anymore," Elizabeth said, and now there was some strength to her voice. "Daddy, that's all over now. All over."

He looked up at her.

She had always been slender, like her mom, but was even more so now.

Though he didn't want to say it, he did.

"Maybe the lack of food. Maybe that's why you're late."

"No, John," and for the first time Makala spoke. "I found a test kit. It's positive. She's going to have a baby."

As she said the word "baby," Elizabeth and Ben, like so many across the ages, looked at each other and smiled.

John looked at them, again how slender she was, losing weight. Though he was a Catholic, even a non-practicing one, the thought of abortion flickered, even though it was anathema to him. Having this baby might kill her.

"I need to think," John said, and stood up, heading to his office.

He stopped at the doorway and then looked back.

"We have to evacuate in one hour. So start packing. . . ." He couldn't say any more and left the room.

He sat down at his desk. The bottle behind it, gone, damn it. He fumbled in his breast pocket and pulled out the smokes. He took one out and lit it.

Numbed, he looked out the window, at the backyard where Jennifer was throwing a stick to Ginger, who though moving slowly still was trying to play.

"John?"

He looked up. It was Makala.

"Am I intruding?"

"Yes and no."

"Can I join you?"

He nodded and she took the chair by his desk.

"What are you thinking?" she asked.

He sighed.

"The whole world has gone to hell. You know I killed two men this morning?"

"I saw the bodies. And they deserved it."

"And Zach?"

"I'm sorry, John, about him. He died well, though."

John lowered his head. Was it only hours ago? he thought.

"There's a barbarian horde coming this way and by tomorrow they might overrun us. If they do, all this will be moot. Jennifer out there will be dead, if lucky you and Elizabeth dead, all of us dead. The country . . . dead."

"That's why you have to accept what happened with Elizabeth."

"What? She's a kid, Makala. She was going to be a junior in high school, that son of . . ." He hesitated. "Ben a senior. My God, Makala. Accept it?"

"Kids younger than them have been getting pregnant for thousands of years. Especially in wartime."

"Not my baby."

"Yes, your baby," and she reached out and touched his knee.

"Listen, John. You know and I know there isn't much chance. And they know it, too. They think they're in love. For God's sake I hope they are in love. They want that taste of life as much as you did, as I did, as any of us do."

He looked at her and found he couldn't respond.

"Give them your blessings. I know it will be hard. But do it. I know the risk she faces as much, maybe more than you do. Give her that blessing for her to carry with her and give her strength."

He saw tears in Makala's eyes.

"She's a good kid, John. You and Mary raised her well. Don't turn this into a moral question now. They were two scared kids, the world going to hell around them; it was all but inevitable it would happen. If not for this damn war, it'd of been different. But it's not. And you have to accept that."

He nodded. "Tell Ben to come in here."

A moment later Ben was at the door, standing straight, eyes wide. John motioned for him to come into his office.

"Sir. You can do what you want to me, sir. Just don't blame your daughter."

And at that moment John softened. He could see the kid half-expected to see a shotgun or face a damn good thrashing. He had the guts to take it.

"You love my daughter?"

"More than anything in the world, sir."

"Well, so do I. Her and Jennifer."

"I know that, sir."

John nodded. He didn't want to think too much further about how Ben loved her; no father really would. But John could see that, though seventeen, Ben was trying to be a man at this moment and would have to be a man in the days to come.

John stood up, hesitated, then extended his hand.

"Thank you, sir," and Ben's voice cracked a bit.

John nodded.

"Just don't call me Dad yet," he finally said. "I'm not ready for that."

"Yes, sir."

He knew Elizabeth, in the next room, had heard the exchange, and she came through the doorway and flung herself into his arms.

"Thank you, Daddy."

Now he did fill up. Her voice still sounded like his little girl.

He saw Jennifer standing in the doorway as well, smiling.

"So you're not going to kill them?" Jennifer asked, and that broke the tension for the moment.

"No, of course not, sweetie."

"OK," and she was gone.

He felt there was some sort of ritual required now, and as Elizabeth slipped out of his arms he took her hand and placed it in Ben's hand.

"Once the next few days are over, well, since our priest disappeared, we'll ask Reverend Black to do the marriage."

Elizabeth smiled and leaned against Ben's shoulder.

"But we got other worries now. Like I said, we're leaving this house within the hour. Girls, you better pack what you can fit into the car. Ben, get down to your family and tell them to get out as well; have them come up to the Cove for now. They can stay with us if need be."

Elizabeth and Ben looked at each other.

"You can do your good-byes later; there isn't time to waste. Tell your folks I'll drive your family up to the Cove in an hour, so be ready."

He hesitated and suddenly it truly hurt, what he was about to say next.

"Ben. We're going to be attacked, most likely early tomorrow morning. You'll have to fall in with the town reserve guard."

"Yes, sir."

Elizabeth started to cry.

"Daddy, can't he stay with us in the Cove?"

"Absolutely not," Ben replied forcefully.

She looked at Ben and then back at John, eyes filled with tears.

"It's his duty now," John said softly.

Ben looked at Elizabeth, hesitated, then kissed her lightly on the lips.

"I'll see you later, sweetheart."

She couldn't reply, hugging him fiercely.

"Elizabeth, go help your grandmother and Jennifer pack."

She hesitated.

Ben broke free from her embrace.

"I'll be OK, sweetheart. Go on now."

Crying, she left the room, and Ben turned back to face John.

John opened his gun cabinet. Scanned the weapons and pulled out one of his best, an M1 carbine.

"You know how to load and handle this?"

"Remember, sir, you took me shooting with it last year."

John checked the clip, it was full, and there was a box of extra ammunition for it.

"Take this; you're going to need it."

Ben nodded.

"Report to Charlie Fuller. Tell him I've assigned you to be one of his runners."

"Sir, you are not keeping me back, are you?"

John lied with the shake of his head.

"You'll be in the middle of it, son."

Ben nodded solemnly, hefting the carbine and looking at it.

"Let me help Elizabeth first if you don't mind, sir."

"Sure, you got a few minutes."

He looked at John, eyes solemn.

"If anything happens to me, sir . . ."

John forced a smile.

"You'll be OK, Ben. Now go help Elizabeth."

"Yes, sir."

Ben left the room and Makala was standing at the doorway, smiling.

"You did the right thing," she said.

"Let me think about it."

To his surprise she came up and kissed him on the lips.

"I better get up to the conference center and evacuate the folks there. From what I just heard, I assume that will be in the middle of it."

John nodded.

"I'll drive you up there. Charlie should be sending up some vehicles to get people out. We're evacuating everybody from here clear back to the town. Once you get your patients out, report to Doc Kellor. I think you'd be most useful there."

"Is it going to be bad?"

John nodded again.

"Real bad, I think."

She squeezed his hand and went back to help the girls pack up.

He looked around. What to take? The guns of course. Seven rifles, including the original Civil War Springfield and the replica Hawkins .50 flintlock. Throw them in the trunk of the car for now. He scanned his office. What to take? The portrait of Mary of course, and as he picked it up he thought of Makala in the next room. Neither would mind, he realized with a sad smile.

He took the picture out of its frame and slipped it into his pocket. He then checked the loads in the Glock and the shotgun and shouted for his family to get moving.

CHAPTER TEN

The entire mountainside north and south of the interstate was burning. He gazed at the inferno, feeling nothing, even though his home was somewhere within that blaze.

Scattered shots still rang out. A holdout band of the Posse was barricaded inside a single-story house facing the interstate on a side road a couple of hundred yards back from the gap. It was a key position because it looked down on both the interstate and the flanking approach of the abandoned paved road and the railroad.

Two of his militia sprinted towards the building, approaching it from a blind spot, where a truck was parked. They crawled under the truck, came out the other side, and rolled up against the side of the building. One opened her backpack; the other took out a Zippo, flicked it to life, and touched the fuse.

Inside was a ten-pound charge of black powder, packed into three-inch PVC pipe, nails mixed in. The girl stood up and threw it through the smashed window, then collapsed backwards, shot in the chest.

He could hear screaming inside the building, someone standing up, trying to throw the backpack out, a fusillade of fire dropping him.

The explosion seemed to tear off the side of the house.

With harsh, guttural screams a dozen militia were up, charging, pushing through the wreckage and into the smoke-filled house.

Seconds later several Posse poured out the front door; none made it more than a dozen feet.

Two more houses to go at the top of the ridge. A couple of dozen hold-outs within, surrounded now on all sides. A barrage of Molotov cocktails rained onto the buildings; from within one there were bursts of automatic weapons fire.

The assault teams waited. In just eight hours they were veterans, no dumb-ass heroics, no "follow me" charges. One of the buildings finally started to burn, and then the second, suppressive fire pouring in through every window to keep those within down.

It took ten minutes, a dozen more Molotovs tossed against the side of the wooden structure to feed the flames, which finally went into the eaves of the house. It was ablaze now. Screaming from inside. The front door burst open and the militia was waiting. Half a dozen were gunned down as they came out. The last two out were women, falling to their knees, hands up.

No one fired and they crawled away from the inferno, then fell on their faces, crying for mercy.

One house left, the one with the automatic fire. John, watching the fight, had a gut sense of who was in there.

He picked up a megaphone.

"I want prisoners from that house!" he shouted.

The house was ablaze.

"Come out and we won't shoot!" John shouted.

Seconds later the door burst open and six men and a woman staggered out, throwing weapons aside.

"Down on your knees, hands over heads!"

They did as ordered and the student militia circled in around them.

The thunder of the battle was dying away now, a burst of shots from down near the second railroad tunnel, a volley from up on Rattlesnake Mountain, the louder sound now the forest fire sweeping both sides of the interstate, driven by a westerly breeze.

He looked around, some of the militia coming out from cover, standing up cautiously, looking around, most ducking when a sniper round zinged down from the ridge atop the pass. It was greeted seconds later with an explosive roar of fire and then silence. One of the militia then standing atop the ridge, rifle held high, waved the all clear.

John rose up from the side of the bridge over the interstate, walked around to the side, and slid down the slope and onto the pavement of the interstate, his action almost a signal that the war was over.

Dozens more were standing, dazed, silent.

He looked up the road to the pass but a hundred yards away. It was a road paved with horrors. At nearly every step there were bodies twisted into the contortions that only the dead could hold, rivulets of blood pouring off the road into the storm gutters. It was a seething mass as well, hundreds of wounded.

He turned and looked back down the highway towards Exit 66 and raised his megaphone.

"Medics! Bring up the medics now!"

They had been waiting several hundred yards to the rear while the last of the Posse were wiped out from the ridge, which they had successfully seized in the opening round of the fight.

There must have been someone local with them, either willing or unwilling. Two hours before dawn fifty of them had emerged on the little-used Kazuma Trail, known only to hikers and mountain bikers, a path that led from the Piedmont below to the highest point on the crest overlooking the interstate and the flanking roads.

Seizing the half-dozen houses up there, wiping out the defenders in a matter of minutes, they had enfilading fire down onto the gap itself, with the defenders there pinned, unable to fire back.

Minutes later the main assaults came in, fifty vehicles up the flanking road, men and women on foot going through the railroad tunnel, and a column of nearly two hundred vehicles roaring up from Old Fort, led by a diesel truck with a snow plow mounted to the front.

The forward barrier fell, and then the next fallback position, where he was standing now, the bridge over the highway, since the houses above were perfect positions to fire down on it.

Though they were caught off guard by the surprise seizure of the houses and ridge above the gap, the rapid retreat had been part of his and Washington's plan all along.

Washington was a superb marine, a superb trainer and leader, but John did realize now that all the crap about his being colonel . . . Washington had been right on that, too.

Washington's plan was a classic defense on the high ground and John had vetoed it.

"Almost as bad as losing would be our winning too easily," he had said. "We repulse them at the crest, they'll take losses, retreat, and then do one of two things: either head off somewhere else or wait until the time is right and get us, and I think it would be the latter. Whoever is leading that band cannot afford even a single defeat; his own people will turn on him, kill him, and then come back yet again."

John's worst nightmare was that after a sharp defeat the Posse would pull back to Old Fort, simply spread out a bit, loot, probe, and keep them on guard twenty-four hours a day and wait them out. They'd make a mistake; there'd be a weak spot; the enemy would catch a guard asleep, attack the position at night in the middle of a storm. No, John wanted them over the ridge—let them take the gap—and then to lure them into a classic killing ground.

"The mountains to either side can give us a Cannae, or a classic Mongol envelopment," he argued, and students who had taken his classes and were now officers sitting in on the planning just the day before instantly grasped it.

"Once in, I want them all in, and then I don't want one of them to get out alive."

It was the plan that Washington warned would triple their casualties but John argued in so doing they would annihilate the Posse rather than just drive it back, with the threat of a return.

The tragedy was that the first platoon of Company A, guarding the gap, was cut off in the opening move and not one of them made it out. That had nearly triggered a rout as the survivors of the second platoon gave way too quickly at the second defensive line, the bridge at Exit 66 and the nursing home overlooking it.

It had been near run then, the attackers swarming forward, sensing victory, pushing hard, squeezing in where Route 70 ran within feet of the interstate, the very place where John had first met Makala, her Beemer now upended and piled into the defensive barrier line across the main line of defense, where the interstate curved up on a bridge that crossed the railroad tracks. It was a bridge poorly designed for traffic, every ice storm someone always spun out on that bridge, but if whoever had designed it was thinking of a battle, it was superb. It was like a hill with no flanks to worry about, atop the bridge a clear field of fire for a mile back up the road, behind the bridge a sharp slope up to where the old town water tank was, another superb position, and the flank there protected by a wide cut through the forest for the passage of high-tension lines, thus creating an open killing field against any of the Posse trying to get to the tower.

And then the trap itself. Concealed up on each flanking ridge, back near the gap, Company B, armed with the best long-range weapons the town could provide, high-powered deer rifles with scope mounts. Every house to either side of the interstate, several hundred homes, including his own, and a trailer park were rigged to burn, buckets of gas placed within each. Students who were not trained as soldiers were now pressed into service, so that when the signal was given, the siren on the fire truck sounding off, combined with signal rockets, they were to go into action, moving fast on mountain bikes or mopeds, setting each house ablaze. He had bet on the usual breeze picking up through the gap, as the air farther down below in the Piedmont heated and began to rise, drawing down air from the pass in a cool continual breeze. Luck was on their side as well in that it had been a tinder-dry summer.

The hundreds of fires merged together into an inferno, acting as the blocking force on each flank, flames driving eastward, cutting off retreat except back onto the interstate or the railroad, which were now kill zones.

At the other end of the box, to the west, at the interstate bridge waited what was left of Company A along with them every citizen of the town who could carry a gun, concealed behind the reverse slope.

It had been a bloodbath.

Once his outer defenses fell, the second wave of the Posse swarmed in, hundreds of vehicles pressing over the crest and, as John hoped, undisciplined enough that, sensing victory, they were now just rushing forward to start the looting and slaughter.

The fight at the bridge had almost been like something from the Civil War, hundreds of men and women rising up from concealment, leveling rifles and blazing away, shredding everything in front of them. Posse vehicles crashed into the barrier line and the fighting had turned hand-to-hand. And then along the opposite slopes fires ignited and began to spread, and as the last of the vehicles crossed in, Malady's team shut the back door, using the two automatic weapons provided by Tom, complete with six thousand rounds of ammunition, backed up by citizens who had produced "illegal weapons" and students armed with a couple hundred of the dangerous homemade grenades.

The force on the bridge had nearly given way, though. For several crucial minutes John had been down, knocked out by an explosion. But someone had rallied the ill-trained backup force, and they were charging forward regardless of loss.

All that was left then was the killing, the closing in of the box, and when cornered their opponents knew their fate and fought with a mad frenzy. This was not the type of fight where surrender was a way out, and they knew it. There would be no escape for them, no pulling back to wait and to then lunge back days or weeks later. They were all going to die this day, and tragically, for Black Mountain and Swannanoa, it was going to cost dearly to do that killing.

Washington had warned of that before the battle, suggesting a false escape path for the routed who could then be hunted down later in a second killing zone farther down the mountain, but there was no other way, John realized. If they left an escape valve, a sound idea with a well-trained force but risky with the assets he now had, the surviving Posse just might break through and indeed escape, and then it could be months of a bitter guerilla war against the vengeful survivors.

It had turned into seven horrid hours of taking ground back, a step at a time, a bloody step at a time.

The medics were coming forward at the double. Wounded from earlier in the attack who had managed to hide and not get murdered, those wounded in the relentless push back, lay by the hundreds along the road. From up on the south side the fire was rolling eastward and screams could be heard, those trapped up there and now burning to death. It made John think of the Battle of the Wilderness in 1864. One could read of that fight in the history books and feel remote somehow. Not now. Even if they were all Posse burning up there, it was horrific.

And behind him Tom's men now came, deployed out in open order, and every few feet one would stop, lower his pistol, and fire.

The Posse wounded were to be summarily executed, and that was a task John wanted the police and older men of the town to do, not his own kids. They were hardened now, but he never wanted them that hard.

John slowly walked up the sloping road towards the crest and at last found him, a knot of students gathered round his body, heads lowered, some weeping.

Washington Parker was dead, killed in the opening minutes of the fight. The way he lay here seemed almost Christ-like, arms spread wide, heartbreakingly a young female student, dead as well, nestled under his arm as if in his final seconds he was trying to protect or comfort her, or maybe it had been the other way around.

Washington had insisted upon being in the front line, arguing with John that the kids needed him there especially to be led in the difficult task of feigning withdrawal, and along with the rest of the first platoon Washington had not come back.

John had held a hope that perhaps, just perhaps, Washington had managed to hole up someplace but knew it was unlikely.

John drew closer.

The man died as he would have wanted, John realized, leading "his men," from the front, and John felt guilt, having fought the battle from the rear line, as a commander.

Washington's "soldiers" were slowly filing by, battle-shocked kids actually, faces strained, sweat soaked, more than a few bandaged, coming down now out of the flanking hills and up the interstate, gathering in, and all now filing past their sergeant.

As each passed they slowed, and John watched them, hearing their whispered farewells.

"Thank you, sir." "Be with God now, sir." "I'm sorry, sir."

With frightful intensity it reminded John of the famous column written by Ernie Pyle back in World War II, about the death of a beloved officer and how his men reacted.

One of the girls knelt down, touched Washington's face, and then walked on. Some were silent, some offered a prayer or thank-you; others swore out of pain and bitterness.

John fell in with them and walked up. All he could do was come to attention, salute, and then move on. The sentimental side of him was dead at this moment, still in shock. He'd cry for Washington later on, alone.

More shots from behind, the sound of the horn of a Volkswagen Bus honking as it sped off, weaving around the wreckage, hauling wounded back to the main hospital in town.

More vehicles backing up, the old farm trucks, the diesel truck now rigged to a flatbed so that several dozen could be loaded aboard at once.

"John?"

He saw Makala coming forward and without thought he grabbed hold of her tightly. She began to shudder with tears.

"Thank God. There was a rumor you were dead."

He shook his head.

Yes, his face was burned. The Posse actually had made up some primitive bazookas, fired from pipes welded to several trucks, and a round had detonated on the bridge, knocking him unconscious for a couple of minutes.

She broke from his embrace and stepped back, holding up her hand.

"Track my finger with your eyes," she said, moving it back and forth, staring at him closely.

"John, you might have a concussion. And you got some second-degree burns."

"The hell with that now. Take care of the others."

She nodded, stepped back, and went over to one of the wounded, a girl, a volleyball player from the school. She was crying, curled up, clutching her stomach. John watched as Makala knelt down, brushed the girl's forehead, spoke a few soothing words, and then with an indelible ink pen wrote "3" on the girl's forehead. Makala leaned over, kissed the girl gently, and then got up and went to a boy lying by the girl's side. The boy's leg was crushed below the knee, and he or someone else had slapped a tourniquet on him. He was unconscious. Makala put a finger to his throat to check his pulse, wrote "1" on his forehead, and stood up.

"A one! Here now!" she shouted.

A stretcher team sprinted up, one of the boys looking down at the girl shot in the stomach and slowing. And John could see the agony in his face. The two had dated a year ago, in fact had been something of "the couple," until she broke it off. At a small college, everyone knew about the lives of the others, sometimes not so good, sometimes rather nice.

"Over here! This one here! Move it!" Makala shouted.

The boy, tears streaming down his face, was pushed forward by the girl at the back of the stretcher. They loaded on the boy with the mangled leg, turned, and started to sprint back down the road. Makala was already up to the next wounded, pen in hand. She was now, as the ancients might have said, the chooser of the slain: 1 for priority treatment, 2 for delay till all 1s were taken care of, 3 . . . 3 simply meant they were going to die and effort was not to be expended on them for now.

None of the student soldiers going into the fight knew about this triage, though the students assigned as medics did, as did all who were now helping to clear the battlefield, but it did not take long for the receivers of this to figure it out.

A girl was lying in the ditch against the median barrier, multiple gunshot wounds having stitched her body. Makala barely paused to look at her, wrote a "3" on her forehead, and moved on. The girl looked at John, crying.

"What did she write? What did she write?"

John knelt down by her side. It was a wonder she was still alive, the gunshot wound to her upper thigh having shattered her femur. How the femoral artery was not torn was beyond him. She was also shot through the chest and stomach, blood frothing her lips. He didn't recognize her. Most likely a freshman who had yet to take his class.

"She wrote '2,' sweetheart," he lied. "Others worse hurt than you. Help will be along shortly."

She tried to smile, to nod, but was already beginning the gentle slide into the night. John leaned over and kissed her on the cheek.

"Go to sleep now, honey. You'll be OK."

She reached out and snatched his hand, her grip remarkably strong.

"Daddy?" she whispered. "Daddy, help me."

"Daddy's here."

She began to shake uncontrollably.

"Now I lay me down to sleep," he whispered.

I pray the Lord my soul to keep . . . , she mouthed the words. The shuddering stopped. . . . She was dead.

John brushed the hair from her sweat-soaked forehead, kissed her again, then gently released her grip and turned away.

Distant shots echoed from the hills and more closely, from behind, as Tom's men continued to kill the Posse wounded.

Ahead, smashed into the side of the gap, was the smoldering wreckage of Don Barber's recon plane. During the worst moments of the fight John had seen Barber fly over, coming in low, tossing satchel charges, taking out one of their tractor-trailer trucks, and then suddenly wing over and go in.

John had specifically ordered Don not to tangle in the fight, to stay high, to keep doing recon, and in the opening hours he had done just that, flying up, observing, swooping back down over the town hall and dropping a note attached to a streamer with the latest update regarding the enemy moves, then going back out. The info had been crucial, keeping John posted on which direction the Posse was pouring in from and, most important, knowing when their full force had been committed before the closing of the trap.

But as he had feared all along, Don could not stay out of the fight and had decided, at last, to play the role of ground support fighter.

Don Barber was tangled into the wreckage . . . dead. He was wearing his old uniform from the Korean War. John slowed, saluted him, then pushed on.

A line of prisoners was being led along the westbound side of the road, hands tied behind backs, all roped together, roughly thirty of them, including the last survivors flushed out of the burning house.

A guard leading them looked over at John and he motioned for them to move towards the truck stop at the top of the pass, the place he was heading.

The truck stop was actually a turnoff lane at the very top of the crest, a mandatory pull over for all commercial vehicles, especially 18-wheelers. Trucks that pulled in were not allowed to proceed until the drivers had examined the map of the long descent that marked out "runaway truck lanes" for vehicles that might lose their brakes on the way down. A traffic light was hung across the lane, timed to let trucks through at safe intervals or to stop them completely if there should be an accident farther down the mountain. Of course all that was now in the distant past. To the good fortune of the town, at the start of the crisis one of the trucks stalled there had been loaded with snack crackers, but those were long gone as well.

It had been the command post for the barrier line established what seemed to be an eternity ago and was now where so many were heading, as if by instinct.

John continued on the road, several students falling in around him, all with weapons poised, acting as a guard. There had been a student assigned to him early, but that young man had been killed back by the Exit 65 ramp, taken down by the blast that had knocked John unconcious.

The prisoners were herded over into the truck lane, where a couple dozen more prisoners waited.

As the second group approached, those already there looked over anxiously. Some stood up staring at the short slender man in the lead, white, gray hair cut close, tattooed arms, ugly face twisted up from what looked to be an old knife wound, one of the final group flushed out of the burning house.

Malady, still alive, arm in a blood-soaked sling, came up to John.

John smiled and extended his hand, which Kevin clutched with his left.

"Good job, Kevin, damn good."

"I lost a lot of kids, though," he replied sadly. "It got real ugly once these bastards knew they were cornered. Kids were reluctant at first to shoot somebody who was down and looked dead, or badly wounded, but they learned real quick. . . ."

His voice trailed off.

He looked at the young soldiers standing around, gazing cold-eyed at the prisoners.

"You interrogate any of them?"

"Oh yeah, they're spilling their guts, pointing at each other. Everyone claiming they were forced into it. That piece of shit over there is their leader."

Kevin looked over at the ugly man.

"Amazingly, that bastard is the leader. Apparently a big drug player in Greensboro, contact guy for major shipments of coke and heroin coming up from Florida. He might look soft, but they're all scared of him, even the worst of the lot. They say he claimed to have the inside line with Satan himself, that God had abandoned America and Satan now ruled and he was the appointed one sent from hell to pave the way for Satan's reign over America."

"The stories about cannibalism?" John asked.

Kevin nodded and spat.

"They're all true."

John walked over to the leader, who gazed at him and then actually smiled.

"So let me guess, you're the general here?"

John did not reply.

"Masterful plan. I bet you're the professor, aren't you. I heard about you yesterday from a prisoner we took. A sweet girl she was, captured her yesterday."

John froze. The girl they had most likely lost in the skirmishing on the dirt road.

"I see a touch of military history in this fight. The la Drang Valley perhaps, lure in, get close up, and envelop? Saw it in that movie and on the History Channel."

"And you walked right into it," John said sarcastically.

"Yes, I did; indeed I did. I guess he decided it thus."

"He?"

"Satan of course."

The man turned and looked at the other prisoners.

"Did I not tell you that if you failed to offer your souls to him fully and in all things he would abandon you? Now you are indeed doomed to the fiery pit of hell. For God has cursed this world and because you failed me, Satan shall turn away from thee as well. Your reign by his side will be replaced by eternal punishment for your lack of faith.

"These dogs will show you no mercy. Rather than feasting tonight on their flesh, as Satan wished for you, instead you will be carrion for the dogs and crows . . . or perhaps . . ."

He looked over shiftily at John. ". . . they will feast on your flesh."

John, his Glock half-raised, was tempted to blow the man's brains out right there.

The other prisoners looked at him wide-eyed. Some started to cry; others knelt down, heads lowered, resigned to their fate.

It was so damn strange, John thought, how sometimes the most unlikely, an ugly little man like this one, could hold such power. He had a tremendous command presence, his voice sweet, rich, carrying power. So strange how some had that, could spout utter insanity and others would follow blindly.

"Cannibals," John said coldly.

The man looked up at him, face twisted into a smile that almost seemed warm and friendly.

"My friend. You know enough about what has happened to know that this nation is doomed except for those chosen few with the strength to live. The flesh of the weak is the holy sacrament to us, the living, to survive and to have strength, to allow us our triumph of the will."

He looked away from John and back to his surviving followers.

"For I have walked up and down and to and fro across the land and have considered this country that once was. Remove thy hand from it, protect it not, and the land that once worshipped thee will curse thee. And thus it was true and the land is now indeed cursed and we are the ones sent forth to cleanse it."

He then looked back at John.

"That girl we captured yesterday. She was indeed sweet, the best I think I've had. Well fed before she became our sacrament.

"You know the natives of New Guinea used to call their foes 'long pork.' Well-fed flesh actually tastes like that . . . pork."

John raised his Glock, muzzle touching the man's forehead.

"Go on, you bastard," he whispered. "Be like me; drink my blood once I am dead as I would have drunk yours. I know you are hungry. You do it, and all who follow you will join in, for they are hungry, too."

John hesitated, then backhanded the man with the muzzle of his pistol, knocking him down.

John turned and looked at the hundreds who were now gathered round.

"You heard it from his own lips."

No one spoke, all filled with shock, revulsion.

John looked around.

"Rope."

One of his students came forward, a coil of rope in hand . . . the knot already made. John motioned to the aluminum crossbeam that supported the traffic light.

The rope went over the beam. Several already had the man up. He had expected to be shot and at the sight of the dangling noose he began to struggle, kicking, screaming, as they dragged him over and tightened the rope around his neck.

John walked up to him, almost spoke to him, but the hell with that. There would be no last words.

"By the power vested in me by the citizens of Black Mountain and Swannanoa I declare this man to be a condemned criminal, a murderer, an eater of human flesh. He is not even worthy of a bullet."

John stepped back.

"Hang him."

They hoisted him up and it took several long minutes of spasmodic kicking before he finally died. His followers watched, terrified. Several fell to their knees and started to cry that they had repented and wished to be saved, one calling for a priest to hear his confession.

John looked at them and then turned away. He saw Tom standing there, grim faced.

"Hang as many as you can; shoot the rest of the bastards. I want a sign painted onto the side of the truck over there: 'Cannibals.'"

Tom nodded and within minutes half a dozen more were hoisted up.

The others now saw their fate, there were screams, pleas, and John stood there silent, watching.

"John?"

Makala was by his side.

"For God's sake. A couple of them aren't much more than kids. Most likely got sucked into this. Stop it."

He didn't speak.

"John, this is a lynching now. This is out of control. It's what you tried to stop this town from becoming. Look at us."

He looked down at her and then back around at his young soldiers, the townspeople who had fought, and saw the savage light on more than one face.

Ten of the prisoners were led away from the side of the truck stop, most pleading, screaming . . . and were shot. Their bodies were tossed over the railing, dropping down the sheer cliff to shatter on the rocks below.

A minute later, another ten were shot, their deaths greeted with angry shouts of approval.

And it was as if at that moment a film was winding through John's memory. Old grainy film, Russians hanging from makeshift gallows in that cold winter of 1941; the etchings of Goya, Spanish prisoners pleading, holding up their hands as French soldiers of Napoléon gunned them down; naked prisoners being led to a pit by the SS, kneeling down, shot, bodies tumbling forward. It was the face of war, of all wars, and now it was here and it was us against ourselves, John thought, as we fought for the last scrap of bread and now even for the bodies of the dead.

There were eight left, Tom's men picking them up, dragging them to the edge of the ravine.

John stepped forward, Glock out, and Tom, seeing him approach, stepped back, assuming that John was reasserting his old position as the town's executioner.

He looked at the eight. Several stood defiant, the same as the punk with the snake tattoo long ago. John looked into their eyes wondering, wondering why. Was this inside all of us? He turned and looked back, the hundreds gathered falling silent, and on more than one he now saw that same cold gaze. And he slowly turned back.

Makala was indeed right. Three of the prisoners, one a girl, were not much more than kids, fourteen, fifteen at most, though all three had that distant look of coldness and ice. He wondered if they were like that long before all this had ever started, gangbangers, as Washington had said, kids who would kill even then and think it a joke.

Next to them was a woman in her early twenties, shaking, so terrified that a trickle of urine was running down her leg, pooling at her feet. The next was an old man, eyes vacant, crazed, and beside him was a Hispanic kid, lips moving, the Spanish all but unintelligible but now obviously praying a Hail Mary.

"Kevin."

Malady came down to John's side.

"Get out your knife."

Kevin looked at John, hesitated, but then obeyed.

The eyes of one of the three defiant men widened. "Shoot me and be done with it," he said coldly. "But not the knife, man."

"Cut their bonds."

"What?"

"I said cut their bonds."

Kevin stepped behind each and cut their hands free. None of them moved.

John looked back at his students, his neighbors, his friends.

"It's over," he said.

There was a murmur of complaint from the crowd.

"What's to prevent those bastards from coming back tonight and trying to cut our throats?"

John shook his head.

"I was wrong."

"For killing them?" someone shouted.

"They killed our wounded without mercy!" a girl cried, one of his students, a girl who had been a Bible major long ago.

"And we have killed theirs. Washington and I ordered it because there is not even a fraction of the supplies needed to take care of our own."

"Cannibals!"

John nodded.

"Yes. Some undoubtedly yes. I won't bother to ask these, because they will lie to save their lives."

He wearily shook his head.

"I'm stopping it because I started to love it. I hate them. I hated that bastard hanging there more than I've ever hated anyone in my life. . . .

"But I will not become him. . . . I will not let us become them. Because God save us, we are on the edge of that now, here at this moment."

He did not wait for a reply but turned back to face the prisoners.

"I'm not going to go through some bullshit ritual of you swearing to me that you will leave, never return, and repent."

The Hispanic boy started to nod his head, went to his knees, and made the sign of the cross repeatedly.

"Remember what you saw here. Don't ever come back. All of you, if you survive, will carry the mark of Cain upon you forever for what you've done. If you come across other bands like yours tell them what happened here, and tell them they will face the same defeat.

"I ask but one thing. We've given you back your lives. Do not take any more lives, for then you surely will be damned forever."

He started to turn away.

"Go!"

Six did not hesitate; they simply turned and ran. The boy on his knees looked up at John wide-eyed and moved as if to kiss his feet. He backed away from the boy and motioned for him to get up and leave.

"Gracias, señor." He turned and ran off.

The young woman who in her terror had urinated just stood there, unable to move.

"Go," John said softly.

"Where?"

"Just go."

"I'm sorry. God forgive me, I'm sorry. I don't know if I can live now with what I've done. I'm sorry."

Sobbing, she turned and slowly walked away.

John turned and faced the crowd.

"Cut those bodies down," he said, then paused. "Except for their leader. I want a sign under him. 'Hung as punishment for leading the gang known as the Posse, murderers, rapists, and cannibals. May God have mercy on his soul and all who followed him.' "

John holstered his Glock and walked back to the rest, his soldiers, his neighbors, his friends parting as he passed, many with heads now lowered.

"You were right, John," someone whispered.

His soldiers. He looked at them as he passed. Some were now beginning to break down. Postbattle shock, perhaps what had just happened here as well.

Some started to cry, turning to lean on one another for support. Others stood silent. More than a few were kneeling, praying, others wandering back now, stopping to roll over a body, then collapsing, crying, hugging a fallen friend.

John felt weak, sick to his stomach.

"John, let me take you back into town."

It was Makala, who had come up alongside of him, slipping her hand into his.

He stopped and embraced her.

"Thank you for stopping me," he whispered. "I was out of control."

"It's OK, sweetheart. It's OK."

She leaned up and kissed him, the gesture startling, for so many were walking by him now, seeing this and respectfully not looking directly at them.

He suddenly did feel weak, as if he was about to faint, and had to kneel down.

"Stretcher!"

He looked up and shook his head.

"John, you have a concussion. You're suffering from shock; you need to lay down."

"I must walk out of here. Just help me."

He leaned against her, walking across the battlefield.

A battlefield, he thought. Memories of photos of the dead at Gettysburg, bodies lying in the surf at Tarawa, the dead and wounded marines aboard a tank at Hue. Always photos, but never in a photograph was there the stench.

The battlefield stank not just of cordite but also the coppery smell of blood, feces, urine, vomit, the smell of open raw meat, but this raw meat was human, or once human. Mixed in, the smell of vehicles burning, gasoline, rubber, oil, and, horrifying, burning bodies, roasting, bloating, bursting open as they fried.

The forest fire to either side of the highway had been a tool of battle but an hour ago. Now it was a forest fire raging, the heat so intense it could be felt from hundreds of yards away, moving with the westerly breeze, already over the crest of the mountain, moving down into the valley towards Old Fort, bodies, the enemy but also his own, roasting in those flames.

Now that it was over, hundreds were moving about, looking for loved ones, sons for fathers, mothers for sons, young lovers and friends looking for lost lovers and lost friends.

Film, yet again film. The scene from the Russian film *Alexander Nevsky,* after the battle on the ice, the mournful music, the haunting twilight effect of the lighting, wives and mothers weeping, looking for their fallen loved ones.

Again, though, this was no film; this was real. A boy, one of the tougher kids from the ball team, collapsing, lifted up the shattered body of a girl, cradling her, screaming, friends standing silent around him and then suddenly pinning him down as he dropped her, pulled out a pistol, and tried to shoot himself.

John staggered on.

A line of vehicles on the highway ahead. Wounded being loaded onto the flatbed trailer. Makala motioning for help. Hands reaching out, pulling him up, Makala climbing up by his side.

The sound of the diesel rumbling, exhaust smoke, they started to move, picking up speed as they cleared the ramp for Exit 65, the driver holding down the horn as the trailer came up State Street and then stopped in front of the furniture store in the center of town. All the furniture had been moved out, tossed into the street, except for the beds and sofas in the main display room.

But the facility was already overflowing.

"All ones here!" someone was shouting. "Twos over here!"

Four of the ones, all of them on stretchers, were lifted off and rushed inside.

John looked at Makala.

"I need to go in there."

"John, it's a concussion, not too bad, I hope. I think it's best I just get you home and into bed. You should be all right in a week or so. Jen can take care of the burns."

"No. I have to go in there. Those are my kids . . . my soldiers."

She didn't argue with him. A couple of townspeople helped him down. The last of the wounded off the truck, the driver revved it up, swung around the turn to Montreat Road, then turned through the parking lot of the town hall complex to race back to the battlefield.

John stood outside the door, hesitated, took a deep breath.

He let go of her embrace, stepped aside from her, and walked in.

He almost backed out but then froze in place.

It was the hardest thing he had ever done in his life up to this moment. Worse than holding Mary as she died, worse than anything.

"Jesus, give me strength," he whispered to himself, and then he walked in.

Dozens were on the floor, all with ones marked on their foreheads. Some were crying, others silent, trying to be stoic. Fortunately for some, they were unconscious. Every wound imaginable confronted him.

He walked slowly through the room. If any made eye contact he stopped, forcing a smile. Some he recognized, and he was ashamed of his lifelong inability to remember names. All he could do was bend over, extend a reassuring hand, and kept repeating over and over: "I'm proud of you. . . . Don't worry; they'll have you patched up in no time. . . . Thank you, I'm proud of you. . . ."

He left that room and in the next one he truly did recoil and Makala came up to his side. He looked at her, wondering how in God's name she had ever handled what he was looking at.

The two towns had nine doctors and three veterinarians Day one. One had since died. There were eleven tables in the room and on each was a casualty and around each was a team at work, the veterinarians as well in this emergency.

The anesthesia saved from the vets' offices and the dentists' offices was now in use. He saw Kellor at work and the sight was terrifying. Kellor was taking a girl's leg off just above the knee. The knee was nothing but mangled flesh and crushed bone. Her head was rocking back and forth, and she was weeping softly.

Horrified, John looked at Makala.

"We're using local for amputations," she whispered. "We have to save the general for the more serious cases."

"More serious?"

But he did not need to be told. Head wounds, shattered jaws, chest wounds, stomach wounds, though, were being triaged off because there were not enough antibiotics to treat them after the operation, if they even survived that.

He went up to the girl on the table. She looked up at him, wide-eyed, panicked, eyes like a rabbit that had just been shot, waiting for the final blow, and his heart filled. He knew her.

He grabbed her hand.

"Laura, isn't it?"

"Oh God, I can feel it," she gasped.

"Hang on," John said.

The sound was terrifying. Kellor was now cutting the bone with a saw. John spared a quick glance down. It was a hacksaw, most likely taken from the hardware store. My God, they didn't even have the right surgical tools.

"Oh God!"

John squeezed her hand tight, leaning over, looking at her.

"Look at me, Laura; look at me!"

She gazed up at him.

"Laura, remember your song 'Try to Remember'. . . ."

" 'The kind of September . . .' Jesus, please help me!"

The sound of sawing stopped; someone assisting Kellor lifted the severed leg off the table. Kellor stepped back from the table.

"Nurse, tie off the rest. . . ." He pulled aside his surgical mask and looked over at John, then down at Laura.

"Laura honey, the worst is over," Kellor said. "We'll give you another shot of painkiller shortly."

Sobbing, she nodded, John barely able to let go of her hand.

Kellor looked at John as they turned away.

"We're out of painkiller except for some oxycodine," he whispered. "God save her and all these kids."

Kellor tore off the latex gloves and let them drop to the floor.

"Nurse, I'm taking five minutes; prep the next one."

John felt guilty leaving Laura, but Kellor motioned for him to follow him out of the operating room.

"John."

It was Makala.

"I'm needed here now. I'm finished with triage up at the gap."

He nodded to her, but she was already turned away, motioning for an assistant to pour some rubbing alcohol on her hands.

John, following Kellor, walked past the other operating bays. The floor was slick with blood, and as John looked down he was stunned to see that it was covered with sawdust, an assistant throwing more down on the floor even as the doctors continued to operate.

As they passed the last table one of the doctors, a woman, stepped back.

"God damn it!"

She tore off her gloves stepped back, and leaned against the wall, sobbing, and then looked over at John, glaring at him as if he had intruded into a world that he should never have ventured into.

Two assistants lifted the body off the table, the boy's chest still laid wide open from her frantic attempt to save him.

Kellor took John by the arm and led him out of the room.

"A friend of her daughter's," he whispered. "They were neighbors."

The next room was set up as a postop, barely any floor space left. There was a precious small supply of plasma that had been saved from the clinic over in Swannanoa. Half a dozen bottles were hooked up, not necessarily to those who needed it the most but instead to those for whom a single bottle could ensure survival.

Some volunteers from the town who had not been in the fight were now sacrificing their own lives. They had volunteered to donate blood. In their weakened state not more than half a pint would be drawn, but even that was too much for so many of them. But they volunteered anyhow.

Those who knew their type were being matched up with the wounded. The letters had been marked on the chests and backs of those who had known their blood type before the fight with a grease pencil. The blood transfer was direct. To John it looked absolutely primitive, using old-fashioned rubber hoses, squeeze balls, and needles, the donors lying on cots higher than the patients receiving the precious fluid.

Kellor led John through a side door and out into the open air. After the last twenty minutes, it was impossible for John to believe that there was still a world out here of sunlight, a warm summer breeze . . . but then he saw the long line of bodies in the parking lot behind the store . . . the dead.

He fumbled in his pocket. There were but two cigarettes left. With trembling hands he pulled out one and lit it.

Kellor looked at him, started to hold up a finger.

"Makala already diagnosed me. Concussion."

"And some burns. You better get some ointment on that face and sterile bandage. Have Jen boil a sheet and cover it. You can't risk another infection. You're still weak from the last one."

"Sure, Doc."

"John, we're going to have a terrible problem in a few days."

"What? What after this?"

"Disease. I was up at the battle site after you pushed them back from the bridge. Saw some of the Posse. Talked to a few of them before . . ."

His voice trailed away.

"Before Tom's men shot them."

"Go on."

"John, their camp was loaded with disease. Flu, hepatitis, I think some exotics as well, typhoid perhaps. You look at their bodies you could see they weren't much better off than the people they were terrorizing. I think we're going to have some kind of epidemic here in a matter of days and it will be far worse than the last one. All that blood splattered about, many of them obviously drug users, we might be looking at hep B and C, maybe even HIV."

"Tell Charlie," John sighed. "I can't bear any more."

"Charlie?"

John looked at him.

"John, didn't you know? Charlie's dead. He was killed in the fight at the overpass."

"Oh Jesus. I told him to stay back here. He was too weak. His job wasn't in the front lines."

"You knew Charlie," Kellor said with a sigh. "He wouldn't stay back, not at a time like that."

"Damn."

"John, you're in charge of this town now."

"What?"

"Charlie appointed you. He told me just before he died. Kate was in here, witnessed it, and agreed. You're in charge now under martial law."

John sagged against the wall.

"I just want to go home right now."

Kellor nodded and put a reassuring arm around him.

"Things will run by themselves for the rest of the day. I'll take care of it. And John . . ." He hesitated. "I think you should go home."

"Why?"

John took the last puff of his cigarette and tossed it to the ground.

Kellor reached into John's breast pocket, fished out the last, the last of all his cigarettes, and offered it to him and helped him light it.

"My God, what else?"

Kellor reached into his pocket and pulled out a ring, a high school ring.

"What is this?" John asked.

"Ben's ring."

He couldn't speak. He just held it, looking down at it, flecks of dried blood coating it.

"He died an hour ago. He was triaged off as a three, but I saw him by the bridge and brought him back anyhow, John."

Kellor nodded to one of the bodies, one of the few with a sheet covering it.

"He was a good kid, John. A damn good kid. Stayed on the bridge even as it was getting overrun. A lot of people saw it, saw how he rallied people about to panic, shouting for them to charge, and then he went down. I thought you knew. You passed within feet of him when the counterattack started."

John couldn't speak.

Kellor sighed.

"John, he'll leave behind a child you shall be proud of. Proud that Ben was the father. Someday I'll come up and tell Elizabeth about him. Hell, I helped to bring him into the world seventeen years ago."

He shook his head.

"We might of lost the fight without kids like him, a lot of kids like him.

"John, he asked me to tell you that he was sorry if he had disappointed you. And asked that you love the child he and Elizabeth will have."

Kellor began to cry.

"Damn all of this," he sighed, then looked back at John.

"Now go home to Elizabeth."

John could not speak.

He walked over to the body and was about to remove the sheet, but Kellor stopped him.

"Don't, John; remember him as he was."

John looked down at the body.

"You are my son," he whispered. "And I will take care of your baby; I promise it. Son, I am proud of you."

Woodenly John turned and walked away.

Going around the building, he came out onto State Street. Another truck was pulling up from the front, half a dozen wounded in the back, three of them with twos marked on their foreheads, the others with ones.

He walked around them, barely noticing.

"Colonel, damn it, we won!"

He didn't even bother to look back at who was speaking.

His old Edsel was parked in front of the town hall. A crowd was gathered round. Someone had written on the bulletin board but one word: "VICTORY!!!!"

Some began to ask questions as he approached, others asking for orders, others asking what they should do now.

He did not reply; he simply got into the car. The keys were in the ignition, the engine turned over, and he backed out.

The radio was on. Voice of America.

"This morning, a containership from Australia docked in Charleston. Our allies have sent us over a million rations, a thousand two-way radios, six steam-powered railroad locomotives—"

He switched it off.

The barrier was still up at the gate into the Cove, two students guarding it. He rolled to a stop.

"What's the news?"

He looked at the girl holding a pistol.

"Sir, are you OK?"

"We won," was all he could say.

The girl grinned and saluted, motioning for the other student to move the Volkswagen that blocked the gate back.

John drove through and turned onto Hickory Lane, rolling to a stop at number 12, Jen and Tyler's house.

As John pulled into the driveway, all four of them were out the door, Jen, Jennifer, Ginger wagging her tail . . . and Elizabeth.

He sat in the car, unable to move as they came running down to him.

He looked at Elizabeth, all of sixteen and a half. No outward sign yet of the life inside her, still not much more than a child herself.

Jennifer reached the car first and then stepped back.

"Daddy, you look terrible!"

"I'm all right, honey. Just a little singed."

Elizabeth was beside her now, Ginger up between them leaning in, wanting to lick him.

God, but two months ago this was the way it was. Come home after a lecture and office hours, if a Tuesday or Thursday when he had a 2:30 to 4:00 class the girls home ahead of him. Always the dogs would come piling out, Jennifer with them, his teenage daughter at least still following a bit of ritual and joining them with a hug and kiss.

He was unable to move, to get out of the car.

Jen was now up looking in.

"What happened?"

"We're OK," he finally said. "We won; they're gone."

Jennifer shouted and grabbed hold of Ginger, dancing around.

"We won; we won; we won!"

He stared ahead . . . the victor returning from the wars, he thought. The triumph, the parade, the ovation. The stuff, yet again, of film, but now, this the real reality of it?

"John?"

Jen was leaning in through the window.

"You're hurt."

"Nothing much. Concussion, some burns, I'll be fine."

"Daddy, where's Ben?" Elizabeth asked.

John looked past Jen to his daughter.

"Let me out," he said softly.

Jen opened the door and as they exchanged glances he could see that Jen knew. She could read it in him.

He stepped out of the car and slipped his hand into his pocket.

He remembered that the ring was caked with dried blood. Frantically he rubbed it with his hand.

"Daddy? I asked you about Ben. Did you see him?"

"Yes, honey."

John walked towards the door, Jen rushing ahead to open it.

"Then he's OK?" Elizabeth asked. "I knew he'd be OK."

John could hear the wishful strain in her voice.

He walked into the house. Jen had opened all the windows, airing out the stale, musty smell that had greeted them. Sunlight flooded in through the bay windows that faced the creek that tumbled down through their backyard.

It had been Tyler's favorite place in the house, the bay windows open unless it was freezing cold, the sound of water tumbling over rocks, the deep, comfortable sofa facing it.

John sat down.

"Elizabeth, come here."

"Daddy?"

She was beginning to cry even as she sat down beside him.

He reached into his pocket and drew out the ring.

"Ben wanted you to have this," John said, fighting to control his voice, to not let the anguish out.

She took the ring, cradling it in her hands. He had done a poor job of cleaning it. Flecks of dried blood rested in the palm of her hand.

"Someday," he said softly, "someday you will give that to your child and tell them about their father, what a wonderful man their father was."

She buried herself in John's arms, sobbing, hysterical, crying until there were no more tears to give.

The shadows lengthened. He could recall Jen bringing him some soup, saying it was sent down by the chaplain from the college and she had been over to see Ben's parents, who had moved into an abandoned house. John remembered Jennifer's voice, in what was now her bedroom, talking to Jen, crying, then saying a prayer, the two of them reciting the Hail Mary together. The sound of Ginger paddling back and forth, then finally climbing up to sleep alongside Jennifer, sighing as she drifted off to sleep.

As darkness settled, Elizabeth came back out, nestled against his shoulder, and cried herself to sleep.

He held Elizabeth throughout the night, and would hold her until the coming of dawn.

CHAPTER ELEVEN

DAY 131

There was a ghost-town feel to the village as John drove into Black Mountain and did his new morning ritual of circling through the downtown area to see if anything had happened during the night.

Makala, sitting beside him, silent; most likely, he thought, going over the plan they had for the phone call.

Windows to once proud shops along Cherry Street were streaked and dirty. His old favorite, Ivy Corner, had burned two weeks ago, the fire an accident caused by some squatters. The fire had been allowed to burn since it threatened no other buildings, and John had let the squatters go without punishment.

Bits of paper, dust, leaves, swirled in the street with the autumn breeze. At the corner of State and Black Mountain a teenager had a booth, made up from an oak desk that had been thrown out of the furniture store when it was converted to a hospital. He had two plump squirrels and a rabbit hanging from a pole. "Squirrel seven bullets, rabbit twenty bullets, willing to barter," read a hand-lettered sign.

As food grew scarcer, the price was going up. But bullets were scarce now as well.

John's earlier prediction that cigarettes might very well become currency had been wrong. Nearly every last one had been smoked long ago. He still felt the pangs for it. It was bullets that were now the currency of choice, especially .22 and shotgun shells.

In his own hunting he had set the .22 rifle aside, going over to the .50-caliber Hawkins flintlock. One of the reenactors from John's old Roundtable group had started up a business of making black powder. The reenactor had figured out how to scavenge and process saltpeter and sulphur and the lead for the bullets; that could be found in any old car battery.

John circled past the military hospital. It was empty. The wounded who still needed treatment had been transferred up to Gaither Hall, which was being heated by the retrofitted boiler. Makala now ran that hospital, tending to the nearly forty who were still struggling to survive.

The casualties had indeed been high, over 700 dead, 120 of those students, and 700 wounded, of whom a third had died, and some were still dying, even now.

Nearly a third of the students had thus died in the battle or afterwards, another third wounded. A horrific price. In class, so long ago, when he spoke of Civil War battles where a regiment would lose two-thirds of their men in a battle, it had always been numbers. Now it was real, so terribly real. Both Jeremiah and Phil had died in the fight, and so many others of his kids, as John had once called them.

Just yesterday he had attended another funeral, of the girl Laura who had lost her leg above the knee. She just could not beat the subsequent infections.

The funeral had been a heartbreaking affair. Only a handful showed up, those with the strength to show, and as she was laid to rest, the surviving members of the choir sang the song that somehow had become associated with the college and the battle: "The Minstrel Boy."

"The minstrel boy to the wars is gone,
In the ranks of death you will find him . . ."

The dead from the battle were all interred in the veterans cemetery at the edge of town, one slope of the cemetery given over to their graves. There had been talk that someday a monument would be erected to them . . . someday.

Everyone agreed they needed a special resting place and not just the golf course.

There was still the occasional skirmish that needed the militia. A small band of a couple dozen raiders made the trek over the Swannanoa mountains and hit down along old Route 9, and a week later an expedition was led by John down into Old Fort to root out the few remaining members of the Posse, most of them wounded, who had somehow escaped. Six more dead for the college as a result. As for Old Fort itself, barely a civilian was left alive after the treatment the Posse had given them.

Those of John's troops who were still left were indeed hardened now.

Regarding Kellor's prediction about another epidemic, he had been right. Days after the battle, what some were now calling the plague month began.

There were nearly three thousand new graves at the golf course, one of them for Doc Kellor. The medical staff had been particularly hard-hit; there were only two doctors and one vet remaining. It had indeed been like the plague in years of old, most physicians heroically standing to their duty until they were felled, but one had just fled, hiding in his cabin, and was now an outcast, the town pariah.

The simple combination of disease and starvation had created a death rate as terrible as that of the Black Death of the fourteenth century. Added in were hundreds with hepatitis A, others carrying B and C, which would kick in later, the usual injuries, the minor cuts that led to amputation and death.

It was the dying-off time and by yesterday's count just over forty percent of the two communities, which had been alive little more than four months back, were still alive. As a war, it was the most horrific since the Middle Ages. The legendary twenty-five million dead in the Soviet Union during World War II had been but one-seventh its population.

And yet now briefly they were swimming in food. The carefully guarded cornfields had yielded a bumper crop. Every apple orchard was striped of its fruit, even the wormy ones. Pumpkins had fleshed out to fifteen, twenty pounds or more, and would not just be used this year for carved decorations. The college scavengers were bringing in bushel baskets of nuts, pinecones, sunflowers, and in some places finding remains of orchards up in the woods where a homestead had been a hundred years ago, the long-forgotten trees stripped clean.

But the food had to be carefully counted, for it would need to last until the coming of spring. And what seemed like a bounty was, in fact, barely enough, actually not enough, for all to get through the winter.

As for meat, there was now almost none, still the occasional squirrel, rabbit, raccoon, or possum, but deer, bear, even wild boar had been hunted to near extinction. Yet again, the false memories of the supposed life on the frontier or up in the mountains now, that all one needed to do was get a gun, walk for a few hours, and then drag back a hundred pounds or more of meat. But when thousands were thinking the same thing, in an area even as extensive as five hundred square miles, and hunting season was now 365 days a year, the game was all but gone.

Hunting parties from the college were going up into the high mountains for three and four days at time and, more often than not, coming back empty-handed. The forest had been hunted clean.

So there was food, but there was no balance to the food and the dying continued, even as apples were carefully hung to dry, corn stacked up in dry sheds, all covered by armed guards twenty-four hours a day. The few elderly in the community still alive were pressed into service to teach the now all but forgotten art of canning. The problem was, there were hardly any proper canning jars and gaskets, which sealed them, to be found.

Every day he had been terrified for Makala, who was in the thick of it, but she had survived untouched. She had avoided their house during the dying month, only coming down to check when John was finally hit by it and then Jen, though through luck, or good nursing, the flu symptoms had run their course in a few days. Elizabeth had caught it as well, and John did not feel uncomfortable that, being pregnant, she was entitled to the now very rare antibiotics and additional rations to see her through. Fortunately, it had not touched Jennifer.

But for her, the risk of flu was no longer the concern.

It was Jennifer all were focused on now. The remaining insulin had finally lost all potency two weeks back, more than a month earlier than John had planned for. With the final bottle Makala risked several injections that finally totaled 800 units to bring Jennifer's blood sugar level back down from 520 to 145. It was now back over 600, climbing, and six days ago she had collapsed. All the symptoms that Kellor had long warned John about were now full-blown. Extreme thirst at first, nearly uncontrollable urinating, a simple scuffed knee that had never really healed over now raging with infection, red streaks up nearly to her groin, her fever soaring to 103. Her immune system had failed, kidneys were failing . . . her precious little body was shutting down.

He knew he should drive up to the gap to check on the guard there, but that had to wait. The drive around town had fulfilled John's duty for the moment, though as he turned the corner past the ruins of the Front Porch he could see, up the street, two bodies lying out along the curb, waiting to be picked up, and made a mental note to call Bartlett.

John pulled into his usual slot in front of the town hall and got out, Makala joining him.

Judy was actually the person who was the center of the town as the switchboard operator, having risen from the quiet role of a secretary. She knew every call coming in and out, lived at the office, and at night monitored the battery-powered radio, pulled out of the blue Mustang, listening for news from the outside, which she would then post each morning on the whiteboard outside town hall.

As he walked in he could see the latest, a report that Asheville supposedly had a reliable two-way radio link with Charleston. Four emergency supply trucks had arrived in Greenville, South Carolina, and one was promised to Asheville by the end of the week. She had not posted the news, though, when she had called into him just after dawn, that a helicopter had landed yesterday evening at Memorial Hospital, reportedly carrying a load of medicines.

That knowledge would trigger an attempt by those still capable of moving to get into Asheville, and he knew that Asheville would not let any of them through the barrier near Exit 53 that was now a permanently fortified position, definitely payback for their defiance regarding the refugees back in the spring. The few refugees from outside trying to get farther west were allowed through, but anyone from Swannanoa or Black Mountain seeking to cross the line to barter was blocked.

He walked into the office, Judy looking up from her switchboard.

"Hi, boss."

"Judy, connect me to Memorial Hospital. Put it through to my line and the line in the conference room."

"I'll get on it."

John went into his office, the office that had been Charlie's. John had not changed it all that much, the only addition a framed Polaroid picture of the survivors of what was now called the First Battalion, Black Mountain Rangers. Eighty-one soldiers, standing in front of Gaither Hall, the picture taken a week after the battle. They looked twenty years older than the kids in another picture beside it, the annual graduation photo of all the seniors, taken just two days before "The Day." Some were in both photos. The kids in the graduation photo looked fresh, ready to go out and take on the world with enthusiasm and joy. The rangers, they looked as if they could take on the world, by killing. The picture always made him think of a painting by Tom Lea, a combat artist of the Second World War, of a shell-shocked marine at Peleliu called *The Two Thousand Yard Stare.*

"Boss, I got a line open. Pick up."

John lifted the rotary phone off the cradle and there was a crackling hum.

"Memorial Hospital." The voice sounded faint, distant.

"This is Black Mountain calling," Judy said. "Can you connect a call to the hospital director, Dr. Vance, from Dr. Matherson, director of public safety in Black Mountain?"

Makala had advised Judy to use John's old title. Doctors of the M.D. kind looked down on doctors of the Ph.D. kind, but still, it would help to get through.

"Please hold," came the voice from the other end.

John looked across at Makala, who was standing at the crank phone in the conference room.

Five minutes passed, then ten. He sat on his desk, waiting nervously, heart racing, the only sound static and then a distant voice.

"Vance here."

"Dr. Vance. This is," he hesitated, "Matherson, director of public safety for Black Mountain."

"What do you want?"

He could hear the exhaustion in Vance's voice. John looked over at Makala and nodded. He was afraid if he continued, emotion would take over, and the man on the other end had no time for emotional appeals.

John had sat in the same spot now since Charlie's death. Decisions about who got rations and who did not. The condemning to death by execution of twenty-two people for looting of food, in one night fifteen of them had killed off two head of cattle, and, horrifyingly, one for cannibalism. Fortunately, he was now able to delegate that terrible deed to someone else, three people, one from Swannanoa, one from Black Mountain, and a professor from the college.

John had listened to so many appeals, and always he had to judge based upon what was fair, and fairness was who might be able to make it through to next spring and who was now triaged off.

"Dr. Vance, this is Makala Turner. I was head RN with the cardiac surgical unit at Overlook in Charlotte. I worked directly with Dr. Billings. I'm now head of all emergency treatment here in Black Mountain."

That line was carefully prepared by her, to create a sense of equality and draw from the tradition of mutual professional respect.

"Billings, how is he?" And then a pause, a realization most likely of the absurdity of the question.

"Doctor, on the day things went down, I was coming up to Memorial to attend your briefing on the new cauterization method for control of P.A.T. arrhythmia."

A pause.

"Seems like a million years ago," and John could hear the voice on the other side soften.

Makala had thought this out well. He looked over to her, but her back was turned to him, avoiding eye contact.

"Nurse Makala . . ."

"Turner," she said. "Dr. Vance, we have a situation here I think you can address."

"Go on," and John could hear the tension come back into Vance's voice.

"We got word that a helicopter load of medical supplies was airlifted to your hospital last night."

A long pause . . . "Yes, that is correct."

"Dr. Vance. We have a girl, twelve years old, type one diabetic."

"And she's still alive?" There was an incredulous note in his voice.

"She's been carefully monitored and is a tough kid. Her father was able to obtain enough insulin to last five months, but the stock has degraded and all potency is gone."

"Amazing she lasted this long."

John stiffened, again looking at Makala, the way she was now so clinically talking about Jennifer.

"Dr. Vance. Was any insulin included in that shipment?"

There was a pause.

"Was there any insulin?" John asked, cutting back in, his voice tense.

"Yes."

A pause on the other end.

"How long has she been without insulin?" Vance asked.

Makala quickly turned, looked at John, and shook her head.

"Last injection four days ago."

It was a lie; it had been over two weeks.

Silence on the other end.

"Blood count?"

"Three hundred and ten," again a lie; it was over twice that now and still climbing.

"Dr. Vance?" Makala asked.

"Yes."

"We can send a vehicle to pick up a vial, just a thousand units. It will save her life."

He sighed and with that sigh John knew. How many had heard him sigh in the same way before rejecting their tearful appeal for but one more bowl of soup or the release of but two or three pills of Cipro or the few precious Z-pac antibiotics locked away in a safe?

"Save her life for how long?" Vance finally replied. "A month? The insulin received might be all we'll get for several months. It's already been designated for those who can survive on far lower doses than type one diabetics need."

"Dr. Vance, we can have her at the hospital in an hour. Just one injection to stabilize her. We've heard the road might be open down to Columbia and from there to Charleston; we'll risk driving her down there if you can help us stabilize her."

"You and I both know the road is not open. A dozen people from here tried to get through just to Greenville yesterday and were wiped out by raiders in Saluda Gap," Vance replied, "and even if you did get through, there's no chance she'll be given more. The authorities in Charleston have listed insulin, along with a couple hundred other drugs, as A priority, meaning to be distributed in extreme need only to those under the age of forty-five and over eighteen with high probability of survival and the ability to work in some manner. They sent me exactly five vials."

Frustrated, John thought of Don Barber's plane.

"Is there a means to fly her out?" John interjected forcefully. "Surely you must have planes down at Asheville Airport that are still flying."

"We did, but we don't now. We lost the last two a week ago. The pilots just took off with their families and disappeared. And even if we did have that means, I'd prioritize a hundred other cases first for airlift, even if we had it."

Makala waved for John to shut up and there was a long pause.

A long pause that drifted into nearly a minute of silence.

"I'm sorry, but the answer is no. Now, if you will excuse me . . ."

John stood up.

"We are talking about my daughter!" he shouted.

"I suspected that," Vance replied. "And suspect as well that it's been far longer than four days since her last injection."

"Please, Dr. Vance. Please, it's my daughter. Just one injection."

"John, isn't it?"

"Yes."

"John. Like I said, they sent up five vials. I've got two kids in this hospital now who have standard childhood diabetes and are barely hanging on, but God forgive me I'm withholding the medicine even from them because I've got nearly thirty adults with varying degrees of diabetes that can survive a lot longer with just a low dose. I might need this stock for the rest of the year to try and save some that can be saved."

"Please for God's sake."

"John. Please listen. One injection for your daughter will not change the final diagnosis; it will simply postpone the inevitable. My God," he said wearily, "do you think I want to tell you this? John, I have enough anesthesia for maybe twenty operations and we need hundreds. Painkillers, even just some damn aspirin . . ."

His voice trailed off.

Makala was waving John off, signaling him to be quiet.

"Dr. Vance. Makala here. I've been treating this girl since all this started. She's a tough kid, a survivor. We can save her life."

"For how long?" Vance replied, and now his voice was getting cold. "Type one diabetics. A hundred years ago they died within weeks after pancreatic shutdown. That's the world we are back in now, maybe for years to come."

Again a pause.

"Nurse Turner. You understand triage as well as I do."

"Triage?" John shouted. "You are talking about my daughter, god damn it. You will not triage her off."

"Sir, I am sorry for you. I truly am."

"Damn you, listen to me! I can mobilize a hundred well-trained infantry and by God we will be there in an hour and by God you will give me that insulin. And if need be I'll blow up the water main to your damn town."

A long silence.

"Are you listening to yourself?" Vance said. "Would you really do that?"

"Yes!"

"I don't think so, John. I've heard a lot about you, John; you are not the type to get innocent people killed if you try that stunt. And if you do, the Asheville militia will meet you at Exit 53, and this hospital is cordoned with troops as well. If you blow the main thousands of innocent people will suffer.

"I'm sorry for you, sir. God save us, I'm sorry for all of us, sorry for those who could have prevented this and now must carry that on their souls. . . ."

His voice trailed off, breaking into a muffled sob.

"Good-bye."

The line clicked off.

"No!"

John swung the phone around, tearing the wire connection out. Filled with impotent rage, he held the phone, and then flung it against the wall.

"John, please."

Makala was in the room, tears streaming down her face.

"Damn all of this. Damn this country. Damn all of this," and he collapsed into his chair, sobbing.

"Come on, John; let's go home. She needs us there."

He finally stood up. In the hallway Judy was standing by the switchboard. She had heard every word and was silently weeping. Tom, gaunt, face pale, was silent, standing in the hallway beside Judy, looking at him.

"John, I'm willing to go up there and try and get it for you," Tom said softly.

Makala shook her head.

"No, Tom, we're going home. Can you see to things the next few days?"

"Sure."

"Judy, hold any calls to the house."

Makala drove John home. As they passed through the guard post, manned as always by two students, John said nothing, acknowledging nothing, the students watching him, eyes wide, as he and Makala drove through, for they could see he was crying.

Jen was outside the house as they pulled up, Makala helping John to get out. She didn't need to be told.

"How is she?" Makala asked.

"Drifting in and out. Breath is fruity smelling like you said it would be. She's no longer urinating; I can't get water into her."

"John."

It was Makala, hands grasping him tight.

"You have to do this now. I want you to go in there as if everything is fine. She is not to know you are afraid. If she asks about medicine, tell her it's coming shortly. She cannot know you are afraid."

He nodded.

"You ready?"

"Yes."

He walked up the front steps and opened the door, then paused.

"Hail Mary full of grace . . . ," he started to whisper, the prayer going silent as he stepped into the house.

The alcove that faced towards the creek had been converted into the sickroom, a bed set up, raised up higher with books underneath so Jennifer could see out the window, watch the creek and the bird feeder. Elizabeth had finally stirred out of her shock as this crisis came and had spent several hours cracking pinecones, gathering handfuls of the precious seeds to fill the feeder, and keeping by Jennifer's bedside, reading to her.

Ginger, now nothing but skin and bones, barely able to walk, had crawled up onto the foot of the bed.

Jennifer turned and looked towards him.

"Daddy?"

"Here, my pumpkin."

He came over and sat by the bed. She was clutching Rabs tight, and arrayed on the far side of the bed were the three Beanie Babies she had snatched as they evacuated the now-lost home . . . one of them Patriot Bear, the gift for her twelfth birthday.

"Will I get well?"

"Sure, sweetheart, you'll be up and running in no time. Makala and I ordered some medicine and it will be here soon."

He was afraid to look up at Makala, who he knew was standing in the doorway. If they made eye contact he feared he'd break.

Jennifer turned away, features pale.

"You're lying, Daddy. You never could lie to me."

"No, honey. It's the truth. You'll soon feel well."

She said nothing, just looking at him.

"Sweetie, would you like me to read to you?"

Head turned away, she nodded.

He stood up, scanning the bookshelf, and saw two books and his heart filled. Both had obviously belonged to Mary, one from early childhood. He opened them. Inside one was inscribed. "Merry Christmas, sweetheart . . . 1976." The second had in a childish scrawl, in pink crayon, "My book, Mary."

He set the second book to one side, returned to Jennifer's bed, opened the first, and started to read. " 'When Mr. Bilbo Baggins, of Bag End . . . ' "

And then he stopped.

No, not this one. She had seen the movies when they had first come out and was young enough then that it had frightened her.

He put *The Lord of the Rings* aside and picked up the second book. It had been Mary's favorite as a child and it was why Rabs, now nestled in Jennifer's arms was named Rabs. On the day Jennifer was born he had placed Rabs in her crib and Mary had cried at the sight of the snowy white rabbit from a story she had loved in her own childhood days. Rabs, now so dingy gray from years of being held, kissed, and loved, was nestled in Jennifer's arms.

"The Adventures of Rabs the Rabbit . . ." he began, swallowing hard as he turned the first page, remembering so many nights when Mary would read Jennifer to sleep with this wonderful old classic that mother and daughter had so loved and cherished together.

"One day, when Jennifer, and her best friend Rabs had nothing else to do . . ."

The real name in the book was Kathy but Mary had always used Jennifer's name, the same way when she was a child, her mother had used hers. He looked up at Jen, who stood silent by the foot of the bed, who unable to speak, could merely nod her head. He felt such love and pity for her at this moment for all that she had lost as well.

And he began to read.

The house was silent throughout the day, except for John softly reading, pausing when Jennifer was obviously asleep.

The shadows lengthened, the windows still open, the cool air drifting in, but he did not close them, the soft rushing of the brook outside the window soothing with its gentle murmur.

Jennifer stirred, Makala trying to get her to drink. She wouldn't, so Makala just sat by the other side of the bed, moistening Jennifer's lips with a damp towel.

"Daddy?"

She looked up at him, eyes open.

"Sweetie?"

"Remember your promise?"

"Which one was that angel?"

"Let me stay close to you . . . and keep Rabs warm and with you; he loves you too . . ."

"Of course, of course," and control did finally break. Crying, John leaned over and hugged her, kissing her forehead. She tried to put her arms around him but couldn't, and as he took her hands he could feel how cold they were.

He tucked Rabs back under her arms, floppy head of the much loved stuffed rabbit resting on her chest.

Makala sat on the other side of the bed, gently brushing Jennifer's brow. Elizabeth had led Jen away, the two in the next room, sobbing. Jennifer was no longer sweat soaked and he knew what that meant. Makala slowly let her hand drift to Jennifer's throat, felt the pulse, and looked over at John.

He picked the book back up, it was nearly finished, and he continued to read, turning the page with one hand, holding Jennifer's hand with the other.

He could feel her hand getting colder and he read now, almost in a fast monotone, turning the pages, and then reached the last one.

"And so Rabs, nestled in Jennifer's arms watched as she went to sleep. 'Some day you will be all grown up,' Rabs whispered to her, 'but I will love you forever. And far, far away, we will play again some day. Sleep tight Jennifer, and I will see you in the morning.' "

"John," Makala whispered.

He couldn't speak.

"John, she's gone."

He knew. He had felt her slip away before he had turned the last page.

She was buried in the garden, her grave near the bay window, very close by to him as promised. At nighttime Rabs rested on the windowsill inside the house, keeping vigilant watch. He had spent a fair part of the day outside, just sitting by her grave, holding Rabs, talking to Jennifer as if she were sitting before him, again his little girl of five, the fur on Rabs still not completely worn off as it now was, Ginger, barely able to move, lying by his side.

It was towards evening and Makala came to sit by him.

"I'm worried about Elizabeth," she said. "She needs to eat."

"There's nothing to eat," John replied, "other than the rations at the college."

"John, she's in her third month. It's crucial now, perhaps the most crucial month of all. The rations are mostly carbs. She needs protein, meat, as much as we can force into her."

Makala fell silent, leaning against his shoulder, and he knew what she was saying.

It was not a hard decision at all now. Not hard at all. He went into the house and came out a minute later, carrying the .22 pistol. He handed Rabs to her.

Ginger was lying by Jennifer's grave as if keeping watch.

He knelt down and picked Ginger up. She was so light.

"Come along," he whispered. "You can still save a life, my dear friend. And besides . . . Jennifer wants to play with you again."

How doth the city sit solitary, that was full of people? How is she become as a widow? She that was great among the nations, and princess among the provinces, how is she become tributary?

BOOK OF LAMENTATIONS 1:1

CHAPTER TWELVE

DAY 365

The phone ringing by his bedside woke him up, the light streaming through the window; it was just about dawn.

He could hear crying in the next room, little Ben, Elizabeth shushing him.

John picked up the phone. It was Judy and he listened, finally sitting up.

"I'll be down there as quickly as possible."

Makala was snuggled up by his side, half-awake.

"Come on, love; get up now."

"What?"

She opened her eyes and looked around.

"Not even dawn yet."

"Up. We got to get into town, all of us."

He pulled on the old stiff trousers lying by the side of the bed and rubbed his chin, suddenly wondering if he should shave. Absurd, he had not shaved in more than six months.

It had been warm enough a week ago for all of them to have a bath. He had built a roaring fire, scooped water from the creek to heat, and then filled what had once been a small outdoor fishpond. By the time the girls and the baby had finished, the water was a dark scummy gray, but John didn't care, the first at least tepid bath since late autumn.

The following day Makala and Jen had scrubbed clothes along the bank of the creek the old-fashioned way, a flat rock and an antique scrub board scrounged out of the basement. All had walked up to the college that evening for an actual spring dinner feast, 140 of the surviving students, Reverend Abel offering a service in the Chapel of the Prodigal, the choir putting on a musical performance, and then what was supposed to be a one-act comedy about someone finding a television that still worked . . . It had fallen rather flat, too painful, though the audience did laugh politely.

Ben had of course been passed from girl to girl, and for more than a few it was practice. The autumn and winter had resulted in more than a few pregnancies and rather quick marriages by Reverend Abel.

The dinner, of boiled corn mixed with apples, garnished with ramps and the first dandelions of spring, had at least been filling.

After the dinner, music, and play he had met with Abel, Malady, and the surviving faculty to talk about trying to get at least a few courses up and running . . . but the conversation had fallen away. It was time to struggle to bring in the first greens, to get hunting parties out, to maybe, just maybe, get the turbine project finished at the dam and finally hook electricity back up. Courses could wait until the fall.

He walked out into the living room, Elizabeth standing by the window, watching the sun rise, Ben nuzzled against her, nursing.

She did so look like her mother as she looked over her shoulder and smiled at him contentedly, that Madonna-like face all new mothers have when nursing a child.

"Morning, Daddy."

"How is he this morning?

"Hungry little devil."

"Get something on a little more presentable than that old bathrobe; you're going into town with me now."

"Why?"

"Just do it; wake up Jen and tell her to get moving as well."

He walked outside; the air was chilled, the sky overhead clear. The trees were really leafing out now, though farther up the slope of the mountains it was still winter and Mitchell was still snowcapped.

Strange, a year ago today. Precisely a year ago.

He walked round the side of the house and saw a fresh tulip beginning to blossom. He snapped it off and placed it on Jennifer's grave.

"Good morning, my little angel," he whispered, and looked back to the window where Rabs sat gazing down protectively.

Next to her grave was another, smaller. Very little had been buried there, but he felt he owed Ginger that for her sacrifice. Elizabeth had found a faded ceramic dog and placed it there for Ginger shortly after Ben was born.

"Dad, what is it?"

Elizabeth was outside, holding Ben.

"Just get in the car."

The old Edsel, the miracle machine, was still running, though just barely, the rings going. He turned it over and it revved to life, black exhaust blowing out. Their remaining stock of gas was increasingly contaminated.

Jen came out, helped by Makala. The two had indeed bonded over the long winter; the starving winter it was now called by those who had survived it. Jen was failing. Though she stood proudly straight a year ago, osteoporosis was taking over. She was developing cataracts also but could still see well enough to at least read, which had become her source of comfort during the long cold winter months spent next to the fireplace.

The firewood. Though he argued against it, students made sure the house was supplied . . . and provided extra rations for Elizabeth as well.

Jen got into the back alongside Elizabeth, and Makala climbed into the front seat. He backed out and started towards town.

"What the hell is it?" Jen asked a bit peevishly. "Did someone get a bear?"

That had happened three weeks ago and had been the cause of an actual celebration in town. Bear stew, enough to feed a thousand when some of the precious dried corn and apples were mixed in.

A thousand, 960 actually, was the number now, at least as of yesterday afternoon.

The starving winter, as Kellor predicted, had taken down most of the rest of the survivors. The months of cold, increasing solitude as already weakened neighbors died away, fires going out, the weak far too weak to crawl out, bring in wood, and relight the flame . . . curling up and then just going to sleep. The death rate soared once more.

Just yesterday, at the town council meeting, Makala, now head of public health, had raised the terrible issue of burials. It had broken down by February. There were too many dead and too few left with the strength to bury them. It was estimated that hundreds of homes might now actually be morgues, the entire family dead. A hundred or more bodies were lying in the graveyard, decaying.

The decision was made to burn them, the grisly task to be seen to by those who would accept triple rations as payment.

That now was a horrible irony as well. With so many dying during the long winter, there was now actually enough food to see the rest through to summer.

John drove down Black Mountain Road, the road that had been his daily commute for so many years. There was no longer a guard at the gate, too few left to man it, along with the outposts and barricades. At the intersection to Flat Creek Road he had to take a turnoff. The ice storm of two months ago had dropped dozens of trees in the town, the next block still impassable; there was no one with the strength to clear the trees.

The First Battalion did still have strength, but he had kept them strictly to other tasks, to be the army, guarding the passes throughout the winter and guarding the food supplies. Their survival rate had been just about the highest. Black Mountain had lost close to eighty percent of its population in exactly one year, the college just over sixty percent, including the casualties from the war. Part of it was the resilience of kids in their late teens to early twenties, part of it the strict discipline, created by Washington Parker, continued now by Kevin Malady, and the slow, heroic sacrifice of President Hunt and his wife, who died from starvation, a month after the battle, so that "our kids" could have another meal.

That memory had stayed with them, bonded them, inspired them.

And as for the bonding, the campus chaplain had to perform eight weddings and a couple of the girls were coming close to due . . . and like Elizabeth, two of them would be mothers who lost the fathers in the war.

Cutting around the fallen trees, John pulled back onto Black Mountain Road, continuing in towards town. A number of houses had burned during the winter and were gutted-out shells, others just abandoned, all within dead. The few with life still inside had yards already planted with this spring's "Victory Gardens"; there wasn't a lawn to be seen.

The town was quiet, more a ghost town now, but still had some survivors and many of them were heading down to the center of town, some of them nearly running. They all looked like survivors of a death camp, skeletal, children lanky, with swollen stomachs, nearly every man bearded, nearly all in clothes several sizes too big.

John drove faster now, heading down the center of the road, the sides filled with debris, broken branches from the storms, cars abandoned since the first day.

And as he came around the bend to the center of town he saw them and at the sight of them Elizabeth, Jen, and Makala all let out a shriek, screaming so loudly that Ben burst into tears.

John pulled into the town hall complex, not even bothering to find his parking slot. Hundreds were gathering, some even running.

He got out of the car and looked at them. . . .

A Bradley armored personnel carrier was at the front of the column, fluttering from a pole strapped to its side . . . the flag of the United States of America.

Behind the Bradley was a column that stretched back down the road for several hundred yards. Humvees, a couple of dozen trucks, five 18-wheelers, another Bradley, most all of them painted desert camo, all of them flying American flags.

"Here he is!" someone shouted, pointing towards John.

The cry was picked up, the people of his town parting as he slowly approached, eyes clouded with tears as he gazed up at the flag.

An officer was standing in front of the lead vehicle, surrounded by nearly a dozen of his own troops who should be back at the gap, the First Battalion of the Black Mountain Rangers, talking with soldiers decked out as soldiers as John remembered them, Kevlar helmets, a mix of uniforms, though, some desert camo, some standard camo green, a few in urban camo. And yet it was his kids, his soldiers, who looked to be the tougher of the two groups, lean, hawk faced, eyes dark and hollow, weapons slung casually, the regular infantry obviously a bit in awe of them, especially the girls, who seemed as tough as the guys they were with.

Nation Makers, he thought. He could see it now. His former students, like the soldiers in the Howard Pyle painting, ragged, half-starved, and yet filled with grim determination unlike anything seen in America in over two hundred years.

The lead officer next to the Bradley, John could see the star clipped to his lapels, was actually in his dress uniform, as if to distinguish him, to make him stand out clearly.

"Here's Colonel Matherson!" And at his approach the soldiers of his own militia came to attention and presented arms. And to his shock, the

GIs standing around them with all sincerity came to attention and saluted.

The crowd surrounding them fell silent.

John slowed, stopped, looking at the one-star general, came to attention, and saluted.

"Colonel John Matherson," he said.

The general returned the salute, broke into a grin, and came forward, hand extended, grabbing John's, shaking it.

"I know you, Matherson. Attended your lectures at Carlisle and did the staff ride with you to Gettysburg. Your lecture on Lee as operational commander at Second Manassas was brilliant. That was back in the 90's."

A wild cheer went up as if this simple handshake was the reuniting with the old world. The crowd surged around them, soldiers suddenly finding themselves being kissed, hugged, more than one of them obviously disconcerted, since many of those showering affection had not bathed in months and more than a few were crawling with lice.

John smiled, looked at the general, the face vaguely familiar, but could not place the name, finally looking down at the nameplate . . . "Wright."

John wondered what Wright was seeing. Americans? Or starved skeletal survivors, the type of survivors that America had seen all around the world for nearly seventy years, had offered generous help to, but never dreamed would finally come to their own land?

"This column is heading to Asheville. I'm to take over as military governor of western North Carolina until such time as civilian authority is reestablished, but I wanted to stop here first."

The cheering crowd did not hear him, but John did.

"You're not staying?"

"Headquarters will be in Asheville, but yes, we are staying in the region."

A sergeant standing atop the Bradley held up a microphone and clicked it.

"May I have your attention please?"

Everyone fell silent, looking up at him with awe. It was the first voice amplified by a loudspeaker that they had heard in a year.

"Excuse me," Wright said, and he climbed aboard the Bradley, the sergeant extending a hand to pull him up.

"My name is General Wright. I am an officer in the army of the United States of America and we are here to reunite you with your country."

The cheering lasted for several minutes, Makala was up by John's side, hugging him, many were crying, and then spontaneously one of the militia girls, a member of the school choir, began to sing:

"Oh, say can you see, by the dawn's early light . . ."

Within seconds it was picked up by all, and all wept even as they sang.

The general stood with head lowered, and there was no acting as he brushed the tears from his face.

"I have been assigned to be military governor of the region of Western North Carolina. My headquarters will be established by the end of the day."

"You're not leaving us?" someone cried.

"No. Of course not. I'm asking you now to move to the rear of this column and please line up patiently. Each of you will then receive three rations, what the army calls meals ready to eat."

Another wild cheer.

"We have a medical team with us who will try and lend a hand with any serious cases of the moment. All children, expectant mothers, and mothers of infants will also receive a three-month supply of vitamins."

Vitamins, John thought. My God, so American. Something good from a small bottle. It lifted him even more than the food. Elizabeth had come through her time but just barely. The vitamins for her and the baby would be lifesavers.

"This column must depart in one hour for Asheville, but I swear to you as a soldier of the United States of America, we are here to stay. By next week another supply column with more food and medicine should arrive."

He handed the microphone back to the sergeant and jumped down, returning to John, while the sergeant started to direct the crowd to move, the troops with him helping. John watched them go, a medic already up to Elizabeth, stopping her, looking at her and the baby. The mere sight of that again filled John with tears. Soldiers were already passing out single sticks of chewing gum to children, who upon learning about the treats were swarming round.

As the crowd flooded past, the general motioned for John to walk with him.

"How bad was it here?"

"Very bad," John said.

"Yeah, I saw your greeting card at the top of the pass."

John suddenly felt embarrassed. The corpse of the Posse leader had hung there thoughout the winter, bones picked clean in a matter of days by crows. Part of the skeleton still dangled there. The ravine below had been a feasting place for scavengers for weeks, nearly a thousand bodies dumped there.

"We followed the wreckage of their trail clear from Statesville to here. You did a hell of a job wiping them out.

"I saw the ashes of the fire on both sides of the interstate. It burned clear down to Old Fort, or what was Old Fort. You did that to trap them."

John nodded.

"Good plan, Colonel."

"History teaches something at times."

"How many survivors here? One of the first things we'll need done is an accurate census; then ration cards will be issued out."

"I already have cards issued."

Wright smiled.

"These will be for federal rations."

"Right," and John nodded, wondering if he was suddenly feeling a resentment that he had just lost control after so many painful months of struggling to keep his town alive.

"What percentage survived here?"

"Around twenty percent, maybe a bit less if we count those who came in after it happened."

Wright shook his head.

"Is that bad?" John asked nervously, wondering now if he had failed.

"Bad. Christ, it's incredible up here. Places like the Midwest, with lots of farmland and low populations, more than half survived, but the East Coast?"

He sighed.

"Here in the East, it's a desert now. Estimates are maybe less than ten percent still alive. They hit us at the worst possible time, early spring. Food would run out before local harvests came in, and a lot of crops, especially farther north, had yet to be put in the ground."

He looked off.

"They say in all of New York City there's not much more than twenty-five thousand people now and those are either savages or people hiding and living off scraps of garbage. A thermonuclear bomb hitting it directly would have been more humane.

"Cholera actually broke out there last fall and the government decided to abandon the city, just isolate it, and no one was allowed in; the few in were not allowed out. A friend of mine stationed there on duty said it was like the Dark Ages."

He sighed and forced a smile as if realizing he was rambling, talking about something best left unsaid.

"You did good, Colonel Matherson, real good. We ran into a few refugees on the road, bitter that you wouldn't let them in, but one old guy, a vet, said he admired you folks, that word was you actually stuck together while the rest of the country went to hell."

He nodded, unable to speak.

Wright stood silent, then lowered his head, his voice a whisper.

"They say nearly everyone in Florida is dead. Too many people, too little land devoted to food."

"What about all the oranges and cattle land?"

"Everything broke down. People killed the cattle for a single meal, and in that heat by the following morning most of the meat was rotting and swarming with flies. So they ate it anyhow and you know what then happened."

"The ocean? All the food out there."

"Incredible as it sounds, pirates made it all but impossible for any kind of serious fishing. It was like something out of the seventeenth century. The coast is riddled now with pirates; the navy is hunting them down. A couple of small towns, especially along the keys, set up good defenses, only one road to block, and their own navies to guard the fishing boats, so they got through relatively OK, but the hurricane last fall knocked them over pretty hard."

"Hurricane?"

He had all but forgotten that natural catastrophes that had once riveted the nation and caused massive outpourings of aid would still continue and if striking but a hundred miles away be all but unheard of.

"Another Katrina, bull's-eye right on Miami, a smaller one Tampa–Saint Pete a few months later."

He fell silent for a moment, looking off.

"This time around, though, no outside help to come pouring in like in New Orleans. It was a death blow for those still alive.

"Add in the heat without AC. Few houses down there today were designed for living without AC. Add in twenty percent of the population as elderly, so many dying in the first days that they say that in some of the retirement towns the dead carpeted the streets, again like something out of the plagues of old. Disease just exploded in that climate; that's what killed most of them before starvation even set in . . . food poisoning, heat exhaustion, bad water or no water, then malaria, West Nile, they say typhoid and dysentery ran rampant in the Miami area, even reports of bubonic plague. . . ." He paused.

"Cannibalism even, like your Posse types . . . but also a lot of people driven mad with hunger. Cults sprang up, one damn near like the Aztecs, into human sacrifices to atone for the wrath of the earth spirits, others some weird play on the Last Supper and Communion, that this was now God's will and it was OK to eat the dead. Others, well, just wackos."

John sighed. The Prozac nation on withdrawal, he thought, remembering Kellor's warning.

"The only ones left there now the barbarians and a few small communities with good tactical positions, like yours, and a good leader, like you."

There was something about the way the general spoke that caught John. Why was he focusing on Florida?

John looked at him, felt he shouldn't but had to ask.

"Sir, your family. Are they OK?"

The general looked back at him, eyes bright.

"I was with Central Asian Command. You know our stateside command is in Tampa—Saint Pete. I shipped over to Iraq month before we got hit."

He sighed.

"Wife, three kids, daughter-in-law, and two grandkids lived in Saint Pete. Haven't heard a word since it happened."

"I'm sorry, sir."

"Yeah, we are all sorry now."

John could not speak.

"Voice of America never said anything about that."

The general shook his head.

"Did you think we'd actually tell you the truth?" he sighed.

John bristled.

"So what the hell is the truth?"

"We had our asses handed to us, that's the truth. Just several bombs, and we had our asses handed to us. With luck there might be thirty million people still alive in what was the United States."

"What do you mean, was?"

The general shook his head.

"Course you wouldn't know; we're not talking about it on Voice of America. You can write off the Southwest, including Texas, unless we can dig up another Sam Houston and Davy Crockett. During the winter, Mexico moved in. Claimed it was a protectorate to counter the Chinese."

"What?"

"China. Oh, they came with aid, plenty of aid for the few survivors after sixty days of anarchy and disease. And now there's five hundred thousand of them on the West Coast, California to Washington State, clear up to the Rockies."

"Who?"

"Chinese troops. Here to help us of course," Wright said, his voice bitter. "Oh, they're giving out aid, even helping with some rebuilding, but there's no sign they ever plan to leave."

"So it was them?"

The general shrugged.

"We'll never know, most likely."

"What?"

"John, three missiles total. One launched from a containership out in the Gulf of Mexico and burst over Kansas, Utah, and Ohio. The cargo ship, typical, had Liberian registry and had docked at half a dozen places, including Oman. We think the weapons might have been loaded aboard there, a medium-range missile capped with a nuke inside an oversized container. That ship, by the way, blew up right after the launch, no one survived, so it fits the terrorist model. Another over Russia, launched from another containership from near Iceland, same scenario, the ship blew up right after the launch. We don't know why over Russia rather than over Central Europe. Maybe its guidance was screwy, but that did mean England and parts of Spain were spared. Last one burst lower, but still high enough to knock out Japan and Korea.

"Some say it was China, others North Korea, which by the way is now a glowing slag heap, others the terrorist cells, others Iran, a fair part of that glowing as well. Maybe it was all of them; maybe it was none of them. Maybe it doesn't matter now; they did it, and they won."

"What do you mean, won? Damn it, Voice of America kept saying we were winning."

"Sure, there's a lot of rubble heaps around the world where once there were cities, us lashing out, maybe rightly, maybe just blindly. But did that change things here?

"I was deployed back here, from Iraq. The entire navy is here as well on the East Coast at least. Nearly all our overseas military is now back here, trying to sort things out, rebuild, and defend what's left.

"John, I saw Baltimore and Washington burning in the night, the smoke a pillar visible a hundred miles away," and he spoke now in almost a monotone.

"My God, it was like something out of the Bible. It was medieval."

Washington, and for the first time in months John thought of Bob Scales in the Pentagon.

"Remember General Scales? Commandant of the war college while you were there?"

Wright nodded his head. "The bastards lucky enough to be assigned the government emergency relocation sites, some of them got out, the rest . . . Well, Washington like I said turned medieval. I don't know what happened to your friend. I'm sorry, but he's most likely gone unless he was assigned to the bunkers out in Maryland and West Virginia."

Wright looked off again.

"There's a cult that has taken over parts of three states in the Rockies. Their leader claims he's the Messiah and when the world is saved all the lights will come back on, and tens of thousands now follow him.

"The Posse you faced? There's one like it ten thousand strong that still rules Pittsburgh and raids a hundred miles out in every direction. We're getting set to stamp it out, but it will be as bad as anything we faced in Iraq several years back . . . and my God, these were once our own people. I lost eight, killed wiping out a nest of them in the ruins of High Point three days ago.

"Oh, we might of gotten even, John, but America a world power? They won; we're finished. We've retreated from around the world, trying to save what's left, and for those that hated us that's victory even if we flattened their country in retaliation, and John, frankly, we might never know who really did it to start with.

"There were no red meatballs, swastikas, or red stars on planes dropping bombs this time. Just three missiles launched from freighters out in the ocean, which then were blown up.

"My God, there's maybe two hundred and fifty million dead in America alone, as bad, maybe worse than any *Dr. Strangelove* nightmares we talked about during the Cold War. We were so damn vulnerable, so damn vulnerable, and no one did the right things to prepare, or prevent it.

"We're back a hundred and fifty years."

"No, not a hundred and fifty years," John sighed. "Make it more like five hundred. People alive in 1860, they knew how to live in that time; they had the infrastructure. We don't. Turn off the lights, stop the toilets from getting water to flush, empty the pharmacy, turn off the television to tell us what to do."

He shook his head.

"We were like sheep for the slaughter then."

The general reached into his breast pocket and pulled out a pack of cigarettes. They were English, Dunhills.

Wright offered the pack and John fought hard, then remembered the last one he had smoked.

"I quit."

"I haven't," and the general lit up.

He blew the smoke out, and though it smelled so good to John, he didn't ask. He thought of Jennifer, who always nagged him about it. No, don't think of that, he realized.

"I have to get this column moving, John. Will you come up to Asheville in a few days so we can talk more?"

"Sure. But will you be confiscating vehicles?"

Wright looked at him in confusion.

"Nothing, just a little problem I had a very long time ago. And by the way, once up there, fire the schmuck running the place. I'm willing to bet you won't find him underfed, nor those around him."

Wright nodded.

"And for God's sake, get the hospital open to the community again. . . . I just wish you'd gotten here seven months ago. . . ."

He couldn't speak.

"Who?"

"My daughter."

"I understand."

John looked into Wright's eyes and could see that indeed this man did understand, torn by a worse agony almost. Jennifer slept in John's backyard, Wright would most likely never know what happened to his family and therefore could only imagine the worst. Another thing about Americans lost, John realized. We knew, we always knew where those we loved were, and if they were lost in a war we had a nation that would spend millions just to bring a fragment of a body back. There were over two hundred million bodies now . . . and no one could even spare the time now to name them.

Wright turned away from him for a moment.

"I'll leave a supply of MREs in your town hall so you can get them out to those not here," he finally said, looking back.

"Thank you."

"I'll leave one medic as well with some supplies. We have some antibiotics, the vitamins of course, painkillers. He can set up sick call once the column has left."

"Insulin?" John asked coldly.

"No, why? Diabetics? They're all dead now anyhow," and then Wright froze. "I'm sorry, John."

He could only nod.

They shook hands and Wright started to turn away.

"General?"

He looked back.

"Is this for real?"

"What?"

"I mean this. Today. Or is it nothing more than a flash in the pan? You'll stay awhile, but things will continue to break down, collapsing in, and then it's just the end. The old line, 'this is the way the world will end, not with a bang, but a whimper.' "

Wright hesitated.

"My friend, I don't know. All our elaborate plans . . . all our dreams? I no longer know."

The general turned and went back to the Bradley. Its engine fired up, troopers returning to their vehicles, engines turning over, except for the last of the tractor trailers, where rations were still being passed out.

The column started to roll forward and John watched as the flag snapping above the Bradley passed by.

Instinctively he came to attention and saluted, civilians placing their hands over their hearts, his militia presenting arms, again, more than a few crying at the sight of it.

Fifty stars, he thought. Will we ever be as we once were? And the voice within whispered the terrible truth.

He took Makala's hand, looked down at her, and smiled as if to reassure, and she smiled back, as if to reassure, and each could sense the lie in the other.

"Look at this, Dad!"

It was Elizabeth, clutching two bottles of vitamins, a canvas bag, military, slung over her shoulder.

"Some guy kissed Ben, said Ben reminded him of his own son. The poor guy just cried and kept hugging Ben, then gave me a dozen rations! They're in the bag. They even gave me a five-pound can of formula for Ben. It's over, Dad; it's really over!"

"Of course it is, sweetheart," he said, smiling. In her joy she looked again to be like a child.

"Let's go home."

And they walked back to their car, drove home, the girls going inside, Elizabeth laughing with excitement.

He went into the house, picked up Rabs, then went outside to sit by Jennifer's grave.

The world had changed forever, the America they knew . . . never to return.

"It is not a matter of *if,* it is a matter of *when.*"

GENERAL EUGENE HABIGER, USAF (RET.)
FORMER COMMANDER-IN-CHIEF,
U.S. STRATEGIC COMMAND
MAY 2002[1]

AFTERWORD

ELECTROMAGNETIC PULSE: A BOLT FROM THE GRAY

The fall of the Berlin Wall and collapse of the Soviet Union marked a distinct turning point in my navy career. The Boeing E-6 strategic nuclear command and control aircraft I flew would no longer fly continuous airborne alert postured for a "bolt from the blue" nuclear attack. I continue to hope that if military anthropologists ever decide to study pre–Cold War hunter-gatherer groups, my rather unspectacular career will be noted for only two significant statistics: no aircraft lost and no nuclear holocaust on my watch.

Growing up in Los Alamos, New Mexico, I was captivated by the subject of nuclear war and somehow it became my career path. I leapt at the chance to tour the Nevada Test Site as an ensign. As I took in the images of a nuclear ghost town and the enormous crater left by the SEDAN event, measuring nearly a quarter of a mile across and deeper than a football field, the tremendous destructiveness of nuclear weapons became real for me. I would devote much of my life to balancing the day-to-day duties of standing ready to fight a strategic nuclear war with the angst of the anticipated aftermath—devouring all I could on the subject.

I read Pat Frank's classic apocalyptic 1959 novel *Alas, Babylon* and was encouraged by man's defiance of annihilation and ability to cope in a post-attack nuclear world. The image of Slim Pickens as Major T. J. "King" Kong in *Dr. Strangelove* provided dark comic relief every time I inventoried a double-locked safe of nuclear codes. After being promoted to captain, I reread Nevil Shute's classic, *On the Beach,* and wondered if I had the courage of the submarine captain Dwight Towers to gracefully face the end of civilization.

I wish my imagination would have allowed me to just sit back and enjoy my friend Bill Forstchen's novel *One Second After* as another science fiction story but I could not. It was an emotional and gut-wrenching read—because it could actually happen.

An Electromagnetic Pulse (EPM) explosion over the continental United States would have devastating consequences for our country. The detonation of a nuclear weapon produces high-energy gamma radiation that travels radially away from the burst center. When the detonation occurs at high altitudes—greater than twenty-five miles—the gamma rays directed towards the earth encounter the atmosphere where they interact with air molecules to produce positive ions and recoil electrons called Compton electrons after the physicist who was awarded the Nobel Prize in 1927 for his discovery of the Compton Effect. The gamma radiation interacting with the air molecules produces charge separation as the Compton recoil electrons are ejected and leave behind the more massive, positive ions. The earth's magnetic field's interaction with the Compton recoil electrons causes charge acceleration, which further radiates an electromagnetic field as an instantaneous electromagnetic pulse.[2]

Additionally, a high-altitude nuclear burst also produces a relatively slow magnetohydrodynarnic EMP, whose effects are like those from geomagnetic solar storm disturbances causing the flow of very low frequency current into the earth and into long transmission lines. The reality of the damage to electrical and electronic equipment by EMP has been established in various nuclear tests and by the use of EMP simulators.[3]

The intense and invisible energy pulse cannot be sensed by people and doesn't damage the human body. Unlike a lightning strike, an EMP explosion is both much faster in producing damaging power surges and much broader and far-reaching in causing simultaneous burnout and failure of electrical and electronic systems over a large area. A well-designed nuclear weapon detonated at a high altitude over Kansas could have damaging effects over virtually all of the continental United States. Our technologically oriented society and its heavy dependence on advanced electronics systems could be brought to its knees with cascading failures of our critical infrastructure. Our vulnerability increases daily as our use and dependence on electronics continues to accelerate.

As former Speaker Newt Gingrich describes the potential catastrophic consequences of an EMP attack over the United States, he notes that "this is not idle speculation but taken from the consensus findings of nine distinguished American scientists who authored the *Report of the Commission to Assess the Threat to the United States from Electromagnetic Pulse (EMP) Attack*."[4]

Unfortunately, the *Report of the Commission to Assess the Threat to the United States from Electromagnetic Pulse (EMP) Attack*[5] was released the exact same day the 9/11 Commission's report directed most of America's immediate attention to the rearview mirror to find out why we failed to prevent the horrific terrorist attack of 2001. As television commentators pored over the 9/11 report and offered in-depth analysis of the "failure of imagination," the stark warnings and recommendations of the EMP commission went largely unnoticed into the back-logged pile of congressional failures of implementation.

So why are we reluctant to realistically address the threat of an EMP attack? Skeptics will continue to regurgitate bureaucratic babble such as "while it is technically feasible, it is highly improbable," or "we do not have any credible intelligence indications and we must remain focused on near-term concerns" and other canned responses of downplayed threat perceptions prevalent prior to 9/11.

Fortunately, while there is no clear objective method for analyzing relative risks and costs for comparing large-scale disasters, there is a high value to preventing, preparing for, and being able to recover from large-scale disasters such as hurricanes, floods, and regional power outages. The thorough work of the EMP commission provides a clear look at the nature of the problem, mitigation strategies and recommendations. The solution "is feasible and well within [our] means and resources to accomplish."[6]

One of the EMP commissioners, Dr. Lowell Wood, noted nuclear physicist involved with EMP weapons for three decades, characterizes an EMP event as a "continental time machine that would move us back to the nineteenth century." When questioned that the technology of a century ago could not support our present population, he unemotionally replied, "Yes, I know. The population will shrink until it [can] be supported by the technology."[7] Farming expertise, horses, and mules would be in short supply. As EMP weapons do not distinguish between military and civilian targets, it is especially critical that our electrical power infrastructure be hardened against EMP.

An EMP attack should not be viewed as a Cold War "bolt from the blue" but prepared for as an anticipated asymmetric "bolt from the gray." We have been warned that our country is "vulnerable and virtually unprotected against an EMP attack that could damage or destroy civilian and military critical electronic infrastructures triggering catastrophic consequences that could cause the permanent collapse of our society."[8] One second after an EMP attack, it will be too late to ask two simple questions: what should we have done to prevent the attack and why didn't we do it.

Captain Bill Sanders, U.S. Navy

NOTES

1. Bill Keller, "Nuclear Nightmares," *New York Times Magazine,* May 26, 2002. From an interview with General Eugene Habiger, USAF (ret.), on nuclear terrorism scenarios.
2. Gary L. Smith, Testimony Statement, U.S. House of Representatives, Subcommittee on Military Research and Development, July 16, 1997.
3. Samuel Glasstone and Philip J. Dolan (eds.), *The Effects of Nuclear Weapons* (Third Edition), United States Department of Defense and the Energy Research and Development Administration, 1977, p. 522.
4. Newt Gingrich, Testimony Statement, U.S. Senate, Committee on Homeland Security and Governmental Affairs, November 15, 2005.
5. *Report of the Commission to Assess the Threat to the United States from Electromagnetic Pulse (EMP) Attack*, Volume I, Executive Report 2004, available at http://empcommission.org.
6. Ibid., 3.
7. Lowell Wood, Testimony, U.S. House of Representatives, Committee on Armed Services, July 22, 2004.
8. Roscoe G. Bartlett, Letter, October 19, 2004.

The views expressed in this essay are solely those of the author and do not reflect the official policy or position of the Department of Defense or the U.S. Government.